THE CASTLE OF WATER AND WOE

BRIARWOOD REVERSE HAREM, BOOK 3

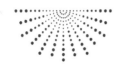

STEFFANIE HOLMES

BACCHANALIA HOUSE

ISBN: 978-0-9951222-7-7

❀ Created with Vellum

To Andy,
For teasing me about not being able to say 'penis'
and doing all the crazy things
I only write about.

Sisters in metal, forever.

Gravitation cannot be held responsible for people falling in love. How on earth can you explain in terms of chemistry and physics so important a biological phenomenon as first love? Put your hand on a stove for a minute and it seems like an hour. Sit with that special girl for an hour and it seems like a minute. That's relativity.

— ALBERT EINSTEIN

MAEVE

"*D*id you really need all these clothes?" I moaned, dropping an armload of Kelly's shopping bags in a heap underneath our table at Happy's Diner. One toppled over, sending a red bra skidding across the linoleum toward a table of stern-looking women holding their coffee cups with their pinky fingers out and sniffing as they railed about their grandchildren's various piercings.

Arthur shuffled inside Happy's, laden down with even more bags. His boot scuffed the bra, looping the strap around his foot so that when he spun around to shove the bags under our table, he kicked the bra up into the air. It sailed across the room, heading straight for one of the lemon-faced ladies. Arthur lunged for it, catching it between his enormous hands right as one of the ladies turned around. He bowed to her, waving the bra in front of his face while she stared in horror, then slumped down in the booth beside Kelly and presented it to her with a flourish.

She giggled and accepted the bra, tucking it back into her bag. "You just gave that lady a heart attack."

Arthur picked up the menu. "If the food in this place

doesn't already do it. Look, this burger has *four* patties. You Americans are bloody insane."

"Mock all you want, Aragorn," I waved my fork at him. "But I know you're totally going to order that burger."

Arthur shut the menu. "Hell yes."

"Your boyfriend is brilliant," Kelly giggled as the waitress came back to give us two baskets of loaded fries and take Arthur's order.

"He is at that," I grinned at her as I watched Arthur try to fit the entire bulk of his shoulders into the narrow booth. Across the table, Arthur raised an eyebrow at me. I kept my face impassive. Her statement was *technically* true. Arthur was my boyfriend now. No way in hell did Kelly need to know about the other four boyfriends I had back at Briarwood Castle in England.

How I was going to keep my polyamorous relationship a secret from my somewhat religiously-conservative sister when she was living at Briarwood was beyond me, but luckily I had some time to consider the problem. Kelly needed Arthur and I to stay with her in the States for the immediate future to help her petition for emancipation, get a passport, and generally put her life together before she could come live with us in England.

And my multiple guys wasn't even the biggest secret I was keeping from Kelly. No way could I even begin to explain I was actually a powerful witch with the ability to manipulate and travel in dreams, and that my birth mother was also a powerful witch and my birth father an evil fae king who was trying (unsuccessfully so far) to reclaim the earth for himself and make me rule by his side.

Phew. My head spun just thinking about it.

Before I left for America, we managed to secure the gateway to the fae realm with magical wards, so my father Daigh would not be able to come through it any time soon.

But he still lurked just behind that doorway, waiting for his chance to strike. We had no way of stopping him permanently yet, but my boys back at the castle were hard at work on looking for answers. Maybe by the time we got on the plane to England with Kelly, the fae wouldn't even be an issue any more.

Wishful thinking, I was pretty sure, but if anyone could make a wish come true just by thinking about it, it was probably a spirit witch.

Arthur's hand snaked across the table and pinched a handful of fries. "None of that," I slapped his hand away. "You've got your heart attack burger coming."

"Just seeing if you were paying attention," he grinned back.

"So I think we should hit that outdoor shop on the corner next," Kelly said, diving into her fries with gusto.

"Why?" I must've missed something important in the conversation, because no way would Kelly ever opt to enter an outdoors' shop unless a hot guy she liked worked behind the counter. Kelly's idea of the 'great outdoors' was walking down the front path, and even then she complained that the desert dust messed up her hair. I couldn't see any reason why she'd need to stock up on waders and fishing hats.

"I was talking to Gabe and Pete at the hostel and they said it's the best place in the city to get a decent backpack from."

I groaned. *The hostel, of course.* We'd bowed to Kelly's crazy request to stay in a local youth hostel, instead of renting a hotel or AirBNB like sensible people. I didn't see the appeal in threadbare sheets and the cockroach-infested bathroom and the "continental breakfast" that consisted of a box of expired Corn Flakes and some powdered milk. Even though we had a private room, it was impossible to sleep with doors slamming and showers running and drunk people yelling down the hallway at all hours of the night.

3

Kelly loved it, though. While Arthur and I tossed and turned on the hard mattress, she'd spent half the night down in the hostel's attached bar, batting her eyelashes and letting complete strangers convince her that what she really wanted to do for the rest of her life was sit in drum circles and carry her possessions around on her back.

"Don't look like that, grandma. This is one topic where you actually don't know everything. Gabe and Pete have backpacked around twenty-eight countries. They know what they're talking about. If I want to do some traveling, it'll be good to have something lightweight to carry around all my clothes."

I kicked one of the shopping bags at my feet. "Even if the manufacturer could somehow bend the dimensions of space, there's no backpack in this universe large enough to accommodate your new wardrobe—" My phone buzzed across the table. I grabbed it before it slid over the edge. Corbin's name flashed on the screen.

"Corbin, hey! We're just eating lunch—"

"Maeve, you have to come home now. It's an emergency."

My chest tightened. Corbin was always so calm and in-control. For his voice to be shaking like that, it meant something was seriously wrong. I immediately recalled the dream I'd been in with Blake where all the guys had been impaled on stakes and burned alive. "What's happened? Is everyone okay?"

"That lady Sheryl managed to pull some strings and organize another baptism for Connor. It's tomorrow at two-thirty."

Phew. So something awful hadn't happened. "Finally, some good news. You had me worried for a min—"

"It's not all good. Blake says he heard from his friend that the fae are going to be at the baptism. They're going to try and take Connor again."

4

2

MAEVE

o. Not again.
We'd only just saved baby Connor from the realm of the fae. My new friend Jane had lived through the worst days in her life, not knowing where her son was or how to get him back or whether she was going mad. No way was she going through that again. No way in *hell*.

Kelly's eyes widened. "Maeve, you look sick. What's wrong?"

I tore myself from my chair and raced out of the diner so Kelly couldn't hear our conversation. "But how's that possible? The fae can't get through the wards. The wards are still holding, aren't they?" *Shit. Have I left my boys back in England completely unprotected?*

"They're definitely still holding, although all your scientific equipment was destroyed. I don't know how this could be possible. Blake swears it's true, but he's not saying anything else until you get back. I'm going to get it out of him if it's the last thing I do," Corbin growled.

Arthur barreled outside after me. He tilted his head close to mine so we could both hear the conversation, his scraggly

Viking beard tickling my bare shoulder. Ordinarily, this would send a shiver of sexual delight right through me – especially after what we'd shared the last couple of days – but not now. Now my whole body shook with fear.

My mind whirred, struggling to put all the pieces together. Rowan and I had wondered if Blake was up to something when we found the last of our sleeping draught gone. Now we knew we were right. "Corbin, don't hurt Blake. Remember, he's part of this coven, too, and he might have just saved Connor's life."

"He's been talking to the fae after we explicitly said not to. We can't trust him."

"He may have his reasons. If he came to you as soon as he knew something was wrong, that's a good sign. It says he wants to help. Just please, promise me you won't kill him until I get back."

"You *will* come? Blake says we're going to need the whole coven to deal with this. He says they'll be stronger than ever."

"Of course we're coming back," Arthur said into the phone. I glanced through the window of the diner at Kelly, who was hunting through her shopping bags. My stomach churned. I didn't want to leave her in Phoenix by herself, but if I didn't go the coven wouldn't have the power it needed. No way was I risking anything when Connor was involved.

"Good." I heard a tapping noise as Corbin did something on his laptop on the other end. "I've just checked the timetable. There's a flight leaving Phoenix within the hour. If you hurry, you might be able to get a last-minute seat."

"I'll call you from the airport." I clicked the phone off and stared at Arthur. "We have to go. The fae have somehow found a way to get to Connor again. We need all of us to stop them."

"What about your sister?"

I squeezed my eyes shut. I really, *really* didn't want to do this. It was my job to look after Kelly, especially after she had just made an attempt on her life after being forced to live with our abusive uncle. I'd promised her yesterday that from now on I would be here for her no matter what. I'd only been in Arizona for three days and already I was abandoning her. "She'll have to join us later, if it's safe. We can't take her with us now and I can't stay behind with her. You need me."

I'm the High Priestess. My coven has to come first.

"Bloody fae, ruining everything. Flynn's right – they are wankers." Arthur picked up my hand and squeezed it. "It'll be okay, Maeve. We'll get the bastards."

My warrior. No matter what we were facing, Arthur waded in on the front lines without fear. The rage that burned inside him – the flame of passion from which his power grew – wouldn't allow him to back down. I hoped his fire would give me the strength I needed to see this through.

I squeezed back, but even the fierceness in his eyes couldn't make my stomach stop churning. *Please let everyone be okay. Please let the fae hold off their attack until we can get there. Please let there be seats for us on this flight.*

"I'd better go give Kelly the bad news," I said, dropping his hand. "Can you bring the car around?"

Arthur ran off and I rushed back inside. Kelly looked up from the table just as the waitress dropped off two slices of brownie cake and Arthur's ridiculous burger. She'd taken a huge bite out of the side of it. "Omigod, Maeve. You have to try this burger. It's even more disgusting than it looks. Do you remember that time Dad ordered it and you lectured him about his gluttony sermon from church and so he had to choke down the whole thing—" Kelly's words died away as she noticed my expression. "What's wrong? Is it Uncle Bob? Has he taken back all his money?"

I shook my head. "It's not that. Kelly, I'm so sorry, but

7

Arthur and I have to go back to England immediately. There's an emergency."

"What happened?"

Good question. I guessed *faeries are coming to take my friend's baby son and I have to go back to stop them because I'm a witch who gains her power from fucking five guys at once* wasn't going to work. Kelly was pretty open-minded, but she was still an Arizona-raised Christian who learned intelligent design in high school. "Um, well, Rowan's fallen down the stairs and he's in the hospital and it's quite serious."

"Do you have to go?"

"He's asking for me and... you haven't met Rowan, but I told you that he's very sensitive. If he's hurt I *need* to be there, I'm so sorry. I'd take you with me if I could, but you don't even have a passport yet, and you've got your appointment with the lawyer tomorrow, and your counselor on Wednesday."

More lies. I'd have to get used to lying to my sister. But at least she'd be safe here in America for now.

Kelly squeezed my hand. After the crush of Arthur's thick fingers, her touch barely registered. "Of course you have to go. Don't worry about me. I'm a big girl, and I've got Gabe and Pete and all my new friends to look after me. Can you drop me at the hostel on your way?"

I wasn't so sure Kelly should be calling all the back-packers her new friends, but I didn't have time to worry about that now. Arthur waved at us from outside. Yesterday we'd had the foresight to exchange the Corvette for a more sensible Honda Fit that could actually seat three people plus all Kelly's shopping, if we didn't mind not being able to move any limbs. Arthur and I had even packed our bags from the hostel into the trunk this morning (lockers at the hostel cost more than a room and I didn't trust any of the hippies who worked there not to steal our stuff). Kelly hurriedly wrapped up the food in napkins, and I threw down money for the bill and tip. We piled in and he sped away.

A few ass-clenching minutes later (Arthur still wasn't a hundred percent used to driving on the right-hand side of the road), we slammed to a stop outside the hostel. Arthur leapt out and started hauling Kelly's shopping bags onto the pavement. Two scruffy-looking Canadian guys – I'm guessing Gabe and Pete – stepped out of the bar and offered to help Kelly carry them upstairs.

"Oh, would you? That'd be ever so kind." Kelly flipped her hair over her shoulder as Gabe sauntered off with her shopping bags. Yeesh.

You wouldn't believe she'd only just come out of the hospital after a suicide attempt. But that was Kelly. She always could bounce back quickly, especially if there was someone around to flirt with.

"Are you *sure* you're going to be okay? The only stuff you own is a car full of wildly inappropriate clothing. We didn't even get you a toothbrush. And you'll need a copy of your birth certificate for the lawyer—"

"Duh. That's why you got me all that money." Kelly held up her purse. "They sell toothbrushes at the front desk. I can buy whatever I need thanks to you, Maeve. You've already given me the one thing I needed the most – a new start. One day maybe you'll tell me what you actually did to make Uncle Bob part with twenty thousand dollars."

I shrugged. "One day."

More lies.

Arthur finished pulling all the bags out of the car. He glanced at his phone and frowned. "Maeve, we've got to go."

Kelly wrapped her arms around Arthur's neck. "It was so nice to meet you. I'd tell you to look after my older sis and make her less uptight and nerdy, but I can see it's a lost cause."

Arthur laughed, his whole body rumbling. "You take care of yourself, Kelly. We'll meet again soon."

Kelly moved around the side of the car, leaned over the door, and embraced me, burying her face into my shoulder. A strand of her golden hair tickled my nose. I wrapped my arms around my sister, breathing in the scent of her new citrusy perfume, which couldn't quite mask the lingering sterile hospital smell. *I nearly lost you. I'll never let that happen again.*

Weirdly, the warm pillar of spirit magic rose up through my belly as we embraced. I poured a tiny bit of that spirit through my hands, splaying my fingers open across Kelly's back. The magic flowed into her, bringing with it all my love and fear and hope for her. *I'll protect you.* Kelly's body sagged a little and she sighed in contentment.

Okay, cool. I didn't know I could do that, *either.*

"I love you," I whispered into her golden hair.

"I love you more, big sis."

After a decade, I pulled back. "I'm calling you the minute I get home."

"I know."

"And I want hourly texts, telling me exactly what you're doing and how you're feeling. If I don't hear from you every hour on the hour I'll be on the next plane back over here, and then you'll really find out how this nerd can ruin a party."

She rolled her eyes. "Relax, Einstein. I'll text."

"And no running off to South America with Gabe or Pete or any other long-haired loser with a djembe and a backpack. You need to stay here and see your counselor and get your petition filed." Kelly rolled her eyes, but I kept going. "And if you *ever* need to talk, day or night, you just pick up the phone. I'll always be there for you. I mean it this time."

"I know." Kelly hugged me again. "I know."

BLAKE

*C*orbin hung up the phone and turned to the rest of us. "They're going to the airport now to get on the first flight they can. Even then, they're going to cut it close. The baptism is *tomorrow*."

Jane sat on the end of the library couch, hugging Connor to her chest. Beside her, Obelix – the fat castle cat – sat on the arm and watched our conversation with a nervous twitch of her whiskers. I got it – the fire in Jane's eyes made me uncomfortable, too. "He's not touching my baby. I'll rip his throat out."

The way she said those words with such righteous venom, her hands clasped around her son, I actually believed she could do it. Was this what the films meant when they talked about a mother's fury? My chest tightened. What would it be like to have a mother? To have someone who would throw herself at the king of the fairies to save you? I'd never know.

"Fecking hell," Flynn breathed. "What do we do until then?"

"We try and head them off or reduce their power in any

way we can. It would help if we knew what the hell we're dealing with." Corbin whirled around to face me. "You'd better start talking. I did what you asked. I called Maeve. Now we need the whole story. How do you know this attack is coming?"

"I'd like to know that, too." Rowan said from the doorway. He held up an empty jar – a jar that had once held a powerful dream-inducing draught that I'd emptied pulling Liah into our world.

Rats – they got me there.

Rowan's gaze darted to the bookshelf – his lips moving silently as he counted the spines, in the same way he did every time he entered the room. He'd already counted them twice since Corbin had dragged us all into the library, but I guess he was extra anxious today. Justified, given the circumstances.

Corbin, Jane, and Rowan's eyes burned into my skin. I'd seen a program on the telly about hostage negotiators that had less dramatic tension than this room. Even Flynn stood rigid, his arms folded, his jovial, almost fae-like features sullen and expectant.

I opened my mouth to tell them the elaborate lie I'd concocted – that Liah had come to me in a dream and given me the information because she was so keen to help our cause. But then I saw the flash of Liah's cold smile as the dark tendrils surrounded her, and the words died on my tongue.

I thought Liah was my friend, that even though she was fae she had some sense of loyalty or filial duty to me. I assumed that because she played with me as a child, she would regard me with affection still. But all the time she'd been playing me so she could take advantage of my stupid human emotions to get information for Daigh. Because of her, we'd lost all Maeve's scientific equipment, and she'd be carrying all sorts of information back to the fae king... information I'd unwittingly given her because I was a complete and utter gobshite.

It was like I'd learned *nothing* in my twenty-one years as Daigh's loyal servant. *The fae lie.* It was the one universal truth about them.

And I'd been about to lie for them. *Again.*

Nope. Not going to happen. I'd made my choice when I helped Maeve rescue those babies the first time, then again when I leapt through the void after her. I'd already thrown my lot in with the witches, and that meant I had to trust them and give them all the information.

"Look," I sighed. "I haven't been completely honest about a few things."

"There's a surprise," Corbin muttered. The cock and balls I'd drawn on his cheek in the early hours of the morning stood out under the bright light of the chandelier. Somehow, I didn't think now was the ideal time to point it out.

"I know it looks bad, but the only reason I kept all this quiet was because I wanted to stay here." I lifted up my hands in supplication. "Full disclosure – and don't get all stabby on me – I *maaaay* have stolen the last of that sleeping draught. I used it to talk to Liah again."

Corbin sighed. "So you explicitly did something we all agreed *not* to do, and stole from our coven to do it."

"I did. I thought if I could find out something useful, maybe bring someone powerful like her over to our side, it would give us the upper hand and finally prove to you all that you could trust me."

"So you lied to us so we'd trust you?" Flynn asked, his lips curling into a smirk that was completely void of friendliness.

"When you put it like that..." I shrugged. "My excuse is that I was raised by the fae. That kind of logic was totally sound in their world. And there's something else. I was

13

worried about her. She was trying to lead a rebellion against Daigh. I thought she was in danger."

"You were thinking about another person?" Corbin looked shocked.

I narrowed my eyes. "Don't sound so incredulous. It's been known to happen. I *am* human, after all."

"So you spoke to your friend Liah and she told you that the fae had found some way around our wards and were coming to attack?"

"Not exactly."

"Well then, *what* exactly?"

I opened my mouth, shut it again. Corbin's gaze stung my skin worse than the citrus juices the Princes used to squeeze into my eyes. I took a deep breath.

Submit yourself, Blake. Show them you know what it means to be human.

"Liah tricked me, okay? She played on my loyalty to get information – about me, about Briarwood, about us – which she gave directly to Daigh. She's the one who smashed Maeve's instruments."

"But *how* did she do that? And how are those fae going to get here if they can't go through the portal?"

"The how of it isn't important." I glanced over at Jane, who hugged Connor tight. "We can't stop them, not where they are now. But we can fight them when they get here. I know you all hate me and you want to throw me back through the gateway and leave me to Daigh's mercy. I don't blame you and I *swear* on the tiny shred of honor I possess that as soon as Maeve gets here and we can *all* talk about this, I'll submit myself to your mercy. If the coven decides you can't trust me, then I'll go. I'll leave Briarwood, no hard feelings, no questions asked. I won't even stop to pick up a farewell curry. All I ask is that *right now* we focus on what's really important – preparing ourselves to battle the fae and save that child from an undeserved fate."

Corbin's eyes flashed. He opened his mouth to speak, but Rowan cut him off. His voice trembled over the words, unused to the strain of carrying a verdict. "Blake's right."

"It's his fault the fae are coming back," Jane shrieked. "They're going to take Connor away again!"

"No, they're not." Corbin placed a hand on her shoulder, his eyes flashing. Jane rested her head against his hand, mollified just by the sheer determination behind his words, although her eyes still burned with anger. It was almost like compulsion, the way Corbin affected people. I'd seen him do it to Maeve, to Rowan, to everyone – made them feel like he held the whole world up on his shoulders for them. It was a little bit annoying.

No one had ever held the world up for me. In fact, my world was dangerously close to smashing to pieces and cutting me up like a fillet.

Rowan gestured at the books on the wall. He kept his eyes on the ground, his voice so quiet I had to strain to catch the words. "We haven't found any answers in these books, so I don't know what another day of looking will achieve. I hate fighting, but we can't run from this. If we don't show up at the church when they're expecting us, they're not going to leave empty-handed. We have a responsibility to this town to protect it."

"How do we know we're not just walking into a trap?" Corbin asked.

An excellent point. Liah had come to me, after all. By telling me to expect the fae at the church, she'd pretty much guaranteed we'd be there. That was obviously what they wanted. "I'm a hundred percent sure that we are. What other options do we have? We could just not show up, but I wouldn't like to see what Daigh did to your little village without us to check him. Take it from someone who knows – he's pretty imaginative when it comes to torture."

Flynn glanced at his phone. "We've got seventeen hours until the baptism. That's enough time to gather a decent arsenal."

"Give me the biggest sword you've got and I'll chop his balls off myself," Jane growled.

"We're going to a *church*," Corbin kept his hand on Jane's shoulder, but he looked like he wanted to throttle us all. "They're not exactly going to let us walk in with a bunch of weapons."

"Ah, but I am a master of concealment," Flynn grinned, pulling up his pant leg to reveal one of his small hand-forged knives sticking out of a sheath. "Arthur's got a bunch of holsters and belts and things in his room. I reckon we can make us all lean, mean, fae-slaying machines."

Corbin looked at Rowan, who was still staring at his shoes. "You sure this is what you want to do?"

Rowan looked up. His face creased with pain that seemed so deep, I wondered if it had a bottom. Fuck. I'd been tortured by my adopted father and I didn't even look that sad. "I don't want anyone to get hurt," he murmured. "Not when we could have done something."

Corbin dropped his arm from Jane's shoulder. He moved across to Rowan, and wrapped his arm around the other guy's shoulders. Rowan's whole body stiffened in surprise. His head shot up, meeting Corbin's eyes with pupils that was as black as his skin.

Corbin flicked one of Rowan's dreadlocks as he stared into his friend's eyes. His expression remained fierce, but there was a new determination there, something that made the edges of his irises sparkle. I wanted to tell them both to hurry up and fuck, but I figured the less I said now, the better.

Finally, Corbin grinned. "Fine. Let's do it. We need every magical talisman, every stone of protection, and every concealable iron weapon we can hide under our Sunday best. We'll show those fae what happens when they come up against the Briarwood coven."

4

MAEVE

*A*fter an uneventful flight filled with tiny packets of pretzels and an ill-conceived attempt to join the mile high club (Arthur's bulk made manoeuvring around him in the tiny bathroom possible only for a dextrous pint-sized acrobat, of which I was *not*), we touched down at Heathrow without incident. Groggy-eyed, I followed Arthur through customs and out into the parking lot, where his ridiculous car still waited for us.

I sank into the uncomfortable seat, all the fears and responsibilities of the coven rushing back to me. America had felt like another world. Now that I was back in England, I remembered what had distracted me from Kelly and my own mourning in the first place. The fae, my father, my mother's painting, Connor's baptism, the five guys and everything we'd done together, learning about my own magic. And now it was all in jeopardy once again if we couldn't get there in time.

Arthur turned the key and glanced at the time on his phone. "If we're hurry, we might just make it. You want some music?" he asked.

"Sure." It would make the trip go faster, and maybe blast out the maelstrom of awful thoughts swirling around in my head.

Arthur put on some band called Iron Maiden. I remembered he'd worn their t-shirt a couple of times. Their galloping riffs and soaring vocals did the trick. I got caught up in the stories of epic battles and things lurking in the darkness. My heart pounded against my chest. Was I riding into a battle of my own right now? What hope did I have against the darkness?

You have the guys. You have the magic. And you have a sensible head on your shoulders. That's going to have to be enough.

I barely registered when we turned off the M1, heading along the homeward stretch toward Briarwood House.

Arthur's phone buzzed. He paused the Discman and hit the speaker button. "Hey Corbin, we're an hour away."

"Good. We're here at the cathedral in Crooks Worthy. We came early so we could hide some protective charms around the perimeter. We haven't seen anything suspicious yet. Come straight here when you can. I've got your sword and some weapons and charms for Maeve."

"How's Jane doing?" I whispered.

"As well as can be expected, given that she thought her baby was safe and now he's in Daigh's sights again."

"But how can Daigh even do this?"

"Blake won't tell us," Corbin growled. "He's been lying to us, but he swears we'll get the whole story as soon as you're here. He almost seems scared."

"He should be scared." Arthur yanked the wheel a little harder than needed. "I'm going to kill him."

"You're not. For all his faults, Blake's on our side," I reminded them both, but my stomach flipped again. What if I was wrong? What if Blake really was still working for Daigh? What if his job was to bring us to this church?

No. I trusted Blake. And more importantly, I trusted myself and my judgement of him. That was what leaders did. I read that in a Sheryl Sandberg article.

"It doesn't matter either way," Corbin was saying. "We're walking into a trap. I just hope we're strong enough to hold them back. But we can't just run away from this, right?"

I realized Corbin was asking *me.* He was trying to remember that I was supposed to be the leader. "Right," I said. "We can't let them take Connor again or hurt anyone in the village. Hold on, we'll see you soon."

Arthur put his foot to the floor, but the old car wouldn't go much faster. In fact, it got the speed wobbles as we bounced down the road and Arthur had to ease off again. I watched the time on his phone click through the minutes too fast.

We'll never make it.

But somehow we did. We made it into Crookshollow without the car falling apart. We zoomed down the high street, zipping past the pub and all the little shops. My eye caught the *Astarte* sign, and I felt a pang. I wished the old witch Clara would talk to us. Something told me she had more power in her pinkie finger than the six of us could conjure in our most epic spell.

We drove out into the countryside, following the signs to the nearby town of Crooks Worthy. My stomach twisted into knots. *Please let Blake be wrong. Please don't let there be a way for Daigh to hurt Connor or anyone else.*

Finally, after what seemed like forever, we entered the village and Arthur pulled over in front of an enormous cathedral. The looming gothic spires couldn't have looked more intimidating if they tried, with their dark stone carvings and dramatic arches. As I got out of the car, I spotted a gargoyle leering over the edge of the roof. Rain pelted down on us, and there was no one waiting around outside. We raced for the open doors.

I skidded to a stop on the slippery marble floor, my breath in my throat. Everything looked normal. At least, what I assumed was normal for a Protestant baptism that wasn't overrun with evil fae. It didn't look as though things had kicked off yet. Jane stood at the front of the church, wearing a figure-hugging red dress that I wouldn't have called Church Appropriate under any circumstances. She bounced Connor in her arms as she chatted to the vicar, who didn't seem to know where to look. Sheryl Brownley bustled around, waving her arms while Corbin and Blake teetered under the weight of an enormous floral arrangement. Corbin had some kind of faded drawing on his cheek. It almost looked like a cartoon cock and balls.

There were a scattering of people in the pews. None sat together, so their spread made the cavernous church appear even larger and more imposing. I noticed Flynn and Rowan seated in the back row. I ran over and slid into the pew next to them. Arthur squeezed his bulk in after me.

"Welcome back," Rowan leaned over and hugged me. A lump rose in my throat as his floury, earth scent washed over me. God, I'd missed these guys.

I pulled away. "No sign of the fae yet?"

Rowan shook his head. Flynn crossed himself frantically. He pushed a long shape across the pew toward us. Arthur's heaviest trench coat, wrapped around some long, hard object.

"I think you'll know what to do with that, Aragorn." Flynn threw a smaller parcel into my lap. I unfolded a short iron dagger from inside my blue jacket. Tucked into the pocket were my four talismans – Corbin's parchment, Rowan's twig, Flynn's medallion, Arthur's dagger. There was a fifth object, as well. I pulled out a long, thin bone.

"That bone is from Blake." Flynn said, wrinkling his nose. "I figured it was safest not to ask him where he found it."

I nodded and replaced all the items. I shrugged the coat over my damp shoulders, sliding the dagger up my sleeve. Through some feat of gymnastics Arthur managed to buckle his sword belt and pull on his trench coat without dropping or exposing the enormous weapon. When he sat down, the tip stuck out at an angle, but I hooked my leg over it to hide it. No one seemed to notice our shuffling.

I watched Corbin and Blake descend the steps from the altar and head towards the pews. Both of them wore huge jackets and thick trousers. Blake walked with stiff legs, like he was pretending to be a robot. As Corbin sat down, a metallic *clink* echoed throughout the church.

They're laden down with weapons. My chest tightened. I glanced around at the few other people present – could we really hope to keep them all safe if the fae came? All the defensive moves and blocks Arthur taught me had flown out of my head. Were we really ready for this fight?

I tapped Flynn on the shoulder. "What's that on Corbin's cheek?"

Flynn gave me a grin, completely devoid of mirth. "Blake drew it on his face while he was sleeping outside his room. We've missed you, Einstein."

The vicar called for silence, and Sheryl sat down at the organ, testing a few of the keys. "I think they're getting started," I whispered, squeezing Arthur's fingers.

I glanced behind my shoulder again. Nothing rapped on the church door. *Where are they?* I knew better than to hope the protection charms would work.

The service started with a hymn. I didn't know the words, but all the guys seemed to. Arthur's hand slid onto my knee. At first, it was a comfort, something to steady myself against while I collected myself. But after a couple of minutes of the

23

priest droning on about baptism and sin, Arthur's fingers grew hot. I tried to focus on waiting and watching, but all I could think about was the other night under the stars and that hand and how close it was to my—

I pinned my legs shut. *Stop thinking about it.*

"Maeve," Arthur elbowed me. "If the fae really are going to show up, we need you to be as magically charged as possible."

"You're right." We should have thought of that earlier. That meant we had to… "I mean, *no!* We can't do that here. This is a *church.*"

"No one will see," he whispered, pulling the edge of his huge coat over my lap. I gasped as Arthur slid his fingers under my skirt, slipping between my already sodden panties. He dipped his finger into my folds, wetting it with the juices that had already spilled there, and rubbed it against my clit.

The ache of my need rose up inside me, followed by the pillar of warmth that meant my spirit magic was activating. Arthur's hand swirled harder and his eyes met mine with a mischievous glint. The fact that the vicar was *right there* – and we were doing this in a totally public location – made it so much hotter.

Arthur's fingers stroked harder. I opened my legs, giving him more room. He responded by switching out his fingers, shoving one inside me while his thumb circled my clit. I bit down on my lip to stop myself from moaning.

Flynn whirled around. He grinned when he noticed Arthur's hand under the coat. "And in an Anglican church, no less. I'll make a Catholic of you yet, Maeve Moore."

I kept my lips clamped shut, because if I opened them, a moan would escape. I kept my eyes fixed on the vicar as he held Connor up and talked about how he would be united with Christ in his burial and resurrection to life.

Oh god… oh god… it feels so good.

"Go ye therefore, and make disciples of all nations, baptizing them in the name of the Father, and of the Son, and of the Holy Ghost…"

The coat rustled. Flynn pulled it up above my shoulder and his hand went underneath, sliding between my breasts to tweak my nipple. He pinched the sensitive bud just as Arthur thrust two fingers inside me. I clenched my teeth as the orgasm claimed me, my body shaking and shuddering against the hard pew. The pillar of power flared against my skin, humming with untapped energy.

"Oh, god," I whispered. Arthur snorted.

Power thrummed in my veins. My fingers tingled. Arthur was right – I was ready for anything now.

But where are the fae? If they don't show up soon, they won't be able to take Connor, as he'll be baptized.

I glanced around the church. Everyone else faced forward as the vicar moved across to the baptismal font. Nothing seemed out of the ordinary.

Maybe Blake's friend was wrong. Maybe they used him to get us away from Briarwood so they could do something else.

The priest raised Connor above his head, then brought him to his breast and dipped a goblet into the water. Connor gurgled. Jane sat in the front with Sheryl, her expression strained. The priest raised the goblet—

"We're actually going to do it," I whispered. *Connor is going to be safe.*

A loud bang made me jump. I whirled around in time to see a shaft of light cross the marble floor. The second wooden door banged on its hinges and angry footsteps marched toward the nave.

"Stop this service at once!" a voice rang out.

A figure stepped into the light thrown by the stained glass windows, followed by another, and another. A whole mob flocked down the aisle – but it wasn't the fae I was expecting.

Instead, they were mostly women in ugly sweaters and wary-looking men waving worn Bibles in their hands. All they were missing was the pitchforks and torches.

At the front of the horde stood Dora, her hands on her hips and a snarl of righteous fury on her face.

"These are witches and fornicators!" she yelled, her voice ringing out through the entire church. "They do not belong here! Remove them now, or we will do so by force!"

5

MAEVE

"*I*f you ladies would like to take a seat," The vicar – who clearly had no idea what was going on – indicated the near-empty church with a dramatic sweep of his wrist. "We'll continue the proceedings."

"We don't want the baptism to continue," an elderly woman sputtered. "Father, do you have *any idea* what you've let into our church today?"

"This humble House of God accepts all sinners—"

"Even fornicators who steal husbands and destroy families?" Another familiar voice spoke up. I swirled my head and recognized Chief Inspector Davies at the back of the mob, her mouth twisted into an ugly scowl.

"That's not—"

"Even *witches?*" Dora screamed, jabbing her finger at me and the guys. "Even the Devil's own children?"

"Please, Dora." A figure in the front pew stood up. I recognized Clara from the *Astarte* shop. Hope surged inside me. Maybe Corbin had called her, in case we needed her help. She swept her black hair behind her ears and met Dora's fearful gaze with a mixture of kindness and pity. "A beautiful ritual is being conducted today. A child is being welcomed into the house of the Lord. Surely you have no quarrel with that?"

"That child is born of bad seed," Dora snapped. "His mother is a curse in this village, beguiling honest men away from their wives and families. The child will grow up in an immoral household. He will learn from that Jezebel and those demon lovers and bring ruin on our fair village!"

"*Hey,*" Jane's eyes narrowed. "That's my son you're talking about."

"Your son is evil. The witches have already corrupted him. The demon they placed inside me told me so."

I got to my feet, raising my hand and pointing it at her. The power Arthur and Flynn had unleashed inside me threatened to escape. Dora's words twisted in my head, digging into my heart. *I'll shut her up. I'll—*

Flames devouring a wooden desk. Uncle Bob's face twisted in agony as I slam his nightmares into his skull all at once.

I can't do it. I can't hurt her like that. Her mind had already been invaded by the fae. If I did the same thing, then I was no better than they were.

My arm wobbled. My righteous anger faltered. A hand fell on my shoulder. "Save your anger for the fae," Arthur whispered.

I nodded, lowering my hand. But it was too late. Dora spun toward me, her lip quivering as she lifted a bony finger and pointed right at me. "This all started when *she* arrived – the daughter of that sorceress. *She* was supposed to be dead, but she came to the castle and all of a sudden my boys are acting strangely, and then my body is possessed by a demon, and the harlot wants her son baptized. Can't you see it's all connected? It's all *her* fault."

"Dora," Clara took a step towards her. Her heels *clack-clack-clacked* on the marble floor. Clara took another step. "I know what you're going through. Your son is in the hospital. The doctors say he might not live out the month, although I can tell you it will be closer to ten days before you must say goodbye. You blame yourself for not accepting him for who he is. You think that if you'd tried to talk to him, to get him to repent his sins, to accept that his love for men was an abomination, that he would never have gotten sick. You think God is punishing you for your son, and that by purging this town of so-called sinners, He will give him back to you."

Dora's lip wavered. "That's not true. My son is perfectly fine. He—"

I glanced at Arthur and Rowan, but they looked just as surprised as I felt. They didn't know about Dora's son. Rowan looked absolutely sick. And from the horrified looks of her followers' faces, they weren't aware, either.

So how does Clara know?

I remembered what she'd said at the shop, that she'd known my mother, that she'd come to Briarwood to perform rituals with our coven. And suddenly I realized, Clara wasn't just any witch. She was a spirit witch. Her powers seemed to center around clairvoyance – knowing things she had no way of knowing. That was the same power my mother claimed. Never mind that quantum physics didn't allow for precognition or premonition… she could be more important in this battle than we'd ever guessed.

Clara stepped forward again, rapping her cane against the marble. The sound echoed right through the lofty nave. "If you say so, dear. But let me say this – it is not your job to mete out judgement. Now, Jane may be as you say, and Maeve and those boys may be witches who dance naked under the moon. For all you know, I could be a witch who dances naked alongside them, my old bones groaning with joy." Clara patted her hip, and smiled a kind smile. "All this sin and depravity and degradation could be going on in this village *right now*, and it doesn't matter a damn – pardon my language, Father. Because you love your son, and you were like a grandmother to those boys for many years, when most of them had never known kindness from a woman."

"But…" Dora's finger continued to point at me, but her hand trembled.

"You are not the final judge," Clara said. "Your only duty to your God is to be the best woman you can be. A woman your son could be proud of. Don't let the last act he sees you do on this earth be one of hatred."

Dora's hand dropped. Her eyes turned down in the corners, and her whole face crumpled. She sagged like a damp cloth. "I…"

"What's happening, Dora?" An elderly woman in the mob asked. "Is all this true?"

"Don't let her fool you, Dora!" Inspector Davies yelled. "She's a witch too, just like the rest of them."

"He's my baby boy," Dora said, tears streaming down her wrinkled cheeks. "The Bible says he's disgusting, but he's my *son*. I can't find the—"

She stumbled over her words as her foot slipped out from beneath her. She crashed against the marble floor. At first I thought one of the guys had done it, but then I felt the floor tilt beneath me. I grabbed the back of the pew to steady myself, but the pew slid across the marble, leaping out of my grasp. The walls rumbled and the whole church lurched as though it were rolling through the ocean on a great wave.

"It's an earthquake!" Inspector Davies yelled.

The floor buckled, slamming my knees into the marble. Arthur fell beside me, landing on his thigh. He crawled toward the aisle, his sword scraping along the marble. He dragged a dagger from his belt.

"Get under the arches!" Corbin yelled. "They're the strongest part of the building."

"That won't help! This isn't an earthquake!" Arthur yelled back.

What made him say that I couldn't see. Chunks of stone fell from the ceiling, crashing around me, sending up clouds of white dust to obscure my vision. I wrapped my arms over my head and tried to crawl behind Arthur. A high-pitched sound stopped me in my tracks.

Through the screams of the mob and the roar of the earth, Connor's wail cut through. I peered under the pews, but I couldn't see anything.

"Someone get to Connor!" I yelled, just as another long rumble slammed me into the pew.

"That's going to be difficult," Flynn called from behind me.

I glanced over my shoulder. A fissure opened up in the marble – an enormous dark crack spreading out across the floor, buckling the pews. The church groaned as the crack warped the walls and pushed up the floor.

It's the fae. But what are they doing? They shouldn't be able to just create a portal like this from another multiverse. The amount of power that would take—

Black fog swirled up from inside the crack, reaching long, ghost-like fingers through the air that snaked toward me. *What is that? It's not carbon...* I tried to focus on the fog, to figure out what it was, but my eyes stung and my vision wobbled. So deep and dark was the blackness inside the crack that my retinas gave up trying to fathom it. The darkness hung weighty in front of me, as though it was a solid wall that rose from the ground, a great weighty mass of pure night.

I staggered back, slamming into someone else. Our limbs tangled up as we both tried to scramble away. The blackness reached toward my throat. I ducked, slamming myself into the marble as a tremendous pressure swelled beneath the

31

ground – as though the crack itself held back something much larger and darker than I could ever imagine.

"Maeve!" Flynn and Rowan called to me from the other side of the fissure. I blinked, focusing on the areas around the blackness where my vision wasn't swallowed up. I could just make them out on the other side of the fissure, crawling backward as the crack widened between us. Chunks of the marble floor toppled into its depths.

I didn't know what the blackness was, but every fiber in my body screamed that if it consumed me, I would be gone.

It's going to devour the whole church, and then what? How can we ever hope to fight it?

"This is but a taste," a voice boomed from inside the crack. "If you do not give back our daughter Maeve and the lands that rightfully belong to the fae by the next full moon, we shall take them by force and scour them clean of the human stain."

Long, green fingers clawed at the edge of the crack. I choked back a scream, my limbs frozen in place. A host of Far Darrigs dragged themselves from the depths and raced across the church, black tendrils cascading behind them like speed lines. The shaking earth didn't seem to affect them. The four-foot high fur-covered fae vaulted over the pews and crashed into the cowering crowd.

Their whirling shillelagh – heavy blackthorn sticks used like batons – made horrible THWACK THWACK THWACK sounds as they slammed into human flesh. I watched, paralyzed with fear, as a Far Darrig whacked an old woman over the head. Her eyes rolled back and she went down. Her head cracked against the marble, sending a splatter of blood across the floor. The fae swarmed over her, their furry paws and rat-like snouts rolling her toward the crack. The tendrils reached out and wrapped around her, pulling her under.

"No!" I surged forward, pushing past whoever had been

in my way. But I was too late. The blackness surrounded her completely and she disappeared into its depths.

Another Far Darrig grabbed Dora, his claws digging into her shoulders. She swung her handbag up and whacked him in the face. He staggered back, his grip loosening, and a stream of water hit him full-on in the face.

"Go, Flynn!" I yelled, whirling around to look at my boy. Flynn's face twisted in concentration as he increased the stream of water, trying to push the fae back.

But the water didn't even slow down the fae. In fact, the stream *bent* around its face, spraying off to the sides and knocking over several of Dora's mob. The Far Darrig threw its head back and laughed, a horrid barking sound that filled my chest with fear.

"It's not working," Flynn yelled, lowering his hand. The stream dried up.

A fireball sailed toward the fae, but at the last moment it veered to the side and crashed into a pew, sending the lacquered wood up in flames. My heart sank into my toes.

"Our magic isn't working!" Arthur cried, dragging a long dagger from his belt. The Far Darrigs chortled as they closed ranks around us.

Arthur leapt at the nearest creature just as it lunged for me. He slammed his dagger through its chest. The fae collapsed in a pile of green blood. Arthur yanked his blade free and turned to grab another. This time, he thrust the blade straight through the fae's nose and up into its brain, killing it instantly. Arthur left the blade inside the Far Darrig, where it smoked and smoldered, and drew his sword.

"Guess we're doing this the old-fashioned way," he yelled, rushing at another fae.

Meanwhile, up by the altar, Corbin wrestled with another Far Darrig, pinning it to the marble and trying to roll it back into the dark fissure. He bellowed in pain as his shoulder touched one of the black tendrils, and the collar and sleeve of his shirt melted away.

My heart leapt in my chest. The magic inside me simmered like a pot ready to boil over. *My coven.* Without their magic, this battle would turn against us at any moment. I needed to save them, and all these people. *I need to get rid of the fae—*

Princess. Blake's voice slammed into my head. *Find yourself a supply of fae nightmares. If I can get to you, we'll show 'em what hell really means.*

I'm here, too, a faint voice echoed after Blake's. It was Clara. *I'll give you what power I can manage.*

I'm on it, I thought back, still unsure if they could hear me. I rushed up to the Far Darrig Arthur had slain, and pressed my hand against its chest. The spiky fur beneath my fingers lurched my stomach. The faintest flicker of life still simmered inside the fae – enough that I could fall into its memories and dreams and pick at the threads of its nightmares—

No.

I yanked my hand away just as the first nightmarish image slammed into me. It was a darkness darker than nothing, darker even than the black fog that crept across the marble toward me. I could see nothing, hear nothing, but every nerve and sinew in my body screamed that inside the darkness was something so terrible I couldn't even comprehend it, but that encountering it would cause me to completely lose my mind.

I flung my body away from the dying fae. I blinked, trying to dispel the unsettling dark. I remembered my uncle's twisted face as he relieved his own horrible nightmares. No way was I going to look into any more fae nightmares. *That shit is going to fry my soul.*

I can't do it, I tried to say to Blake inside my head. *Their nightmares are too much for me. But let's see if your compulsion will work again.*

I whipped around, sliding my dagger out of my shirt and jabbing it at a Far Darrig barreling toward me. Before it could reach me, Corbin leapt on it, shoving his palm against the fae's mouth and trying to pull the air from its lungs with his magic.

"Your powers are useless against me now, *witch*," the fae rasped, digging its claws into Corbin's arm. But Corbin didn't waste time. He yanked a dagger from his belt and plunged the blade into the fae's neck.

"My blade's still sharp," Corbin gasped out, yanking out his dagger as the fae dropped to the ground.

I ducked around them. Green blood splattered across my back. A dark shape lunged at me. I raised my own knife, steeling myself for the Far Darrig's fierce claws to sink into my skin.

"I know how much you want my body, Princess, but this is hardly the time." *Blake.* The dark shape was Blake. I lowered the knife and thrust out my other hand. He grabbed it, wrapping his fingers around mine. His lips moved in some kind of chant but I couldn't hear the words over the chaos around us and the pounding of my own heart. The pillar of power inside me flared up, flowing through my fingers into Blake's, as his power sizzled against my skin and raced through my body. Behind him, I could feel the quiet addition of Clara's power, bolstering our reserves.

Blake's magic swirled inside my skull, probing into the recesses of my mind, wrapping around my thoughts and pulling out what he needed. I focused on feeding him more of my power. Random thoughts flew in front of my eyes. Kelly lying in the hospital bed. Me as a gangly teenager presenting a speech on black holes at an Arizona science convention. Me making demands of Uncle Bob while the fire blazed around us. Corbin and I squeezed into the priest hole. Arthur and I shagging under the stars.

You've been busy, Princess. Blake's sardonic tone pounded inside my head. He was seeing all of my thoughts, learning more about me in moments than I might have told him in an entire lifetime.

Just focus on stopping the fae, I shot back at him. The room swam as more memories danced in front of my eyes, mere flashes too quick to distinguish. My mind blazed with bright light and blinding pain. Instead of shying from the pain, I fell toward it, bracing myself for the disorientation of seeing through someone else's eyes.

My body toppled and spun. My consciousness flew out my ears, but instead of falling into a fae's head, it slammed into a wall of darkness. The shock juddered through my body, rattling my bones and gnashing my teeth together. Blake clung to me, his eyes wide with shock.

"They've blocked us out, too!" Blake cried. "We won't get them like that."

In the moments Blake and I had tried to perform the compulsion spell, things had got even more dire. Several more fae spilled from the inky depths, holding aloft bone knives and shillelagh as they raced around my boys, grabbing the screaming, scattering protesters and shoving them into the void. Screams cut off abruptly as the darkness took Dora's mob one by one, leaving not a trace behind.

Arthur flung himself at another Far Darrig, his blade swinging and slicing. Green fae blood ran down his arms and drenched his trench coat. His hollow eyes and drawn face were the only clue that he was starting to tire. Behind him, Corbin battled a swarm of sprites, whirling his knives around his head, slapping at them with the metal blades while they pecked at his head. Dust and black ink swirled around us like a cloud. I couldn't see Rowan or Flynn through the battle.

Blake still held my hand. He squeezed my fingers tight. "They won't hurt you. Daigh wants you alive. Use that. Get to Jane and Connor. I've got to help the others."

"But they'll kill you all!"

Blake drew a long dagger from his belt and saluted me with it. "I'll give 'em hell for you, Princess."

I gulped back the panic mounting inside me. "Blake, no. Don't let go of me."

They're here for Connor. Save Connor.

His fingers fell away. With a final cocky smile, Blake turned away and rushed into the fray.

6

MAEVE

*M*y heart tore to pieces. I knew in a few moments I would see my boys cut down by these vicious creatures. Once again I would stand hopelessly on the sidelines and watch someone I love perish at the hands of the fae, and all I'd be left with was the hollow grief of their loss.

I'll protect them, Maeve. A sweet, singsong voice that wasn't my own sang inside my head. *Make their distraction count.*

The voice sounded familiar, but I couldn't place it. I didn't have time to wonder who the hell that was or how they were able to get inside my head. I didn't even stop to see how this mystery voice intended to save my boys. If I'd been given an opportunity, I'd damn well make it count.

I pitched forward again, pushing down the fear that battled against the magic in my chest. crawling around the corner of the pew and into the aisle. Chunks of masonry cascaded from above, hitting the floor and shattering into pieces, showering the battle in a glimmering mist. I scrambled to my feet and bolted toward the front of the church, toward Jane and Connor.

"Don't you touch my son!" Jane screamed from somewhere in front of me.

"Stay there, Jane!" I cried, scrambling over the pitching ground. "I'm coming for you."

A Far Darrig leapt down in front of me. Before I could react, it grabbed my shoulders and spun me around, pressing my back against its slimy, furry body and pinning my arms at my sides. I screamed and kicked, trying to position myself the way Arthur had taught me so I could knee him in the groin. I managed to connect with its kneecap, but it didn't put me down. It slammed something into my forehead. My skin seared. I screamed as it held the object there and my head cracked open and my skull burned and all I could see were dancing white lights of pain.

My feet left the ground. More hands grabbed my ankles. I kicked and screamed, but it did no good. My mind flailed for something, *anything*, but the pain was too great. I couldn't call my magic. I couldn't see, couldn't feel, couldn't think.

The Far Darrigs lifted me higher, shuffling across the floor. They grunted and gibbered in some crude language. I managed to pry open one eye in time to see the great wall of black smoke curling toward me. The void called me, pulling my body closer, willing me to succumb.

"No," I gasped.

But I couldn't free myself. They held me over the crack – my body swinging over the gloom. With a jubilant cry, they let go, and I toppled down, down, down into the dark of nothing.

7

MAEVE

*efore I could even scream, I slammed into something hard. My back cracked as pain arced through my body. I flailed my arms out, felt the cool marble of the church floor beneath my fingers. A moment later I glanced up. I was back on the shaking ground in the church. The two Far Darrigs stood over me, staring down at their hands. Grey smoke rose from their fingertips.

The void was gone. It had closed beneath me. *What the hell?*

"You... you've been baptized," one Far Darrig whispered, its voice hoarse. The smell of burning flesh clogged my nostrils. Pain seared through my body. I tried to roll over, but every muscle screamed at me to stop that nonsense. I ignored them. On my third try I managed to get up.

Something about my being baptized had hurt them. I had no idea why that would matter, but at that moment I praised my parents and their crazy Christian ideals with every fiber of my being.

My forehead still stung, but the pain gave me a new

strength. *Whatever they did to me, they accidentally made me into a weapon.*

I lurched toward the fae, holding my hands up like a cartoon zombie.

The Far Darrigs staggered back. I slapped one across the face. *That's for trying to drop me into a void, you bastard.*

Black tendrils shot from its skin, and it made a keening wail like a banshee being sucked down a drain. It shrunk away and I hit the other one. I flailed at them wildly, driving them back, back, back until they teetered on the edge of another fissure. I closed my hand into a fist the way Arthur had taught me and slammed it into the nearest fae's solar plexus. It collapsed backward and sank into the void, the black tendrils consuming its body. As the second one whimpered in terror I shoved it in as well. The last thing I saw before they disappeared into nothingness was their long snouts disintegrating and their mouths open in silent screams.

I stepped forward, unable to believe that I'd somehow got rid of two of them. *Did I kill them or just send them back to the fae realm? What is that black fog?* A tendril curled in the air toward me. My fingers itched to touch it, to somehow discern its chemical makeup. *I'm staring at something that has literally been formed in the multiverse. It's astounding—*

The ground rumbled. I leapt back as more fae poured from the fissure – this time they were tall and slim and humanoid and wearing the green tunics of the Seelie, with curved bone knives on their belts and elegant recurve bows slung over their shoulders. Arthur sliced the head off one as soon as he reached for his quiver. Flynn and Rowan leapt on another one, Rowan flinging the bow away while Flynn stabbed at its chest.

"They've been baptized," one fae yelled as he tried to push Flynn into the abyss. The crack closed up beneath him, and

Flynn's hands broke his fall against the hard marble. "Leave the witches. The others will make an adequate sacrifice."

What the fuck does that even mean? Those who were baptised seemed to be unable to fall into the cracks, but I knew for a fact that I was the only one of my coven who'd been baptized. Why didn't Flynn fall into the hole?

Tears brimmed in my eyes as I realised how hopeless it was. Dead bodies littered the floor – some fae, too many human. Blood – both red and green – stained the pew cushions. The guys were tiring, their swings erratic, their breathing heavy and labored. More fae would keep coming. Eventually they would bring us all down.

You're protected. They can't get to you. Get to Jane. Save Connor.

I turned to run to the altar, but Blake's voice froze me in my tracks. "Liah, what are you doing?"

The words trembled on his lips. I turned, fearing what I'd see.

A tall fae with white-blonde braids that swung almost to the floor faced Blake, her eyes cold and cruel. Her right hand was missing, and a barbaric wooden contraption had been tied to the stump and fitted to the nocking points so she could draw the bow.

But that wasn't what turned my blood cold.

A green-tipped arrow sat in the bow, its vicious point aimed at my chest. The fae pulled back the string until it was taut against her cheek. "Hello, Blake," she said evenly, her voice as chilling as the ocean on a stormy day. "Hello, Princess. I hope you're ready to die."

8

BLAKE

*M*y mouth dried up. The church and the Far Darrigs and the void and the cowering vicar and the clashing of coven and fae ceased to exist. All I was aware of was that poisoned arrow aimed at Maeve's chest.

The world stopped. Liah's lips turned up into a smile.

"You're not supposed to kill her," I said, a last desperate effort to reason with her. "Daigh will be unhappy."

"Maybe the plan has changed," Liah replied, straightening her arm. "Or maybe I know how to wound the princess without killing her. Or maybe I just don't care anymore. Which answer will cause you the most pain? Because that will be the truth."

I didn't even think. I stepped in front of Maeve, shielding her body with mine.

The act was pointless. Liah's arrow would tear through my chest, and the poison would kill me even before the organ damage and blood loss. My corpse would fall over and Maeve would be exposed again, and Liah had had many, many more arrows. And yet, the act didn't *feel* pointless. It felt like the most important thing I'd ever done.

Liah lifted an eyebrow. "Feeling selfless for once, Blake Beckett? Your sacrifice will be in vain."

I nodded, folding my arms across my chest. "I know."

"Blake," Maeve's hand gripped my shoulder, her voice a knife tearing through my chest. My whole life she'd been a story told to me by Daigh, a mythological princess I was supposed to wed so that the fae kingdom could be restored on earth. She'd been my only hope for a life outside my prison. But now that I'd found her, I saw how much more she was. I didn't want to ever leave her. But her life mattered more.

From behind Liah's back Corbin dragged his dagger from a Seelie's skull. He met my eyes. As soon as he noticed the arrow he leapt into action, shoving his way through the battling fae struggling to toss the last of the humans into the fissures. *Maybe my sacrifice will buy them enough time to save Maeve.*

This is how I die, shot through the chest by someone I thought was my friend.

Weirdly, the thought brought no anger or sadness, only peace. I would die today having spoken a truth, having sacrificed myself to protect Maeve, having fought for the coven, for earth – the home I'd never been allowed to know.

It might have taken me my whole damn life, but I'd finally done the right thing.

I lifted my hands, palms facing Liah. I broke into a smile. "Go ahead, Liah. I'm waiting."

Liah's fingers twitched on the bowstring. Her remained passive, her eyes containing only that callous coldness she'd possessed back when I found her beside the sidhe, Daigh's rune carved into her arm and the broken pieces of scientific equipment at her feet.

She didn't loose the arrow.

I sucked in a breath. It was a perfect shot. She had me completely at her mercy. So why did she hesitate?

Corbin slammed into her from the side. Liah's face crumpled as they sailed across the room. He slammed her into a pillar. They slid to the floor, limbs and bow and dagger tangled together. Liah's rope pinned her arm, and she swore and screamed as she battered Corbin with her one good fist. None of the other fae moved to help her, and Corbin quickly pinned her other arm.

"We've got all we can," a Seelie warrior yelled. "The rest will follow in the Slaugh. Fall back!"

I glanced around. He was right. Most of the humans had disappeared – fallen by the shillelagh or the bone blade, their bodies taken by the darkness, leaving behind only dark trails of blood where they had be dragged across the floor. The only corpses that littered the church were the fae we had slain.

The rest of the fae started to leap into the fissures. They dragged the bodies of their dead across the stained marble and tossed them into the void, then leapt in after them. The black abyss curled around them, dragging them down to the place we had no hope of reaching.

Liah kicked and struggled. Corbin bent over her, his lips curled back into a nasty snarl as he raised his dagger—

"Don't kill her," I cried. "Let her go with the others."

Wait, where the fuck did that come from?

She betrayed you. She lied to you. She just tried to kill Maeve. She doesn't deserve mercy.

Corbin paused, his blade hovering inches from her neck. Liah hissed through her teeth.

"Let her go," I repeated.

I'm going to regret the hell out of this.

Corbin growled as he swung his arm and tossed Liah away. She sobbed as she hit the marble and skidded into the fissure. "Blake—" she choked out, but the void stole her words as it consumed her, her body disappearing into the blackness.

I sank to my knees, sucking a breath in through my lungs – lungs that should have been perforated by Liah's arrow, but weren't.

It didn't make sense. Liah had made it clear she was with Daigh. The burns from touching Maeve's scientific equipment and the raw cuts from Daigh's rune still marred her flesh. So why did she threaten Maeve?

And why didn't she follow through on her threat? Liah could have killed me, but she hesitated. *Why?*

MAEVE

*B*lake looked shellshocked. I rushed to him, but I'd barely grazed his shoulder when someone behind me yelled. "Maeve, help!"

When will this nightmare end?

I whipped my head around. Jane cowered against the altar, cradling Connor in her breast. Looming over her, holding a long bone blade in her hand and reaching for Connor, was Sheryl Brownley.

What now?

"Stay away from her!" I sprinted across the buckling ground, the earth tossing me off balance. I half leapt, half-fell into Sheryl, knocking her to the ground. We wrestled over the knife. Sheryl clawed at my face, raking long nails down my cheeks. I bent her hand back until tears pooled in her eyes and her fingers loosened. She was definitely human, then. I grabbed the blade and held it to her throat.

She simply smiled. "Go on, *witch*. Spill my blood on the steps of this altar. It does not matter. The fae king has his sacrifice."

Corbin appeared by my side. Long cuts crossed his arms

as he reached for Sheryl. My heart soared. *He's alive.* He dragged Sheryl to her feet, shaking her shoulders. "What have you done?" he demanded, his eyes flashing with barely-controlled rage.

"Nothing you wouldn't have done had you been in my shoes, dearie," Sheryl answered pleasantly, as if we were discussing the proper method for making a pot of tea. "Delivering that whore Aline Moore's daughter into their hands would have been the ultimate triumph. But alas, she has been baptized, and so they cannot touch her... for now."

"What do you mean, they cannot touch me?" It didn't make any sense. I'd always been baptised and the fae had handled me before in their realm. They had dragged me in front of Daigh. So why did touching me burn them up now?

But Sheryl ignored my question. She lifted her chin high, proud and defiant even as Corbin tightened his grip on her. "You can't hold them back forever. It's only a matter of time before your coven falls. You made the wrong choice by rejecting your father, Maeve Moore. I, on the other hand, will be rewarded for my loyalty."

"You did this?" Corbin blinked. He didn't believe her. But I did. It was too perfect. Sheryl had arranged the baptism for us. She had all the parish records. She knew all the local gossip, so she'd learn the identity of every newborn child who wouldn't be receiving a baptism. She'd been watching Connor from the *start*.

"Of course I did this, dear," Sheryl smoothed down the front of her dress, staring defiantly between me and Corbin. "Someone had to ensure the fae king had the appropriate, unbaptized sacrifice. I know everything that goes on in this county, everyone's little secrets and dirty laundry. And I knew that within that mob Dora brought to stop Connor's baptism the first time, at least fifteen of those so-called right-eous people had never been baptized of the Lord. I expected them all to turn up today. And Maeve here was kind enough to provide me all the tools I needed to ensure they would be protected from your coven's magic."

"But how?" And then I remembered. *My purse.* When Jane and I first went to speak to the Crookshollow vicar, I'd left it unguarded while I took Kelly's phone call. Sheryl must have scooped out all the objects she needed; Flynn's medallion, Rowan's twig, Corbin's parchment, Arthur's blade, and something of mine. Each object was imbued with the residue of our energies. She must've used the objects to create a spell to protect the fae from our magic before she pretended to find my purse behind that pillar.

I bet she ate my cookies, too. Bitch.

"But why?"

Sheryl laughed. "Why? Because the fae are Angels of God come to scour the evil from earth. Only the righteous will inherit the new Kingdom of Heaven. It is no place for witches and fornicators and people who don't pay their Council tax."

"You think the fae are sent from God?" Flynn demanded. "Bloody hell, you're mad, woman."

"Of course. They are the Angels of Justice sent to purge the earth of sinners, to bring the righteous to paradise and to make this broken land a place where the spirits of the dead can dwell."

Anger surged inside me at this woman for being so stupid as to fall for fae tricks. But mostly, my rage was reserved for Daigh. That he could take this woman's faith and twist it like this, that he could take a good person and get her to do this evil thing, that he could lay the deaths of others squarely upon her shoulders.

"Their blood is on your hands now," Corbin said. "Where does that leave you in the Kingdom of Heaven?"

"Oh, I won't be seeing God's Kingdom," Sheryl said. "God

does not allow murderers such as I to dwell in his eternal glory. But I go to my new dwelling place in peace, knowing I have done God's Will, and that I will soon see my husband again."

She lowered her head and broke into a run, heading straight for me. Corbin stepped in front of me, but I elbowed him aside. "No," I cried. "She's—"

But it was too late. Sheryl Brownley leapt into the fissure, her skirt and petticoat flaring up around her as she topped into the inky black depths.

*A*s I stared in horror, steadying myself against the altar, the earth rumbled and the edges of the fissure pulled tight again. Screams tore from the crack as the marble floor repaired itself over top of its victims. Inspector Davies tried to claw her way out of the void, but a sharp piece of marble sliced through her hand as she searched for purchase on the slick marble floor, and she was torn back into the crack once again. The tiles sank back into place. The puddles of blood dried up and faded away. It was as if the whole thing had never happened.

"No. Give them back!" I sank to my knees and pawed at the ground, trying to get to the fae. But the marble had completely closed over into a smooth floor. The rumbling stopped.

Jane still cowered against the altar. I rushed to her, wrapping her in my arms and gazing down at little Connor's face. We kept him safe, but at a terrible cost.

So many people... all gone.

Flynn and Rowan picked themselves up from the back of the church and made their way toward us, stepping around buckled, broken marble and masonry. Corbin wiped green fae blood from his face. Arthur slid his sword back into its scabbard, his eyes hollow. Blake sank down beside me, his usually casual face pale and drawn.

One by one, my boys shambled their way up to the altar and collapsed beside us, wrapping their arms around Jane and I, resting their heads against mine. Rowan's face was streaked with tears.

I couldn't cry. I was too numb.

I counted them all. Jane, Connor, Corbin, Blake, Arthur, Rowan, Flynn. Even Clara sat on the steps, her hands trembling as she clung to her black shawl that had been ripped to shreds. The priest stared with hollow eyes across the church, where a handful of people crawled out from behind the pews. All of them had torn clothes and filthy skin and horror in their eyes. But all gloriously, beautifully alive.

If only it wasn't at such a horrible cost.

"How did you guys not get killed?" I choked out, wrapping my arms around Flynn. Rowan fell against us, his breath warm on the back of my neck. The others piled on, and soon I was engulfed in the warm, hard bodies of my coven.

My boys. They're alive. But only just.

"It was the darndest thing. I was fighting a Far Darrig when something splashed in my face, and this girlish voice inside my head chanted the Lord's Prayer." Flynn ran a hand through his fiery hair, now caked with stone and plaster dust and splattered with fae blood. "I thought it was you working some kind of magic."

I shook my head. "Not me. I was too busy trying not to die."

"The same thing happened to me," Rowan said. "The water splashed on my face just as one of the fae tried to throw me in the void, and I hit the ground instead."

"Me too," I squeezed him harder. "It was as if I bounced

off and the Far Darrig who touched me went up in smoke. Sheryl said something about them not being able to take me because I'm baptized. But they were fine touching me in the fae realm, so I don't get it."

"Maybe because it was us who went there, not the other way around. But that doesn't explain how we were saved – none of us have ever been baptized..." Corbin's face twisted. "That was it. Someone – or something – baptized us in the middle of the fight. But I didn't think that was possible. You have to be a priest or something."

"What about all those other people?" I demanded. "Why did this mystery person not save them, too? Now Daigh has them and he's going to use them as his sacrifice. We have to go after them. I can drag them back through my dreams and—"

Blake shook his head. "They're gone, Princess. Not even you can follow them to that place."

My whole body shuddered. *We couldn't save them. Now Daigh has everything he needs to raise the Slaugh. What can we even hope to do now?*

A few other people crawled out from behind pillars and under pews, their bodies bloody and broken. They huddled together at the back of the church. The vicar crept out from behind the vestibule. "Is it over?" he asked, his whole body trembling. "Have they gone?"

"They're gone, but it's not over," I croaked out. "Not even close."

My phone rang. I pulled away from our huddle and dragged it out of my pocket. Kelly's picture flashed on the screen.

I'll always be there for you.

In the midst of the broken church, I pulled the phone to my ear and managed to croak out a greeting. "Kelly? Is every-thing okay?"

"Hey, sis. Yeah, I'm good. I'm great, in fact. That's what I wanted to talk to you about. Is this a good time?"

I burst out laughing. I couldn't help it. Corbin looked up in concern, but Arthur just squeezed me tighter. "Oh yeah. The best time. What's up?"

"I just wanted to tell you that today went really well. I met my new lawyer and she's lovely. She seems to think I've got a very good chance of having my petition for emancipation approved, especially given the state of my finances and your statement. And she helped me put my passport application in, and pulled some lawyer tricks to get me a special emergency passport that only takes a couple of days. And I've had the best day hanging out with Gabe and Pete and all the backpackers. We went to the Desert Botanical Garden and Old Town Scottsdale. I can't believe I've lived in Arizona all my life and I'd never been to Old Town Scottsdale! So I've decided that's what I want to do."

"What is?" My head spun. Bile rose in my throat. *So many deaths on my hands. Thank god Kelly wasn't here to be another one of them.*

"I'm going to be a backpacker. I'm going to travel the world with my possessions on my back and do odd jobs when I need money and make friends everywhere I go."

"You... *what?*"

"I'm going to be a world traveler! And, the best news is, I can start from England." Kelly's voice rose with excitement. "I've already been to the British consulate today and got my travel visa sorted. Gabe helped me do it. And Candice says I don't need to be in the country for my petition to be lodged. There's nothing keeping me here, which means I can come to Briarwood even earlier than we thought. I'm getting on a plane in two days. Isn't this awesome?"

"But..."

"I want the bedroom right under yours so we can gossip

about those hot tenants all night. I can't wait to meet them! And since you're not doing much except hanging around reading boring astronomy books, I'll take you to see all the sights – Big Ben, Hadrian's Wall, Buckingham Palace, let's do them all!"

My head throbbed. *Two days.* I thought I'd have weeks until Kelly got herself organized enough to come to England. Kelly had no idea I was really a witch. Now she was coming to Briarwood, right in the middle of my messy relationship with the guys and a full-on war against the fae.

What the hell am I going to do?

MAEVE

y sister is coming to Briarwood.
Right as the fae have captured people for their blood sacrifice.

This is going to go horribly, woefully wrong.

I huddled in a circle with Jane and the rest of my coven at the back of the church, gazing out over the smooth marble floor that had only half an hour ago been torn down the middle with a great dark fissure, through which poured an army of fae warriors who stole away several people – including the old castle housekeeper – to use as a human sacrifice.

Horror and panic rose in my gut as the scene repeated over in my head – the terrifying rumbling through the ancient church as the fae tore open the earth, the snarl and snap of sharpened teeth as the Far Darrigs scampered across the church, the screams of innocent people as they were pulled into the black abyss.

I leaned against Arthur, looping my arms around his neck and letting him take my weight in a way that couldn't have been comfortable. Right now, he was the only thing keeping my trembling body upright.

Magic still hummed in my veins, desperate for release. We needed to get back to the castle, to do... *something*. But the police wouldn't let us leave. They'd arrived on the scene after one of the neighbors heard all the screaming, and found at least twenty people had gone missing and those who remained telling a crazy story that made no sense. They were questioning Flynn right now, while paramedics tended to the vicar. He'd gone catatonic from the shock of seeing his church carved open down the middle like a Sunday roast.

I can't say I blamed him.

"Everyone got it?" Corbin hissed. He was the only one talking. He'd switched to solve-the-problem-and-protect-the-coven mode immediately, trying to concoct a story for the police that would marry up with what the others said *without* giving away that the cause was supernatural. Considering the Far Darrigs were essentially four-foot tall talking rats, that was some tall order. He must have come up with something, because he was looking at everyone expectantly. I nodded, even though I hadn't heard a word he'd said.

All those people are dead. I couldn't save them. And now Kelly is coming here and putting herself right in the middle of it.

"Flynn's coming back," Arthur said in a flat voice, his arms tightening around me. I sunk deeper into his thick trench coat, feeling the heavy weight of his sword brushing against my leg. It was hard to believe that only a half hour ago he was swinging that sword around like a Viking, slaying any fae that crossed his path. At least he'd managed to calm his rage now. If the police discovered that blade on him – its edge darkened with fae blood – or any of our other weapons, we'd be in a world of trouble.

"They want to talk to you next," Flynn said, as he rejoined

the circle and patted Blake on the shoulder. His usually-jovial expression burned with weariness.

Corbin turned to Blake, his eyes wide as though he'd just remembered our newest coven member was there. "What are you going to tell them? You can't say you're the son of Darren and Colleen Beckett, or they'll find out about the murder suicide and—"

"Relax, Mussolini. I've got this." Blake shot me his wild grin as he sauntered off after Officer Judge.

"He has so *not* got this," Corbin fumed. "He's going to say something stupid and get us all in trouble. With Inspector Davies gone, they're going to be out for our blood."

Inspector Davies. My chest burned. I looked over at Jane, who bounced Connor on her shoulder, trying to keep him calm with all the commotion. *She's such a good mother.* Jane always put Connor's needs before her own. Even though she'd been terrified when the fae had targeted her son for their vile sacrifice, she'd held it together so she could find a way to keep him safe. Not for the first time, I wondered if my mother would have been the same, and then hated myself for wondering because it felt like I was betraying the Crawfords.

Inspector Davies had instigated a witch hunt against Jane because her husband had partaken of Jane's services. I hated her for that, but that didn't mean I wanted her to suffer through whatever the fae were currently doing to her.

My stomach twisted again. *All this death... and there's no way to make it right again.*

Blake came back a few minutes later and tapped me on the shoulder. "You're next, Princess."

My brain wasn't registering any instructions, but my body moved across the room of its own accord and sat down opposite Officer Judge and a new Detective Inspector. I touched the bare skin of my arm, but I couldn't feel the press of my fingers against my skin. I couldn't even feel my magic anymore. Everything was numb and cold and dead, just the way I'd been when I first learned my parents had been killed.

My mouth felt as though it had been stuffed with cotton. I don't know how I managed to push air past my vocal chords when all the air had been driven out of me. I heard myself running through a cleaned-up version of everything that happened, so I must have managed it somehow. Words flew out of my mouth in some semblance of order, but I didn't remember any of them. I kept my gaze trained on the haunted look in Officer Judge's eyes. Her boss toppling down into that black abyss played in my head on a continuous loop.

"Your little group has been involved in another recent incident." The new inspector – whose name was Wallace – glanced at his notes. "Only a few days ago, you found Ms. Forsythe's baby in the bushes outside Briarwood Castle. Now, we find all the same parties have witnessed this unusual phenomenon."

"We're all friends, so we all came here for Connor's baptism," I said. "We were supposed to have it in a church in Crookshollow a few days ago, but Dora and her group of witch hunters kept us away. If it hadn't been for Dora and Inspector Davies, we wouldn't even have been in this church today."

"Witch hunters?" Officer Judge's face twisted.

"It's just an expression. They didn't approve of Jane. They were harassing her, trying to prevent the baptism. Apparently the Middle Ages are alive and well around here."

Inspector Wallace looked at his pad again. "You just returned from overseas?"

"Yes. I was in Arizona on a family matter. Arthur and I came here straight from Heathrow."

"Tell us about the... creatures... that came out of the

crack?" Officer Judge asked, her mouth turning down at the edges.

"I didn't actually see any creatures," I heard myself saying. "There was definitely black, curling smoke pouring from the crack. I wondered if perhaps it was some kind of natural gas released when the earth moved. It could have been hallucinogenic. Some kind of sinkhole or thermal activity underneath the church, maybe?"

"We've got a geologist coming down from Oxford to survey the site," she said. "Trust me, we're taking this *very* seriously, Maeve. Please, don't leave the country again without informing us first."

Her gaze sizzled the last of my frayed nerves. I couldn't move from the chair. Officer Judge had to call Corbin to come drag me away.

"We're going home," he whispered in my ear as he wrapped his arm around my shoulder. I nodded, leaning into his chest, wishing I could sink right into his starched white shirt and disappear forever.

We trudged outside. Arthur's stupid old car was parked diagonally across three spaces. We'd been so desperate to get there in time that he hadn't even bothered to park it properly. *And it was all for nothing.*

"We're going to have to make two trips," Corbin sighed.

"No need," Blake swiped Corbin's phone from his pocket. "I discovered this fascinating thing called an *app*. There's one that calls an automobile to answer your beck and call, like a servant-on-demand."

"You really need to grasp the concept of the sharing economy," Corbin snapped, snatching his phone back and calling a ride share.

Flynn laughed. "It seems to me our friend Blake is getting the hang of being a human just fine and dandy."

I thought of what he'd done today, leaping in front of that arrow. *In more ways than one.*

Arthur pulled open his door and folded his enormous frame into the driver's seat. "This slave is leaving right now, if anyone needs a lift."

I grabbed for the passenger-side door just as a sharp finger tapped my shoulder. I spun around. Clara stood behind me, holding her black shawl tight around her shoulders. Her expression was stern. "I think I'd better come with you, dearie."

Corbin looked ready to argue, but he snapped his mouth shut. *Damn right, it's not your decision any more.* I was High Priestess now, and it was time I took responsibility for what that meant. And that started with listening to this little old lady.

"You're right." I held open the car door for Clara and she climbed inside, adjusting her hat in the rearview mirror. Corbin climbed in behind her, and I sank down beside him, and we tore off.

I didn't register anything about the ride back to Briarwood. One moment we pulled out of the churchyard and the next Arthur careened through the gatehouse and squealed to a stop outside the Norman keep.

I dragged my feet across the inner courtyard in a daze. *How did this happen? The fae weren't supposed to be able to get here unless they came through the gateway. And Blake and I sealed the gateway with our spirit magic. They wanted Connor, so why did they take all those other people instead? Why did they need so many? How had everything gone so horribly wrong?*

The front door groaned on its hinges. Briarwood welcomed us home with a cold draft blowing from one of the high, narrow windows. Clara shuffled across the flagstones in front of me, her intelligent eyes darting around the entrance hall, taking in the sweeping staircase, gilded portraits, and towering suit of armor.

"Briarwood," she breathed, the word catching in her throat. "It's been so long."

"I need a curry," Blake said, pushing past us and heading toward the kitchen. Corbin grabbed his collar.

"Not so fast. We're going to the Great Hall and you're going to explain to everyone what the fuck just happened."

"But—"

"*Now.*" Corbin hauled Blake into the hall. I dragged my feet after them. The way Corbin looked, Blake's life might be at stake, and I wasn't going to have any more death today.

Corbin threw Blake down on the couch. "Start talking, before I give that smartarse face a real human makeover."

I grabbed his arm. "Corbin, we should at least wait for the others—"

"Yeah, Arnold will be pissed if you rip my throat out without him," Blake shot back.

"People *died* today," Corbin yelled, his hands balled into fists at his sides. "Can you possibly stop being a fucking twat for just a single second and be actually useful?"

"I *was* useful. I was the one who told you the fae were going to be at the church. If it wasn't for me, that screaming baby might've joined them. I get credit for that, right?"

Connor's shriek echoed through the great hall, as if underlining Blake's point. The others must've arrived. Arthur moved to Corbin's side, his arms folded and his face twisted with menace. Flynn walked around the other side of the sofa, his expression dark.

"Don't threaten Connor," he said. "You said you'd explain it all when Maeve got here. Well, she's here. Start talking."

"You took the last of the sleeping draught," I said, slumping down into the beanbag opposite him. I knew I should be angry at him for lying to us, but after everything that had happened today, it seemed like it barely even mattered. "You spoke to Liah again."

Blake nodded. He fixed his eyes on mine. For the first time since I'd met him, he showed none of his swagger or bravado. He looked utterly defeated, which was exactly how I felt. "I didn't just speak to her. I brought her back with me."

"Jesus fucking Christ!" Corbin yelled.

"Hey." I fixed Corbin with what I hoped was a withering stare. "I know you feel betrayed here. But can we just let Blake tell the whole story first? Then we can decide whether he gets the tar and feathers."

Flynn whistled. Arthur glanced at me in surprise. I guess no one ever told Corbin to shut up. Corbin nodded. Blake continued.

"I did the same thing you'd done when you brought all the guys back into this world. Only I did it from outside the grounds so Liah wouldn't get hurt by the castle's wards. I hid her in the wood – on the Raynard's property, since she couldn't enter Briarwood, and I took her some food."

"The curries," Rowan breathed. Blake nodded.

"And I stole some fruit, too. We talked a bit. Liah was all keen to join us against the fae but then she went down to the village and saw the buildings and the roads and cars. That made her angry. She told me she wanted to go back. I thought—" he took a deep, shuddering breath. "I thought I could still convince her to fight for us. When we were kids I could convince her to do anything. It was me who encouraged her to pick up a bow, and of course she excelled at it immediately.

"So anyway. I told her some stuff about you guys, about the castle. I showed her the gateway. Then yesterday I went down to see her, and she wasn't in the forest. I found her at the sidhe. She'd destroyed all Maeve's equipment. She had burns from touching the metal all down her arm from doing it." Blake's eyes darkened. "On her other arm she'd carved a rune into her flesh. Daigh's rune. She wouldn't do that unless she was on his side."

"And then what happened?"

"She told me she was going back to Daigh, that after what she'd seen she couldn't possibly fight on the side of the humans. She went back through the gateway he'd made for her, and as she was leaving she told me that the fae were going to be at the church for Connor's baptism, and that's when I ran to tell you."

"Okay, but then how did she go back to Daigh through the gateway with our wards in place? Don't tell me – the same way the fae got into the church. What was that hole in the floor and the black fog?"

"That fog is the blackest, darkest magic – like a primordial soup for demons. The cracks are another kind of gateway, similar to the one between earth and Tir Na Nog, only that one was made by witches and this one was made by something entirely different."

"Who?"

"Somehow – and I don't entirely understand how he did it, but it's evil and mad and *brilliant* – Daigh has gone direct to the source. Direct to the place where he will raise the Slaugh."

"Meaning?" Corbin glared.

"*Meaning*," Blake's eyes narrowed right back. "The fae are in the underworld."

MAEVE

I couldn't help it. I snorted back a laugh. "Blake, be serious."

He looked up at me, his eyes blazing. "I am, Princess. I know you don't believe in things you can't empirically measure, but think about what you saw today. That crack in the earth, the black fog seeping out. You know that the fae cannot cross over from Tir Na Nog into our world except through the gateway at the sidhe. But they did, which means they're not in Tir Na Nog anymore. In the words of my new favorite author Mr. Conan Doyle, you need to make deductions."

"Seriously? An underworld, with fire and brimstone and demons and pitchforks?"

"The pitchforks were an invention of the renaissance painters," a croaky voice spoke up. "But the rest of it is true, to an extent."

I whirled around. Clara stood in the doorway, balancing a tray with a tea pot and several cups and saucers.

"The underworld Blake's speaking of is not the same as the Christian concept of Hell," Clara explained, shuffling into the room and placing the tray down on the table. "It's like a waiting room. The souls of the dead go there to endure punishments for their sins and await their final judgement."

"Purgatory?" Flynn asked.

"That's the most recognised of it's descriptions on earth, yes. It is from this place where the Slaugh will get their riders, but they must first strike a bargain with the creatures in charge for the use of those unfortunate shades. That bargain has been paid in the blood of the innocent tonight." She stared up at the ceiling, her eyes wide. "Ah, it's so wonderful to be back in this beautiful Hall. A few more swords than I remember, but otherwise it's exactly the same."

"Who is this person?" Arthur demanded.

"Clara owns the *Astarte* shop where Corbin and I got those books from the other day," I explained, reddening slightly as I remembered the title of one of mine: *Sacred Polyamory*. "She also knew all our parents, and even helped them with some of their spells."

"I remember you, young man," Clara said, poking Arthur in the chest. "You owe me three quid for that dreamcatcher you got tangled in your beard. The feathers are rumpled, so I can't sell it. Your mother wouldn't approve of such behavior from her son."

Arthur looked shocked. It might have been the mention of his mother, but probably it was the fact that an old lady one tenth his size was bossing him around.

"How do you know anything about this?" Corbin demanded, swinging around to face Clara with all his fury simmering.

"Sit down, dearie," Clara said to Corbin, thumping the cushion on his favorite chair. "You're going to pull something with all that strain."

"But what are you—"

"Now, now." Clara gave his chest a shove, pushing him

down into the chair. She lifted the teapot and started pouring out cups. "I know you're all scared and you want answers. What you saw today was not something human eyes were meant to comprehend. But all this yelling and swearing won't help matters. We all need to calm down. Here," she shoved a cup and saucer into Corbin's hands, then turned to Arthur. "Now, do you take milk and sugar?"

SMASH.

"We don't have time for tea!" Corbin screamed, dropping the cup at his feet. His voice reverberated around the hollow hall. Obelix leapt down from on top of the fireplace and fled into the entrance hall. "The fae are about to raise the Slaugh and our magic is useless against them!"

"Please, use your indoor voice," Clara scolded. "And yes, you have time for tea. The fae have made good on their bargain with the beasts who dwell there. The unfortunate souls who were taken today are already dead, their blood forming the final ingredient for the spell to unleash hell on earth. However, they can only raise the Slaugh on the first night of the full moon, and we still have fifteen days until then. That gives us plenty of time to figure out how to stop them."

I remembered the fae saying they would see us again on the full moon.

"As for the fae's immunity to your powers, you have Sheryl Brownley to thank for that. I saw her toss a charm that must have blocked your magic."

"She made it when she stole my purse," I said. I filled the guys in on the day I misplaced my purse at the church.

"Thankfully, the spell is temporary, and we can protect against it in future," Clara sipped her tea. "But if the fae are cooperating with demons and spirits of the underworld, they may attack with other weapons. They will be gaining tremendous power from their new abode, but they are also

71

being changed by the foulness of that place. This is why the touch of a baptised person hurts them now."

"How do you know all this?" Corbin demanded.

A thought occurred to me. "Clara, you said you used to help the Briarwood witches with rituals. You helped the coven with the spell that banished the fae twenty-one years ago, didn't you?"

She nodded. "I did, and I wasn't the only one. We had covens all over the country lending their magic to help stop the fae."

"So you could help us recreate the spell?"

This time, Clara shook her head. "Probably not. Only the High Priestesses of the covens and Aline's Magister and assistants were privy to the inner circle where the spell itself was cast. As a solitary witch, I remained in the outer circle to lend power. Aline was very careful to keep the details secret for some reason. But just knowing what they did isn't going to be enough, anyway. First of all, the fae weren't as close as they are now. But that's beside the point. The actual spell – the ritual – isn't the important thing. It's just pageantry that channels the power. Your mother led the ritual – she was its heart, and even her power was barely enough to hold them back. She was the most powerful spirit user of her age, and she died as a result. If Daigh is in the underworld, then he is infinitely more powerful than last time. We need someone with an even greater spirit ability to lead us, and I know of no such witch."

"We've got Aline's daughter." Arthur put his arm around my shoulders.

Clara looked at me and nodded. "Yes, we do. But are you all aware that performing this ritual is very likely a death sentence for all of you? It will most certainly kill Maeve."

I'll die?

Clara's words bounced around inside my head, growing

louder and harsher and more terrifying. I glanced at the others, and saw from their expressions that this hadn't occurred to them. But it should have. After all, most of our parents had died during the ritual, or been irreversibly changed by it.

I thought of the cemetery where we'd buried the Crawfords – their simple stone grave marker with the words *Weep not, for we are angels now*. I imagined my own stone next to theirs, probably with some stupid religious quote on it. I'd never get to go to university, or have a paper published in *The American Journal of Physics*, or go into space. I'd never read all the books I wanted to read or have a celestial body named after me, and Kelly... Kelly would lose *everything*. She'd already lost so damn much.

I don't want to die. I'm not ready to die.

There had to be another way. And we had fifteen days to find it.

Clara held a cup of tea out to me. I took it, my hands shaking.

"Maeve dying is not an option," Corbin said. "And even if she can't yet control the full extent of her powers, she has five Magisters. Aline only had one. That's got to count for something. If you say we've got fifteen days, then that's plenty of time to find an answer."

"I have one more question," Flynn waved his arm in the air.

"This isn't a classroom, young man," Clara said. "You don't need to raise your hand to speak."

"Sorry. You remind me of the schoolmarm back in the Old Country. I just wondered, was it you who did that magic that protected us all back at the church?"

Clara shook her head. "I cannot lay claim to that miracle. I was too busy trying to stop Sheryl getting to that child. It was a very clever piece of magic, performing an emergency baptism like that."

"Emergency baptism?"

"Yes. It is part of canon law that if a person is in danger of death and wishes to take the sacrament, than any layperson not normally authorized is able to perform the ritual of baptism. All they would need to do is splash each of you with holy water and say the simple words as laid out in the Book of Common Prayer."

"We all heard a voice inside our heads. It said the Lord's prayer," Flynn said, his eyes wide. "It was a woman's voice, all melodic-like. And I definitely felt something wet on me forrid. But we weren't anywhere near the baptismal font."

Clara tapped her fingers against the edge of her teacup. "It could have been one of the fae who possess telekinesis and compulsion. Or it could have been a spirit witch. But the only spirit witches I know who were in that church were Maeve and myself."

If it wasn't Clara, and it wasn't me, than who... I wondered briefly if it could have been Liah, but after the way she'd pointed that arrow at my chest, I didn't think so.

Then I remembered the voice I'd heard. Light and melodic, the words sung more than spoken. The voice telling me it had protected my boys.

I knew I'd heard it before.

I leapt to my feet, my mind whirring. Nothing about this made sense. It went against absolutely everything I knew to be true about physics and the universe and life and death. And yet—

"Maeve?" Rowan's dark eyes were wide with concern.

"I just... give me a minute," I stammered out. I shoved my cup back into Clara's hands and darted for the stairs. *This is insane. This is the most insane idea I've entertained since I entered this castle. I can't explain this away with theoretical physics.*

I wound my way up, up, up the spiral staircase to the first floor hallway and my mother's portrait. The words she'd written for me in her letter reverberated in my head.

There are so many things I wish to tell you, but there is so little time. I will die tonight, of that I am certain. I saw my own death many years ago. The power of premonition is an ugly gift, and I pray that you will not inherit this curse from me.

But was it precognition? Had she really seen her own death, or did she just believe that because she knew she was the only one capable of stopping the fae? Why did she keep all the witches – even her own coven - out of the ritual? Was it 'destiny,' or did she make really make a choice?

Did she choose death over me? Is she now haunting me?

"I hope for your sake you're a victim of retrocausality," I yelled up at the portrait. "You were supposed to love me above all others, like Jane does Connor, and I think you *chose* to leave me. But now I might have to make the same choice, and I'm scared, and even if I did still have parents, this situation is woefully out of their sphere of interest. If it really is you haunting me and saving my boys, then I need answers, because ghosts don't exist and paintings don't talk and I'm so fucking *scared*—"

My words died on my lips. I stared up at the painting, seeing for the first time that night that my mother wasn't staring out of the wall with her sparkling eyes and mysterious half-smile. Once more, her face had been twisted into an expression of extreme horror.

"Maeve," Corbin's footsteps clattered up the stairs behind me. "Don't listen to Clara. We'll find a way to—"

Corbin's words died on his lips. He'd seen it, too.

13

CORBIN

"*S*ee?" Maeve yelled. "I wasn't just imagining it."

I couldn't find the words to answer her because I was too stunned to see that face staring back at me. Aline's eyes were wide, filled with terror. Her mouth hung open, exposing the pink of her tongue and the black depths of her throat in a scream of silent horror. Even her posture seemed to have shifted ever so slightly, her limbs tight with tension.

This is insane. That painting has smiled down from this wall my entire life. How does it now look so completely horrifying?

Just as Maeve had already told me she'd done, I ran through the possible rational explanations in my head. *It's not the light shining on it in an unusual way. It's not a portrait from underneath showing through thin paint.* I tapped the heavy gilded frame, wondering if someone had come into the castle when we were at the baptism and exchanged the painting for a copy just to terrify us. But the frame was so heavy it would require at least three people to lift. There wasn't an elevator in Briarwood, and we hadn't been gone long enough for anyone human to complete that trick.

And even if someone *had* managed to exchange the

painting both times, that didn't explain how Maeve had seen it last time and then moments later, it had transformed back.

So then what the hell am I looking at?

Maeve inched closer. I grasped her arm, my head spinning. *This is just insane.*

Footsteps clattered up the stairs behind us. "Mary Mother of Jesus," Flynn whispered as he too saw the face in the painting.

"That's not possible," Arthur hissed.

"No way," Blake echoed.

"Aline certainly looks upset," said Clara.

Okay, so everyone had seen it. *Either we're having some mass group hysteria, or... or the painting really has moved.* Right. I gulped back my fear. No time for that. We had to figure out what was going on.

I sucked in a deep breath, pushing the fear further down until it was a flicker of a shadow on the edge of my mind. Now that I could focus again, my mind started to whir through possibilities.

It had to be some sort of magic. That was the only explanation. It couldn't be a fae's doing, because they wouldn't have been able to get inside the castle to enchant the portrait. Judging by the dust on the frame, the portrait hadn't been moved outside. So that left us with a couple of possibilities – it could be some sort of ghost-related phenomena. The castle was certainly old enough to have a resident poltergeist, and although we'd never noticed any activity like that before, I couldn't rule it out.

The other possibility – and this was much more likely – was that a witch did it. And I had a pretty fair idea of which witch that might be.

I whirled around and faced Blake. "You did this."

Blake shook his head. "Think again, Mussolini."

"Stop calling me that. This is a glamour, and you're the only one of us who can perform that magic. You told us so."

Maeve's fingers tightened around my arm. "Corbin, don't do this," she hissed.

I wrenched my arm out of Maeve's grasp and folded them across my chest. "Go on, Blake, tell us all how you're really still working for Daigh, how you're here to do things like this to terrify and distract us so your king can slip past our defenses."

Blake folded his arms. "He's hardly slipped past anything. I'd say he's rode in on a huge golden chariot waving a sign saying, 'look at me! I'm coming to kill all humans'!"

"Corbin," Maeve's voice was sharper this time. "This subject is old. Blake's on our side, end of story."

Why is she still so willing to trust him? Blake had never helped us for any other reason than to save his own skin.

Except for just before, when he told the truth about contacting that fae, and at the church, when he threw himself in front of that arrow meant for Maeve.

Bloody hell. I didn't want to trust Blake. He was a complete wanker and it would be so much easier to punch him in his stupid sneering mouth. But I didn't have the final say anymore. Maeve did. And that was right and proper. If only she'd see Blake for what he really was.

But... if it weren't for him, Maeve would be dead right now. All signs pointed to Blake being on our side. Unlike Maeve, I didn't make my decisions solely based on empirical data. I trusted my gut to lead me in the right direction. And right now my gut was screaming that this guy couldn't be trusted.

Clara waved her hand over the portrait. "This is no glamour. There's magic here, but it's much older. It seems to be mixed through the paint itself. I've never seen anything like this before."

"Almost as if it came from another realm," Arthur muttered. I nodded in agreement.

Blake shot me an amused look that made my blood boil. "Once again, my innocence is proven to the person who really matters here – *our* High Priestess. Can I go to the kitchen now? Fielding this constant suspicion does build up an appetite."

Maeve touched Blake's shoulder. She glared at me, and I felt her power sizzling behind her words. "We have to stop this bickering. People *died* tonight. I know we're all upset about that, but if we lose it with each other then we're never going to stop Daigh." She fixed each of us in turn with her dark eyes, and my anger withered. Admiration surged in my chest, and a bit of shame. Trust Maeve to bring us all back to what was really important. I glanced at Blake, who was flicking strands of his long black hair over his shoulder and not looking the least bit sorry. Could I ever trust the guy? For Maeve's sake? For the coven's sake?

I'd have to bloody well try.

I stuck a hand out under Blake's face. "She's right. You're in this, whether I like it or not."

Blake stared at my hand as though he was afraid I'd strike him with lightning.

"You shake it. It's a human gesture of camaraderie."

Blake still looked confused, but he took my hand and we shook. I may have crushed his fingers a little more than was polite, but it was a start.

Maeve gave a little smile. If she was happy, it was worth it.

I stared up at Maeve's mother, who still looked out with that petrified expression. "Okay, then. We know this portrait is magical. It's moving on its own. This magic might be something we can use. Does anyone have any idea what it might be and why it's in Aline's portrait? Flynn, you're an artist. Any thoughts?"

Flynn ran a hand through his mop of red curls. "Painting leprechauns?"

"Just a medium of seriousness while the whole world is at stake would be appreciated, Flynn," Maeve huffed.

"Sorry, couldn't resist. My totally serious, not-remotely-humorous guess is that if there's magic in the paint then the artist must've put it there."

Of course. I turned to Maeve. "You brought a book about Smithers, didn't you? Have you read it yet?"

"Only the first half of it – his biography. The rest is all wank about art."

"I'll give you wank about art," Flynn grinned, grabbing his crotch.

I ignored him, because that was what you did with Flynn. "Can you grab the book?"

"Corbin," Maeve looked like she was trying very hard not to throttle me. "You're not going to find an answer to this in an art compendium."

"All the same, I want to see it."

Maeve darted up the stairs to her bedroom and returned with a slim, hardcover volume. I flipped through the pages, skimming the short biography. Robert Smithers was a recluse, kind of last generation's Banksy. He claimed to be an orphan, and there was no record of him before his first painting appeared wrapped in brown paper on the doorstep of a London dealer. That dealer was so taken by Smithers' superior brushwork that he offered representation immediately. Smithers' first exhibition received the Turner Prize, and he was offered a place at the Royal Academy of Arts. The story caught the attention of the press, and Smithers became what passed for a superstar in the art world, even though he declined to appear in public. Reportedly he moved around the country in order to keep hidden from the press. Smithers produced some three hundred works during the six years he created art, then abruptly stopped, disappearing for three years before showing up again in Wiltshire where he committed himself to a psychiatric facility. He still remained there today.

There was a single picture of Smithers at the front of the book. He sat in a cafe, a cigarette dangling from his mouth, half his face hidden in the shadow of a brimmed cap. A pair of skinny arms stuck out from a checkered work shirt, the sleeves rolled up to his elbows. The caption stated that the image was taken shortly before his disappearance, which was the same year the last Briarwood coven stood up against the fae.

Coincidence? I didn't think so.

"Let's see that picture, young man." Clara pushed my arm aside and tipped the book up for a closer look. "Yes, I thought so. I've seen this man before. He was present at the rituals I attended at the castle all those years ago."

What? "You're telling me that Robert Smithers is a witch? That he was in the Briarwood Coven?"

"That's exactly what I'm telling you. In fact," Clara squinted at the picture. "Yes, I think so. He was Aline's Magister for a time."

"His name isn't in the coven history—" *Because he used a pseudonym. Of course.* An artist like Smithers who wanted to remain reclusive and mysterious wouldn't necessarily want any record of his days at Briarwood. I thought back to the list of coven members I'd memorized, and one name leapt out – Herbert Missort. A man I'd never been able to find any information on. Now I knew why.

In fact... in my mind I pictured the letters HERBERT MISSORT. I rearranged them until they spelled the name

ROBERT SMITHERS. An anagram. How childish. But I hadn't seen it.

Maeve stared at me, her eyes dancing with excitement that mirrored my own. She *got* it, the thrill of solving a great academic puzzle. The pieces were slotting together.

"What are you two cooking up?" Flynn demanded.

In a rush of excitement, I explained what I'd figured out. Robert Smithers was a witch, and he'd somehow painted magic into this portrait so it moved... but maybe only when Maeve was around. What did this magic *do?* What was it trying to achieve?

Rowan touched the edge of the canvas, his eyes closed. "I think this is earth magic," he whispered. "I can reach inside the pigment and feel the raw ingredients."

Maybe Smithers was an earth user. That explained a little. Earth and Water witches often took careers in the arts – something about being in tune with the natural order of the world made them able to create work that spoke directly to the soul. But I'd never heard of artists imbuing magic directly into their work before.

"This doesn't say where he's institutionalised. And even if we find out, it's unlikely they'll just let us in to speak to him. This says that he hasn't done any press since he stopped painting." I flipped through the book until I found the page with Aline's portrait. "But this is hanging in the National Gallery along with some other works of Smithers. I think we need to see it."

Flynn looked scandalized. "You mean the National Gallery in London?"

"The very same."

"Fierce. I'm always down for a wee jaunt in Old Smoky." Flynn grinned. "Maybe I'll teach all you heathens to appreciate fine art."

"Your art is many things, Flynn," Arthur said. "But it is not fine."

"But Corbin, we can't go off on some wild painting chase!" Maeve snatched the book away. "What about the fae? What about all those people they took?"

Clara placed a hand on Maeve's shoulder. "I'm afraid they're gone, dear. You can't bring a soul back from the underworld, not without sending another in its place."

"So we're just supposed to sit here and do nothing?" Maeve's voice rose an octave. Her usually bright eyes swam with pain. Death laid heavily on her conscience. I knew what that felt like. I knew how that ate away at you until you were a hollow shell.

I moved toward her and opened my arms. I expected her to stand her ground, but instead she collapsed into me, her body shaking. "You heard what Clara said. We have until the full moon before the Slaugh come to find a way to stop them. I think this might be important, Maeve. This painting has hung in this house for more than twenty years and it never moved before. You show up and it starts going haywire, and it may even be protecting us. And now we learn that the painter was really a witch who was present at the ritual that stopped the fae last time? We have to investigate this."

"But what about Kelly? She's arriving in two days time!" Panic wracked Maeve's voice.

"Get her to meet us in London. She wanted to have an adventure, right? We'll show her all the sights – Buckingham Palace, Big Ben, St Paul's Cathedral, The British Museum. We'll all go down together. It will give us a chance to investigate this, and maybe talk to some of the other covens in the city, try and get some help." I grinned. "Who knows? Maybe amongst all the worrying about the end of the world, we might actually get the chance to have a tiny bit of fun."

Flynn waved a hand in front of my face. "Fun? Who are you and what have you done with Corbin Harris?"

I laughed. "What do you say, High Priestess?"

Maeve glanced up at her mother's face twisted in horror. Something passed over Maeve's eyes. "I guess we're going to London."

14

BLAKE

"We're going to be late for the train if you go into the village now," Corbin yelled after me as I slung my new leather jacket over my shoulder. While Maeve had been in Arizona, Flynn showed me how to order things off the internet. I found the jacket in an online marketplace where people placed wagers on items they wanted – a practice I was very familiar with from the fae realm. Lots of people wanted this jacket, but I won. I always won.

Flynn banned me from using his credit card again, but as the soft leather crinkled across my shoulders, I decided it was worth it. I think my new hero Sherlock Holmes would have liked this jacket.

"I'll meet you at the station," I called back to Corbin as I shoved my new phone (another internet purchase) and some of those parchment rectangles I'd nicked from Rowan into my pocket. "I just want to get my fix of curry before we head away in the metal box on the rails."

"They do have curry in London, you know."

"I'll give the key to Clara while I'm there. That will be helpful. I'll be back soon!" I pocketed the heavy ring of castle keys Corbin had left by the door to drop at *Astarte* on the way to the train station. I slung the small rucksack of my worldly possessions over my shoulder and sauntered out the door before Corbin could go running to Maeve so she'd forbid me from going.

"Blake, don't be ridiculous. You—"

I slammed the heavy wooden door behind me, breathing in the dewy air and relishing the instant quiet of nature. I knew that for all his posturing, Corbin wouldn't follow me. Weirdly, admitting my lie about Liah seemed to have made him warm to me. Well, he initiated that hand-squeezing ritual, and he hadn't said anything about the cock and balls, although he'd managed to scrub it all off. He still yelled at me every chance he got, but I'd once been tied to a rock in the middle of Daigh's sidhe for four days – the yelling just amused me. Last night was the first Corbin hadn't slept in front of my door. Maybe my dashing wit and sparkling personality would finally win him over.

A tiny sliver of something that might have been guilt jabbed me in the side of my stomach. I did want the coven's trust, after all. And yet here I was, lying to them again.

This is the last time, I swear. I just need to know for myself.

The walk into the village was as invigorating as always. I didn't know why humans bothered to strap themselves into those weird metal contraptions they called cars. Imagine being able to walk in any direction for hundreds of miles and see completely new things around every corner. Bliss.

I waved to two women jogging down the road toward me. "Top of the morning to you!" I'd picked up lots of useful human customs from the telly.

One woman looked up from their conversation. When she noticed me, her expression turned to stone. She grabbed her friend's arm and yanked her to the other side of the road. They turned down a side street and sprinted away, turning back over their shoulders to shoot me filthy looks.

Strange. I looked down at my leather jacket, black jeans, and new Doc Martin boots (another internet purchase. Flynn hadn't seen the bill for them yet). It couldn't be that they thought I was ugly. I must've been missing some kind of social cue.

The village loomed ahead. I walked quickly, aware that I didn't have much time. As I made my way down the high street, practicing my wave and greeting, several people crossed the road. No one answered me. *Very strange.*

Shops stocking every manner of magical implement lined the main street, but I remembered exactly where Clara's shop was. The bell on the door tinkled as I went in.

The shop was deserted save for the old woman, who looked up from a shelf of figurines she was arranging. "Ah, Blake. I wondered when you'd show up here."

Her statement was meant to freak me out and make me wonder how she knew I'd turn up. I wasn't going to give her the satisfaction. Instead, I thrust out my arm in a flourish. "I have arrived."

Clara walked over to the shop door and flipped the sign over, so the word CLOSED faced the street. She turned the lock in the door. "Not that it will make much difference. No one in this village will shop here after word got around I was at the church yesterday. Follow me." She shuffled through the shop to a back room.

Okay, this was getting weirder and weirder. Why was she acting as if she already knew exactly what I wanted? I glanced toward the door, wondering if I should leave. But no, I'd come here to get answers, and I wasn't going to walk away empty handed.

"I've already brewed some tea for us," she said, fetching a kettle and a couple of cups.

"You're quite the modern day Sherlock," I said with fondness. I'd grown to admire the character. He reminded me a little of Maeve. I perched on the tiny stool Clara provided, my knees thrust awkwardly up in the air. "Do I have to tell you why I'm here, or have you deduced that as well?"

Clara handed me a steaming cup. "You want to contact your friend Liah in the underworld. Sugar?"

"Just one lump. Okay, old lady, I'll bite. How do you know that?"

Clara plonked one sugar cube in my cup. "Milk?"

I shook my head.

Clara grinned. "I've spirit powers of my own, don't forget. Also, I've been talking to Liah. The dark energy around her reaches to me. She tells me that my puny human conception of hell doesn't do justice to the true horrors that await my soul."

I smiled, because that was what she expected me to do, even though her words twisted in my gut. "That sounds like Liah. Did she have any other message? Did she say anything about me?"

Clara paused. "She said that next time she will shoot that arrow straight through your heart."

"Why didn't she? She had the perfect chance. And why did she try to shoot Maeve, anyway? Daigh wants her alive."

"Ours is not to wonder why," Clara stirred her tea.

"Damn right. I'm not wondering – I want answers. Say if I wanted to speak to her, could I do that somehow? I'm guessing I can't just dream myself down there?"

Clara shook her head. "Even if you could, she doesn't want to hear from you."

She hesitated. Why did she hesitate? "You can't help me at all, then? This visit was a complete waste of time."

"Not entirely. You came to give me the key."

Sighing, I tossed the key into her outstretched hand.

Clara had agreed to watch over Briarwood while we were away, feed Obelix, and monitor the wards to make sure they remained intact.

Clara tucked the key into a pocket in one of her many skirts. She reached for a vial on the shelf beside her. "The Underworld may be a place that only the spirits of the dead can enter, but it's really much closer to earth than *Tir Na Nog*. I have made you a single dose of spirit draught. It's like the sleeping draught you used at Briarwood, but allows your living essence to travel as though you were a dead soul. You will be able to enter the Underworld, but only through your nightmares. On the other side you will be as a shade, faceless and nameless. No one will recognize you, but you will also not be able to speak to anyone, including Liah. You must be careful, for you will be indistinct from any other shade, and what the beasts do to others there they can also do to you. I suggest you use it wisely."

I stared at the small vial in my hand, trepidation creeping into my veins with every word she spoke. "I just wanted to know if... if things had been different, would she have stayed here and fought with us?"

"No." Clara patted my hand, closing my fingers around the vial. "Now, you best hurry up, or you'll be late for your train."

15

ARTHUR

"*A*ll aboard!" Flynn cried, waving his arms around like a conductor as he danced along the Crookshollow station platform.

"We're already *on* the train, Flynn!" Maeve called out the window. Beside her, Jane snorted back a laugh.

"Shite!" Flynn took a dramatic leap off the platform, flapping his arms like a duck. He landed on the top step of the train and pitched forward, nearly barreling into a staff member.

I climbed on after him, pushing past the staff member as she launched into a lecture about the dangers of horsing around on the train – probably a lecture Flynn needed to hear every day of his life. I sank into the seat behind Maeve and Jane, who collapsed into giggles as they watched Flynn get a well-deserved bollocking.

Across the aisle, Corbin and Rowan sat together. Corbin had his nose buried in a book, and Rowan was scanning reviews on his phone to choose the best high tea in London.

High tea. The National Gallery. Jesus bloody Christ. Maeve was talking about taking Kelly to the Natural History

Museum and St. Paul's Cathedral. Corbin had already called ahead and got us a meeting with the Soho Coven. It was all sounding like a wonderful trip.

I stared down at my hands, willing them to stop shaking. But of course my body wouldn't obey that command. The ball of fear tightened in my chest, pushing out the fire so it simmered under my skin. This time it wasn't rage that fanned the flames, but horror.

Everyone else was in such a jovial mood, laughing and fooling around, looking forward to the trip to London. It was like they'd all just forgotten what happened two days ago.

Twenty-two people disappeared beneath the floor of that church. Twenty-two people have had their bodies broken and their blood drained in the torture chamber of the underworld. Twenty-two families would have to live with the horrible crushing grief of losing a loved one, of not even knowing what happened to them, and we were fucking laughing?

And I couldn't save them.

I'd fought against those fae with all my might. I'd stabbed four of them through the guts with my sword, and stomped on another's face until it stopped moving. I'd drenched myself in their blood, and still it wasn't enough. I still had blood on my hands – human blood.

I couldn't be excited about this trip to London. I didn't think I'd ever be excited about anything again. Not when I saw bodies toppling into the void whenever I closed my eyes, or heard their screams everywhere I went. Not even heavy metal could drown out those screams.

Flynn dropped down beside me. "Looks like you're stuck with me as a seat buddy. I hope you like house music because I intend to turn my headphones right up until one of these polite toffs snaps and goes on a murderous rampage—"

"Actually, mate," my stomach lurched. "Can you scoot a sec? I need to take a slash."

Flynn ducked out with a dramatic sweep of his arm, narrowly avoiding swatting a passenger in the face. I left him to explain himself to a huffy-looking woman (maybe he'd get his murderous rampage sooner than he expected), and locked myself in the loo.

I sat on the lid of the toilet and studied my face in the mirror. Huge black circles ringed my eyes. Even my beard looked weirdly limp and lifeless.

You're useless. You've got one job in this coven. You're the warrior, the muscle, the guy who swings the sword and slays the enemies and keeps the innocents safe. And you can't even do that.

I rolled up my sleeve. My fingers brushed the long cut I'd made when I was frustrated about the group sex thing, wanting Maeve and wishing I didn't. Staring at that deep cut made my eyes burn with shame.

Now everything with Maeve and the guys was... well, not *sorted* exactly. We hadn't had a chance to even talk about the group since Maeve and I got back from Arizona. But after everything Maeve and I went through in Arizona, I knew she was close to me in exactly the way I wanted. I had her and she had me and it actually didn't matter what she did with the others.

But all that was overshadowed by what happened at the church. The horror of everything I'd seen and the helplessness I felt to stop it ate away at me. *Twenty-two people died, and if you don't find a way to stop the fae soon, there are going to be a lot more names on that list. This is only the beginning.*

I closed my eyes, but that was worse. From the darkness behind my eyelids, twenty-two pairs of eyes stared back at me in silent accusation. *You killed us.*

I was going insane.

How can I lift my sword again, knowing this is the result? I can't face more faces every time I close my eyes. What if Maeve gets killed, or one of the guys gets killed and it's all my fault?

Beside me, the toilet paper roll burst into flame. Cursing, I yanked the holder off the wall and knocked the flaming roll into the loo, where it sizzled and went out, thankfully before the smoke detector started beeping.

"Shit." I slumped against the wall, the tile cool against my cheek. I was a danger to everyone around me.

You're the warrior. You can't lose it now. You have to get this under control.

I dug around in my pocket for my knife. Corbin said I couldn't bring my sword down to London, but I wasn't going to walk around unarmed. I carried a small dagger Flynn had made for me, the blade carved with the same runic message I wore on my skin. A verse from the *Hávamál* – an old Norse poem – part of a section dealing with Odin's teachings on living well as a man, translated for me by Corbin.

Cattle die,
kindred die,
we ourselves also die;
but the fair fame
never dies
of him who has earned it.

A warrior's deeds live on after his death. It was the only thing about a person that could ever be immortal. What would my legacy be upon my death? That I let everyone I loved fall because I couldn't fight? That I burned up a train bound for London because I couldn't keep it together?

I held the blade in my hand, feeling the familiar weight and heft of it. I ran my finger along the edge. Already, a sense of relief rushed over me, and the fire inside me simmered down.

Control, that was what I needed.

No, Arthur. I could practically hear Corbin's voice admonishing me. *You haven't hurt yourself in so many years. Why would you go back to this now?*

What you need is me to be strong and brave. I'm not that. I'm falling to pieces. Just one cut, and I'll be in control again.

I placed the blade against my skin.

Maeve's face floated in my vision. What would she think if she knew I was doing this? She kept asking about the scars on my arm. Luckily, when we fucked under the dark of the desert night she hadn't noticed the fresh cut.

I didn't want her to know. She wouldn't understand. Of course she wouldn't, especially not after she'd seen her sister try to hurt herself. Corbin never understood, either. He saw the cuts and they made him think of Keegan. I couldn't explain that this was different in a way that would make sense to either of them.

Warriors bleed. Our blood makes us strong.

Maeve deserved the best of me. She needed my strength right now. She needed me to be ready to leap into action, not this sniveling mess that was falling apart. And if this was the only way I could be her warrior, then I didn't really have a choice.

"I'm sorry, Maeve." I whispered as I pressed the dagger to my skin and drew it back. "I'll be strong enough again soon."

MAEVE

"Wow," I breathed as we pulled into Charing Cross Station. All around me, trains clattered into the different platforms and thousands of people bustled between them while a snooty English lady on the loud-speaker admonished us all to 'Mind the gap' with that air of polite uncaring that the British excelled at. So many people going to so many places, completely unaware that in just fourteen days time their entire world was going to be overrun with the restless dead.

Don't think about it, Maeve. If I started to contemplate the Slaugh in too much detail, I forgot to breathe. Panic wasn't going to get anything done. Panic and stress meant mistakes crept in, and even the tiniest mistakes were disastrous, like when engineers rushed to put together NASA's Genesis probe and installed the accelerometers backward, so the probe crashed in Utah upon reentry, contaminating its precious solar wind samples.

Our coven needed a reasoned, sensible leader who didn't let *anything* get installed backward, which meant I needed to focus on the next tasks in front of me – discovering the secret of the painting, meeting with the other coven leaders, and keeping Kelly from learning about my powers and how I produced them.

Totally easy. No problem at all.

"They had light rail in Phoenix," Corbin reminded me as we swept up a narrow escalator to another platform. In proper English fashion, everyone diligently obeyed a sign requesting pedestrians to keep left, so that anyone in a hurry could run along the right without obstruction. Everyone, that was, except Blake, who stood beside me with his hand on my hip and a growing line of disgruntled commuters behind him.

"Yeah, we did, but nothing like this."

We hopped on the Northern line, which would take us into Camden Town station, where Corbin had booked an apartment for our stay.

After an uneventful twenty minute journey during which Flynn's blaring drum and bass music earned him no less than sixteen withering glares and one long-suffering sigh, we emerged into the street. I couldn't help but gasp at the trans-formation. *London.* A proper city – all gleaming glass skyscrapers and zipping black cabs and Victorian and Geor-gian facades.

I'd flown in to London, of course, but I'd hopped straight into a taxi and had been too nervous and jet-lagged to take anything in. And there was so much to take in. Everywhere I turned, new sights and smells assailed me. Street vendors on every corner sold tabloid newspapers sporting lurid head-lines about the royal family or the long-irrelevant Spice Girls. Horns blasted and tinny renditions of 'God Save The Queen' blared out of the windows of tourist buses. Pigeons fluttered across the pavement, chasing down a kid who was struggling his way through a bag of salted nuts. Blake practi-cally walked down the street with his nose in the air, picking up the scent of curry houses and kebab joints mixed with the familiar aged-wood-and-urine scent of British pubs.

Camden turned out to be a really interesting mix of funky shops and eateries and buskers and homeless people sitting on the curb. At one street corner, a scrawny teen ran up to Rowan and asked him if he wanted to buy drugs. Rowan's eyes bugged out of his head in an adorable way and he hid behind Arthur until the dealer ambled away.

It hit me once again that I'd seen only a very small corner of the world in my life, but right now we were fighting for all of it – for the noisy cities and desert plains and the curry shop owners and the drug dealers. We were fighting to preserve all of humanity in her messy, imperfect glory.

Corbin marched us through a sprawling market selling club wear and gothic corsets, before turning off down a narrow cobbled alley to an unassuming brick building. "It should be down —ah, here we are." He stopped in front of a red door and plugged in a security code. Inside we found a narrow flight of stairs and a lockbox. Corbin plugged in another code to the lockbox and retrieved a key from inside. "Here we go," he said.

"What is this building?" I asked, running my hands over the mottled wallpaper. Huge ribbons had been torn away, revealing several layers of patterned paper underneath, riddled with lewd graffiti.

"It started its life as a workhouse in the 1700s, then it was a brothel during the Victorian era. In the 70s it was a famous squat for artists and radicals."

Flynn groaned. "This whole trip is going to be one long monologue from our very own walking history book."

Corbin lifted an eyebrow. "I chose this place because of you, actually. Apparently, there's a mural in the attic that might be an original Banksy." Flynn's eyes shot up.

"What's a Banksy?" Blake asked, leaping up the stairs two

at a time. Unlike the rest of us, Blake didn't actually own any possessions, so he had only a small canvas tote bag over his shoulder containing a change of clothes he'd purchased off the internet.

"He's a vandal who pretends to be an artist," I said, remembering an article I'd read about him defacing public buildings in New York City. "Daigh would've probably liked him a lot."

"Careful," Arthur elbowed me. "Them's fighting words as far as Flynn's concerned."

"Woman, you have *no* taste," Flynn huffed. "Banksy uses art as guerrilla warfare in the eternal struggle against the upper classes and centralized power. His work is all about claiming power back. As an Irishman, I can relate."

Whoa, that was perhaps the most serious thing I'd ever heard Flynn say. I held up my hands. "Hey, I'm happy to be proved wrong. Want to sneak up later and take a look?"

"Is the Pope Catholic?" Flynn wrapped me up in an enormous hug.

"While this discussion is absolutely fascinating," Blake drawled, "could we continue it inside the rooms? My bag is getting very heavy."

Flynn snorted. Corbin pushed open the door, revealing an enormous living room with high walls, decorated in an industrial style. A row of tall windows lined one side, giving a bird's eye view of Camden Market below. Bare fixtures hung from the thick wooden beams and a bookshelf made from perforated metal jutted out from the end wall, towering over a black leather sofa set and massive TV. A ladder in the middle of the room led up to a mezzanine level.

"This place is crazy," I breathed, which was saying a lot, since we'd all just come from a castle.

"I thought it might be good to get away from dark medieval rooms for a few days. There are three bedrooms, plus a fold out couch," Corbin said, throwing open a door. "I thought you could stay in here, Maeve. That way you can at least hide certain things from your sister behind a closed door."

Corbin stepped aside, revealing a room containing a double bed and two singles. Bare Edison bulbs bobbed from an industrial chandelier, and a giant canvas covered in grey and red splodges covered one entire wall. I dumped my bag on the bed. "Agreed. I'll take this room. Arthur better come in here with me, so Kelly can keep believing we're a couple. The rest of you can draw straws."

"I'm not sleeping with the snoring giant," Flynn declared, pinching my ass as he went out the door. "Even if that does mean I end up on the couch."

"And miss out on Maeve time?" Blake lifted an eyebrow.

"Hey, I can always leave after the snuggling."

"I'll take this one." Corbin dropped his backpack on one of the single beds. Wordlessly, Rowan snuck past Flynn and claimed the third bed.

The room across the hall was really more of a study, but a small double bed had been pushed up under the window. "This is perfect for me," Jane said, setting down her bag. "Connor won't wake you up in the night when he's in here."

"Blake and I'll see which bed Maeve's sister wants when she gets here," Flynn said, gesturing to the fold-out couch and the mezzanine. "We'll take the other."

"Thanks." I leaned over to give Flynn a peck on the cheek.

Flynn lifted an eyebrow. "Remember my magnanimity in the future, Einstein. I've got designs on that sweet ass of yours."

Back in the lounge I clambered up to the mezzanine level. An enormous king-sized bed took up nearly all the space, with a view out the high windows into the street below. Above it, a mirror hung from the ceiling at an odd angle. A gleaming white tub sat in the other corner – no walls around it, just completely open to the room beyond.

A tiny thrill coursed through me, and the pillar of magic inside me flared to life.

"Now you can see why I chose this place," Corbin grinned as he hauled himself over the top of the ladder. I leaned over the railing, looking down into the room below where Flynn and Blake were arguing over whether the splodgy artwork was creepy or genius. Corbin came up behind me, pressing his chest against my back and enfolding me in his arms.

I sank against him, breathing deep as I relished the first moment we'd had alone together since I'd returned from Arizona. The smell of musty books and ink still clung to Corbin's skin, even though we were far away from his library. He drew a line of kisses across my neck, laying them exactly where he knew would make me shiver. I ground my ass against him, feeling the hardness swell through his jeans.

I need you to drive out the pain.

"Careful, Maeve Moore," Corbin growled in my ear. "You work those witchy charms on me, we're not going to get any sightseeing done."

I turned around, pulling him against me and brushing my lips against his. I snaked my hand between us, rubbing his length through his jeans. "The only sight I want to see is this glorious cock."

Corbin laughed against my lips even as he stiffened under my hand. We fell against the bed, bodies entwining, kisses hard and urgent. All the stress and fear from the last couple of days rose to the surface of my skin, seeping out of me as Corbin surrounded me in his warmth. I straddled Corbin, grinding myself against him, suddenly desperate to feel the earthly connection of our two bodies pressed together, to cling to the one concrete connection I had left on this earth.

His hands roamed over my skin, sending delicious shivers

through my body. He tugged up the hem of my t-shirt, and I shuddered as the skin of his hand met my back. His fingers tingled as he traced his air magic across my skin – the lightest breeze that made all my hairs stand on end. God, I wanted to sink into him, to lose myself completely in the pleasure of being with him and just… forget… all the shit…

Something pinched my ass, and I yelped. Someone behind me burst out laughing. "Flynn," I growled, even as my body ached with desire for both of them.

A hand slid around my waist, snaking under my shirt to rub against my hard nipple. I gasped. Flynn's voice rippled against my earlobe. "This is our last chance before your sister arrives to give you a little magical boost."

"That's might be the most sensible thing Flynn has ever suggested," Corbin added.

"Right." My body thrummed with agreement. I slid my hands under Corbin's face, pulling his head up. My lips brushed his and I relished his sharp intake of breath. "And sensible *is* my middle name."

It was my turn to gasp as Flynn nibbled my ear. He rolled my nipple under his finger until it formed a hard pebble that ached for more. Corbin shuffled up the bed to make room. I snapped open the dome buttons on Corbin's shirt, biting my lip with anticipation as it fell away to reveal the beautiful tattoos across his toned chest.

I traced my fingers across the gods and demons battling around bands of Celtic knotwork. Behind me, Flynn slipped my t-shirt over my head and snapped off my bra with one hand, tossing it across the mezzanine so it fell into the bath.

The bed creaked. Rowan climbed on, kneeling beside Corbin as he faced Flynn and I. His hand lingered on Corbin's wrist for several moments before he raised it to my face, cupping my cheek and pulling me to him. He claimed my mouth with his.

As our tongues entwined, Rowan's body trembled. He kept his eyes open, staring at me with such savage intensity it make my chest tighten. His hand against my skin burned with heat, sending shudders of magic straight into me. His kisses drew me deeper, until I was drowning in him, struggling for breath against the onslaught of his desire. All his emotion flowed into me, and the force of his anxiety clamped around my heart.

Is this the crushing pain Rowan walks around with all the time?

The worst of it was, I knew I'd only scratched the surface of Rowan's pain. That boy was so deep he was practically a portal to another universe. He clutched my face, his whole body shaking. I shook too, his pain becoming my pain, even though I didn't understand it.

I drew away, tears brimming in the corners of my eyes. "I'm sorry," Rowan whispered. "It's not you. It's London."

I didn't know what he meant by that, but with Flynn teasing my nipples and Corbin stroking me through my jeans, it wasn't the time to ask. Rowan leaned his forehead against mine, his breath heavy and ragged. Between his legs, his cock stiffened. I reached down and freed him from his jeans, stroking his length with my hands until he moaned.

"Quit hogging the priestess," Flynn cried from behind me. Rowan laughed, but his voice cracked, his laugh so heroically, impossibly sad that it nearly snapped me in two.

I couldn't fall into Rowan, not now, not today. If I did that, I was afraid his pain would break me, and I needed to be together for what was coming. But that didn't mean I didn't need him here. We all needed each other, otherwise we'd never be able to keep going. My body hummed from the contact of his skin, the force of his kisses. I kept stroking him while I turned to kiss Flynn, just as Blake poked his head above the ladder.

"This looks like more fun than arguing about art."

"When it comes to Maeve, I think we're all in agreement." Flynn shuffled me over, giving Blake room to climb up on the bed. Blake shrugged off his leather jacket and slid down beside Corbin, his leg brushing Corbin's arm. I expected Corbin to stiffen, but he just glanced at Blake and gave a little smile. Blake leaned up and took my mouth from Flynn's, kissing me with the wild abandon that was so unique to him – a tempest that unfurled inside me, stealing my breath.

"I'll drink to that," a voice growled from the ladder.

I whirled around, tearing my mouth from Blake's. Arthur leaned against the top of the ladder, watching us all with an intense gaze. Flynn's hand froze on my nipple.

Arthur, please join us.

This was it – the test of the bond we'd forged while in Arizona. I searched Arthur's face for any sign of his earlier jealousy, but all I could see in his eyes was lust. My heart surged.

"I thought you weren't into this?" Corbin said, surprised.

"I changed my mind." Arthur stepped up on the mezzanine, pulling his black t-shirt over his head. My eyes flicked immediately to the crook of his elbow, to the scars that he never talked about. But he'd angled his body to hide them behind his muscular torso. On purpose? I didn't know, but saliva pooled on my tongue as I took in the thick ropes of muscle that bulged under his skin. *To feel that tight body against mine again—*

"Well, I'll be buggered," Flynn said. Then he whipped his arms behind his back, covering his asscrack. "I don't mean that literally."

I swallowed, straining to speak through my lust. "We haven't had a chance to discuss this as a group yet, but in Arizona, Arthur and I sort of had…"

Arthur slipped his arms around me, his hand cupping my

breast. The words flew out of my head. He shot the others a look that explained it better than I would've, anyway.

"So he's part of Maeve's Merry Men now too?" Flynn asked.

"Not if that's what you're calling yourselves," Arthur shot back, his fingers pinching my nipple until I gasped.

"We *never* agreed," Corbin flashed Flynn an exasperated look.

"Fine. What about Maeve's Magisters? Or The Harem of Queen Maeve? Or Maeve's Murder, like a murder of crows... ooooh, or the Briarwood Bruhs?"

I snorted. "Flynn, you are ridiculous."

Corbin winced. "I don't see why we need a name at all."

"I'm not sure what I'm doing about the group thing yet," Arthur said, his enormous arms squeezing me against his chest. "But I'm here now. I'll leave when I need to."

"Can I touch your willy?" Flynn lunged at him.

"Stay a good fist-flying distance away from me, O'Hagan," Arthur growled. The bed groaned as he climbed on, and everyone shuffled around to make room. My heart pounded against my chest, and the ache between my legs raged into an inferno.

"You lot are gross," Jane yelled up from downstairs. *Oops, I forgot she was here.* I heard the wheels on the stroller slap against the wooden floor. "Connor and I are going for a ramble around the market. We'll be back in an hour. Stay away from my bed, and remember, no glove, no love!"

"Have fun!" I yelled back, my words dissolving away as Arthur kissed my neck. Flynn reached around to pinch his ass, but Arthur slapped his hand away.

Corbin took the opportunity to pull me down on top of him, his mouth seeking mine. Hands stroked my naked back as Flynn and Arthur got my jeans undone and slid them down my thighs. Someone kneaded the flesh of my ass while the others struggled to pull the skinny jeans down over my ankles.

"Knickers next," Flynn declared, grabbing for the flimsy fabric. Hands trailed down the bare skin of my legs, sending delicious shivers straight to my core. Fingers wrapped around my ankles, holding my legs wide, while a hand snaked between my legs to stroke my length until I squirmed and shuddered.

"She's as wet as Jacques Cousteau," Flynn declared.

"All in favor of kicking Flynn out if he doesn't shut up?" Arthur said.

"Aye," Corbin murmured against my lips. My hand shot in the air. It was joined by Rowan's and Blake's.

"Fine. I'll just work me own magic down here, nice and quiet-like." Flynn worked his fingers inside me, stroking me long and deep before circling my clit, adding more pressure with each rotation. The power rose inside me, hot and needy and desperate for more.

There were several thuds from behind me as the guys shed their clothes and tossed them across the mezzanine. Flynn, of course, threw his right over the side. "Let's turn her over," Arthur suggested.

Corbin wrapped his arms around my back and rolled, lying my body down against the soft bed. I stared up at the five adoring faces of my guys. Arthur bent to kiss me while Corbin leaned down to take my nipple in his mouth. Rowan took the other nipple, his dreadlocks falling over my chest. Sparks shot under my skin.

Blake bent between my legs, stroking his tongue down my slit before swirling it around the tip of my clit. I bent my hips up toward him, begging for more. He flicked his tongue against me, giving me just enough that my power vibrated against my skin, but not enough to send me over the edge. I pushed

"As you wish, Princess." His hands clamped over my thighs, holding them open, and buried his face into me, hitting the flat of his tongue against my clit with a ferocious speed. I dug my nails into the sheet as the ache rose into my stomach and fire licked at my limbs.

"What can I do?" Flynn moaned.

"Give her something to play with," Arthur said.

Flynn grabbed my hand and directed it to his cock. I slid my fist down his shaft, pumping him in time to Blake's relentless beat on my clit. My whole body thrummed with energy, magic flaring right through my chest, cascading down my arms, flowing straight into my brain, my heart.

Five guys. Five guys all touching me, worshipping me.

So many mouths, each one a conduit for their magic, their emotions. Power flowed into me, stoking the fire of my spirit higher. It radiated out of my body and back into them.

Blake's tongue worked its magic, pounding and pounding until the ache exploded. I cried out as an orgasm claimed me, clamping my thighs over Blake's head as he continued to attack my clit. My whole body spasmed. Red welts blurred my vision. The guys held me through it, keeping me safe, buoying me up for more to come.

When my eyes worked again, I flicked my gaze through all their faces. Hungry eyes looked back at me. Smiling lips, beautiful tortured souls, hungry for more.

"Well, I'm ready to go to sleep," I joked, fluffing the pillow behind my head.

"Oh, no, you don't." Flynn grabbed me under my shoulders and hauled me up so I knelt on the bed. "We've got plans for you yet."

While Flynn's mouth devoured mine, Arthur slid down behind me so my back rested against his chest. His hands encircled my breasts, grazing over my sensitive nipples.

Blake shuffled underneath us, threading his body between

my legs, his thick cock already glistening with need. "Do you have your bag of tricks?" he asked Flynn.

"I never leave home without it." Flynn bent down beside the bed and drew out a bag of condoms. He tossed one to Blake, and another to Arthur. "You'll need that," he added, thrusting a tube into Arthur's hands.

Blake rolled the condom on and positioned himself at my entrance. The wide grin on his face was the most genuine expression he'd ever given me. I sighed as I sank down on him. His cock touched every part of me, and it was like coming home. His grin widened, his mischievous eyes sparkling.

"At last, Princess." He gripped my hips to guide my speed. The hunger in his eyes made my chest ache. Blake may play at the uncaring bad boy, but he'd risked everything to come to Briarwood and be part of our coven, and every day he tried to become a little more human. He wanted to belong, maybe more than any of us. Right now, with him sheathed inside me, I never wanted him to leave.

Flynn stood, straddling Blake on the bed. He rested a hand on the back of my head, guiding his cock into my mouth. I relished the taste of him, all salty and hot and distinctly Flynn. I bent my head back, taking in as much of him as I could, wanting to give him the same pleasure he always gave to me. The pillar of power inside me leapt higher, burning bright.

Something cool landed on my lower back and dribbled into the crack of my ass. Arthur trailed the lube down, inserting one finger inside me. I gasped around Flynn's cock as Arthur pushed his finger past the tight ring of muscle, sliding deeper inside me, allowing me to relax and loosen up.

The other two came around either side of me. Corbin took my nipple in his mouth again, and Rowan mirrored him. Each had a hand on their own cocks, stroking themselves in time with the shudder of my body.

Rowan's eyes locked with Corbin's and he dropped my nipple from his mouth. For a moment, I was sure they were going to kiss. A surge of pleasure wracked my body at the thought of it, that two of my guys cared about each other so deeply that they would be able to be that open and vulnerable in front of me.

Rowan averted his eyes first, his lips going to graze my neck. Corbin blinked, then went back to swirling around my nipple. I didn't have time to be disappointed or wonder if I'd just imagined the tension between them, because Arthur removed his finger and pressed the head of his cock against my back opening. I stopped thinking at all, lost in the wild sensations that assailed my body as my witches venerated me in the only way they knew how.

Blake drew back, giving Arthur more room to get properly inside me. Arthur's breath hit the back of my neck as he sank into me, burying his length inside me. I moaned as he stretched me wide. He started with a little, but as my body sank back against him, he went a little deeper.

"Oh, fuck, Maeve." Arthur's ragged breath teased my earlobe. I moaned around Flynn's cock, feeling him tense in my mouth.

Blake's fingers dug into my hips as he eased himself back up inside me again, rubbing his length down Arthur's shaft from the other side of the thin membrane. "I've got you, Princess," he said, holding me tight to keep my body steady as he drew back and slowly drove himself inside me once more.

Arthur and Blake held me rigid between them as they built up a rhythm. Pinned between them, I could do nothing but surrender as they moved in and out in a steady tempo. From the moment they synced their movements, their cocks like one long member sliding right through me, I lost track of the world. The entire thing was one long orgasm, suspended between them both as they drove out the demons that had tortured me ever since the battle at the church.

Too much.

So much.

Just right.

I closed my eyes, reveling in the exquisite sensation of it all, of being suspended between the five of them, the complete center of their universe. They poured all their pain and rage and heartache into their lovemaking, placing these gifts at the altar of their adoration. I imagined my body taking the strands of their broken hearts and knitting us all together, making us all stronger.

I was the missing piece.

"Oh, Princess," Blake gasped, clenching his lower jaw in an completely adorable expression. His whole body stiffened. His cock hardened inside me as he came, his eyes wide with surprise and delight. He collapsed against the sheets, his chest slick with sweat as he slid out of me.

Seeing Blake lose control like that and feeling the rush of his spirit power in my veins sent me over the edge again. My final orgasm blinded me completely, projecting me into space, burning me up in a supernova.

The magic surged, beating at my skin to be set free. I didn't channel it anywhere. Instead, I focused on holding it close, on imagining it being stuffed into a tiny storage box inside me, like a Pandora's Box ready to be opened when the time was right. I needed that power for what was to come.

When I surfaced, I tasted Flynn's orgasm on my tongue. Corbin and Rowan had rolled away from each other, eyes fixed on me as they came into their hands. Arthur shuddered against my back. Our power sizzled in the air around us. I was amazed the building hadn't burned down.

The six of us collapsed on the bed in a tangle of limbs. I rested my head on Blake's chest, Corbin's head beside me. Rowan curled up against me, his dark skin contrasted against mine. His dreadlocks fell over his face, like a curtain hiding him from the world. On my other side, Arthur trailed lines across my chest with his huge fingers. Flynn curled at my feet like a puppy, tickling my toes.

My whole body ached from the workout it had just endured, but my mind and heart thrummed with energy. When it had just been the five of us, I'd felt completely whole and fulfilled, but with Arthur here as well – it was more than I could have even imagined.

I realized that I was only just waking up to my power. All the things I'd done so far... they were kiddie stuff. I could easily believe the force that hummed through me now could topple mountains and build wormholes to other galaxies.

I wonder what it would be like if we... I shifted my weight so that I sat up against the pillows and cast a gaze over the six content faces. "Hey, so I had this idea..."

"You're going to go downstairs and fry us all some bacon?" Flynn asked, his voice hopeful.

I slapped him lightly across the shoulder. "No. I was thinking that we haven't discussed *it* yet, what with the whole fate-of-the-world-in-our-hands thing, but I think it's time we all get an STI check."

Beside me, Rowan stiffened. Arthur's eyes widened.

"You mean..." Flynn's gleeful face showed exactly what he thought of my offer.

"Yeah. Condoms are a bit of a hassle, and we're going to need an awful lot of them. As long as you all check out and you're all happy with it, I don't see any problem. I'll probably have to do some research on the anal sex part because..." my face flushed. "They don't cover that in Arizona public school sex education. There's probably a clinic here in London we can go to in between all the sightseeing and painting investigation."

The idea sent a delicious shudder through my body. Being skin on skin with all of them, completely naked, body and hearts bound together. It sounded amazing.

Arthur squeezed his body against mine, his beard tickling my arm. "I'd like that."

"And me," Corbin bent down to kiss my lips.

"The prospect doesn't fill me with dread," Blake added. "What's an STI?"

Rowan slid out from under my arm. "I think I'll just..." he floated away before he finished his sentence, grabbing his clothes and clambering down the ladder. I watched his shaking body descend the rungs and disappear from view. A moment later, one of the downstairs doors clicked shut.

Corbin glanced at me, his eyes begging me not to go after Rowan, to let him run. I stared at the empty spot on the bed where Rowan had just been. He always took things so seriously. Was this too much of a step for him? Did it make his anxiety play up?

Or was it something else, something he wasn't telling me?

ROWAN

L ondon.

I slammed the front door of the building and hurried away down the street, conscious that in my haste to leave I'd somehow put on Blake's jeans instead of mine and they hung around my hips.

My legs begged to run, to put as much distance between myself and Maeve and her suggestion as I could. But no matter how far or fast I ran, I'd never escape this city. Once London held you in her clutches, you were hers forever.

Corbin just had to get a flat in Camden. He knew that Haringey was just a few blocks away. All I'd have to do was go through Highgate Wood and I'd be back there, back where the nightmare that was my life began.

No. I couldn't blame Corbin for any of this. He probably didn't even remember, not with everything else he was trying to deal with. *This is all you.*

You're a disgusting pervert. Maeve will find out. They'll all find out. They'll kick you out and you'll have no choice to come back here.

I'd been an idiot for believing I could just fake my way

through this trip. On the train, I tried to pretend I was as excited about London as the others. I even made a show of looking up a high tea I wanted to take everyone to, as if they'd even let someone like me into a fancy place like that.

What they didn't see was me going to the bathroom twenty-six times. I scrubbed and scrubbed my hands, but the fear that they weren't clean – that I wasn't clean, that I'd poison everyone around me – never went away.

At Briarwood I had my routines. If the voice did this to me I could just go to the Great Hall and count the window-panes. I could knead the bread – a-hundred-and-fifty-four quarter turns gave the most delicious loaf. I could wash my hands in the kitchen sink a hundred times a day without anyone monitoring me, and no one had to know just how close I was to losing it on a daily basis.

I turned onto Prince Albert Road, heading for the entrance of Regent's Park. *Nature. Earth.* Towering trees with their roots buried deep. That was what I needed right now. Just a few breaths of fresh air, and I'd be able to—

"Hey, you!" A punk with a nose ring and an anarchist sweatshirt shoved a leaflet in my face. "Stop the fascist pigs ruining this country!"

My heart thudded against my chest. The world disap-peared – all that existed was the kid's worn, gaunt face and the smell, the smell of his clothes – sweat and piss and the distinct vinegar scent that could only be from heroin.

My throat constricted. The kid lunged for me, mouthing something I couldn't hear. I lost control of my limbs. My body contorted, toppling into the street. Horns blazed. A double decker bus shrieked to a stop. A woman screamed. The driver leaned out to yell at me, but I didn't hear a word he said. My legs froze in place. I stared at the kid on the side of the street and the smell… the *smell*… caught in my throat. I gasped for breath but it was inside me, all around me, turning my veins to ice. I was drowning in it, pulled under by the acidic current.

Poison.

Death.

They've found me. They're coming to take me back.

"Shit, bruv, it's just a poster, innit?" The kid yelled after me.

My lungs burned. I gasped and spluttered, but there was no air left in the world. The voice pounded inside my head. *This is the death you most feared – choking on your own tongue like the degenerate you are. Welcome it. Accept it. It is yours.*

No, Rowan, you're not dying. It's just a panic attack, Corbin's voice rang in my ears. *You've had them before. You're okay, just breathe.*

More horns honked. I managed to gasp in a tiny mouthful of air. I crawled to the side of the street, clutching my stomach as it cramped and spun. A woman came up at me and asked if I was all right. I nodded. "I slipped," I choked out. "I'm fine."

She nodded and left, because Londoners always had somewhere to be. I sat in the gutter, each passing vehicle splattering Blake's jeans with more muck, until I could breathe normally again. When I stood up, my body trembled so much I had to hold up the waistband of Blake's jeans so they wouldn't fall down. I staggered into a hookah lounge, desperate to be out of the crowds for a few moments, but not yet ready to return to the flat. The sweet, pungent stench of the molasses-based tobacco smoked in the distinct hookah pipes drove out the memory of the kid's scent.

I pretended to be interested in a display of flavored *Mu'assel*. My mind replayed what had just happened over and over. I hadn't had a full-on panic attack in at least two years, not since the first time I'd met Corbin's mother, just after I got out of rehab for the last time. Even that visit to Corbin's parents didn't set me off, probably because I was too busy worrying about him to focus on myself. I hadn't even been in London for five hours and I'd already gone mental, and all because a kid tried to give me a poster.

Maeve wanted us to get STI checks. She wanted to go without condoms. She wanted to be as close in our bodies as we were in our hearts.

How can I tell her that could never, ever happen?

18

MAEVE

"*M*aeve! Omigod, there you are!"

Kelly rushed across the arrivals lounge, her loud American accent booming over all the quiet British chatter. Her blonde hair streamed behind her, and a brand-new oversized purse stuffed with magazines clattered at her side.

I opened my arms and she fell into them, and all my apprehension about her being here melted away. I was so happy to see her, alive and happy and not in a hospital bed.

"Welcome to Jolly England. How was the flight?"

"I've been trapped in a tiny tin can for fifteen hours. My hair looks like straw and I'm all sweaty and gross and the guy next to me smelled like stale doughnuts." Kelly smoothed down her hair. "I'm never getting on a plane ever again."

"Aren't you planning to backpack around the world? How are you going to get to other countries – litter bearers?"

"I figure I'll just take the trains. Gabe told me Europeans are nuts for trains. Trains are romantic. Haven't you ever seen that famous film?"

"Which one, *Murder on the Orient Express?*"

"Maeve!"

"*Snowpiercer?*"

Kelly swatted my shoulder. "I'll know it when I see it, but there was definitely a train, and some hot guys were on it. I'll just ask to get a ticket on the hot guy train, not the murder express."

I grinned. Kelly hadn't changed a single bit. "Come on, let's get you back to our apartment."

"We have to find my backpack first."

"I cannot picture you with a backpack." Kelly was not an outdoorsy kind of girl. At her summer camp last year she faked sunstroke and sat in the first aid tent all week while guys fell over themselves to bring her glasses of water. The idea of her lugging her possessions across Europe in a backpack was as funny as NASA misspelling the name of the space shuttle *Endeavour* on their launch site banner.

We picked our way through the crowd to reach the luggage carousel. One single bag sat on the conveyor belt, going around and around on its lonesome – a bright pink backpack with glittering golden straps that was about the size of a small car.

Behind me, Arthur burst out laughing. "It looks like Barbie's brought the whole bloody dream house on vacation."

I struggled to keep down my own laughter. "Are you seriously going to lug *that* across Europe? It's not aerodynamically sound."

"You're such a worrywart. Look, it's fine." Kelly grabbed the straps and hauled the bag off the carousel. The weight of it sent her flying backwards. She slammed into a businessman dragging a tiny wheeled case. He glowered at her and yanked his case away.

"Sorry!" Kelly yelled. Kneeling on the ground, she bent over backwards and slid her arms into the straps, but when she tried to get to her feet, the backpack wouldn't follow her. Her arms and legs flailed in the air like a beached turtle.

I couldn't help it – a loud snort burst from my mouth. Arthur's face had already gone pink from trying to hold in his laughter. Our eyes met and that sent us both over the edge.

"Oh... my... god..." I held on to Arthur and clutched my stomach as tears rolled down my face.

"Fine, don't help me then," Kelly huffed, as she managed to roll onto her side.

"I'm sorry," I wheezed, my stomach hurt from laughing so hard.

How can you laugh when twenty-two people just died?

The laughter died in my throat. I couldn't forget the real reason we were in London. In thirteen days the fae would raise the Slaugh. We needed answers, and allies, and we were here to find both. Kelly wasn't a guest of honor, she was a distraction, one who had to be kept in the dark as much as possible.

"I'll take that for you." Arthur bent down and scooped up the straps, hauling first one, than the other, over his shoulders. Even he winced at the weight.

"Oh, thank you so much, Arthur. I don't know what I'd do without you." Kelly batted her eyelashes. I flung my arm around her shoulder, my whole body shuddering with laughter as Arthur tottered toward the Tube station, nearly keeling over from the weight of the bright pink pack.

"See?" Kelly winked at me. "Europe is full of hot men eager to impress a young lady from Arizona with their muscles. I'm going to be totally fine."

If one person could make it all the way across Europe without having to carry her own backpack once, it was Kelly.

She glanced around. "Where are the other hot guys?"

"They decided to wait at the apartment. You'll meet them soon."

I hoped. Rowan still hadn't come back when I left. Corbin went out to look for him, but he said Rowan might not want to be found. The look in Corbin's eyes said he knew what was going on in Rowan's head, but when I pressed him about it he just sighed and said Rowan would tell me when he was ready. I hoped that would be soon. The sadness and panic in Rowan's eyes as he fled down the ladder scared me.

We crammed onto the tube and rode on the Piccadilly line to Leicester Square, where we changed to the Northern line. Kelly chattered the whole way about the flight and the airline food and the people she'd met at the youth hostel. It didn't seem to matter to her that neither of us said much back.

It took us nearly an hour to get her through Camden Market to the apartment. She kept running off to look in the shops. I had to explain to her what a hookah pipe was and stop her spending a third of Uncle Bob's money on a sparkling red gothic ball gown that looked like something from a fairytale book. Arthur bowled over three teenagers and two living statues with Kelly's enormous bag.

Since our apartment didn't have an elevator, Arthur had to lug Kelly's backpack up three flights of stairs. Sweat poured down his face when he finally dropped it in the doorway. He collapsed on the couch, struggling for breath.

"You can't just leave it in the doorway," Corbin said as he came out of the bathroom and saw the bag protruding out into the hall.

"I can and will." Arthur wiped matted hair from his brow. "It could be one of Flynn's modern art installations. Call it *Guy Slips Disk for Chivalry*. I don't care. I'm not moving it."

"Boys, don't fight. I'll take care of it myself." Kelly tugged on one of the straps, but the bag didn't move an inch. She stepped over it. "Later."

Corbin laughed. "You must be Kelly. Maeve's told us so much about you. I'm Corbin." He held out his hand, but Kelly ignored it and swept her arms around him in a huge hug.

"Omigod, our fairground hero, we meet again. You were absolutely the most amazing person ever, saving Maeve from the fire like that and helping me nurse her back to health. A regular Florence Nightingale, only with infinitely more muscles. Maeve's told me hardly anything about you, except that you're a total brainiac and you're really hot. But I knew that already. Honestly, I thought you were the one she'd end up dating, but it's probably for the best that she chose Arthur because if you're as brainy as she says then the two of you would have really boring children—"

My cheeks flamed red, but Corbin only laughed more. "I can see we're going to have our hands full with you."

"We were going to give you the mezzanine," Arthur added. "But no way am I lugging that bag up the ladder. It's a monolith from *2001*."

I laughed, but the reference was lost on Kelly, who'd never wasted the rare moments our parents weren't monitoring our TV time by watching science fiction films. "Who's in that room?" Kelly pointed to the tiny double bed under the window in Jane's room.

"I am." Jane appeared at the doorway. She wore a black tank top and old-fashioned pedal pushers, her hair tied back with a polka-dot scarf. She shuffled Connor to her other arm and smiled at Kelly – a rare, genuine smile. "I'm Jane. And this is Connor."

"Aw, isn't he cute?" Kelly rushed over. A few moments later she had Connor in her arms, cooing as she dangled a tiger toy in front of his face. "Don't worry about it. I'll take the fold out sofa. I sleep pretty deeply, anyway. Nothing wakes me up once I'm gone."

"You don't know how relieved I am to hear that," Arthur said, with a glance at the pink backpack.

I glanced at Corbin, trying to keep my voice steady. "Is Rowan around?"

"Yeah, how is he?" Kelly asked. "Is he okay?"

I remembered just in time that I'd told Kelly he'd been in a car accident. "Yeah. His injuries weren't as bad as we first thought. He was discharged, but he's got a concussion, so he has to rest a lot."

Yet another lie. This time I just wish I knew what I was lying about.

Corbin nodded. "He's in the room having a nap. He'll be out when he's ready."

The message was clear – don't disturb Rowan now. At least he was safe and here with us. I wished I could just read Corbin's mind and figure out what was going on, but that wasn't my power. I had the distinct impression that if I could get inside Rowan's head, I'd end up lost there.

"Where are the others?" Flynn and Blake weren't anywhere to be seen, either.

"They weren't here when I got back. If I had to guess, I'd say they went out for food."

Luckily, Kelly was too busy with Connor to care that much about the whereabouts of the other guys. She bounced over to the couch and flung herself down. "So, when can we start sightseeing?"

How could she be this chipper after a long haul flight? "You don't want to rest a bit first? We could order in some food and—"

"No, Maeve. This is my first time in another country. I want to *explore*. You promised we'd go and see all the London things."

I thought of the meeting Clara had arranged for us with Isadora, the leader of a London coven, in a couple of hours. "I can't today. Corbin and I have an appointment to do with our research project, but—"

"I can't believe you're not even in school and you're *still* studying. What is this all about, then? You discover a new type of space dust?"

"No, actually. It's to do with my mother." Briefly I explained that I'd seen the portrait of my mother in the castle, and that it was painted by a famous artist. "I want to learn more about the artist, but he's in an institution now, so we can't go talk to him. Maybe I'll discover more about my mother. That's why we're in London."

"That's so cool. I want to come."

Shit. "No, you can't. This is a meeting with a… um, reclusive historian. It took Corbin all week just to convince her to let the two of us visit. If I bring another person she won't see us. Plus, you'll find it insanely boring, trust me. But the other guys are free, so they could take you somewhere. What do you want to do first?" I asked Kelly.

"Big Ben! No, the Tower of London! No, Buckingham Palace! Can we see the changing of the guards?"

"I bring sustenance!" Flynn yelled as he and Blake barged through the door, stacks of takeout containers balanced precariously in their arms. The now familiar smell of curry and naan bread wafted across my nose, and my stomach growled.

"I guess we're eating first," I said. "Kelly, this is Flynn and Blake."

"Greetings," Flynn tipped his hat to Kelly. She wrapped her arms around his neck.

"Eeeee! You're Scottish! I've never met a Scottish person before!"

Blake snorted. Flynn launched into a long diatribe about

the difference between the Irish and Scottish that had Kelly in giggles.

I glanced across at Arthur, my sole "boyfriend" while Kelly was around. The corners of his mouth turned up. So far so good, right? I mean, Kelly had only been in the door ten minutes and I'd already told so many lies I could run President Trump's Twitter feed. Keeping this secret from her wasn't going to be easy.

But what choice did I have?

19

FLYNN

*M*aeve had taken Mr. Serious (I quite liked Blake's Mussolini nickname, actually, but I think Corbin would throttle me if I made that catch on) to meet the leader of the Soho coven, which meant the rest of us were on entertain-the-sister duty. Which was going to be difficult, considering Arthur was being even more sullen than usual (although he seemed to have perked up recently. Having a sixsome with Maeve and your closest mates tended to put a smile on one's dial) and Rowan wouldn't look her in the face. Jane had her hands full with Connor, and Blake kept saying weird things that made it clear he'd never lived in human society before.

Luckily, I was a world-class entertainer. The Flynn-meister to the rescue once again. I'd make sure Kelly enjoyed her time in England if it killed me. After everything she'd been through, the girl deserved to have some fun. And fun was about all I was good for.

I sure couldn't do anything to save all those innocent people from dying. All the jokes in the world couldn't bring them back or make it okay. But Maeve needed Kelly distracted, so the king of distraction was here to serve.

"Where are we going?" Kelly asked as I shoved everyone out the door of the flat and down to the Camden Town Tube station. "Can we go to Buckingham Palace first? Let's go everywhere, just leave out all the boring stuff."

"Your wish is my command. One whirlwind London tour, coming right up!"

I checked my watch as we crowded on to the Tube. We were much too late for the changing of the guard, but the palace was still a great site. It wouldn't be as crowded now, and it would be a quick stop on the way to our second destination.

"It's the palace!" Kelly cried as she raced across the street to stand with the small crowd outside the iron gates.

"Good guess. This is where they keep the Queen." I gestured to the security around the gates, ordering people back when they got too close to the Beefeaters. "They got all this security because no one wants Queenie getting out and about. She's a bit forgetful, you see – forgivable at her age, since she's exactly two hundred and forty-three years old, and the palace has seven hundred and seventy-five rooms, so if she takes a wrong turn on the way to the loo she ends up in another post-code. And if she gets out it takes them *ages* to find her and lure her back inside. I've seen them out here at night, holding their torches and rummaging around in the bushes for her. They wave big wads of cash around on sticks to coax her back inside. She loves money. Sometimes, if it's a quiet day and you listen really hard, you can hear her squealing as she swims around in her giant pool of money. Fun fact for when you come back: on Valentine's Day Queenie operates a kissing booth. Just be careful you don't try to get out of paying because she keeps a brick in her purse and she ain't afraid to use it."

"Jesus, Flynn." Arthur groaned. "You're going to give our guest the completely wrong idea about this country."

"Hey, who's running the tour here? Kelly specifically asked me to leave out the boring stuff."

Kelly laughed. "Thank you for obliging. You're much better at this than Maeve. She'd be yammering on about all the scientists the Queen's given money to, and all their achievements, and why exactly she agrees and disagrees with their theories, and before I know it I've fallen asleep on one of those guys with the funny hats and I'm in a world of trouble."

Maeve. Just hearing her name made me think about how drawn her face was, how much she hated lying to her sister and being away from the castle when the fae were so close. She wanted so desperately to find a way to stop them. I know she was turning the information from Clara over and over in her head, thinking about how she would have to die in order to stop the Slaugh.

No. Maeve is not going to sacrifice herself. It wasn't going to happen, we couldn't let it. There had to be another way. But how to find it? I felt so helpless. I had nothing to contribute except stupid comments and fake city tours. I had to stand aside and let Maeve and Corbin figure that out, and it made me feel sick to my stomach.

Nothing I did could ever be enough to keep her. It was just the same as before. I could make her laugh, but when she was facing this horrible fate, what good did that do? What good could I possibly do?

It was just as well I kept my distance. It was hard enough seeing her stumble and being helpless to stop it. If I got too close—

"Tell me more about this Queen of yours," Blake grinned, punching me in the arm and bringing me back from my dark thoughts. I plastered a smile on my face and gestured to the nearest sentry.

"Here you'll find a member of the Queen's Guard, a fully operational soldier charged with guarding the Queen's residences in London. At eleven am each day, the guards change places in one of the greatest mysteries of the British Empire: Changing the Guard. The bells ring and they swap 'em out. Where do they go? What do they do? What is under those massive hats? Nobody knows. My theory is they go off to charge their batteries. The guards are called Beefeaters because of their quite legendary ability to maintain a grudge, or 'beef,' with tourists who stop to wave in their faces and make them break character. One time I saw this couple run up to try and take a selfie and the Queen herself came out and hit them with a brick. True story."

"They're actually *not* called Beefeaters," Arthur corrected. "This is the Queen's Guard. The beefeaters are the Yeoman Wardens who guard the Tower of London and give the tours and look after the ravens—"

I waved a hand in front of his face. "Details, details. Now, let's move on before Arthur turns into Corbin and gives us a fascinating lecture about the production process for the Queen's favorite type of brick." I turned to Kelly. "Where to next? Saint Paul's Cathedral? The Tower of London? The British Museum?"

Kelly wrinkled her nose. "No museums. Besides, Maeve will kill me if I go to a museum without her. She needs someone to listen to her rants about incorrect science displays."

Arthur's face darkened at the mention of Maeve. Rowan stared at his feet. Even Blake – who I expected to be at least excited to be out and about in the Big Smoke – looked off in another world. They were all thinking what I was thinking, that Maeve was trying to find a way to save the world and we weren't with her.

"Rightio, Tower of London it is. Follow me!"

I marched everyone to the Tower, determined that I'd find some way to distract them all from their ugly thoughts. Because nothing took one's mind off the horrors of an impending fae invasion like learning how human beings love to torture each other.

After we paid for our tickets I led Kelly into the courtyard, the rest of the group trudging behind looking like they were all about to go to their deaths. I'd fix that.

I cleared my throat and swept my arm up at the tower behind me. "The Tower of London is all that is left of England's short-lived attempt to win the space race. Built in 1984 by Morrissey, this rocket was meant to carry the Empire to the stars and beyond. English scientists have posited a theory that if you plant a flag in another country you own it, so if you just leave a flag floating in outer space you will own it as well. Unfortunately, one of the neighbors complained to the local council about all the noise the engines were making and so they scrapped the whole thing. Now they mainly use the tower to house the crown jewels and imprison failed footy captains, which you Americans know as 'soccer' because you're heathens."

By the end of my little speech, we'd accumulated a small crowd of tourists who stared at me with rapt attention, which only made Kelly and Jane snigger. A large American man tapped his watch. "Are we moving into the tower now? Can we still see the engines and the control room?"

"He's not a real tour guide!" Arthur yelled, his body rumbling with suppressed laughter.

"Maybe I should consider a change in career," I grinned as the tourists moved away. I kept up my ridiculous commentary as we made our way through the different displays. Kelly loved every minute of Flynn's Alternative Tower Tour, shrieking in her loud American voice at all the right places. Even Jane was laughing. It was all going well.

That was, until we came across a display of medieval alchemical equipment and a scale model showing how the scientists and philosophers of the day imagined the universe. Kelly passed by the display with little interest, but I lingered, taking in the artful arrangement of the pieces and the elegance of the equipment.

Maeve would have loved to see that display. But as long as her sister was here with us, we'd never get to have a day out all together like this. One of us would always have to be with Kelly, giving her the sunshine and glitter version of what was going on. And given the ever so enthusiastic expressions I was getting from my fellow coven-mates, that person was probably going to be me.

We had less than two weeks before the Slaugh came a'riding, and Maeve was thinking she was going to die. Shouldn't she be able to enjoy her time with her sister? She clearly hated lying, but shouldn't she be able to be completely herself around Kelly?

Maeve said there was no way Kelly would accept her powers or her relationship with all of us. I wondered if maybe she was placing too much importance on her parents' influence. Kelly seemed cool and not at all like the stuffy Christians I'd met. Maybe Maeve was just too stressed out by the whole fae thing to really see clearly. I decided to feel Kelly out.

"You know," I said, as we toured a display of royal bedchambers. "Many of the British royals took multiple partners. It was considered prudent, for if an heir wasn't born by one, there was always another shot. Henry the Eighth had six wives—"

"But not at the same time. You're being ridiculous, Flynn." Arthur glared at me pointedly. "That's not true at all."

I stomped on his foot, but Arthur was so damn big he probably didn't even feel it. "Even if it's not true – which I'm not definitely saying either way – don't you think it's a cool story? I love the idea of a Queen luxuriating on this bed surrounded by all her loyal suitors."

Kelly wrinkled her nose. "Really? I think it's horrible."

"You don't like the idea of a harem of guys all looking after you, tending to your every whim? You'd never get bored. You'd always have someone to talk to or hang out with or fuck."

"Look, maybe it was okay in ancient times, but we know better now. Marriage is one man, one woman, period. It's a partnership, two people with their souls intertwined."

"And you can't intertwine more than one soul?"

"That's not how it works," Kelly said. "You ever heard how too many cooks spoil the broth? There would never be any kind of accord. Besides, if you had children, how would they know who their real parents were? I want my children to grow up with a mother and a father. No confusion. Honestly, I'd think anyone who was doing that is kidding themselves that they'd be happy in that situation."

"Ooookay then." Wow, that was not the words I was expecting to come out of this girl's mouth. Arthur shot me a look. *See? Maeve really does know her sister.*

"Plus, think of all the diseases," Kelly added. "If you're not being faithful to one guy, than how can you trust them all to be faithful to you? You'd end up riddled with STIs, and it would just be so gross."

A weird wheezing sound came from behind us. I turned around to see Rowan clutching his chest and gasping, as though he was struggling to breathe.

"You okay, mate?"

Rowan's face had gone as still as stone, his eyes a million miles away. Arthur rushed to his side, glaring hard at me.

What? I didn't do anything. But that was the problem, wasn't it? I shuffled aside as a big crowd of tourists pushed behind us, feeling completely helpless.

"I just need a moment." Rowan slumped down on a bench. Sweat trickled down his face. He kept pounding his chest, as though he somehow needed to restart his heart again.

"What's going on?" I'd never seen him look this sick before.

"He's having a panic attack," Arthur said. "I saw him have one once before, when you were living in Arizona. We should take him home."

"Why?" Kelly wiped Rowan's cheek. He flinched away at her touch.

Arthur shrugged. "Beats me. It might just be all the people. When he starts breathing properly again, he might be able to tell us."

A panic attack. I glanced around the room, wondering what had set him off. He'd been quiet and jumpy ever since we got to London, and then after he ran away earlier... something about the city had made Rowan's anxiety flare up. Had I made things worse with my city tour? That'd be just my bloody luck.

"I'm... fine," Rowan wheezed.

"Okay, big fella, let's take you back." Arthur looped his arm under Rowan's shoulder and pulled him to his feet.

I slid my arm under the other shoulder. "Nice job, mate, faking a heart attack just to get out of listening to the rest of my tour. I'd be impressed by your acting skills if I wasn't mortally offended."

Rowan made a choking noise. Over his shoulder, Arthur glared at me like he wanted to throttle me. I gave him a huge grin, but that did nothing to ease his scowl.

We were basically helpless. If the painting didn't give us any answers, and the other covens wouldn't help support us, there was no fecking way we'd be able to stop the Slaugh. If we weren't laughing, what the hell were we going to do?

20

MAEVE

There are so many things I wish to tell you, but there is so little time. I will die tonight, of that I am certain. I saw my own death many years ago. The power of premonition is an ugly gift, and I pray that you will not inherit this curse from me.

I read the words of my mother's letter over and over as the train clattered through the tunnels, until the words blurred together and became a blob of ink, like a Rorschach test that showed the inner workings of my mother's mind. If only I could decode it and figure out what she was thinking.

Premonitions don't exist. An effect can't predate its cause. Things aren't destined to happen – the very fact that the fae exist in the multiverse proves that. My mother didn't know she was going to die. So was it selection bias and unconscious perception at play – as the High Priestess, she was the center of a dangerous spell, and therefore the most likely to die – or did she know consciously because she chose *to die?*

Did my mother choose to die, rather than fight for me? Would I have to make that choice, too?

"Maeve." Corbin's hand settled on mine. "No matter how many times you read it, you're not going to make more sense out of it."

"I don't know why it's bothering me so much now," I said. "I feel this insane need to resolve it in my head. I mean, why did she even write this? Why did she think it would be a comfort to me to know that she didn't even fight for me?"

"Because she didn't know that you'd be *you*, and that you'd see this through the lens of your scientific knowledge," Corbin said. "Maybe she thought that if you knew she could see her own death you'd find it a comfort."

"Do you believe that?"

"It's not important what I believe."

I folded the letter again and slipped it into my purse. "I just wish I could ask her myself."

Corbin squeezed my hand. "You can't. But maybe we'll get some answers from our research. We're about to meet one of the most powerful witches in England. She was there the night of the ritual. Maybe we'll get lucky, and she'll know where Robert Smithers is hiding."

I nodded. The thought was so odd. After twenty-one years of not knowing my mother, I was about to meet a second person who hadn't just met her, but had worked magic with her.

We got off at King's Cross station and walked a couple of blocks through beautiful Victorian terraces with ornate iron fences and lavishly-tended gardens. The cars parked in the street were all luxury models. Audi. Ferrari. Tesla. Designer labels dazzled from shop windows. We crossed the street into a beautifully manicured public square, surrounded on all sides by theatres and restaurants and more grand buildings.

"This is Soho, part of the West End," Corbin explained in what Flynn described as his 'history professor' voice, gesturing to a beautiful old theatre on the corner of the square. The billboards out front advertised a season of Shakespearean plays. "All the big theatres and entertainment venues in the city reside here. It's also been the heart of London's sex trade since the late 1700s."

He pointed up at one of the buildings across the square. "That's 21 Soho Square, home of the White House – one of the most notorious historical brothels in the city. Photographers used to hide on the streets outside to try and snap pictures of famous people going inside so they could blackmail them."

"How do you *know* all this stuff?"

"My dad wrote a book about the history of prostitution in Britain. It came out about a year before he left Briarwood. He refused to let me read it, but a couple of years later I ordered it off Amazon." Corbin gave me a tight-lipped smile.

"Sneaky. Was it any good?"

"Yeah. It was. I had no idea my dad was such a good writer. He knows how to talk about history in a way that's interesting and humorous, without disrespecting the material."

Just like you. "Hey, why don't you write a book? A history of witchcraft, or of Briarwood Castle. You could sell it at the gift shop after the tours."

"I wouldn't know how."

"You could try. You could ask your dad for—"

Corbin shook his head. "Dad's made it perfectly clear he doesn't want to speak to me ever again. I can't say I blame him."

"But why, though? It's not as if it's your fault that your brother died."

"Yes, it is."

Corbin's words pounded inside my head, and even though his voice was as soft and stoic as if he were reciting some historical fact, the pain behind them tore me up. I stopped walking, dragging him to a halt as well.

"That can't be, Corbin." I met his eyes, searching for the killer he seemed to think lurked there. But that killer didn't exist. "You've got to tell me what happened."

"It's in the past. It's not important now."

"It is. It might be the most important thing you ever tell me. Why do you think you're responsible for Keegan's death?"

"Because I am." Corbin's voice shuddered. His fingers knitted between mine. He inclined his head and started walking again, the steady beat of his steps seeming to calm him, perhaps in the same way the pounding drums of heavy metal music calmed Arthur. "Keegan and I had a huge fight the night before he died. We were down in the garden. He told me he hated me because Mum and Dad loved me and not him. He said he hated us all and he wished he was dead. I thought it was just one of his episodes, so I turned my back and left him to rage and vent. He didn't come to dinner and I didn't see him in the evening, but it was pretty typical of him to hide somewhere when he got upset. The next day, he wasn't at breakfast. Mum sent me out to look in all his usual hiding spots, and I... I found him hanging in the woods behind the castle. Here we are."

Corbin dropped my hand. He swung around a large decorative concrete urn and leapt up a short flight of steps toward a fancy terrace home, leaving me frozen in shock on the street.

What the hell?

Corbin's words – spoken so easily as he dropped that bombshell, carrying no trace of the torture behind them – slammed into me, conjuring the image of a lone figure swinging from a rope looped around one of Briarwood's towering oaks. A sibling lost, a family broken. A brother who felt he let down the one person he was supposed to help.

So much of who Corbin was became clear to me. No wonder he rarely left the comforting darkness of his library. No wonder he never walked on the grounds unless it was coven business. No wonder he rarely slept. He must see that image behind his eyelids every time the lights went out. No wonder he wore himself out trying to keep the coven together, giving us every piece of himself and holding nothing back for his own happiness. Because he feared that if he missed a single clue, if he messed up again, he'd be seeing another person he loved hanging from a rope.

All that he bore with his easy smile. All that guilt that had been heaped unfairly on his shoulders he had turned into goodness, because of the person he was.

That broke my heart to pieces.

I raced up the steps after him and slammed my hand over the brass knocker. "What are you doing?"

"Our meeting's in three minutes," Corbin said calmly, turning back to the bright red door. "I'm knocking."

"You can't just drop that bomb on me and then expect us to walk into this meeting as though everything is totally fine."

"You asked me to tell you."

"That's not the point. We should go somewhere and talk about this."

"What's there to talk about?" Corbin's face remained impassive. He looked like he was discussing the weather. For some reason, his indifferent expression tore at my heart more than seeing him upset ever did. "Talking won't bring my brother back or make my dad talk to me again."

"No, but maybe I can help somehow. Maybe we can find a way to reach your family together—"

"It's okay, Maeve. Really, it is. I understand. Dad had to

cut Keegan down from the tree. Whatever I feel about it, they feel it a hundredfold, because they lost two sons that day. They felt like they had to bury me when they buried him, so that they wouldn't crush me under the weight of their own guilt. I won't burden them with any of mine. We don't need them to defeat the Slaugh."

"But they were there that night. Clara said my mother had two assistants. Maybe it was them. Maybe they remember the ritual."

"The ritual isn't important, remember? The power is. And we have Clara now, and Isadora – if today's meeting goes well. And we have you."

"But—"

Corbin pried my fingers off the knocker. "Isadora was very specific. We were not to be a minute late or we would forfeit our meeting. *Please*, Maeve. I've already got too many deaths on my hands today. Don't make me dredge this one out of my conscience, too."

Too late.

I yanked my hand away. Corbin grabbed the knocker and let it drop. He looked visibly relieved. My stomach twisted as I watched him. How had he lived with that guilt for so long and still kept going? If Kelly had taken her life, I'd have lost myself completely. And how could his parents allow him to continue blaming himself? Could they not see that their silence only served to prove their condemnation? I could practically see the noose he wore around his own neck – a cord braided from his own honor and despair.

The door swung open, revealing a woman who seemed to entirely consist of legs and teeth, wearing a figure-hugging shift dress that could have paid my first year's tuition at MIT. She flashed us a smile that didn't reach her eyes. "Do come in. The mistress is expecting you."

Inside, the house was more spacious than I expected. The

woman took our coats and hung them on a black rack to the side of the entrance hall. Modern monochromatic art gleaned from stark white walls and black crystal chandeliers dangled from the high ceiling above our heads. The only color in the entire space was a violent red carpet stretching up the staircase. The overall effect was jarring, making the furniture appear the wrong size for human use, as if we were standing inside some fairground funhouse.

Now is definitely not the time to be thinking about fairgrounds.

"The first landing, last door on your left." The woman flicked a hand of perfectly-manicured talons at the staircase. "Don't keep her waiting."

I followed Corbin up the stairs, taking in as much of the weirdness as I could. On the first corner of the staircase was a weird black blobby sculpture that made the things Flynn made look like fine art. At the top of the landing we entered a narrow hallway containing five doors on each side. Faint noises trailed up through the doors – the whisper of voices, the creaking of furniture, the soft tinkle of piano keys. How many people were in this weird house? I half expected a clown or an ax-murderer to leap out at any moment.

"What is this place?" I whispered to Corbin. My skin prickled as though someone was watching me.

"Remember what I said before about Soho being a red light district?" I nodded. "Well, this is the sort of establishment you might find in such a district."

"You mean this is a *brothel?*"

"Sssh!" Corbin's eyes danced around. "*Don't* use that word here. This is an extremely upmarket establishment. There might be foreign rulers or Monte Carlo billionaires behind those doors. It's also one of the few safe places in the world witches can come to openly convene together."

"I don't understand."

"I'll explain later." He rapped three times on the last door on the left. A voice inside purred, "Come in."

"Wait!" I grabbed Corbin's arm. "I've never met another witch before as a coven leader. How do you do it? Is there some sort of secret handshake or ritual I'm supposed to know?"

"All our rituals are unique to our covens. Blake was right when he said the rituals are just elaborate ways of chan-nelling power. Just talk to her like you would a normal person." He pushed open the door and stepped back. "Ladies first."

I stepped into the room, not sure what I was going to see. Like the rest of the house, this room was something out of a Lady Gaga video – completely decorated in white on black. Black sofa and two chairs with white edging. Slim black desk with white laptop. Gleaming white bar along one edge with rows of glasses that splattered rainbow prisms over the wall. More weird art. Only a luxurious red carpet underfoot and the prisms splashed across the walls by light hitting the crystal drinkware gave any color.

A woman sat behind the desk, her swan-like neck bent toward the keyboard as she tapped at the keys with impos-sibly long nails, each one sharpened to a deadly point and coated in a red lacquer so sleek it looked as if it should be on a car commercial. Long, straight hair – every strand perfectly in place – was swept back into an elegant bun at the nape of her neck. Black-framed glasses sat on the end of her slightly ski-jumped nose. She didn't look up as we came in.

Isadora. It was Just Isadora, Corbin had informed me earlier. No last name – at least, none that she trusted to the witching community. High Priestess of the most powerful and influential covens in Europe, and also the most well-connected. If we got Isadora, Corbin and Clara both said, we would get others.

"Mmmm," she purred as she continued to tap at the keyboard. "Close the door, please, I'll be finished in a moment."

Corbin closed the door, and gestured for me to speak. The woman hadn't stopped typing. I mouthed at him, *what the hell am I supposed to say?*

"You could begin by telling me who you are and what this visit is in aid of," the woman said without looking up.

Corbin elbowed me in the ribs. I stepped forward. "Um... right. I'm Maeve Moore, High Priestess of the Briarwood Coven. We're here because—"

"American," she sniffed, in the same way someone might remark about off-seafood. She finally raised her long neck, glaring at me from down the slope of her nose. Eyes like ice water regarded me, then turned to Corbin. "Might you have found someone of your own stock, my dear? I could have given you one of my girls, you know."

"That's quite all right," Corbin said, stepping back behind me.

I glared at him. *That's quite all right? She just said that to me and that's the best reply you can come up with?*

But then I remembered we needed this woman to lend us the power of her coven, and to help us find Robert Smithers. I tried to ignore the surge of annoyance that flashed against my skull. "We came to speak with you about the fae. I understand your Soho coven helped Briarwood stave off a fae attack twenty-one years ago?"

"We lent a hand to a fellow sister. What of it?"

"Aline Moore was my mother."

Isadora blinked. She reached up and pushed her glasses up her nose. "That's not possible."

"How do you mean? I'm right here." I waved a hand in front of my face. "Not a hologram."

"You're supposed to be dead."

21

MAEVE

*M*y heart thudded in my chest. "That's news to me."

Isadora shot Corbin a look. "I thought her name was for ceremonial use. The child died in the ritual twenty-one years ago. I saw it happen with my own eyes."

"Nope, not dead." *This doesn't make any sense. Why would she believe she saw me die in the ritual? I wasn't in the ritual.* "I was adopted out to a family in America. I only recently returned and learned about my powers."

"It's true. She is the daughter of Aline Moore," Corbin said.

"And her power? Does she have Aline's premonitions? What does she see of the future?"

"I'm right here." I gritted my teeth. Why did she speak to Corbin as though I wasn't in the room? "And premonitions aren't real. They are caused by selection bias and unconscious perception of—"

"Maeve is a dreamwalker," Corbin said. "Probably the most powerful we've ever known. I've also seen her use compulsion with another witch on several fae at once."

Isadora opened her mouth, but I spoke over her. "But that's not important now. The fae are trying to raise the Slaugh again. We have tried to hold them off but have been unsuccessful. They are now residing in the underworld, waiting for the full moon to arrive. Our coven is not as strong as it was back then, therefore we are asking for your help again."

She looked up at me and sighed. "The full moon is in thirteen days time. You've left this late to inform me. Had you come to us sooner…"

"We didn't realize how bad the situation was until they were already in the underworld. We believed we'd succeeded in halting their progress, but we were wrong."

Her red lips formed a frown so formidable it made my heart sink into my toes. "You're the guardians of the gateway. You needed to be on top of this."

"Yes, well, I've had this job for less than a month, so—"

Isadora steepled her fingers. "Very well, daughter of Aline. If you are asking me to place my coven in danger, then I must hear your plan."

"I—" I glanced at Corbin, but he shook his head. I got it – he couldn't speak for me, he wasn't the coven leader. I was. My gut told me that telling this woman we didn't have a plan wasn't going to cut it. "Well, we're going to do the same thing you did last time."

She studied me again. "Is that so?"

I nodded.

"Then you will fail." She raised her glass to her lips and took a sip. Not a speck of her lipstick rubbed off on the rim. "As your mother has clearly failed, if you are standing before me."

"Excuse me? My mother died to save the world from the Slaugh. She didn't fail—"

"Do you even know what ritual you are asking me to help you perform?"

"Er, we're a little fuzzy on the details. None of the original coven are able to tell us anything about it. But we've got the basics from Clara Raynard—"

"A second-rate witch – she was not in the inner circle that night. She knows nothing. As for you... you do not have the stomach for what must be done."

"If you mean to sacrifice myself, we're trying to find a way to avoid that. If you could help us with the ritual—"

She laughed, the sound completely devoid of mirth. "No, dear, it is not you who needs to be sacrificed."

"What, then?"

Isadora fixed me with those violet eyes. "A mother must plunge a knife into the heart of her own child."

*M*y heart stopped beating.

"What – what did you say?"

"You must sacrifice an innocent. And the only true inno-cents are children who have not yet had the chance to sin. The fae are trying to do something unnatural – to force the restless dead to walk across the earth and kill the living. In order to make that happen, they must bend the forces of nature until they break. The only way to combat that kind of power is to also do something unnatural. In Aline's case, she killed her own child." Isadora frowned at me. "Except she didn't."

My mind reeled. My mother hadn't just gone into that ritual knowing she would die. She'd gone into it ready to kill *me*.

Bile rose in my throat. *How could she—*

How could *anyone?* It was inhuman. It was monstrous. The room spun, the stark white like a siren pulsing inside my head. I covered my mouth with my hands.

Corbin was at my side in a moment. "Can we sit down?"

With a flick of her wrist, Isadora motioned to a long

white chaise lounge under the window. Corbin led me over to it. My body had gone numb. I couldn't feel his hands on me. Isadora stood at the bar for a moment, mixing something in one of the crystal glasses. Ice cubes tinkled, the sound like gunshots. She came over and handed us each a glass of something red. I lifted it to my lips and sipped. Alcohol burned my throat, but the drink tasted like ash. I choked, nearly bringing the mouthful back up again.

Corbin rubbed my shoulder, but suddenly I didn't want comfort. Rage surged through me. How could my mother be a part of that? How could *anyone?* This woman in front of me had been a part of that ritual, and now she was offering me a drink like... like...

"How could you do that?" I demanded, finding my voice. I tossed the glass across the room. It slammed into the wall and fell to the floor, where it smashed into a thousand pieces, splashing the red drink across the crisp white paint like a bloodstain. "How could you murder a child?"

"Do they not teach you philosophy in your hideous American schools?" Isadora shot back. "Witches are governed by the laws of nature, which are utilitarian in principle. That utilitarianism must be applied across all sentient species. We cannot place the suffering of one child and the mother who bore her over the lives of every living being on earth."

She sounded just like Uncle Bob or Dora, trying to justify cruelty with religion. "I thought witches were different, that centuries of persecution might've taught you something about compassion and justice. But you're just as cruel as the fae you tried to destroy." I sat back, folding my arms. "You know what? Fuck it. Let them come. I'm done trying to fight for a world that just wants to hurt and maim and kill in the name of dead philosophies or invisible gods. Let the fae torch this place and start fresh. They can't be any worse than we are."

"Maeve." Corbin tried to take my arm, but I jerked away, the movement causing bile to rise in my throat.

Isadora's body sagged. Her face aged ten years in a moment – lines appearing around her perfectly made-up eyes, her bow-shaped lips turning down at the edges. "No one wanted it. We didn't think we had a choice."

"That's bollocks and you know it. There's always a choice." *Don't throw up. Don't throw up. Don't...*

She turned away, staring at the juice dribbling down the wall. "I suppose I best tell you what happened that night."

"It would be helpful, yeah."

"At least two hundred witches converged on Briarwood Castle." Isadora spoke to the wall, her arms hanging at her sides, red talons bright against her black silk dress. "This was highly unusual. We do not congregate outside our own covens, for we do not have need of the large rituals any longer, and it makes it too easy for ordinary humans to observe our powers and persecute us. Each coven has its own duties and guardianships. We rarely share information or contact each other, outside of establishments like this.

"When the Briarwood coven realized the fae were close to raising the Slaugh, they contacted all the covens they could find and begged for our help. Even though they grossly disregarded our protocols, the situation was too dire to ignore. So the witches came – from all corners of the British Isles, from Germany, from Slovakia and Finland, even as far afield as Turkey.

"We went down to the sidhe. Twelve High Priestesses gathered in the inner circle, our bodies pressed together so no one could see what went on in the center. The rest of the witches formed a larger circle around us. Aline Moore led the ritual, with her magister and two witches to serve as assistants. Aline had given birth only hours before. She had to be carried into the circle by her Magister. She held the baby in her arms."

I imagined my mother as I knew her in the painting, her beautiful face wrecked with exhaustion, her body pushed past its breaking point. She wore a white dress that fluttered in the breeze, the hem already streaked with blood from the birth. In her arms I wriggled and begged for milk, tipping my head toward the woman who was supposed to care for me.

My stomach heaved. I coughed, struggling to keep down the curry I'd foolishly eaten before we left. *How could she do this? How could she make all these people complicit? She's evil. My own mother is—*

"Who was her magister?" Corbin asked.

"A witch named Herbert, I believe."

I glanced at Corbin. He'd guessed right. *Herbert Missort – Robert Smithers.*

If only it mattered.

My head pounded. I didn't want to know any more. I didn't want to hear how my mother tried to murder me.

"Then what happened?" Corbin asked.

"The skies darkened. Voices traveled on the wind, the whispers of the restless dead rising, preparing to ride. We chanted together, channelling our power into Aline. She declared her intentions to the four corners and the five elements. Her magister charged her powers in the usual way. She raised the knife. She plunged it into your heart."

My mind whirled even as I struggled to hold down my stomach. What had my mother done to me? Had I survived by accident, by chance, or by design? Did I have some secret twin sister who she killed off in order to save me? Had she somehow sacrificed herself so that I could live?

Was I just grasping at straws, hoping for some explanation that could excuse what she did? But how... how could there ever be an excuse?

I gripped Corbin's knee. The room spun. I leaned forward, knowing I was only moments from passing out. *I wish we'd never come here. I wish I'd never come to Briarwood and found out what I am, that this horror is part of my heritage. More than anything, I wished I could speak to my mother, demand answers.*

"But how is that possible?" Corbin demanded. "Maeve is here, very much alive."

Isadora shook her head, still staring at the wall. "I don't know, but I saw it. I saw the blood spurt from the wound, the life drain from the child's eyes. I have seen that image in my nightmares ever since. Aline slumped forward as her body filled with magic, and the earth rumbled and split open, but we held firm and the heavens parted and the sky cleared, and the wind and rumbling stopped just as the light in her spirit went out. She died in that moment – releasing the power she had obtained – and the voices on the wind ceased their tortured howls."

I gasped for breath as my heart pounded against my chest, as if it was reminding me it was still part of my body. "There must... be another way."

Isadora spoke, her voice louder. It took me a moment to realized she had moved beside me. "If it is as you say, and the fae are in the underworld, then it's already too late. If Briarwood wishes to make a last stand in a pointless display of futile magic, then we will stand with you. But I must see a solid plan before I will place our coven at risk."

A child. She means she needs to see the child we plan to kill.

My stomach lurched, my throat burned, and with a gasp, I threw up across the red rug, my stomach heaving as it emptied itself of my lunch. Tears streamed down my face.

Corbin's hand swirling on my shoulder did nothing to relieve the horror or humiliation of that moment.

Isadora made an annoyed clicking noise with her throat. She went over to her desk and pushed an intercom button. "Katie, bring in the cleaning trolley. You'll need gloves, too, for the broken glass. Another guest of mine has demonstrated poor self-control."

Corbin held back my hair as I spat the remnants of bile on the carpet. "What's your duty?" I gasped out.

"Pardon?" Isadora couldn't keep her disgust out of her voice. She had joined a ritual to murder a child and she was disgusted by *me*? Fuck her.

"The duty of the Soho coven. If we guard the gateway, then what are you responsible for?" I couldn't resist adding, "I hope it's philosophy education for future witches."

"Secrets. We are responsible for secrets."

"I don't understand."

She sighed. "Of course you don't, American. Follow me."

Corbin helped me to my feet. I stepped around the puddle of puke just as the woman who answered the door bustled inside, dragging a beautiful silver trolley stacked with cleaning supplies. She got to her knees on the carpet, swinging her ass in the air as she dabbed at the stain.

We followed Isadora out into the hall. She pulled a keychain from her belt and opened the door immediately opposite. I peered around her, fresh bile rising in my throat as I took in the room beyond.

It was a bedroom decorated completely in black and white. Black walls, white wainscoting. White-painted metal bed frame covered in black silk sheets. But what had me reeling was the two figures on top of the bed.

A naked man sprawled on his back across the bed, his hands gripping the thighs of a woman as she rode him in a languid, gentle rhythm. Her ample curves spilled out of a white corset and garters, and white lace gloves pulled up past her elbows. Her gloved hands danced sensuously over his neck, not touching his skin but waving just above it. Each time she lifted her body, she pulled her fingers back, and the man wheezed as if he struggled to breathe.

She's an air witch, I realized with a start, fresh bile rising in my throat. *She's using her power to suck away his breath with each thrust, emptying his lungs so... so...*

Isadora slammed the door shut. I grabbed Corbin, anchoring myself against his unshakeable frame. I wasn't a prude, but something about seeing that witch stealing that man's breath made my already empty stomach clench and cramp.

"Isn't that... illegal?" I breathed, remembering snatches of breakfast conversation with the Briarwood lawyer Emily, who explained that in Britain a person couldn't consent to bodily harm through sexual practices.

"The only law recognized inside these walls are the laws of nature," Isadora said. "We cater to exclusive predilections here, and many of our clients are lawmakers who would not wish to see theirs exposed if this house were made public."

"You blackmail people."

Isadora smiled. "My witches extract secrets, many from the witches who visit us, many from ordinary humans. We store them all for when we need them."

"Anything that could help us now?" Corbin asked.

Isadora gave me one of those cold smiles. "Yes."

I waited for her to elaborate. She didn't.

~

"Well." Corbin fitted his hand into mine and squeezed hard. The giant red door slammed shut behind us. "That didn't go as well as I hoped."

"You're telling me." My legs wouldn't stop shaking. I didn't trust myself to tackle the steps back down to the street.

"Maeve, I'm sorry. I didn't know that was what this ritual involved. My parents told me to keep secret the fact you were still alive from other witches, but I thought that was just for your safety – in case the fae got to them. You know I'd never ask you to—"

"I know."

"There's another way. There's got to be, and we're going to find it."

"Corbin, can we not talk about this for a bit?"

"But—"

I yanked my hand from his. "I have to go back to that house and put on a happy face for Kelly and pretend that I didn't just learn my mother was supposed to stab me. I mean, what if she *did* stab me? What if me surviving was a fluke? What if she isn't a hero sacrificing herself at all, but a monster?"

"Hey, hey, this isn't like you – talking about heroes and monsters like this is a storybook. Use your logic, Maeve. It always steers you toward the truth. The point is, you *are* alive. That means something in the ritual didn't work properly, but even then, the Slaugh never rode. If we can figure out why that is, we can do it again." Corbin reached for my hand, but I shrugged away. Right then, I didn't want anyone to touch me.

We rode back to Camden in silence. My mouth tasted of curry and bile. I unfolded my mother's letter from my pocket, but I couldn't get past the first line – rage blinded my vision.

I clasped my hand over my chest, feeling my heartbeat through the thin fabric of my shirt. Did a knife pierce my chest by my mother's own hand? Isadora said she had seen it, and her careful words made me believe she would not lie.

How am I alive?

Kelly bounced on me as soon as I entered the flat, telling me in long, breathless sentences all about her afternoon of sightseeing. I listened with half an ear, nodding in all the right places as I tried to check in my my guys, sending them messages with my eyes that only they would understand.

I need you.

Flynn and Jane sat on the fluffy rug, playing with Connor like nothing was amiss. Arthur sat on one end of the couch, a wadded ball of agitation with his headphones plastered over his ears and his fingers drumming against his knees. Rowan peeked out from behind the door of our room. He was the only one who caught my gaze, and his whole body shuddered when he saw my expression. He held the door open, beckoning me to him.

At least he hasn't run away again.

"I've got to go get cleaned up," I smiled to Kelly. It wasn't a complete lie – I was desperate to brush the taste of bile from my teeth. "I'll be out in a second, and then we can think about dinner."

"We've already taken care of it," Kelly said. "Flynn's done a big order of sublami—"

"Souvlaki!" Flynn piped up without looking up from Connor's shape-matching game.

"—and other weird stuff from a Turkish place around the corner. I've never had Turkish before. I'm excited." She hugged me again. "You look more tired than I am, and I was the one who flew across the Atlantic Ocean today. Go shower or whatever. I'll call you when the food comes."

"Thanks, sis." My empty stomach growled. I hoped the food would stay down. I pushed the door open and slid into the bedroom, clicking the door shut behind me. Rowan sat on the edge of his single bed, staring at the window, hugging his knees to his chest and resting his chin on his hand. His dreadlocks fell over his shoulders like a curtain.

"Are you okay?" I asked, flopping on the bed beside him.

He shook his head. "I had two panic attacks today."

"Why? What happened?"

"It's fine. I'm over it. But I just… I can't do this sightseeing stuff around London."

"'It's fine' is not an answer to 'what happened?' Rowan, I really need you to do this for me. If Kelly thinks something is up, she'll dig around until she catches us. At least if she's here, I can keep an eye on her. I've got you guys to help me keep her safe. But if she finds out the truth—"

"I know. Flynn was asking her about polyamory today, and he got a big lecture about how marriage was between 'one man and one woman.'"

"What?" *Great, just what I need – Flynn sticking his nose in with all the subtlety of Elon Musk launching a Tesla into space.* I told them all not to bring up that stuff with Kelly. I didn't want to even put the idea into her head. It figured explicit instructions would go in one ear and out the other with Flynn.

Rowan nodded. "It's fine, he was making up fake guided tours, and he happened to do one about the royals having multiple partners. I don't think she suspects anything, but she does have strong opinions."

"Is that why you don't want to hang out with Kelly anymore?" We hadn't actually talked openly about Rowan's feelings for Corbin, but I could see them written all over his face every time they were in a room together. I always thought Corbin was completely clueless, but earlier, when we were all on the mezzanine, he was staring at Rowan like he was seeing him for the first time and I *really* thought they were going to kiss, but Rowan pulled away. Why did he do that, if it was what he wanted? "I know her worldview is disgusting, but she grew up in a pretty sheltered place and she's never actually *met* someone who's openly gay. I know her – once she found out that about you, she'd never be able to say—"

"It's not that. I swear. I like Kelly. I want to help. I'll do anything else. I just can't go out there again."

I wanted to snap at him that we all needed to be strong now, that some of us weren't shirking away from their duties even if that meant having to commit murder, but then he looked up at me.

Dark rings circled his eyes and tears streamed down his cheeks. His irises swam with that intense pain he carried with him always, the weight of his past dragging him inside himself, shutting him off from me.

I reached up and stroked his cheek, kissing a salty tear just as it rolled over the edge of his chin. What was it about the city itself that had Rowan so scared?

"I'm sorry," he whispered. "I know I'm weak."

"There's nothing weak about you, Rowan. I'll make some excuse to Kelly and find you something else to do. But I want to know *why*. I know it's hard for you to talk about this stuff, but I need to know what it is you're so afraid of out there." I squeezed his hand. "We're in this together, Rowan. Me and you and all the guys. We can't help you if you shut us out."

"I don't want to lose you."

"Well, at least we're in complete agreement about that. I don't want to lose you, either, which is why it's so important you tell me what happened. Help me understand. It's about when you used to live in London, isn't it?"

Rowan curled up into a ball, hugging his legs to his chest and burying his face between his knees so he didn't have to look at me. "If I tell you, you won't want me here anymore. You'll make me leave the coven, and I—I'll be alone again."

My heart broke hearing him talk like that. "Don't make the mistake of putting words in my mouth. I'm telling you that I'm not going to do that, so spill. This is where you lived before Corbin brought you to Briarwood."

He lifted his head slightly, his eyes meeting mine. Pain etched across his beautiful features. "I grew up very close by, in Haringey. I've walked these streets so many times, and being back here now – it's like I see ghosts everywhere. When I ran out this morning, a boy came up to me with an anarchist pamphlet, and I jumped into the street to avoid him. It was a full-on panic attack. I nearly got hit by a bus. Then I had another one at the Tower of London. It was something Kelly said—" he noticed my expression and rubbed his cheek against mine. "No, it's not her fault. It's just that she summoned another ghost. They're everywhere in this city."

"These aren't the first panic attacks you've ever had, are they?"

Rowan shook his head, his deadlocks fanning over his shoulders. "You know about the counting, and some of the other tics I have."

"Like cutting all the vegetables into perfect squares?"

"Yes," he smiled, and my heart twisted with his pain. "Exactly like that. Sometimes I wash my hands a lot, or I do two hundred sit-ups. Or I pluck leaves off the seedlings in the garden so they each have an even number. Doing those things helps stave off the attacks. It's like, my brain tells me that something terrible is going to happen to someone I care about unless I go through these rituals. If I don't count the windows every night, the guys will all die in a fire. If I don't cut the vegetables perfectly symmetrical, Corbin will be poisoned. Even if I know it's bonkers, I can't control the need to get them right. If I don't do them, my stomach goes all tight and my chest caves in and I can't breathe. The guys always just let me do my own thing, and I haven't had an attack for a couple of years now."

I kissed him. Rowan was so beautiful, inside and out. I couldn't imagine what he described – being convinced that something terrible was going to happen, living in fear every single day, believing that you were solely responsible for stopping it.

"So why now? Is it the Slaugh? Is it what we saw at the church?"

"That's part of it, but it's also—"

The door burst open, and Flynn, Blake and and Arthur barreled inside. Flynn shut the door behind him. Rowan rubbed his eyes and scooted away from me, covering himself with the blanket so no one could see his face.

"Your sister and Jane have gone out shopping at the market while Connor has his nap," Flynn said. "Quick, give us the lowdown on what Isadora said."

With my hand on Rowan's knee, I told them about the ritual and the fact I was supposed to be dead, and that Isadora knew some kind of secret, but she wouldn't say what.

"Clara texted earlier," Arthur said. "She says Obelix is doing very well, and the wards are still intact. No one in the village will speak to her, and the tourist office has stopped directing people to visit the castle. She hasn't found Smithers' yet, but she *has* found another High Priestess willing to meet with us – Gwen O'Shea of the Avebury Coven. Apparently, one of Gwen's witches has access to records that could help track down Smithers."

I shuddered. "I don't know if I want to meet any more of my would-be murderers."

"Gwen's not like Isadora. Apparently, she was particularly intrigued when Clara said who you were. She said she never believed your mother had killed a child, and she'd be honoured to help another Moore woman defeat the fae."

A tiny flicker of hope surged inside me. Under the blankets, Rowan squeezed my leg.

"Okay," I breathed. "Tell Clara to set up the meeting. And in the meantime, none of you say a word about this to Jane. I don't want her thinking Connor is in any kind of danger from us. Got it?"

Flynn saluted.

"None of this makes sense to me," Arthur said. "We're sure that whatever magic lingers inside your mother's portrait was what performed the emergency baptism on us in the church. And you have that letter from your mother, where she says she knows she will die that night. *She* will die, not you, Maeve. None of it marries up with what Isadora told you."

"I know. We've going to the National Gallery tomorrow. Maybe Smithers' paintings will give us some answers. If not, we'd all better find a god or a philosopher and start praying, because we'll have ten days until the Slaugh ride and I'm all out of ideas."

23

MAEVE

I walked across parched ground, the earth beneath my feet covered with a lattice of cracks. Here and there, blackened circles and broken arrow tips denoted a battlefield stripped clean of her dead. On my left, a towering wall of tangled briar penned me in. To my right, the ground sloped up, disappearing into a violent orange sky.

My body ached with an acute sense of loss. Someone was supposed to be with me. I could still feel their fingers wrapped around my arm. I glanced behind me, but I was completely alone. I tried to call out, but when I opened my mouth, a horrid, bitter taste hit my lungs. My stomach heaved. I doubled over in a coughing fit.

The air... the air is poison.

Tears stung my eyes as I struggled for breath. *You have to move. Head downhill.*

Crouching low and spluttering into my collar, I inched forward, heading toward the briar. Here, the air was a little easier to breathe, and I crawled along the hedge, scraping my knees raw on the bare, ruined earth and tearing long cuts in the skin on my arms when I got too close to the thorns.

When I thought I couldn't go on any longer, the hedge opened out into a short tunnel. I peered inside, but couldn't see the end through the tangled briar. Fresh air blew from inside the tunnel, and that was enough for me. I crawled inside, sucking in thick lungfuls of air. Goosebumps rose on my arms as the temperature dropped. After twenty feet or so, I was able to breathe enough that I could get to my feet again.

The tunnel opened out into a wide clearing, surrounded on all sides by walls of briar so high they blocked out any light from the sun. Thorns tangled over my head and snaked across the ground, snaring my bare ankles as I stepped around them.

Dark shapes rose out of the earth at the center of the clearing. My heart leapt into my throat as I recognized them.

Six long stakes stuck up from the ground, propped at a forty-five degree angle with the use of triangular wooden frames. Their tips pointed toward a black lump on the horizon. Over the tops of the briar I could just make out the highest turret and the ramparts of Briarwood, broken and blackened from a recent battle.

Six lumps hung from the stakes, charred and mangled.

Six bodies.

My stomach heaved. Bile rose in my throat. *Turn away. Run.* I whirled around. There was nowhere to run. The briar had closed around me, sealing me in.

"No," I gasped. "No, no."

I clamped my hands over my eyes, but their broken, blackened faces were seared into my mind. Flynn, Arthur, Corbin, Rowan, Blake... Everyone I loved, tortured and killed, their skin burned away, revealing the muscle and tissue beneath. White, lidless eyes bulged from their faces, begging me to save them. But there was nothing I could do. It was over, they were all dead and I... I was completely alone.

Alone.

I lowered my hands, turned around. Six stakes. Who was the sixth?

The final figure waited at the end of the line, shrouded in the shadow of the briar, its features obscured by thorny vines snarled around the stake. Who else would never walk the halls of Briarwood or wrap their arms around me again? Who else had sacrificed themselves for this cause? Who else's death would I carry in my heart?

I tried to walk towards it – wanting and not wanting to see – but it was like walking through molasses. I clenched and yanked and barely lifted my foot off the ground. The shape was impossible to make out.

Who are you?

Are you me?

I reached out, dragging my leaden legs and swiping my hands at the branches, trying to push them aside. *Nearly there, just a couple more—*

"Maeve?" A voice called me through the briar. I jumped, toppling backward, my feet sliding out from under me on the dry ground. I hit hard, my head bouncing against the nearest stake, tossing my brain around inside my skull. The world spun and disappeared.

A rough hand shook me. I grabbed at it, allowing it to pull me up. My eyes flew open, my surroundings completely confused. *Where am I? Where's the briar? Where are the stakes? Why does the ground suddenly feel all soft and squishy?*

"Maeve, are you awake?" Arthur whispered.

Awake?

My eyes adjusted, and I realized that I was tucked into a double bed. *That's right, I'm in the London apartment.* Something warm stretched out beside me. Rowan's dreadlocks peeked out from a pile of blankets, splaying over my pillow, his arm draped over my side. Arthur crouched beside the bed, his thick fingers curled around my shoulder, his eyes wide with concern.

"I was having a nightmare," I mumbled, reaching for my phone. My body trembled with the memory of the staked bodies. *Why did I have that dream again? Who is the sixth figure?*

"I know. You were thrashing around a bit."

I moaned as I glanced at the clock. 11:05. I'd only been asleep for three hours. After our Turkish dinner, Flynn put a movie on, but Kelly had crashed out on the couch before the opening credits were finished – the jet lag finally caught up with her. Flynn and I tucked her in, and the rest of us decided to take advantage of the early hour to catch up on our own sleep. We hadn't had much of it lately. Rowan had crawled into bed with me (Arthur didn't even protest; he must've seen how badly Rowan needed the comfort), and I'd fallen asleep in his arms, as safe as I could ever hope to be in this mess.

So why was Arthur waking me now? And why was I having that horrible dream again, the one Blake had shown me all those weeks ago?

I bolted upright, suddenly terrified. "Did something happen? Is Kelly okay?"

"She's fine," Arthur patted my shoulder. "Get dressed and meet me in the lounge. I have a surprise for you."

"Arthur—"

"You'll love it, trust me. Come on, we have to hurry."

As quietly as I could, I slid out from under Rowan's arm and picked through my backpack for something to wear. Arthur hadn't given me any details about this surprise, but he was wearing black jeans, his heavy boots, and a Blood Lust hoodie, so I assumed it was relatively casual. I threw on some skinny jeans and a lilac sweater and slipped out of the bedroom, tiptoeing around the couch where Kelly snored from a nest of blankets.

Corbin stood beside Arthur at the door of the apartment, also dressed in black. "You're going to stick out like a porcupine in a nudist colony," he said, gesturing to Blake's new leather jacket lying over the end of the sofa. "Take that instead, luv. Trust me."

I pulled on the leather jacket, sniffing the collar. It smelled like Blake – like fresh cut grass and burning incense and blood-drenched battlefields. As I poked my fingers through the too-long sleeves, I felt as though I had donned a suit of armor.

Arthur grinned. "We're ready."

"But where—"

"Ssssh!" Corbin grabbed my hand. We clattered down the stairs and out into the night. Sometime while I had been asleep the sky had opened up. Rain fell in thick droplets, drenching my hair. I wiped my pink bangs out of my eyes as we jogged past a club, the air briefly filled with driving dance music before the rain swallowed us again. The wet pavement reflected headlights and blinking signage on the bars and nightclubs, throwing up prisms of light like another city existing beneath the cobbles. My sneakers squelched as they filled up with water.

Black cabs lined the street, waiting for their next fare. *Good, we can get out of the rain.* But Arthur led us right past them. "It's only a couple of blocks," he said.

"*What* is?"

"You'll see."

On the next block, Arthur stopped in front of a kebab shop to fumble in his jacket. Something rumbled under my feet, vibrating beneath the sidewalk. I grabbed hold of Corbin, sucking in a breath as my stomach sank to my knees. *The fae have come back.*

"Maeve, what's wrong?"

"Can't you feel it?" I glanced around, searching for the

STEFFANIE HOLMES

first sign of the fissure tearing through the earth. "The fae are here. They've followed us!"

My heart pounded. *We have to get the others. We have to—*

Corbin laughed. "No, luv, it's just the music. We're right above it."

The music? What's he talking about?

Arthur pulled tickets out of his pocket. We followed him to a narrow staircase leading down below the street. A bouncer at the door stopped us. "You're just in time," he said. "I think they're starting now."

What's starting?

After checking our IDs and tickets, the bouncer waved us through and we descended into the gloom. I ran my fingers along the graffiti-covered walls, wondering what the hell Arthur and Corbin had got me into. Hot air swelled up from below, and music pounded up after it, a thumping bassline that drove right into my heart, making my bones jangle and my teeth clatter together. A very familiar bassline...

Holy shit.

We emerged in a cavernous room, packed with people surging toward a long stage shrouded in fog. No wonder heat rose from the crowd like an inferno. I was already sweating under Blake's jacket, but no way was I taking it off. Corbin was right – in the sea of black-clad fans, my lilac sweater would stand out a mile.

We pushed our way through long-haired guys dressed like Arthur and girls in corsets and PVC. No one turned to look at us. All eyes focused on the swirling fog while the bassline hummed in the air. A few moments later, a guitar joined in. Hundreds of arms raised in the air, their fingers formed into some kind of two-fingered symbol I remember from a bible study group being the 'sign of the devil.' For a moment I thought the guys had taken me to a satanic ritual, and my stomach flipped at the thought I might soon be witnessing a goat sacrifice. Then I saw a figure emerge from the fog – a black guitar swung low on his hips, long dark hair draped over his face. His fingers whipped along the strings like he was caressing a lover as the familiar riff soared over the crowd.

Blood Lust.

Arthur's favorite band – the band we blasted together to drown out our fear – were standing right in front of me. I'd played their latest album on repeat on the plane to Arizona, losing myself in the music. It made me feel like I wasn't really helpless.

And here they were, in the flesh.

The drums came in with a violent crash. The bassist swung his enormous, muscled body across the stage. A soulful, tremulous note reverberated through the venue as the instrumentalist struck the bow against his cello. The lead singer leapt into the center of the stage, dressed in his trademark frock coat and cravat. The spotlight caught his porcelain skin as he wiped a strand of wavy dark hair from his eyes and ripped into a bloodcurdling scream that sent a tremor through my whole body, right down to my toes.

The pillar of magic inside me flared to life. A thousand needles of pure energy darted through my skin, trailing threads that reached to the stage, stitching the music to me, and me to the musicians, and to the other fans in the crowd. Seeing Blood Lust in the flesh made their music flare to life. The melody dragged me up and spat me out.

Arthur and Corbin sandwiched me between them, the warmth of their bodies feeding the fire inside me. Arthur flicked his head forward, his hair whipping around as he thrashed his head in time with the pounding drums. It looked painful, but also... my body itched to copy him. I settled for nodding my head, unable to keep a smile from creeping across my face.

Corbin threw his arm around my shoulders. Arthur followed, trapping me between them. They jerked their bodies forward and I followed them, thrashing and jumping in time with the music. Corbin's face shone with pleasure and Arthur's wild smile melted my heart. For both of them, the music helped them drive out the pain and rage and guilt that hovered over their heads like a sword of Damocles. Corbin looked more relaxed than he had in weeks, and Arthur... he practically shone with happiness.

Other people around us banged their heads like Arthur. Long hair flew in all directions. Others jumped up and down or rocked their whole bodies in time to the unrelenting drums.

"I'll get us some drinks," Corbin yelled when the first song finished. He disappeared off towards the bar area along the side of the crowd. Arthur grinned and gripped my hand, pulling me deeper into the crowd, toward the stage. The closer we got, the more tightly pressed the people, brushing up against each other with careless familiarity. Normally, this would make me nervous, but the thick, damp air surged with raw energy, and it swept me up with it. In front of us, right near the stage, it was a savage pit of wild animals as the crowd whipped into a maelstrom, bodies crashing against each other and even flying through the air, held aloft by the hands of their comrades, boats adrift on an ocean of chaos.

Corbin returned, holding three drinks. He handed me something fruity with a strong taste of rum. I sipped it, holding the glass tight against my chest so no one would knock it with their elbows. Arthur tossed his head back and downed his beer in a single gulp.

After a couple more songs, Arthur squeezed my hand and yelled in my ear. "I'm going up front. You want to come?"

My eyes widened. He was going in there? Into the pit of crashing bodies? "I think I'll stay here!" I yelled back.

Arthur nodded then disappeared into the crowd. His large frame pushed through the other patrons until he was sucked into the churning, whirling maelstrom.

Corbin shifted so he stood behind me, his arms wrapped around me. His body shifted, bouncing in time to the furious beat. I let my body slacken, allowing my limbs to fall into rhythm with his. We moved together, caught up in the thrill of the powerful music. Corbin's lips brushed my neck and my whole body lit up.

My heart hammered against my chest as his kisses drew out something wild and unbidden inside me. I wanted to find a room to ourselves, blast the music, and fuck until this swelling in my chest burst out of me like a supernova. I leaned back and whispered in his ear. "I want you."

"What?"

"I want you. *Now.*"

Corbin looked confused. "I don't think they'll play 'Falsehood Disavow', because it's from their first album—"

Jesus Christ, he's hopeless. "Let's go somewhere and fuck!"

I yelled so loud the guy next to me turned his head and grinned. Luckily, Corbin got the message this time. He grabbed my wrist and yanked me back, shoving his way through the surging bodies. We passed the sound desk and merch stand, and ducked into a black hallway leading to the bathrooms. The music still pounded around us, filling my heart, bleeding my emotions all over my skin.

Corbin wasted no time. He pinned me to a wall, his mouth finding mine. I devoured him, tangling my fingers in his hair and jamming his head against mine. We kissed with desperate need, like the last two people alive on a defunct space shuttle hurtling toward earth. His teeth grazed my lip and the sharp pain only sparked me harder.

The music shook the wall so it rumbled against my back in time with the pounding of the bass and drums in my ear. I wrapped my legs around Corbin, grinding my hips against his already rigid cock.

Corbin pawed at my jeans, but he couldn't tug them down while my legs were around him. He leaned back and I slid my legs back to the ground. He unzipped his fly and rooted around in his pocket for a condom. *He's just like a Boy Scout, always prepared.*

I whipped my head around to check that no one was coming to the bathroom as I pulled one leg out of my jeans. Someone could come down the hallway at any moment, but I didn't care. I needed Corbin, *now.* I needed to feel him inside me the way the music was inside me. As soon as I freed my leg, I tried to pull it out of my panties, but Corbin grabbed my legs and threw me up against the wall again.

I dug my fingers into Corbin's back as his hands roamed all over me, his kisses consuming me, lighting a fire straight to my core. He reached down behind me, pushing the thin fabric of my panties aside. His hand supported my ass while he guided himself inside me.

I threw my head back as Corbin entered me in one hard stroke. Our eyes met as he thrust his hips up into me, his mouth open, his lips moving but the words soundless against the onslaught of heavy fucking metal.

His thrusts lit me up like a comet. We burned together, inside and out. Corbin's blue eyes blazed with a dark storm, violent and primordial. His mouth crushed mine, raw with frenzied need and a glowing determination – as if he somehow planned to drive out the demons that haunted me with his touch, with his cock.

And I *knew* with a sinking, sickening crush in my chest, that this boy who held us all together would one day undo me. That the strength Corbin carried in his heart would tear me to pieces, and I might never be whole again.

But in that moment, I couldn't care less. I didn't want to

think. I needed to forget the crushing weight of responsibility and the ritual that would transform me into a monster. My body shattered, the aching heat inside me burning up until I became a raw, bare mess of atoms, dancing to the sound of thundering drums.

Every thrust rocked through my body along with the music. Corbin's nails dug into my ass as he rose up to meet me, shoving me hard against the wall with every stroke. I knotted my ankles together behind his back, dragging him deeper into me. His teeth slid down my neck, the pain only fueling the fire inside me as it burned hot.

Hard. Fast. Heavy. Exactly what we both needed to drive out the demons.

"I love you!" I cried out, the words flying off my tongue before I'd even thought them. My heart constricted. Corbin's eyes blazed across mine.

"I love you!" Corbin screamed back, and with a hard shove and a shudder, he came, his face contorting as he lost control. I clenched around him as my body disintegrated into atoms and stardust, and I hovered on the edge of space, weightless and lost.

I came back to earth, my heart racing. Corbin collapsed against me, panting hard. I slid down the wall, anchoring myself against Corbin as I forced my legs to take my weight again. With shaking hands I shoved my foot back into my jeans, zipping up the fly just as two girls came running down the hall.

My head swam with force of the words I'd just spoken and the strange knowing sense that the closer I got to Corbin, the harder he would break me. But I had no idea what that meant, and I still didn't care.

Corbin ducked into the men's toilet and disposed of the condom while I straightened my clothes and raked a hand through my short hair. He came out and we rejoined the crowd, hanging a little further back by the sound desk to watch the finale. The set finished with the lead singer throwing down his mic stand and flailing his body like he was fed up with the world. Only, when he came out to the front of the stage to take a bow, he smiled from ear-to-ear. His long hair plastered to his porcelain skin and his classical cravat and frock coat were drenched with sweat. Looking at him now, I could see why there were rumors he was a vampire.

I cheered and jumped and whistled along with the rest of the crowd as the band took their final bow. My thighs ached and my ears rang and my whole body buzzed with incredible energy. I didn't want it to be over.

The drummer tossed his sticks out into the audience, and a scuffle broke out at the front as the crowd surged to reach for them. Worry panged in my chest as I thought of Arthur up there, but of course he was probably the biggest person in the pit. I didn't have to worry about Arthur.

For the ninety minutes Blood Lust played, I hadn't had to worry about anything at all.

The band disappeared and the house lights went up. My body buzzed from the thrill of the music and the taste of Corbin on my lips. I said that I loved him.

I'd never said those words before to anyone except my parents and Kelly. I'd thought them about Arthur, but I hadn't been able to say them, not yet. I should be afraid of the weight of them on my lips. The danger of loving someone when I'd seen how quickly they could be torn from you, when I knew that being what I am might force me to do to them. I didn't care. I was done.

I love Corbin. I love Arthur. I loved all of them with the wide-eyed wonder of a scientist – the same way I felt when I learned something new about the majestic complexity of the universe, the way I felt when I stood in the dark Arizona desert and gazed up at the stars. Far away and impossibly close, tantalizing mysteries begging to be unravelled, so much infinitely larger than my own feeble body and yet made of the same stuff, so vast and complex that I would spend my whole life falling into them and never ever reach the other side.

Corbin nuzzled my cheek with his. "You okay?" he asked.

"Never better." It was the truth. I loved and I was loved. Even after everything I'd already lost, and everything I might lose in the future, I didn't have to be afraid of it now. I had everything.

I watched the dwindling crowd for Arthur, a need to tell him those same words welling up inside me. But I couldn't see him anywhere. Corbin pulled me close to him, and pressed his lips to mine. The room and the noise melted away.

"You really enjoyed the concert?" he asked as he pulled back. "All of it?"

"I really did. I can't say I get all of this heavy metal stuff, but yeah – it was amazing." I grinned up at him. "Does this mean I get to drag you to a country music festival next time we're in Arizona?"

"Not on your life. Oi, there's Arthur."

Arthur pushed toward us from the back of the venue, a broad smile across his face and his entire body streaked with sweat. His clothes clung to him, revealing the curve of his muscles. My heart skipped a beat at the sight of him striding toward us, leaving the battlefield in his wake. *My warrior.*

"I got us all t-shirts," he boomed, handing me a black shirt featuring an enormous image of a girl in a red dress outside a gothic-style house, holding a raven in her hand. The bird's beady eye glared out at me, and the band's name dripped in blood from above the image. I loved it immediately, although

I wasn't sure where I'd ever wear it. Dripping blood didn't really go with the rest of my wardrobe.

Arthur wrapped his arms around me, and I sank into him, his sweat clinging to me. My heart raced. "Thank you," I whispered in his ear.

"I knew you'd understand," he whispered back.

Should I say it now? I toyed with the idea as I ran my fingers down his arms, relishing the thickness of his muscles. "You've torn your shirt!" I exclaimed, holding up the tattered corner of his longsleeve.

"Yeah," Arthur grinned sheepishly. "It can get a bit brutal in the pit."

The material flopped back, giving me a view of the white scars across Arthur's arm, just beneath his elbow. A fresh cut crossed over top of them, following the same direction, a thin line of red near its tip where it had bled recently.

"What happened to your arm?" I asked, pointing to the new cut. Corbin, who was walking ahead, whirled around. His eyes narrowed when he saw what I pointed to.

Arthur covered his arm with his hand. "It's nothing. I cut myself sharpening my sword. It happens."

"But what about all the other cuts—"

"Maeve, don't worry about it." Arthur thrust his arm behind his body so I couldn't see it. He tugged me toward the door. "Now tell me, what was your favorite song?"

Arthur and I traded memories from the show all the way back to the apartment. Corbin remained silent. His heavy boots landed in every puddle with a vicious *SLAP*.

A wave of exhaustion swept over me as soon as I stepped through the door. I glanced at the clock on the kitchen wall. It was nearly two am. Corbin and Flynn and I had our meeting at the National Gallery today at eleven. I *had* to get some sleep.

I'll find a private moment and tell Arthur in the morning. I'll tell all of them as soon as I can. I glanced over at Corbin, who glowered from the doorway while Arthur poured himself a glass of water. Maybe Corbin was having second thoughts? You weren't supposed to tell another person you loved them during sex. I saw that once on a romantic comedy film Kelly loved. Guys would say anything in the heat of the moment.

Had I royally messed up?

Arthur hugged me and planted a kiss on my forehead. "You want me to carry you to bed?" he asked, wrapping his tree-trunk arms around me.

I shook my head. "Go. Get some sleep. I'll be a few minutes. I just want to wash the sweaty crowd off my body."

"You don't want company in the shower?" Arthur lifted an eyebrow.

Yes. But I needed to talk to Corbin. I shook my head.

"Okay. Goodnight, Maeve Moore. I'm glad you liked your surprise."

As soon as the door to our room shut, Corbin moved away, his shoulders sagging. He headed for the kitchen. "Hey, wait a second." I reached out and grabbed him, pulling his body against mine. "What's wrong? You're not upset about us, are you? About what I said?"

"No." Concern flashed in Corbin's eyes. "Unless you didn't mean it. Because I completely understand if you said it in the heat of the moment."

I sucked in a breath. "I meant it."

"Good. So did I."

His lips found mine, teasing and sweet, so different from the raw need we'd shared earlier when the music got inside us. My chest swelled, my heart straining against my ribs, ready to break out and fly away.

"So why did you go mopey all of a sudden?"

Corbin jabbed a finger toward the door to our room. *Arthur.* I lifted an eyebrow.

181

"That cut on his arm? It's not an accident," Corbin growled.

"What do you mean?"

Corbin shook his head. "I can't tell you any more, Maeve. It's not my story. But I think you need to talk to him. He's not coping and he's trying to hide it because he doesn't want to show any weakness."

That sounded like Arthur. My chest tightened up as fear crept in again. "I hate this. I hate that people died and everyone is hurting and I'm helpless."

"Just talk to him when you have the chance. I'd do it, but if he's doing what I think he's doing, I don't have the impact on him that you do. If anyone can show him what it really means to be brave, it's you."

After my shower, I crawled into bed next to Rowan. He whimpered in his sleep and pulled me into his arms, spooning my body so his warmth caressed my naked skin. I stared at the closed door of our bedroom, the ghosts of Blood Lust's lyrics pounding in my ears. Arthur snored on the bed opposite.

Corbin's words pounded in my head. *If anyone can show him what it really means to be brave, it's you.* But why? I wasn't brave. I'd been leading this coven for barely two weeks and I was already falling apart. I'd never had to face the cruel truths of life until my parents died, until I discovered my mother had tried to kill me. But Arthur had lived with cruelty like that his entire life. I had nothing to teach him, nothing to offer him except my love.

Arthur's beard hung over the edge of the bed, his hair plastered to his forehead and his lips pursed as he let out a loud, shuddering snore. My chest constricted as I recalled the long, fresh cut across his scarred skin.

My beautiful warrior. What are you hiding from me now?

24

BLAKE

I watched with one eye open from the mezzanine level as Corbin, Arthur and Maeve snuck out of the apartment. I debated following them to whatever sneaky shenanigans they had planned, but decided against it. Tonight I was getting answers if it killed me. Which it very probably would.

Maeve needed a miracle, a way to defeat Daigh without having to sacrifice herself or kill an innocent the way her mother did. No way in hell was I going to let that happen.

In the palm of my hand I held a tiny glass vial that could give us those answers.

The others would be pissed when they found out I'd done it without them, but they'd be just as pissed if I showed the draught to them and told them I'd gone to Clara by myself. Better to have them pissed at me when I actually had something to bargain with.

Wait. You're thinking like a fae again. You and Corbin did that hand-shaking thing that means he's going to stop being suspicious of everything you do. You don't need something to bargain with anymore. This is a hundred times more dangerous than trying to find Liah in the fae realm. Doing this alone is a bad idea, and just because your the Prince of Bad Ideas doesn't mean you should make another mistake.

I turned to the bed where Flynn lay sleeping, the sheets a tangle around his torso. I hesitated, my hand hovering over his shoulder. Here it was, the final test – trusting a human.

I clamped my hand down and shook Flynn awake.

"Get outta mah garden, you gombeen dryshite!" he yelled, slugging his fist at the air.

"It's just me," I grinned, grabbing his wrist and pushing his arm back into the pillow. "Do you want to help me do something that'll piss off Corbin?"

"Fecking hell, yes." Flynn kicked off the sheets. His eyes narrowed as he saw the tiny vial in my hands. "Not more dream-walking? I've seen enough severed hands to last me lifetime, thank you very much."

Quickly, I explained to him what Clara had told me. "We should probably wait for the others," he frowned. "Corbin will—"

I had an idea he'd chicken out on me. Luckily, I'd been observing him carefully over the last few days, ever since I realized he was mad keen on Maeve, and I knew exactly how to push him into complying. "Corbin left with Maeve and Arthur about twenty minutes ago. They were all dressed up."

Something dark passed over Flynn's features. He bit his lip. *Yep, he's got it bad.* "And doing this will help Maeve?"

"I'm not gonna lie to you. I don't know if it will help. But we need answers, and the best place to get them is to go to the source. This draught will get me into the underworld as a shade. They won't be able to see. I'll try to get close to Daigh and overhear something useful."

"Fine. It's your life to bollocks up," Flynn shrugged. "What do I have to do?"

A niggle itched at the edge of my mind, a thought that

said I probably shouldn't use Flynn's insecurities against him. "I just need you to watch me, then in case it looks like I'm in trouble, try to wake me up. If you can, feed me magic so I can keep the connection going longer."

"Can do." Flynn shuffled over so I could lie down on the bed. "Is this dangerous?"

"Hell yes." I uncapped the bottle and drank all the contents. I flopped back down against the bed, calling up a flash of memory of the six of us tangled up together only the other night.

No, can't think pleasant thoughts now. Only nightmares.

That was easy. All I had to do was draw on one of Daigh's many tortures over the years, or recall the torment of his forbidding Liah and I to play together.

I took myself back to the dream I'd had, the only dream I'd ever been able to extract from Daigh's mind. The dream I shared with Maeve – of the world burning and the air poisoned and the members of the coven burned alive at the stake.

The dream that I'd give my life to prevent becoming reality.

Only this time, I recalled the true horror of the dream – the part I fought with each night to make sure Maeve never saw – the sixth person burned and broken on the stakes. The horror that above all else had propelled Daigh to make his stand against the human realm.

Maeve Moore's body hung from the sixth pike, her head hanging limp, her beautiful skin blackened and peeled from her bones, her mouth open in a silent scream.

If the Gods were real, I'd build an effigy to them all if they would burn the vision from my mind. But I had to endure it. The horror of it was the only way I'd get the answers we needed.

I fell into the vision, toppling toward the stakes. The heat of the fires crackled against my skin. My chest open, ready to meet my fate…

My body slammed into something hard. I bounced once, the force driving the air from my lungs.

I forced my eyes open. At first I could see nothing, and my heart thudded as I wondered if I'd somehow got sent to the wrong place. But then my eyes adjusted to the gloom and I found myself in a dark cavern – a little like the inside of a sidhe, only much larger and creepier. Long iron chains hung from the ceiling, extending down and outward like the ribbons on a maypole. At the end of each train was shackled a human from the church and a fae.

A gasp escaped my throat to see them all trussed up like that. Not just Seelie and lowborn sprites. There was Hefeydd, the captain of the Seelie guard. There were four of Daigh's princes – minor ones, but still – and one of his favorite Baen-sidhe concubines. In the center of the room sat a large cauldron bubbling over an open fire.

Daigh stood in the one entrance to the room, his hands clasped in front of him in silent prayer. Was it just the dim light, or did his face look drawn, almost… sad?

I crept around the outside of the circle. Hefeydd was tied to that old housekeeper, Dora, the one that incited the mob against Maeve. Deep cuts crisscrossed her cheeks and her whole body trembled.

"Merry met, my loyal fae," he called out. "I apologize for the cramped nature of your quarters, but our gracious hosts could only spare one extraction chamber."

This doesn't sound good. I searched the faces for Liah, but could not see her anywhere.

"The iron burns," a prince cried out. "Father, loosen our chains!"

"My king," Hefeydd called out, giving Dora a swift kick as he swung around to face Daigh. "Why have you shackled us here, and to these despicable humans, no less? Did we not bring you the required sacrifice?"

"My most humble apologies, my boy," Daigh hung his head. His voice cracked a little. "We brought back twenty-two unbaptized souls from the church. However, that was not the price that was demanded of us. I'm told by our partners that the soul of a child – completely untainted by sin – has a certain exquisite taste that cannot be matched. Except for one – the blood of the fae. Etiquette decrees that we cannot go back on our word to our hosts, and so they have agreed upon this sacrifice as fitting to meet the terms of our deal."

Great gleaming shitballs, he's going to sacrifice them all.

Hefeydd's eyes bugged out. "But you will need me during the final battle, when the Slaugh ride—"

"None of us are needed, Hefeydd." Liah stepped out from behind Daigh, her eyes burning bright as she surveyed the room, her mouth pursed, her expression unreadable. A million conflicting thoughts burned through me at the sight of her. "The battle we fight is greater than our lives, than even our King's life. Sacrifices must be made."

Daigh waved a hand, and the fire beneath the cauldron flared higher, leaping up the sides of the iron pot. The liquid inside bubbled over the sides and dribbled down until it met the leaping flames. Where the two met, shapes formed – limbs and tails and gnashing teeth and long whips that rained down showers of sparks as they cracked through the air. I dug my back against the wall as the fire demons lashed out, wrapping their whips around one of Dora's friends, sinking their needle-teeth into her flesh, not stopping even when her screams became silent.

"Why is that *Seelie* not burning with us?" Hefeydd cried as a demon crept along the chain toward him. "She had an arrow pointed right at the heart of your daughter! She is a traitor! Trusting her will be your ruin."

Daigh smiled. He placed his hand on Liah's shoulder, his fingers curled around her skin. My teeth ground together.

"Of course she will betray me," he said. "That is why I trust her. Because she and I have seen the same vision."

Hefeydd opened his mouth to speak again, but all that came out was a scream as a demon tore off his arm, swallowing the severed limb as the skin burned away and the flesh beneath cooked.

I wanted to tear my eyes away from the torture, but horror froze me in place and held my eyelids open. Demons crawled over the structure, sliding down the chains to devour their victims – human and fae alike consumed in the fires of eternity.

When I finally managed to tear my gaze away, it fell on Daigh and Liah.

Daigh watched the burning bodies. He didn't flinch as the fire demons curled around his sons, their forked tongues tearing out their eyes and flaying away their skin. Their screams scarred my soul, but they didn't seem to faze him. The coldness of his decision would haunt me far longer than the horror I'd just witnessed.

As the fire demons smacked their lips, causing sparks to fly across the barren floor, Daigh turned his back and left. I slunk around the walls and slipped out into a long, low hall, lit with flaming torches. Between each torch was a mirror that shifted and wobbled, revealing different tortures and realms of the dead. The plains of suffering, the archipelago of agony, the topiary maze of mild irritants. I knew them all from our myths. I was more interested in what Daigh was up to now.

Daigh's steps fell heavy as he moved through winding

halls. Liah trailed after him. Her lips moved to speak; it took her several tries before she actually got any words out.

"Master," Liah said. "I have an idea I wish to discuss with you."

Daigh whirled around, his face twisted with rage. "I have spared your life. I do not appreciate my kind deeds being thrown back in my face."

"If I could explain—"

"You threatened my daughter. The only reason you still draw breath is because I haven't decided which torture is most appropriate."

Liah held up her hand. "You can torture me all you like. It won't be worse than what Blake did to me."

Ouch. My stomach clenched as if she'd punched me.

"I never intended to shoot Maeve," Liah continued. "I merely wished to figure out Blake's mind and hers. It worked."

"I don't care about his mind. You had Blake in your sights. You could have taken him down. But you hesitated, too. I should have known better than to trust you, after your friendship—"

"Our friendship is over." Liah's eyes flashed with fire, and with a sinking heart I knew she spoke the truth. "I did not hesitate. I did everything as we planned. I was ready to kill him. But it occurred to me that his death would not serve us."

"I didn't keep you alive to do my thinking for me."

Liah powered on as if he hadn't spoken. "The very fact that Blake leapt to defend her... he cares about her deeply. And the feeling is mutual. I wouldn't have believed it if I hadn't felt it myself. Her spirit magic flared when he was endangered. She cares for him, which means that killing him will ensure she will never return to you."

Daigh's lips flattened. I knew that look. She'd got to him.

"He needs to be punished for his betrayal," he said slowly.

"He will be, if the vision comes to pass," Liah folded her arms. "But you don't always get to be the one to do the punishing. This is much bigger than you and your personal demons."

I grinned at her choice of words. *That's my Liah.*

Daigh's lips curled back into a placid smile. I knew that look, too. Beneath that smile, he seethed with anger. It usually preceded some particularly evil torture. "Careful what you say to me."

"I know what happened last time, why you couldn't raise the Slaugh," Liah said. "I figured it out because of something Blake said to me about a portrait that moves."

Daigh's body stiffened. I leaned forward. *This is it. This is what we need to know.*

"You had the chance to remake the world again, and you blew it all because of a *human*. If the fae knew the truth about what really happened, they'd overthrow you in a heartbeat. I am not helping you out of love for my King – weak fae do not deserve my loyalty, even if they wear the crown. I'm here because I have seen the tortures humans have inflicted on the earth, and I *will* set it to rights. You failed at this once before. You may think you're close now, but you're going to make the same mistake again. When you do, I will step in and lead the fae to victory."

Daigh stepped toward her. Liah shoved the stump of her arm into his face, her mouth twisting back into an evil smile I'd never believed possible of her steel-cold features.

"Lay a finger on me and I'll reveal everything I know. Your own fae will tear you limb from limb," she growled, low and dangerous. "The only way out of this is with me by your side. And you'd do well to remember this advice – your daughter is half-human, so if you want her to join with you, you're going to have to think like one. That shouldn't be hard for you—"

A rough hand grabbed my shoulder, tearing me away from Daigh and Liah. I yelped, trying to turn my body to see my attacker. *I'm a shade. No one can grab a shade except—*

"What the 'ell are you doing here?" A cold voice rasped in my ear. "Shades aren't 'asposed to be in these 'alls."

Shite.

He twisted my shoulder, sending a shriek of agony through my non-corporeal body as he spun me round. The demon pulled me close to his face, studying me with eyes that reflected back all the dark things about myself I'd never wanted to acknowledge. "Let me see, where have you escaped from? You don't look to be one of mine. You one of Tartarus' punks? 'is shades is always escaping. Pretty face like yours, I bet I can beat that pride right out of you."

He dragged me back down the hall. The next step was him tossing me into a torture chamber and who knew if I'd be able to get out of that. I called up every scrap of power inside me, conjuring the image of Maeve's face, of the world and the family I'd left behind on Earth. I imagined Flynn, lying next to my sleeping body. I channelled my spirit toward him, focusing on just three short words.

Wake me up. Wake me up.

Nothing. The demon yanked open a door and dragged me inside. Torches flared around the walls of a wide, circular room. There was no furniture inside, because there was no floor. An enormous dark hole extended across the entire width and depth of the door.

Flynn, if you can hear this, wake me up, now.

The demon raised me over the edge of the hole. My feet scrambled for purchase, but there was nothing below me but that deep, blackened presence. My head spun as wretched, inconsolable anguish crept along my veins, poisoning me from the inside. *This is what you deserve. This punishment is just.*

"A few weeks in the Pit o' Anguish should loosen you up a bit, Sonny Jim," the demon rasped, his fingers tightening around my throat.

This is where I belong now. No sense in fighting it.

The ends of my fingers tingled. Another presence pressed against my back – a void in the hopelessness opening up behind me – a gateway where my nightmares called me back to earth. *Yes, yes, thank you! I promise I will never again mock you about being Irish.*

The demon's grip loosened. His face twisted with confusion as my power surged through his fingers. "What are you trying to do, punk?"

I leaned forward and planted a kiss on the demon's lips. "It's been swell, darling. But you're just not my type."

The demon swiped at me, but its hand fell through my face. The tingling ripped through my whole body. I laughed as I toppled backwards and the void of my own nightmares swallowed me up.

"Blake…" Flynn's wide eyes met mine a few harrowing moments later. "Did you find out anything?"

I sat up, rubbing the burn on my shoulder from where the demon touched me. "Oh, fine and dandy. I was nearly thrown into the pit of anguish, but whatever."

"What's that? A giant swimming pool filled with American beer?"

"You took your sweet time saving me, and now you're making jokes?"

Flynn waved his hand. "That's not important now. The important thing is that you're here with all your limbs attached."

"Not important? Have you ever been left hanging over a pit of anguish? You might think it's pretty bloody important."

Flynn punched me in the arm. "Hey, it's not my fault you sleep so soundly. So did you learn anything useful?"

"Yes." My throat tightened. "Liah told Daigh she knew about the painting of Maeve's mother. He was all ready to kill her for aiming that arrow at Maeve, but when she mentioned it, he completely caved to her. She's blackmailing him, but I don't know what with."

"What does that mean?"

"We thought Daigh was the dangerous one," I said, my mouth dry. "But maybe he's not. Maybe it's Liah."

MAEVE

I woke to the smell of frying bacon. I rubbed my bleary eyes, for a moment transported back to my childhood in Arizona. Mom usually had breakfast on the table when Kelly and I dragged ourselves downstairs – cereal and toast and the usual stuff. But a couple of times a month we'd wake up to the crackling sound and savoury smell – all the evidence we needed to conclude that Dad was in the kitchen, producing towering pyramids of bacon, freshly made waffles drowning in maple syrup, or piles of scrambled eggs like yellow mountain ranges.

I cracked one eye open. Light flooded the room, illuminating the two slumbering figures on the single beds opposite mine. Corbin's face smushed into the pillow, his arm draped over the edge so his fingers trailed on the ground. Arthur was turned toward the window, the sunlight catching on his golden hair as he let out a rumbling snore.

Behind me, Rowan's chest rose and fell against my back, his warmth almost enough to keep me in bed. But he was competing against bacon, and even against my beautiful broken boy, bacon won. I turned over as I slid out from under his arm, balling up the sheets into a Maeve-shaped parcel for him. He looked so peaceful in sleep – his face relaxed, his lips slack, his dreadlocks streaming over the sheets. I grazed my lips across his forehead, then pulled on a blue dress and padded out into the lounge, following the sound of laughter and sizzling.

Kelly leaned over the kitchen island, gesturing wildly as she told one of her crazy stories. Flynn stood in front of the stove, wearing a hot-pink apron with white lace trim as he turned bacon and sausages like a pro. Blake stood with the fridge open, buttering toast with all the aplomb and none of the skill of a TV *sous* chef.

"Einstein, they have bacon in England!" Kelly grinned, beckoning me over.

"I see that." I grabbed a piece off the plate and sank my teeth into the salty meat. "Rowan is going to be so mad. He wants to be the only one showing off his culinary skills."

"Rowan can suck me bollocks. Today is Flynn's turn to shine." Flynn tossed a sausage in the air. It hit the light fixture and bounced on top of the fridge, where it rolled off the back and behind the appliance. "Oh, you wanker."

"Shower's free!" Jane called as she padded through the living room, a towel wrapped around her torso and another tying her hair up like a turban. She gripped a wriggling Connor in her arms.

"Flynn and Blake made breakfast," Kelly yelled back.

"Give me five minutes. I've got to put on my face." Jane's bedroom door slammed shut.

"Don't be surprised if I've eaten yours," Kelly called back, grabbing another piece. She smiled at me. "I love bacon."

"I know."

The look we exchanged said a hundred things that had nothing to do with bacon. A lump rose in my throat. *Will it ever stop hurting?* Everything I did reminded me of my adoptive parents and what had been stolen from us. With Kelly here, it was a hundred times worse. Just seeing her face made it hard to breathe.

I guess I only had to look around me to know the pain never went away. Corbin still carried around guilt he shouldn't have to feel over his brother's death. Arthur still missed his mother with every fiber of his being. And Rowan... I couldn't even *fathom* the extent of his loss.

Flynn must have seen my expression change, because he leaned across the table and tried to feed me a sausage. Laughing, I swatted his hand away. Kelly crunched another piece of bacon, and just like that, I was dragged back to the present.

Which carried a whole new set of problems for me, but at least Kelly was smiling. That was, until I snared another piece of bacon and Flynn pinched my ass. She frowned and averted her eyes. My stomach thudded. *Got to remember, you're only dating Arthur.*

"I had a brilliant idea," Flynn announced, totally oblivious to the change in atmosphere in the room.

"Did your head explode?" Blake asked.

"Ask me bollocks. All my ideas are brilliant. What do you say, Maeve? Before we head out today to look at stuffy 'proper' art, do you ladies want to hunt out this Banksy upstairs with me?" Flynn raised his eyebrow, clasping his hands together and leaning toward me with a coquettish pout.

More than anything, I wanted to crawl back into bed and try to steal another hour of sleep. But no way could I say no to Flynn when he looked like that. "Sure," I shrugged, and grabbed another piece of bacon. "I'm interested to see what all the fuss is about."

Kelly slid off her stool, her voice flat. She didn't look at either of us. "No thanks. I think I'll take advantage of the shower while it's free. Contrary to popular belief, you boys take even longer in there than I do, and there's five of you to get clean."

Flynn curtseyed, holding the edges of his apron out. "You wish you looked this good, doll."

Kelly smirked as she dug a dress out of her bag and headed for the bathroom. "You're going to make some long-suffering woman a really annoying husband one day, Flynn."

I kind of agreed, except for the fact I wanted that woman to be me. "When do you want to go up?"

"How about now?" Flynn tossed down his apron. "We can just leave the food here for the others. Blake wants to come, too."

"Okay, sure." I grabbed Arthur's torn Blood Lust hoodie off the back of one of the chairs and pulled it on. We clambered up two flights of stairs, passing more graffiti and torn Victorian wallpaper and some dark stains on the carpet I didn't want to investigate too closely.

When we emerged on the top floor, I sucked in a breath in amazement. It looked like a scene from a post-apocalyptic film set. The staircase opened out into a vast room – the full height obscured by a crisscross of large industrial steel beams. Two huge windows lit the space at either end, casting grimy light across a hardwood floor littered with debris. Judging from the overturned trash bins and dusty printers and broken swivel chairs, it had once been an open-plan office, but it clearly hadn't been rented in some time. My sneakers scuffed a thick layer of dust, sending clouds swirling around us.

No artwork, though. The walls were a bare mess of peeled white paint and dusty red brick.

"Here," Flynn pointed to a dilapidated kitchenette. A metal staircase led up into the ceiling, and I could see a steel mezzanine up there. Flynn took the stairs two at a time, his excitement infectious. I clambered up after him. At the top, he helped pull my body over a rusted step onto the mezzanine. A couple of bean bag chairs – their upholstery stained and torn – faced each other with a table between them. A single coffee cup sat on top, a brown stain in the bottom the remains of the last drink.

"Holy Mother of Jesus," Flynn whispered, his hand on his mouth. "There it is."

There, hidden in the rafters so it was completely obscured from the ground, was a crude drawing of a man in a business suit, poking his head out of a hole in the roof. A sign hung around his neck that read. "0% interest in people."

"I dig it," Blake said from behind us. He leaned against the balustrade, his hands shoved deep into the pockets of his leather jacket. "Hey, how come there's a piece of paper in here?" He frowned at my ticket stub.

"Arthur and Corbin took me out to a concert last night." I said. Blake's eyebrow rose. A weird, slightly-pissed look crossed Flynn's face. "It was that band they're obsessed with – Blood Lust. It was fun."

Flynn grunted. Blake shrugged. I got the idea that I needed to change to subject.

"I don't get it." I frowned at the simple image, hoping to draw out Flynn's artistic side. "It's just a picture of a guy and a poor excuse for a pun."

Flynn sat down on the metal, crossing his legs and staring at the figure of the man. "I want to make art like this," he said. "You'll see what I mean when we go to the National Gallery today. To most people, art is the stuff you'll see there – portraits and landscapes and religious scenes and battles that hang on the walls and look pretty. But Banksy's art isn't capturing a static moment in time. It *lives*. The very act of its creation and concealment and appearance is part of its story. How did he get it up here? Why did he place this particular piece here, in *this* office? I bet you a tenner there was once a financial institution here. It's guerrilla art, going behind enemy lines to deliver an important message – we see you, and we're not amused."

Wow, that was some speech. I looked back at the artwork, and I thought I could see what Flynn was talking about – the context of the piece and why it mattered. "If I didn't know better, I'd say Flynn O'Hagan was actually being serious about something."

"I am." Flynn nodded at the portrait. "The way you feel about the stars and space and all that shite? That's how I feel about art. Banksy stenciled a girl holding a bunch of balloons and flying through the air on the west bank of Israel. That shit fecking *matters*. That's what I'd like to do."

Wow. This was a side of Flynn I'd never seen before, all stormy-eyed and passionate and hot as all hell. He ran a hand through his red curls and I bit my lip so I wouldn't jump him right there.

"Don't look at me like that, Einstein," he grinned. "You'll make me forget why we came here."

"I thought we came to hunt for this weird graffiti— I mean, *art*."

"That was just a ploy. Blake has something to tell you," Flynn said. "We might have done something really stupid last night while you were at the concert."

I whirled around. *What now?* Blake opened and shut his mouth. He stared down at my ticket stub in his hands.

I sighed. "Go on, out with it."

This time, Blake managed to make his mouth work. His story rushed out, how he got a new kind of draught from Clara before we left Briarwood, how he talked Flynn into helping him use it, how he traveled into the fucking *underworld* as a shade and watched Daigh feed forty-four victims to the demons there and that Liah was blackmailing Daigh and it all had something to do with the painting and what had happened twenty-one years ago, and how he'd nearly been thrown into the Pit of Anguish but Flynn had saved him just in time.

"Jesus, Blake."

"I don't know who Jesus is, Princess." Blake sighed. "But if he's half as bad as I am, I can see why you use his name all the time."

"This is serious! You could have been spit-roasted alive by demons. This Pit of Anguish doesn't sound like a vacation spot."

"You're telling me," Blake shot Flynn an evil look. "But I'm in one piece, and now we know some important details so we can stop Daigh."

"There's something else we know." Flynn lifted an eyebrow. "We're all alone up here."

"Why, I hadn't even noticed. But now that you mention it," Blake peered over the edge of the gangway. "Nope, not another soul."

I put my hands on my hips. "Guys, this is serious. You can't just go off and do your own thing like this. If either of you had been hurt, or if you'd accidentally revealed something more to Daigh—"

"I solemnly swear that I won't be doing anything like that ever again," Blake's eyes flashed. "There's nothing like dangling over the Pit of Anguish to make one reassess one's life choices. In fact, I'd like to forget all about it, and nothing would do that better than making good on Flynn's suggestion."

My breath hitched. "You want to do it here, in the middle of this rubble?"

"Why not?"

Flynn grabbed my hand and dragged me down the ladder. My heart pounded, and the ache inside me flared to life once more. Blake pulled over one of the old office chairs, its wheels squeaking across the hardwood floor. A delicious shiver pulsed through my body as Flynn wrapped his arms around me, stroking my breast through the thin layer of my dress until my nipples stood hard.

Blake dusted off the chair and sat down on it, spreading his legs wide and fiddling with the buttons on his fly. "Climb on board, Princess." He licked his lips.

How could anyone resist that invitation?

I straddled the chair, placing my feet flat on the ground to steady myself. I caught Blake's face in my hands, pulling him against me as my lips met his. Blake's kisses stole my breath, and all thoughts of his journey into the underworld fled from my mind beneath the attentions of his strong hands and sensuous tongue. Being kissed by Blake was like a quantum reaction – you never knew what was going to happen, but something was going to explode.

Behind me, Flynn's arms wrapped around my body, sliding under the collar of my dress to touch my nipples. Blake snaked his hands up my thighs, tugging up the hem of my dress. Flynn's tongue slid over my earlobe and a fresh shiver rocketed through my body.

Blake's fingers reached under my panties, slipping inside me. "She's dripping wet," he smirked at Flynn. "Someone wasn't as opposed to shagging in the middle of the rubble as she made out."

"If you're got all this time to chit-chat, then you're clearly not doing enough with your mouth," I mumbled back, wrapping my lips around his.

"Oh, Princess. You have *no* idea," Blake's tongue slid across my teeth as he stroked a finger over my clit. I moaned against his lips as he battered that little nub with ferocious strokes until my knees shuddered around him. Flynn clamped his fingers over my nipple. I yelped as a jolt of pain arced through my body, but the pain and the pleasure slammed together and exploded in a hard, fast orgasm that left me gasping.

"What do you say, Blake?" Flynn produced a couple of condoms and a tube of lube from somewhere in the depths of his pockets. "Now that Maeve's all warmed up..."

"You just carry those around everywhere with you, hoping you'll get lucky?"

Flynn grinned. "What can I say? I'm Irish. Good luck is in my genes."

"It sure is." I rubbed his crotch until he groaned.

Flynn slid his hands under my dress, hooking his fingers in the elastic of my panties. "Knickers off," he murmured against my ear. I lifted my hips, sliding one leg off Blake so I could kick the offending material away.

"Keep the dress," Blake said, his fingers tweaking my nipples through the thin fabric. "I like it on you."

Flynn handed him a condom and he rolled it on. "I can't wait until I can be inside you without this, Princess," he whispered.

"Me neither," I whispered back. I sank down onto Blake's cock, gasping at the fullness of him warm and tight inside me.

Blake leaned back in the chair, running his fingers down my thighs, over my ass. I gripped his shoulders and lifted my hips, sliding myself up his shaft and then slamming back down, filling myself with his length. I rose up again, enjoying being in control and seeing Blake's blissful expression as he watched me move up and down on him.

"Mind if I... butt in?" Flynn whispered in my ear. I groaned.

"You are ridiculous." But no way was I leaving him out of this. I lifted my hips again, giving Flynn easier access. He squeezed out some of the lube, sliding it down my back, using his finger to rub it in. I heard the condom wrapper tear and Flynn position himself behind me, his thighs rubbing against Blake's. I ground my hips down on Blake again and lifted up, feeling Flynn's cock sliding between my cheeks. With a strangled cry, he pushed forward, his tip sliding inside me.

I sucked in a breath, holding my body still, digging my nails into Blake's shoulders as Flynn worked his way in deeper. "Bloody hell, Einstein," he whispered as he buried his length inside me. "You're amazing."

"Welcome to the magical kingdom of Maeve," Blake grinned, his hands gripping my thighs. He pushed me up, sliding out of me, his cock rubbing along Flynn's from behind the thin membrane that separated them.

"You okay?" Flynn whispered. I nodded, releasing the breath I'd been holding as Blake slid inside me and Flynn drew back, their cocks rubbing together like one enormous length ramming right through me.

So tight.

Too tight.

Just right.

They found their own rhythm – steady, relentless, intoxicating. They tossed me between them, my body their plaything, my mind wiped clean by the waves of pleasure cascading over me. Magic flared in my fingers, sizzling over Blake's skin, pouring from Flynn's lips into mine.

I tossed back my head. Flynn's teeth dug into my neck. Blake leaned forward and wrapped his mouth around my breast through the fabric of my dress, biting down on my nipple.

The orgasm hit me like a hadron collider, the force of it jerking my body between them. My cry echoed through the enormous room, joined by their groans as they both came with powerful thrusts that rocked through my whole core.

Magic swirled around us, hanging in the air like orchard

fruit waiting to be picked. I collapsed against Blake's shoulders, my body trembling from the residual. Flynn danced the tips of his fingers over my body, sending delicious shivers through my body as he trailed over the sensitive skin.

"It was good for you?" Flynn whispered in my ear.

"It was amazing."

"Good. That's all I want. To see you smile." His face tinged with sadness as he stroked my cheek. "You have the prettiest smile."

We slid apart, fumbling for our clothes. Blake tossed his condom into a nearby trash can, and headed for the door. Flynn had taken off his socks, and was struggling to get them on his feet. "Who even needs socks?" he mumbled. His red curls fell over his eye and my heart swelled.

I could tell him now. Why not? I already told Corbin during sex. Maybe that's my thing.

"Come on, you two!" Blake called from the stairwell. "I can hear Mussolini calling us. We'd better hurry back before he comes after us with a dictionary."

"Flynn, I have to tell you something." I took a deep breath. "I realized something last night. All this... what we're doing, I didn't know what it meant at first. I thought maybe it was our magic calling us together, and being with you guys made me forget about the pain of losing my parents. A big part of that was you, the way you make me smile, the way you don't take anything seriously. And I just... what are you doing?"

"Got this blighter inside out," Flynn grinned up at me, pulling his sock off and banging it against the ground to turn the toe out. Thick plumes of dust rose up around him.

I gulped. *Here goes.* "Right, yes. So, I just wanted to say that... I love you."

The grin froze on his lips. His eyes wheeled around, panicked, desperate to look anywhere but me. Flynn's lips moved, but no sound came out. He gulped, tried again, still nothing.

The words hung in the air between us, floating without restraint, unable to be shoved back into my mouth no matter how badly I wanted to.

Say something, dammit. I tried again. "How do you feel about that?"

Flynn stood up, his sock forgotten in the dust. His face turned away.

My heart tore in half down the middle. I placed my hand over my chest in an effort to hold it together, but there was nothing I could do. The pain was on the inside.

"You guys coming?" Blake called.

"Right behind you!" Flynn raced for the door, his arms flapping beside him like he hoped he could fly down the stairs and escape me.

I sank back onto the chair, tears streaming down my face. I struggled for breath as the pain in my chest pressed the air from my lungs.

He doesn't love me. He doesn't care.

I thought Flynn's joking personality was a coping mechanism, a way for him to avoid confronting some of the terrifying things that had happened to us, and that had been a part of his past. But maybe I was wrong. Maybe he really just didn't give a shit about the coven, the fae, any of it.

Traces of his magic sizzled along my skin. I wished I could burn them away. *How can we go on when I know he doesn't give a shit about me?*

FLYNN

*Y*ou *idiot.*

You bloody potato sucking, gobdaw scut.

I raced down the stairs after Blake, Maeve's crumpled face haunting me with every step. *Turn around, go back to her. Throw your arms around her and tell her how much you love her, how much you need her.*

I pumped my legs harder, leaping down the last few steps and disappearing into the street. I sprinted through the market, into Regents Park, my chest bursting, my thighs aching, my dick flopping uselessly against my thigh.

My lungs burned. I had to stop. I collapsed on the grass, gasping for air. What was the point in running? I could run and run across London and into the bloody Thames, and it wouldn't erase Maeve's stricken face from my mind.

I love you too, Maeve. But I'm scared.

I could have just *said* that, but I didn't. Because I was a fecking idiot. Because I looked at Maeve and I saw all the times my ma told me she was getting clean, that this time was going to be different, that we were going to start a new life and she was going to look after me and give me everything I'd ever wanted, and then she shacked up with another druggie scut and left me to fend for myself.

And then she'd gone and died and I had no one, no one.

Now I had Maeve, and the guys, and no way was I bollocksing up a good thing by getting emotionally involved.

If I said those words to Maeve, I'd be setting myself up to heartbreak again. And I just couldn't do it. So that was that.

Even though my chest felt like I'd swallowed a stone.

Maeve would get over it. She had the other guys.

I'd be fine. Totally bloody fine.

MAEVE

"Are you sure you don't mind me going off without you?" I asked as I watched Kelly pull clothes from her monolithic pink backpack and strew them across the apartment.

"Are you kidding? I've already had enough of boring old stuff to last me a lifetime. You and Corbin and Flynn go be nerds and look at dusty paintings. Jane's offered to take me shopping on Oxford Street."

After what happened between Flynn and I this morning, her day sounded a hundred times better than mine. "Connor will enjoy that."

Kelly jabbed her thumb over her shoulder, where Arthur sat on the edge of the bed, playing 'horsey' with Connor. My heart skipped seeing him being so nurturing. He really was a gentle giant. "Arthur, Blake, and Rowan are going to watch him for the day. Jane's pretty excited about having free babysitters. She says she's even going to have wine at the pub. My first English pub, I'm so excited!"

A sharp pain stabbed in my chest. I'd wanted to take Kelly to her first English pub. My sister was here in England after escaping a horrible situation. I was supposed to be around to help her, to show her the sights. And yet we'd barely spoken to each other since she arrived. All the memories we were supposed to be creating together she was having with other people. And while I appreciated my friends stepping up and looking out for her, I felt like it was yet another thing I was missing out on.

It's not important. What was important was that Kelly had a great time sightseeing and shopping and stayed safe and remained none the wiser about my new powers or the brewing fae problem or the fact I'd had a sixsome while waiting for her flight to land.

Corbin yelled from the living room. "Maeve, let's go. We're going to be late."

"Coming." I grabbed my purse and hugged Kelly quickly. "Have fun, and just remember, if you want that twenty-grand to last long enough for your backpacking adventure through Europe, you can't spend it all on cute clothes."

Kelly rolled her eyes. "Relax, big sis. I know what I'm doing."

"No, you don't, but it's fine. Neither do I." I gave Rowan and Blake each a quick hug, and Arthur a lingering kiss for Kelly's benefit (and also, it was hot as fuck). Then I followed Corbin and Flynn out of the apartment and down the street to the Tube station.

Flynn made jokes about modernist painters, his voice as casual as ever, as if he hadn't just stomped my heart into a million pieces. Corbin laughed along, not noticing anything between us until Flynn went to take my other hand and I pulled away. Flynn's face sagged, but I told myself I didn't care.

You never specified that the guys had to have feelings for you to be in the harem. Just because Flynn doesn't love you, doesn't mean you can leave him out of the coven stuff. It doesn't have to change anything.

But it did. It changed *everything.*

We took the Northern Tube line to Charing Cross station, then walked a block to Trafalgar Square. The National Gallery dominated one side of the square, its classical facade the very picture of European majesty.

"Whoa," I said as I took in the towering Doric columns and sprawling grounds. I'd never seen anything like it before. It was so enormous. It was hard to believe that was an entire building just filled with paintings.

"Come on." Corbin squeezed my hand as he led me up the steps and into the towering foyer. Flynn trailed along behind. We skipped past a long line of tourists waiting at the turnstiles and went straight to a small counter in the corner.

"My name is Corbin Harris. We have a private tour booked with Professor Hendricks," Corbin explained to the lady behind the counter. She put a call through and a few moments later, a short fellow with Coke-bottle glasses and a faded blue suit rushed down the grand staircase toward us.

"It's a pleasure to meet you, Mr. Harris," he gave Corbin's hand a vigorous shake. "I'm a huge admirer of your father's work. His latest essay on Victorian puritanism was simply *stunning.*"

"My father is a very accomplished scholar," Corbin said without emotion. "I'd like to introduce Flynn O'Hagan. He's the artist of our group."

"Ah, Mr. O'Hagan. What style do you work in? Modernism? Cubism? No, let me guess... you're an impressionist?"

"I make giant insects out of scrap metal," Flynn said in a completely deadpan voice.

"Ah. Very good." Hendricks' pinched expression showed exactly what he thought of that. He turned to me. "And who is this lovely lady joining you? Are you a fellow scholar of European art?"

"Er, no. I'm an astronomer."

"Maeve has a personal interest in Smithers work," Corbin said. "Her mother is the subject of one of his portraits, *Woman in Citrine*."

Hendricks' eyes lit up, and his whole face broke into a smile. "That is astounding! I am most honored to make your acquaintance. As you no doubt know, Smithers drew and painted the *Citrine Woman* several times. Sadly, most of them are in private collections. We have one of the earlier portraits in our collection. I will show it to you. But first, allow me to delight you with some of the highlights from our collection."

I gritted my teeth. I just wanted to get to the portrait and maybe solve the mystery for good. Corbin squeezed my fingers – I guess we had to humor our guide. We walked through a massive gallery. Every wall groaned under the weight of enormous canvases housed in elaborate gilded frames. They depicted scenes from the life of Christ, which Hendricks explained was because the Church had the money available to pay renowned artists to paint the complex works. He rattled off lists of names and facts with such exuberance that I worried he'd give himself a heart attack.

"This is the Impressionist gallery," Hendricks said, bustling us into the next room. "Impressionists painted everyday subjects – scenes from city life, landscapes, people working and playing – in bold, visible strokes. This subject matter appears mundane to us now, but it was highly controversial at the time because prior to this it was thought these weren't fit subjects for serious art. The impressionist movement started in France during the 1860s with a prominent group of artists—"

Corbin and Flynn were rapt in Hendricks' commentary, but I bit my tongue to keep from screaming at him to hurry up. Questions burned in my mind and I needed that painting to answer at least some of them.

We entered a long, narrow gallery. My eyes were assailed with vivid colors and bold designs. Hendricks swept his arms around. "This is our modern gallery. Here we display works by some of England's favorite living artists, many of whom are reinterpreting or reinventing traditional techniques. Over there is a piece called *Vixen*, by the artist Ryan Raynard. I believe his family estate is not far from your address."

"He's actually our neighbor," Corbin said. "Not that we've ever met him. He hasn't left Raynard Hall in years."

"Yes. He's an enigma, one of the many in the art world. And there is what you came to see; our works by Robert Smithers."

I whipped my head up and froze, arrested by my mother's gaze. Her vibrant blue eyes stared out at the room, the corners of her mouth turning upwards in that slight smile. Her radiant skin shone from beneath her flowing mane – deep brown like the oak trees that lined the gardens at Briarwood. She sat in the same chair in the library, although her posture was slightly different, and in this painting she held a small book in her hands. Runes like the ones on Corbin's and Arthur's tattoos were gilded across the cover.

The same citrine jewels glittered on her body – the ring on her right index finger, the amulet around her long, angular neck, and the diadem sitting in the center of her forehead.

She was so beautiful. Tears welled in the corners of my eyes. I felt like I had collected another puzzle piece of my past, but I didn't know where it fitted or what picture it was showing. Was I staring into the eyes of a cold child murderer, or of a woman who sacrificed her life to save mine?

The painting itself was beautiful, but something about it seemed... off. It lacked the radiance of the piece at Briarwood. Hendricks had said it was an earlier work. Perhaps Smithers was still refining his technique.

"We know her name was Aline Moore, and that she was a well-known bohemian – part of a New Age movement Smithers was involved in. From his letters and sketches, we gather they had an intimate relationship. You say she was your mother?"

I nodded, not trusting myself to speak. Corbin squeezed my hand, so spoke for me. "Aline died during childbirth. Maeve was adopted as a baby. She has no memories of her mother."

"Pity," Hendricks tsked. "Still, she lives on in the artwork. She must have been a remarkable woman."

Must she?

I gulped, steadied myself, found my voice. "Can you tell me, has the painting ever changed? Have you ever noticed it looking different from one day to the next?"

Hendricks looked confused. "What do you mean?"

I tried again. "Have visitors ever said anything weird about this painting?"

"If you are talking about stories of haunted paintings and other 'spooky' things," Hendricks used air quotes around the word *spooky*, "then we've seen our fair share of such tales here at the gallery. But this painting has never been among them. As far as I'm aware, it's a perfectly mundane – although beautiful – artwork that has never once said 'boo'." He laughed at his own terrible joke.

Corbin pointed to a series of three works on the same wall. "I see these are also by Smithers."

"These are weird." Flynn stepped forward and frowned at the paintings. "They're very... erratic."

That was putting it mildly. I tore my eyes away from my mother's portrait and took in the others. The first showed a pack of black horses riding through fog. Cloaked, faceless riders leaned forward over their backs, urging their steeds faster. Tiny lights glowed in the fog, giving the piece an ethereal spookiness that chilled my blood. In the second piece, lithe figures danced naked. I gasped as I recognized the whirling dances, the green costumes and platters of food on bark plates, the rounded mounds in the background.

These are the fae realm. He's painted the fae.

The third picture showed a slumped figure pierced through the heart by a long stake. Its limbs hung limply at its sides, and a crown of briar thorns encircled its head. More of the fae figures danced around the stake, sloshing food and drink everywhere as they enacted their frenzied dance. My breath caught in my throat as I recognized elements from the nightmare Blake and I shared.

Hendricks nodded. "Those are some of the last works Smithers completed before he committed himself. He was painting these mythological subjects then. It's thought his deteriorating mental state accounted for the looseness in the brushwork and the abrupt change in subject matter, but so little is known about Smithers that it's difficult to say. To answer your question, we hold several of his early royal portraits in our collection, but they're currently on loan at the Victoria and Albert Museum. We also have some sketches for these and other portraits. The majority of his sketchbooks and letters are held at the Ashmolean Museum in Oxford."

Letters? My ears perked up. *There are letters?* If Smithers was a witch who was 'involved in the New Age' as Hendricks had put it, then maybe those letters would tell us about the kind of magic he did with the coven. It was worth a shot. "The Ashmolean?"

Hendricks turned to Corbin. "I'm surprised your father didn't mention them – the Ashmolean are very protective of their collections, but he could probably secure you a viewing."

Corbin's face paled. "Yes. That's true. Thank you."

Next, Hendricks took us back to an archive room, and sat with us while we pored over a book of Smithers' sketches and letters to other artists. They included several sketches of my mother's painting – including ones where she reclined on a sofa instead of in the chair – but nothing that showed the horrified expressions we'd seen.

There was nothing about Briarwood or magic or the fae.

The three of us trudged out of the gallery, spirits broken. Even Flynn dragged his feet, his head hung. I was too dejected to even think about him now. I'd pinned all my hopes on the painting giving us a clue, and so far all we'd come away with was more questions.

We'd come up against a dead end. We needed to move forward, and as leader, I had to make that decision, even though it meant pushing someone I loved into doing something he didn't want to do.

"We know what we have to do now," I said, reaching for Corbin's arm.

He pulled it away. "Please don't ask me to do it, Maeve."

"Corbin," I grabbed his shoulders, holding his gaze with my own. "Nothing about this is easy. I'm dealing with the fact my own mother might have tried to murder me. We're all reeling from the massacre at the church and what Blake saw in the underworld—"

"What do you mean, what Blake saw?" Corbin's eyes narrowed. Behind me, Flynn flinched.

"Ah, right, I haven't told you about that yet. It's not important now. What is important is that you get on the phone right now and call your father. Because this shit between the two of you has gone on long enough and we need him to get us into that museum."

Corbin shook his head so vigorously I was afraid it would roll off his shoulders. "I can't."

"I'm your High Priestess. My word is law around here. Call him."

Corbin sucked in a breath. He opened his eyes. The wounds of his grief sliced through his irises. "Okay," he said, the word barely a whisper. "I'll do it."

CORBIN

*C*all.

I stared at the mobile phone on the table, wishing I had the power to fry the motherboard and melt it into a plastic lump. The only thing I could do was suck the air from my lungs, and fear was doing a bloody good job of that already.

My hands shook. I tried to move them from my lap, but they wouldn't budge.

"Corbin, it's not rocket science," Maeve said, nudging the phone toward me. We were sitting in the beer garden at the rear of a pub. Flynn had gone to fetch another round, leaving me alone with Maeve and the phone call of doom.

"How would you know?" I shot back.

"Duh. I went to space camp. I've worked with rockets. Trust me, this is way easier."

Right, I can do this. I've fought fae and looked after everyone and learned fifteen languages and found my own brother's body. This is a phone call.

I grabbed the mobile phone in my sweaty palm and raised it to my face. I clicked the button.

The extension rang once. Twice.

No.

I threw the phone down on the table.

Maeve glared at me. "You didn't call."

"Nope."

"You have to call. You know that, right? We still don't have a meeting set up with Smithers. The letters are our only clue, but we're not going to be able to see them without your Dad's help. You said yourself this might be our only shot at figuring out what happened during the last ritual."

"I know. I just—" I rubbed my temples, remembering the last time I'd seen Dad, only a few days ago, when Rowan and I had gone to my parents house in the Cotswolds in an attempt to convince them to tell us how they'd defeated the fae last time. Dad had entered the house, hung his academic gown in the hall, and breezed past me as though I didn't exist.

I got it. In his mind I was forever tied to the death of his other son – a second death because all his dreams for me died along with Keegan. I squandered my talents hiding in Briarwood working on the very magic that had cost our family so much, instead of going to university as he'd always dreamed of. He'd yelled as much at me more than enough times, and then he stopped yelling. He started pretending I didn't exist. The last word he spoke to me was four years ago. I'd do anything to go back to the yelling.

I buried my face in my hands. "Fuck."

"Corbin, you're stronger than this."

"Apparently not."

"For God's sake. Give me that." Maeve swiped the phone from the table and pressed it to her ear.

I lifted my head. *She can't be...*

But she was. I heard the click of the receiver being picked up and a crisp voice answering. "Yes, I'd like to speak to

Professor Harris," Maeve said. My chest constricted. "No, I'm not a student, this is about a research matter. Tell him it's Maeve Moore on the line."

My fingers gripped the edge of the table. *He'll hang up on her. He'll—*

"Professor Harris? Hello, yes, this is Maeve Moore." She paused. My heart leapt out of my chest and shattered across the table.

This is not happening. How is she doing this?

"Oh yes, I'm very well, thank you, considering everything. I'm just sitting here with your son trying to protect the world from the Slaugh. You know, the usual."

I nearly choked.

"So listen, I'm so glad I got to talk to you. Corbin tells me you watched over me for the first fifteen years of my life. Thanks so much for that. I hope I didn't bore you too much with all those astronomy trips into the desert..." she laughed. What the bloody hell? Maeve Moore was *laughing* with my Dad? "Yeah, Kelly's great. She's actually here in England right now, causing chaos and mayhem wherever she goes."

Another pause. It almost sounded like laughter on the other end of the phone. But that was barmy – Dad hadn't laughed since Keegan died.

"So listen, I don't know how much Corbin's told you about what's going on, but we've discovered something really interesting about Robert Smithers, the artist who painted my mother's portrait. We think we might be able to stop the fae for real this time. There are some of Smithers' letters and drawings in the collection at the Ashmolean museum, and I'd really like to see them, and I just wondered... yes? Oh, sure... mhhhmmm, that will be fine. Thank you for your time."

She hung up.

My heart thudded. "Well?"

Maeve broke out into a wide grin that lit up her whole

face. "Your dad's agreed to show us the archives if we can be in Oxford tomorrow afternoon. We'll be able to look over Smithers' letters at our leisure."

"Wow."

"Yeah. He's also asked us out for dinner with him."

"He… he did?" How was he going to eat with us if he wasn't even ready to talk to me?

"He did." Maeve reached across the table and squeezed my hand. Warmth flooded up my arm and pooled in my chest, and the tiniest fraction of my tension released. "I know things are pretty tough between the two of you, but maybe this is him saying he's willing to patch things up."

"I don't think we could go that far." I couldn't expect Dad to forgive me for what happened. I'd never forgive myself. But after all this time… just like that, he wanted to see me, eat a *meal* with me. I knew I shouldn't hope… but here I was, hoping like bloody hell.

I let out the breath I didn't realize I'd been holding. I squeezed Maeve's hand back, and another jolt of warmth flooded my body. "Bloody hell, you're amazing."

Maeve stood and came around to my side of the table. She slid onto the bench beside me, wrapping her arms around my neck. Her soft, fruity smell overwhelmed me. "I know. Want to show me how grateful you are?"

In all the years I'd watched over her, I never imagined that having Maeve in my life would be this amazing. This girl didn't just command magic, she *was* magic – light and breath and spirit in one feisty package. I brushed my lips against hers. "Your wish is my command, Priestess."

29

MAEVE

I woke up with a start. The remnants of that same horrific dream about being lost in the briar and seeing the stakes burrowed into my head. I threw my hand over the blankets, craving the warmth of Rowan's body, needing the steadiness of his breath to calm me. Instead, all I grabbed was thin air.

Huh?

My heart hammered against my chest. Rowan wouldn't just leave. Not in the state he was in. When Corbin, Flynn and I had returned from the art gallery, Rowan was the only one home with Connor. He said the others wanted to go out, but he couldn't stomach it. He looked so sad and scared.

So where was he now? Had the fae somehow got into the apartment and taken him?

Calm down, my rational self scolded. *You're scaring yourself. He's probably just gone to the bathroom.*

I sat up, eyes wide open, body tensed. After a few moments, my eyes adjusted to the gloom inside the apartment and I noticed the bathroom door was still open, and the light was off. I couldn't hear any water trickling. From the bed under the window, Corbin's breathed with a regular rhythm. A shaft of light from the street outside revealed his serene face. In the other bed, Arthur snored loudly, his beard sticking out at odd angles.

Where's Rowan?

Knowing I wouldn't be able to sleep until I knew the answer, I threw off the bedclothes and padded out into the living room. On the foldout couch, Kelly slept like a starfish, her blonde hair splayed across the pillow like the halos on the renaissance paintings I'd seen at the National Gallery.

As silently as I could, I clambered up the ladder and peeked on to the mezzanine. Flynn and Blake slept side by side. Blake's arm draped over Flynn's naked torso in a way that was so utterly adorable it nearly brought tears to my eyes. I wished I'd thought to bring my phone with me.

But where was Rowan?

My feet hit the floor again, and I turned to look at Jane's closed door. My breath caught as I noticed a dark silhouette standing by the high windows, face bent down toward the street below.

"Rowan?"

He didn't react, didn't even stir. Now that I was closer I could see the sadness tearing up his features. His lips moved as he watched the street below, counting every car and black cab and double decker bus that careened down the narrow road.

"Rowan?" I tried again, reaching out and closing my hand over his shoulder. Rowan shuddered at the touch, his whole body convulsing. His head whipped up.

"Please," he whispered, covering his face with his arm. "I don't want you to see."

"See what? Rowan, what's wrong?"

Rowan bent his head up toward the ceiling.

I wrapped my arms around him. His whole body trembled. "Rowan, something's really upsetting you. You have to tell me everything. I can't help you if you don't talk about it."

"You can't help me. No one can."

"You don't know that. I'm your High Priestess, and I'm giving you an order."

Rowan's eyes rolled back in his head. His body sagged. It was as if my ordering him had taken away the agony of holding back that was tearing him up. When he spoke, his voice was steadier, although it still trembled over the words. "Get Corbin and a coat. It's cold out."

"We're going out?"

"Can't tell you. I have to show you."

I went into the bedroom and slid onto Corbin's bed. My weight on the mattress woke him. He smiled groggily up at me, sliding his arm around my waist. "Mmmm, you're a nice surprise."

"Rowan's upset," I said. "He wants us to go somewhere with him. Can you get dressed?"

Corbin nodded, the desire in his eyes turning to concern. He threw off the blankets and hunted around on the floor for clothes. A few moments later, he stood in front of me wearing nearly the exact same outfit he'd worn when we saw Blood Lust. I found a pair of jeans and a sweater, and I swiped Blake's leather jacket from the back of the sofa and shrugged it over my shoulders.

We followed Rowan out the door, down the stairs, and out into the street. Traffic noise blared in my ears and I pulled the collar of the jacket tight around me to ward off the chill.

Rowan didn't speak. He kept his head down, striding with unusual speed and purpose. He wasn't aware of the other pedestrians on the street, barging right through the center of a large group of drunk guys and causing a woman with a stroller to swerve around him. He stepped out into the road without watching the traffic and Corbin had to grab his arm to yank him back.

"Do you know where we're going?" I hissed to Corbin as we hurried to keep up with Rowan, who headed for the entrance to Regents Park.

"I think so." Corbin didn't offer any more information. I decided not to ask. *Let Rowan tell his story*, that was what Corbin always said.

The park was eerie at night – the trees casting long, spindly shadows across the ground. People appeared along dark pathways and from behind statues and fountains, and I kept looking over my shoulder, certain I felt an unwelcome presence behind us. Perhaps it was just the shadows of Rowan's past, finally ready to be freed.

We came out the other side of the park and walked a couple more blocks. The only light in this area came from the moon and a few grimy streetlights. Towering warehouses and concrete office blocks lined narrow streets. Trash cluttered the drains and rolled across the pavement. Teens and young people darted between shadowed doorways, and cruel laughter punched through the crisp night air.

Rowan led us down to a narrow river – barely a trickle of dirty water in an unnaturally even hollow. Corbin whispered to me that it used to be one of the old canals that connected London to other parts of England before the extensive road and train networks were built. The road passed over the canal, creating an darkened underbridge bordered on both sides with the bare block faces of office blocks. A few people scattered into the shadows when we approached. I clutched Corbin's arm so tightly my nails dug into his skin.

Rowan led us down underneath the bridge. He stared at the brick wall of the abutting office block for a long time, his breath coming out in ragged gasps. Cold air rose off the water, and my teeth chattered. The underbridge reeked of urine. Questions burned in my throat, but I knew I had to wait.

Rowan spoke, still facing the wall. "This was where I grew up."

I glanced at Corbin, not understanding. "There used to be apartments here?"

Corbin shook his head. He didn't answer. He waited for Rowan to fill in the blanks.

"You know both my parents died in the ritual." Rowan's voice shuddered. "They weren't on speaking terms with anyone in their families, and so there was no one willing to take me in. I went into the care system, and I—" Rowan traced his hand over the faded bricks, the lines of graffiti that spoke of a life vastly different to mine. It was a long time before he spoke again.

"I didn't get lucky like you, Maeve. No one adopted me. No one wanted the weird skinny black kid with the tics, except as a way to get their hands on government handouts or a punching bag or..." he shook his head. My stomach clenched. I wanted him to finish that sentence, and at the same time I knew that hearing it would break my heart and his.

Rowan cleared his throat. He kept staring at the wall. "I ran away when I was ten to escape the abuse. I'd run away twice before, but they brought me back. The third time they must have decided I was more trouble than I was worth. Or maybe they couldn't find me. Maybe they figured that if I couldn't survive in a home, I'd be eaten alive out here. They were nearly right."

"Where did you go?" I whispered.

"I came here. This building is a squat, Maeve. This office block has been abandoned for years. It doesn't meet the building code, so the owners can't rent or sell it. They're just letting it slowly slide into the water. Kids who've been rejected by the system come here to live. Some are hiding from the law or the government. Some run anarchist collectives and political campaigns. We dumpster dive for clothes and supplies. We share scraps of food and cigarettes and a laptop. We share needles."

Rowan turned from the wall. The sorrow in his eyes wrecked me. Tears rolled down my face as his words registered.

Oh, Rowan, no.

He rolled up the sleeve of the long sweater he always wore, his sad eyes darting from me to Corbin and back to the wall. He jerked his arm toward me. On his skin I saw something I'd never noticed, something he'd managed to hide even when our naked bodies were wrapped around each other.

My heart stopped as I stared at those tiny dots. *Track marks.*

"This is who I was," Rowan whispered. "When Corbin brought me to Briarwood, I was a heroin addict. I didn't care about anything except getting my next fix. I… there are things I did to get the money and the drugs that…"

Rowan shuddered, dissolving in his memories. My body ached to hold him in my arms, to travel back in time and find a way to bring him to Arizona with me, to give him back all the love he'd been deprived of while I had reveled in it.

Corbin stepped forward and placed his hand on Rowan's shoulder. "Mate, it's okay."

Rowan's eyes widened, and I realized there was more. More horror he had to tell me. I wrapped my arms around him, wanting so badly to pour out something of me into him, to show him that it didn't matter to me who he used to be. All I cared about was that he was my Rowan, and he was beautiful, and he was in pain.

I pressed my palm into his back, sending a sliver of spirit

magic into Rowan, trying to calm him. His body shuddered against mine, and he sank against me as he gave in to the embrace. Corbin's strong arms fell around us both, and the three of us rocked together, bracing Rowan against the onslaught of his memories.

"Maeve should know," he whispered. "Especially because of the STI check-up—"

Recognition crossed Corbin's face. "Ah. Yes, she should."

"Maeve should know what?"

Rowan took a shuddering breath. "A lot of the kids in the squat were desperate for money. It's impossible to get a job if you don't have an address, a bank account. We found other ways. We're standing in a known spot where men can come if they... if they want to pay for sex."

My throat closed. I *knew* I did not want to hear this. But I had to. I had to understand every part of Rowan.

"A lot of the street kids do it. I needed the money and I— I was so out of it most of the time, it didn't matter what they did to me."

"But... you were a minor—" *Oh shit.*

I covered my mouth with my hand. Tears filled my eyes. *My sweet Rowan. To think he had to endure that.*

Rowan rested his cheek against mine. The warmth of his skin stark against the cold night, the coldness in his words. "Maeve, I won't ever be able to stop using condoms with you. I won't put you or the guys in danger like that. I'm HIV positive."

MAEVE

S *hit.*

I stared at Rowan as his words sunk in.

The needle sharing. The stuff he'd done on this very street corner with men who paid money to fulfill their taboo desires. He'd been through all of that, and now he'd carry the scars of it for the rest of his life.

Tears filled my eyes. *Just how much of a life does he even have left?*

"Bloody hell, mate, give her the full story," Corbin wiped a dreadlock out of Rowan's face. "Maeve, Rowan was diagnosed two years ago when I first brought him to Briarwood. He's been taking the medication religiously and for the last year he's had an undetectable viral load. That means there's no risk of him passing on HIV even if he had unprotected sex."

Rowan shook his head. "I won't. I can't."

Corbin rubbed Rowan's shoulder. "It's okay, mate. We understand. You don't have to do anything you don't want to do. Right, Maeve?"

"But what does this mean?" I couldn't hold the tears back. They streamed down my face. "Will we…?"

I couldn't even say the words. The thought of it crackled through my body like lightning, nearly knocking me off my feet. *Will we lose you? Will I have to stand over your grave and say goodbye to you, too?*

"Not for a very long time," Corbin said firmly. "We discovered it early and the medication is working. That's the important thing."

Rowan's tears mingled with my own, pooling inside the collar of Blake's jacket. The three of us swayed together, holding each other upright as we carried Rowan's burden between us. Water lapped against the edge of the canal. Rowan's shoulders shook with silent sobs.

"I love you," I whispered to Rowan. "I'm here for you, always."

Fresh tears pooled in his eyes. "No one's ever—"

"I know, and that's the greatest tragedy, because you're amazing and everyone in the whole world should love you. But you've got me."

"And Corbin?" Rowan lifted his eyes to mine.

"Corbin got to hear those words first." I didn't want to think about Flynn right now.

"No, I mean—"

Corbin bent his head toward Rowan. A moment later, their lips pressed against each other.

The kiss started off chaste, hesitant, lips brushing each other as though they both wanted the option to pull back and pretend it never happened. Then it heated up. Their lips opened. Their tongues entwined. Their eyes blazed into each other as they fell into each other for the first time, filling each other up with their need.

My breath caught in my throat. I wanted to turn away, to give them this private moment. And yet, it felt like it was for all of us. My body sizzled as though both their lips were on mine.

Corbin drew away, breathing hard. Rowan's eyes widened, the whites glowing under the dim moonlight.

It was the most beautiful thing I'd ever seen.

Corbin cupped Rowan's cheek in his hand, pulling his head closer. Rowan's dreadlocks fell over his shoulder.

"Does that answer your question?" Corbin growled.

Rowan's lips moved, but he couldn't speak. I pressed my body against them both, resting my forehead against Rowan. His body trembled again, but judging by the hardness pressing against my thigh, I didn't think it was with fear.

"We're just one big, fucked up family," I grinned, planting a kiss on Rowan's forehead.

"Can I tell a story now?" Corbin asked, breaking the silence.

"Sure," I sniffed.

"This is the story of the last time I came to London, to this very bridge, in fact. It's the story of how I found Rowan. He was the last of the guys to come to Briarwood, and he was a bloody difficult wanker to find. It took me two years to track him down," Corbin said. "I had to do a few slightly-not-legal things to get his file out of the care system, and then of course there wasn't any record of him after he ran away. I went to the last family he ran away from, and they told me to shove off."

"That sounds like them," Rowan choked out.

Corbin continued. "Flynn was in Arizona watching Maeve, so I left Arthur to look after Briarwood and came up to London. I vowed that I wouldn't leave until I found Rowan. I'd just started reading Hunter S. Thompson and I got this idea that the only way I was going to find him was to do a bit of gonzo journalism, so I took myself to the first squat I could find – which happened to be this insane mansion owned by a Saudi oil baron who'd never even set foot in the door – and unrolled my sleeping bag." He laughed. "It turns out among squatters that's a serious breach of etiquette. I got beat up so bad and shown the door."

"How did you find him?"

"I knew Rowan must be an earth user, because of his parents. It's a recessive trait and they were both earth users. So I asked around about someone living rough who had a way with plants. I got beat up even more, but finally a skin-head told me about this guy living down by the canal who grew potatoes and carrots in a tiny garden on top of an abandoned office block, and he shared the bounty with anyone who asked."

That's Rowan. Even when he was at the absolute bottom with nothing, he cared for people, sharing the only thing he had to share.

"I came here and asked around about the vegetable kid, and someone pointed me to a body slumped on a filthy mattress up on the fourth floor, high out of his mind." Corbin grinned. "I waited until he passed out completely, then I bundled him up and carried him out of there over my shoulder."

"You didn't!"

"He did," Rowan murmured. "It was like a fairy-tale. I fell asleep in the squat and woke up in a castle."

"Fairy tale my arse. In fairy tales the fair prince never wakes up and pukes on his knight-in-shining-armor's shoes." Corbin kissed Rowan's forehead. "I had to take Rowan on the Tube. It was so crowded that I banged his head on the doors. He smelled like a slaughterhouse and people screamed at the guards to kick us both off, but I'd paid for our tickets so I told them all to bugger off. I hauled him back to Briarwood and tried to shower him, but I couldn't hold him up, so I just left him in a bed to sleep off the drugs."

Rowan reached out his fingers, tentatively raising them to

Corbin. His eyes swam with tears. Corbin took his hand and squeezed it hard. I wrapped my arms around both their shoulders, feeling Rowan's kindness and Corbin's steadfastness coursing through me.

"And then what?" I whispered.

"What do you think? I searched 'how to detox a person from heroin' on the internet, followed the steps until he stopped throwing up, and then I took him to a drug center. Six painful months of rehab later, he was the handsome creature you see before you now."

"All thanks to you," Rowan murmured.

"You didn't make it easy, you bastard. He ran away twice to come back here. I dragged him back. He smashed a bunch of priceless furniture at Briarwood, even tried to jump out the tower window." Corbin smiled again, but this time his smile was tinged with sadness. "It was almost like having Keegan back."

"You saved me," Rowan whispered.

"You saved yourself," Corbin replied.

We clung together in silence, listening to the lapping of the water and the pounding of each others' hearts, until Corbin said, his voice husky. "Are we going back to the flat?"

The weight of the night's revelations hung in the air, sizzling between us. Rowan and Corbin exchanged a glance so rife with hunger I imagined them as two explorers lost in a desert who'd just found water.

Rowan tugged my hand. "Come on," he said with a smile that lit the night brighter than fireworks, brighter than a comet screaming across the sky.

Holding his hands, Corbin and I let him drag us up to the street. I'd follow Rowan to the ends of the multiverse if it meant I could see that smile again.

In the next block Rowan pulled us into a dingy hotel lobby, the air thick with stale cigarette smoke. He went over to the front desk and asked for a room for the night. His fingers shook as he pulled out a wad of crumpled notes and counted out the right amount.

The three of us held hands in the elevator. No one spoke. I didn't know what would happen when we got to that hotel room. All I knew was my heart raced a hundred miles an hour.

Rowan's hands shook so badly he couldn't get the key into the lock. "Give me that," Corbin took the key and opened the door. I followed the boys into a cramped room with a bed and a TV and a stunning view out the window into a brick wall. On the street below, two people screamed abuse at each other.

Corbin took Rowan's wrist in one hand and mine in the other, and yanked us both close to him. His eyes blazed with need. He pulled Rowan's head to his and wrapped his mouth in a sizzling kiss.

"What do you say, Rowan?" Corbin pulled back and winked at both of us. "Want to make another of Maeve's dreams come true?"

"You saw, didn't you?" Rowan whispered, resting his fore-head against Corbin's.

He meant the dream where they'd kissed, the dream where I'd first realized that Rowan was bisexual and that he had feelings for Corbin. I hadn't known at the time that Corbin reciprocated, and from the shell-shocked look on Rowan's face, he hadn't known, either.

Corbin smiled. "I've always seen you, Rowan."

Rowan broke away to press his lips against mine. I could taste the heat of Corbin's kiss on his lips. "Thank you," he whispered.

"What are you thanking me for? We're here because of you, Rowan. All this is because we love you. We're here to hold you up so none of us drown."

Rowan sighed against my lips and my heart soared. Corbin came around behind me, pressing his firm chest against my back. While Rowan tenderly cupped my face, Corbin laid a trail of kisses along my neck, his hands dancing over my body, skimming my hips. I shrugged off Blake's jacket, tossing it to the floor. My sweater and Blood Lust t-shirt followed shortly after.

Corbin pulled the two of us down on the bed, kneeling down on the other side of Rowan and tipping his head back in a searing kiss. While the boys tore their shirts off and lay back, exploring each others bodies with their hands and lips, I undid their jeans and yanked them off, adding them to the pile of clothes on the floor.

I freed Rowan's cock and slid my hands down his shaft. He moaned against Corbin's lips, his fingers tightening against his shoulders.

I wanted to taste Rowan, too. I bent toward his cock. He handed me a condom and I rolled it on, sliding my lips over the tip of his cock. It was weird doing this with a condom, but if it made Rowan comfortable, that's what I wanted. He hardened inside my mouth, and he tilted his hips to give me better access. I tilted my head, sliding my tongue along the length of him and taking in as much as I could fit, which was barely half of his enormous length. What they said about black guys was apparently true, although Rowan defied stereotypes. All my guys did.

I increased my rhythm, gripping Rowan in my hand and pumping him as I swirled my tongue around his tip. I couldn't see his face – Corbin's body obscured it – but from his moans I gathered I was doing something right.

A hand twisted in my hair. "Do you want to swap?" Corbin asked.

Did I want to watch Corbin get Rowan off? The ache

pounding between my legs answered that question. I grinned. "Sure."

I scrambled up toward the pillow, meeting Rowan's hungry lips with my own, tasting Corbin on his tongue. He wrapped his arms around me, his fingers dancing trails across my skin.

"Forgive me if this isn't quite right. I've never done this before." Corbin wrapped his hand around the base of Rowan's shaft and stroked him slowly over the condom. Rowan gripped my shoulders so hard his nails dug into my skin. I kissed him deeper, tangling my fingers in his dreadlocks, pulling him closer.

Rowan's fingers teased my nipples, brushing over the hardened buds until they ached with desire. My lips vibrated with his moans. I peered across his body and met Corbin's eyes. Desire hummed inside my body as I watched his lips wrap tight around Rowan's shaft.

So hot.

I met Corbin's eyes, and the same fire that flared inside me burned in his gaze. We could give Rowan this gift, this night, together.

Corbin tipped his head back, sliding Rowan deep into his mouth. Rowan came with a shudder, his whole body convulsing like he'd stuck his cock in an electrical socket. His teeth clamped on my lip. Magical energy poured through his skin and rolled into my body, stoking the fire of my power higher still.

He collapsed back against the sheets, his muscles completely relaxed, his face frozen with sleepy bliss. Corbin tossed the condom, and he and I snuggled on either side of Rowan, touching each other across his body.

"That was…" Rowan breathed.

"We know," Corbin grinned.

I sent a flicker of spirit magic out through my palm into

Rowan's stomach. He sighed as the energy coursed through him and his own earth magic fed back into me.

"The best news is, we paid for the whole night and it's only—" Corbin checked the clock on his phone. "—1:23 am. This doesn't have to be over yet."

"I don't want this night to ever be over," Rowan whispered, as he claimed my mouth in his.

In our room away from the world, I lost all sense of time and space. The boys took turns going down on me, licking me and fingering me until I came so many times my body became Jell-O. When they were ready to go again, they shuffled up the bed – one on either side of me. We fell over each other, a tangle of lips and limbs and nerve endings stretched to breaking point.

Corbin leaned over the side of the bed and yanked another two foil packets from the pocket of his jeans. He tossed one to Rowan. "Gentlemen's choice," he said.

"I don't have any lube," Rowan whispered.

"Well, don't look at me," I shrugged. "I'm not going to be the one to pry that tube out of Flynn's cold, dead hands."

"It's fine," Corbin said. "I've had a lot of firsts tonight. I'm not quite ready for that one just yet."

Rowan pulled me on top of him. He handed me the condom and I rolled it onto his cock, noticing the head already glistening with his desire. I fell into his deep eyes as I lowered myself on top of him. From this angle I could take him in slowly, lifting myself up and pushing him deeper than he'd ever been before. He was so big. It hurt so good.

Corbin straddled Rowan and placed his cock against Rowan's lips. He winced a little as Rowan took it in his mouth, but his hesitation turned to groans as Rowan took him deep.

We moved together, pounding and pulsing, thrusting and slamming and drowning in each other. Time stopped, giving us this night that went on forever, an endless loop of plea-sure and healing and love. When I finally came, the entire earth wobbled on its axis.

We collapsed in a heap, breathing hard, unable to move and not wanting to be the first to break our bond. More than sex had happened tonight.

I only just closed my eyes when my cell rang and jolted me awake. Rowan didn't stir. Corbin moaned and threw a pillow at the phone, which was vibrating its way across the bedside table.

Arthur's face grinned at me from the screen, his beard sticking out at all angles. I'd snapped the picture during one of our sword-fighting lessons. His eyes shone with mischief, mainly because he'd just slapped me on the ass with the flat of his blade. I grabbed the phone and pressed it to my ear. "Mmmmmph?"

"Where the hell *are* you?" Arthur demanded. "I woke up and you and Corbin and Rowan were gone. What the fuck, Maeve? Way to give us a bloody heart attack."

"Relax. I'm fine. We're all fine. We just had an... errand to run."

"Well, get back here before I have to explain to Kelly why my girlfriend has run off with two of my best friends. Flynn booked us all appointments for STI checks at a clinic down the road in an hour. Where have you been all night, anyway? Rowan didn't drag you to some reggae concert, did he?"

"Where have I been?" I blinked. "To the stars and back."

31

MAEVE

*C*orbin tried to insist the two of us go up to Oxford to meet his dad alone. I disagreed. He was already nervous. Having the others around with their jocularity might help to distract him. And since my word now over-ruled his, he didn't get to argue. Plus, I didn't think I could convince Kelly to stay behind in London while I jaunted across the English countryside.

Watching him wringing his hands and staring straight ahead as our train rolled through the beautiful Cotswolds countryside, I wondered if I'd made the right decision by insisting the others came with us. Flynn was, of course, completely oblivious to Corbin's anxiety, pulling funny faces for Connor and causing Kelly and Jane to burst into fits of laughter.

Flynn's eyes caught mine and I looked away. We hadn't spoken since the Banksy incident, since I'd told him I loved him and he'd collapsed in on himself. I'd deliberately taken the last appointment at the clinic this morning so I could avoid talking to him. Every time I saw that smirk on his face I wondered if he was laughing at me.

On the seat opposite us, Rowan glanced up from the medieval cookery book I given him. On our walk back to the apartment, we discovered a tiny bookshop tucked behind the corner kebab shop, and I bought the cookbook for Rowan and a set of illuminated manuscript prints for Corbin – gifts to remember our perfect night.

Rowan's eyes shone brighter than I'd seen them since the first time I kissed him. He hadn't done the STI check, and he'd told the rest of the guys why, and they were cool. He reached across and squeezed Corbin's leg. "You're strong," he whispered.

Corbin nodded. He didn't look like he believed it at all.

The train rolled into the Oxford station. We all got up and grabbed our bags and jackets. All of us except Corbin, who remained in his seat, staring straight ahead into nothingness.

"Corbin." I jabbed him in the ribs.

He grunted and didn't move. I grabbed his backpack from under his legs and shoved it into his arms. "Come on."

No response.

A uniformed British Rail attendant was making her way down the carriage with an amused expression. "Corbin, *please*."

He squeezed his eyes shut. "Fine," he sighed, and stood up. He looked like he was going to the gallows, instead of visiting one of the most beautiful medieval cities in the world.

I didn't breathe easy until Corbin was off the train and it had shunted away. I didn't want him jumping back on at the last minute.

We stepped out of the train station – a sweeping expanse of modern glass and a roof Arthur described as an 'upturned Viking ship' – and headed straight into the heart of the city. I kept stopping in my tracks, awed by the splendor and romance of the place. Towering spires pierced the heavens, and around every corner was another grand medieval building or secret cobbled alley or quaint bookshop.

"Check this out, Flynn." Arthur pointed to a brochure in a souvenir shop crowded with tourists. "There's a haunted pub tour of Oxford."

Flynn grabbed up the brochure. "I know what we're doing this afternoon."

"That one doesn't start until this evening." Rowan flicked through the other leaflets on the display. "There are lots of other walking tours."

"Corbin and I have our appointment at two," I said. "But I'd be down for a walking tour first. The city is so beautiful. I'd love to see more of it and learn about the university."

Kelly made a face. "I don't want to see a stuffy university. Look, there's a chocolate shop. Can we go there?"

"Kelly, you don't come to Oxford to eat chocolate—"

"Yikes, twenty quid?" Flynn frowned at the city walks brochure. "And there's not even a pint at the end?"

"We don't need a walking tour," Corbin snapped, snatching the brochure out of his hands. "Follow me."

I glanced at Flynn, who lifted an eyebrow. "What's got his knickers in a twist?"

"You know what. Stop being so bloody insensitive." I grabbed mine and Corbin's backpacks and chased after him. "Come on, you guys. We'd better not keep our tour guide waiting."

~

I love Oxford.

Corbin spent the morning marching us down

cobbled alleys and through beautiful college courtyards. Around every corner was another medieval building or gorgeous Victorian facade covered with creeping wisteria. Tourists crowded down Broad Street, ducking in and out of the tiny shops selling books and academic dress and teapots and Alice in Wonderland souvenirs. Cars were limited in many areas of the central city, and the whizzing bicycles made the whole place feel collegiate and timeless. Enormous stone gates marked off the different colleges of the university – Corbin explained that there were thirty-eight in total, and each one was like a tiny institution into itself. When you joined the university, you also joined a college, and that was where you lived, dined, and took your classes. Because it was summer, visitors could look in on some of the colleges, and Corbin snuck us into an enormous one called Christ Church, which even had its own cathedral.

"This is amazing," Kelly gasped as we walked into an enormous, dark paneled dining hall with a high, vaulted ceiling and tables set with glowing lamps and shimmering silver. "It looks like the dining room in Harry Potter."

"That's because the author was inspired by this room," Corbin mumbled, scuffing his boots across the floor. "It was also the seat of Charles I's parliament during the English Civil War."

"It's beautiful," I squeezed his hand. "Imagine eating meals here every night, surrounded by other students all talking about what they learned that day."

"It's not all its cracked up to be," Corbin grumbled. "The cooking isn't as good as Rowan's."

He meant more than he was saying. This place must carry all sorts of memories of his dad, and maybe something more… something about a life he could have had? I wanted to say something comforting, but Flynn was calling me.

"Look at this, Einstein," Flynn jabbed a finger at one of the many portraits on the walls. "Your namesake used to hang out here."

The portrait and plaque described a visit Albert Einstein made to Christ Church college when he was in hiding from the Nazis. My heart raced as I scanned some of the other names on the walls. So many famous scientists and thinkers had walked these halls, eaten mediocre dinners at these long tables, learned and lectured and invented and thought here.

It all looked and sounded so magical. My chest panged as I thought wistfully of the MIT acceptance letter still hidden at the bottom of my suitcase back at Briarwood. Even if I had the money to pay my own tuition – since the fae screwed up my scholarship – I couldn't go back to the States until the fae situation was under control, if it ever would be. And would going to MIT mean leaving the guys? My heart ached at the thought of it.

But I'd always intended to go to college. Getting my degree and joining the space program was my dream, and I hadn't considered until this very moment what being the High Priestess of the Briarwood coven meant for that dream. I glanced over at Corbin, at the haunted look in his eyes when he looked up at the spires. I could have been looking at my future. *He deserves more than this, more than Briarwood. And so do I. But how can we protect the gateway* and *have a life?*

Corbin's next stop was a tiny Saxon tower where we clambered up a narrow spiral staircase to emerge on a windy roof overlooking the city's dreaming spires. Corbin pointed out different sights and more of the colleges, including Merton, where his dad taught. He glanced at his phone. "Only one more stop, and then we have to go," he said.

He dragged us past more quaint shops and through sprawling university courtyards with signs ordering everyone to keep off the lawn (a warning Flynn ignored, earning us a stern warning from a college porter), to a fore-boding building that dominated an entire city block.

"What's this?" I asked.

"*That* is the Bodleian Library. It's one of the largest academic libraries in the world, housing over twelve million books. The majority of the library's archives are stored in tunnels and caves underground. Anyone who wants to gain admission to the library has to recite an oath not to damage any of the books or smoke tobacco inside."

"Bor-ring!" Flynn yawned. "It's time for a pint."

I glared at him. Couldn't he see how much this place meant to Corbin, how much he needed the distraction? But Flynn was, as usual, totally oblivious. *He doesn't need any of us,* I realized. Not in the same way Rowan or Corbin or Arthur or even Blake rely on the coven. *Flynn's here for the adventure and the sex, nothing else.*

And so what? He had a right to be here on his own terms. Flynn could do what he wanted – it shouldn't bother me, but it bothered me heaps.

Corbin glanced at his watch. "I wanted to show you inside but we don't have time. We have to go."

"We'll see you guys at the apartment for dinner," Arthur squeezed Corbin's shoulder. "Good luck, mate."

Rowan didn't say a word, but his eyes swept over Corbin, saying everything for him. Corbin was the one who stepped forward and embraced Rowan, holding him close for a moment longer than was strictly friendly. Arthur's lifted an eyebrow at me, and I nodded. Kelly glanced around Arthur's shoulder, but her expression was dark.

Is she okay?

Rowan wrapped his arms around me next. I breathed in his comforting scent, fresh dew and autumn leaves and flour.

As soon as we were around the corner and out of Kelly's

line of sight, I grabbed Corbin's hand and squeezed. "It's going to be fine," I said. "Your dad's willing to meet you. That's a good thing. Even if we don't get any useful information out of the archive, today is still a win."

Corbin nodded miserably. "I hope you're right."

32

CORBIN

J dragged Maeve up the steps of the Ashmolean Museum. The building was more modest than the museums we saw in London, and I briefly wondered if she'd find it as interesting as I always did. But then I remembered why we were here, and another shiver ran down my spine. Dad was getting older – he must've had a senior moment on the phone to Maeve earlier, forgotten who she was and what she represented. As soon as he saw us he would turn away and refuse to speak, and we'd be right back where we started again.

Except worse, because the faint flicker of hope flaring in my chest at the thought that Dad might be reaching out, trying to reconnect, was about to be snuffed out again.

At the front desk, it took me three tries to get out to the docent I needed to speak to Professor Andrew Harris. She buzzed us through and we picked our way around the Egyptian exhibit to the archive room, where Dad was 'supposedly' waiting for us.

I'd believe it when I saw it.

I pushed the door open and there he was, sitting at a table

with archive boxes strewn around him. He'd taken off his academic dress, and wore a wool jersey and grey trousers that looked oddly informal for an Oxford don. His dark hair had greyed around his ears, a fact I hadn't noticed last time I'd seen him. His eyes behind their horn-rimmed glasses were bright, if a little shifty.

"Corbin," he said, extending his hand. I stared at it in shock. It wasn't the warm, heartfelt greeting I'd hoped for after the last five years, but he was *talking* to me. He offered to touch me.

I took his hand and we shook, his hand was warm, soft, the tips of his fingers slightly rough from a lifetime of sifting through ancient books. I hoped he couldn't feel the tremors in my grip.

"Dad. Thanks for seeing us. This is Maeve."

"Of course." He smiled, but the smile didn't quite reach his eyes. *He is nervous. That makes two of us.* "Hello, Maeve. It's lovely to meet you at last."

Maeve's smile was genuine. She tucked a strand of her pink bangs behind her ear and shook Dad's hand vigorously. "Thank you so much for getting us in here today, Professor Harris. It means a lot to me and Corbin."

"Call me Andrew. And it's my…" Dad cleared his throat. I guess he couldn't quite stomach the word *pleasure*. "I've set out the books for you."

"Thank you." I pulled out a chair for Maeve and sat down opposite her. "You can leave us here, if you have work to do."

"Nonsense. I may be able to assist." Dad pulled out the chair beside me. He glanced at me, and dared a tiny smile. "Besides, the museum won't let you look at these unsupervised."

"Ah."

"So why the sudden interest in Smithers? You've never been bothered with the artwork at Briarwood before."

"It's fine, Dad." I opened the first case and pulled out a stack of yellowed papers, which mostly looked to be sketches. Maeve slid a binder filled with letters across the table and flipped through them. "You don't want to know."

"Corbin, if you tell me what's going on, I might be able to help."

"I didn't think you'd want to know, because…" I lifted an eyebrow toward Maeve, who was already engrossed in one of the letters.

Dad gave me a tight-lipped smile. "I'm trying. Go on, son. If I need you to stop, then I'll tell you."

I met the ocean of pain in his eyes, and that flicker of hope flared another inch higher. "Do you remember the big portrait of Aline on the upper landing of Briarwood? Ever since Maeve started living with us, she's noticed it moving. I know it sounds insane, but I saw it with my own eyes. The features on the painting went from serene to terrified. And we found out from Clara at the *Astarte* shop that the artist, Robert Smithers, was a witch so…" I gestured to the table. "I don't know what we hope to find, but there's got to be something here that will tell us what's going on."

Dad leaned back in his chair, steepling his fingers together. "The painting moved? It's not a fae glamour?"

"That was my first thought, too, especially since—" I was about to explain about Blake, but stopped myself. I didn't want to bombard Dad with too much stuff, not when he actually sounded *interested* in something involving the fae. Instead, I coughed into my sleeve. "But it's not. The magic is part of the paint."

"Andrew, you must have met Smithers when you were at Briarwood," Maeve looked up, smiling at him. "Can you tell us anything about him?"

"Smithers… yes, I remember him." Dad stroked his chin.

"He was very odd, and for a coven of witches, that's saying something."

My stomach flipped. *He just said the 'w' word right in front of us. Who is this person, and what has he done with my Dad?* "Odd how?"

"Most of the time he was a normal artist – charming, charismatic, in love with the sound of his own voice. The women in the coven were utterly in love with him, including your mother, although he had eyes only for Aline." Dad smiled wistfully. "When he came to live at Briarwood, we saw a different side of him. We had to call him Herbert in front of the castle staff or whenever we were in public, which wasn't often – he hated leaving Briarwood. He had the room at the top of the tower as his studio, and he'd lock himself inside for days at a time without food or water, only emerging when he'd created a new piece. He sketched frequently, but I never saw him touch paint to canvas outside that room, and he didn't allow anyone to watch him work. He talked to himself – whole conversations where he argued back and forth for hours. He would sometimes walk into a room and stand there stupefied. Halfway through a conversation he'd suddenly forget what he was talking about."

"What about his magic?" Maeve asked.

"He was a water user, so when he got confused and frustrated he'd flood the castle. I remember a beautiful Georgian end table that had to be tossed after it sustained heavy water damage during a particularly heated argument he had with himself. Most of us grew afraid of him, but of course Aline was High Priestess, and he was her magister. She was fiercely protective of their magical bond."

Maeve's head whipped up. "Hang on, you mean they were lovers?"

"Oh yes. Aline never told us who your father was, but we always suspected Robert. But when you were born, you didn't exhibit as a water user, so we had to discount that. Your mother had some other lovers, and I'm not sure she knew your paternity."

Maeve glanced at me, her eyes wide. I knew she was wondering if we should tell him that we knew who her father was. I gave my head a tiny shake.

"Do you know any of those other men?" she asked. "My mother's lovers?"

Dad shook his head. "Many of them came and went with the night. Others she met outside the castle walls. You have to understand that Aline was a force of nature, a wild woman in the true sense of the word. She could not help but collect men like trophies."

I watched Dad as he spoke to Maeve. His shoulders relaxed. He leaned forward, his eyes dancing the way they did when he talked about Beedle the Bard. He'd barely said five words to me since I'd decided to remain at Briarwood. When I came back for Christmas he would only address me through Mum. Now, Maeve's presence had opened him up.

Maeve folded her arms across the stack of letters strewn in front of her. "Okay, Andrew. I'm going to say something here, and I'm not sure how it's going to go. But it's kind of eating me up inside."

My stomach clenched. I knew exactly what Maeve was going to ask.

"We spoke to Isadora in London. She said that on the night of the ritual... the night my mother died, that she stabbed me. And I just—"

Dad's eyes widened, his jaw tightening. He gripped the side of the table as it was the only thing keeping him upright.

"It's okay, Dad." I said quickly. "You don't have to tell us anything you don't want to."

"No." When Dad spoke, his eyes fixed on mine. "We've

been silent about this for too long. Maeve, you deserve to know your history. After all, history is what defines us."

He took a deep breath. "Aline took Bree – that's Corbin's mother – and I aside a few days before the ritual. At that point, she hadn't revealed any details of the magic she'd be performing, only that she had a way to beat the fae. All we knew was that in order to combat them, Aline would need to do something reprehensible. She had a vision several days earlier and it had made her reserved, melancholy. We'd offered to help her plan the ritual, but she said she needed to do that on her own." He gave a short laugh. "That was Aline, always needing to figure things out on her own, to do things her way."

"Sounds like someone else I know," I grinned at Maeve.

"Hello pot, have you met kettle?" she shot back.

Dad smiled. "On the night in question, Aline locked the door of the library and revealed to us what she had seen in her vision – that her daughter would be born the night of the ritual, and that she would carry her newborn child into the center of the circle and plunge a knife into its chest."

Maeve's face paled. I reached across and took her hand, squeezing her fingers.

"I expected Aline to be upset, but she seemed determined, focused, oddly detached from her words. She said she'd finally figured out what the vision meant. And then she told us the second part of the vision, the part where she died."

"We didn't want to hear it. We tried to talk her out of the ritual. I swore we could find another way, that there would be something buried in the library's books that would help us. Aline shook her head, that haughty expression on her face. 'You've already read every book in this library,' she said. 'If there was an answer, you would have found it already. No, I will die that night. I am resigned to it and I don't want to talk about it a moment longer. We have too much to do.' And she handed me a sealed letter and gave us both specific instructions on what we had to do on the night of the ritual."

"That night, the witches gathered around the sidhe. The High Priestesses made up the inner circle, along with Maeve, Bree, Robert, and I. All the other witches crowded around the outer circle, lending their power. Aline called on the elements and the old gods. We raised our power – a great cone of energy, more powerful and volatile than anything I'd ever conjured in my life. When the ritual was at its height, Aline took a knife, and she held it above your chest. She screamed and a blinding flash of light struck the center of the circle. I reached beneath her and grabbed you, and as fae warriors swarmed from the sidhe and the circle broke into chaos, I fled with you in my arms."

Dad reached across the table and clasped Maeve's hands in his. His gaze flicked to me as he said, his voice solemn. "Your mother didn't try to kill you, Maeve. She did everything in her power to keep you safe. But she wanted everyone else to believe you had died."

MAEVE

$\mathcal{W}$ ith trembling fingers, I pulled my mother's letter from my pocket and tossed it on the table. Wordlessly, Corbin's dad picked it up and unfolded it, his eyes flicked across the words as he held the corners in the tips of his fingers, like it was a precious manuscript or a bomb. His expression changed, his mouth slackening, his eyes filling with moisture.

"I never knew what it said." Andrew wiped the corner of his eye. A tear streaked down his cheek.

"Corbin kept it safe for me," I said.

"That he did." He wiped his eyes again. "I'm sorry. I didn't expect to—"

"It's okay."

Andrew sucked in a breath. "You probably want to know the rest of the story."

Was he kidding? I was *dying* to hear. "Only if you're ready to tell it."

He folded the letter over again, running his finger over the broken seal. "Aline told me to keep this letter safe for you, and we did for all those years, and I guess Corbin kept it after we left. But you probably want to know about the rest of that night. The ground shook as the fae came for us. Witches screamed. Arrows whizzed past my head. I wanted to turn around and help, make sure Bree was okay, but Aline told me to keep going no matter what I heard. I raced into the woods with you under my arms, across Raynard's land, and to the car that we'd parked on Holly Avenue earlier that day. We bought you a brand new car seat in the morning, and I had some formula in a Thermos ready for you. I hit the pedal as soon as you were strapped in. Halfway down the M1 to London I got a call from Bree. She was weeping. 'Aline's dead,' she kept saying. 'So many of us are dead.' I asked her if she wanted me to come back, if they needed my magic. 'The fae are gone,' she sobbed.

"I kept driving. I broke so many road rules to get to the orphanage as quick as I could. All the way, you barely made a peep. You waved your hands a little and gurgled when I took a corner a bit fast, but otherwise, you were a quiet little thing, just staring at me with those intelligent green eyes."

"She still does that," Corbin said. "It's unnerving."

Andrew laughed. The tension in Corbin's shoulders relaxed a little. Andrew continued. "These days, people can't just dump babies anonymously at an orphanage like a fairy tale, but Bree had found this old-fashioned place run by a cloister of nuns who didn't have the strictest admin processes. You were so tiny, smaller than I remember Corbin being as a baby. When I handed you to the Mother Superior you looked up at me with this wide-eyed expression, like you knew exactly what was going on and you'd already decided to forgive me, and I nearly snatched you back and brought you to Briarwood."

"Why didn't you?" Corbin asked.

"We offered to adopt Maeve as soon as Aline told us what she was planning. But she wouldn't have it. 'If you're suddenly looking after a newborn baby that's not yours, people will guess, and all of this will be for nothing. No one can know, not the other High Priestesses, not our coven, and *especially* not Robert.' She wept as we made the plans for your adoption." Andrew pointed to the corner of the letter, where small water stains marred the paper. "She cried those tears as she wrote this, but she said it was the only way to keep you safe."

"What happened after you left the orphanage?"

"I got back to Briarwood and the place was chaos. The remaining witches had sealed the gateway before more fae came through. Whatever Aline had done, she'd stripped them of much of their magic – they couldn't raise the Slaugh. We'd won, but it was a hollow victory. There were bodies everywhere – the earth stained red with the blood of the greatest witches of our time. The other High Priestesses were packing up their covens, threatening to sever all ties with Briarwood. Isadora screamed that she would not be party to dark magic. I had no idea what she was talking about until the others told me that they'd seen Aline kill you. I knew that wasn't true, but I couldn't tell anyone.

"The Briarwood coven disintegrated. The parents who remained couldn't bear continuing on, knowing what Aline had done and how many had died. We didn't blame them. They needed space to mourn their dead lovers and Aline's betrayal. Bree almost told them so many times what Aline had really done, but we wouldn't dishonor her wishes.

"Bree and I wanted to leave the castle, too. Without the coven, the community we had built, Briarwood was big and empty and filled with shadows. But we had a duty to Aline, and to the world. We were the only ones left to guard the gateway. Aline made provisions for us – perhaps she had seen the coven's disintegration, too – and she set up a trust to allow us to continue at Briarwood without worrying about money. We raised our family there, and we kept an eye on the gateway, and everything was fine, until—" his eyes swiveled to the ceiling.

"She knows, Dad." Corbin said quietly. "You don't have to talk about it."

"Right." Andrew jerked his head forward, his voice shaking a little. "After that, we couldn't stay. You may think us cowards for leaving the gateway unguarded and forgetting our promise to Aline. But we didn't care if the fae destroyed the earth. It was dead to us already."

"I don't think you're a coward," I whispered, wanting to take his hand in mine but not sure if that was appropriate. "Just the opposite."

Andrew swallowed. "So there you are. You're all caught up. Tell me a little about yourself, Maeve? Did you have a good life?"

I told him about growing up in Arizona, about camping overnight in the desert and falling in love with the night sky, about bickering with Kelly, about Matthew and Louise Crawford and the love they showered on me as though I was their own child. My voice choked when I came to their deaths, and how Corbin had protected me at the county fair and looked after me at Briarwood.

By the time I stopped for breath, Andrew's eyes glistened. He removed his glasses and wiped them with a cloth, then dabbed the cloth into the corners of his eyes. "Aline would have been so proud of you, both of you."

Corbin beamed. He reached for his dad's hand, but Andrew drew away to pick up one of the papers. "We should get on with this task."

We pored over the letters for hours. First, Corbin and his dad divided them into piles according to their type, taking all the ones between Smithers and other artists and galleries and leaving me a stack written in my mother's scrawled hand. The coven must have believed the letters would someday become public, because they went to great lengths to avoid outright admitting to being witches. The envelopes were addressed to Herbert Missort, but in the letters themselves she used Robert's real name. The language only made veiled references to the coven and their work, and she talked a lot about a Historical Society, which I figured out was a code word for the fae.

Robert,

I hope things are going well in London. I miss you. Spring is always the loveliest time of year at Briarwood. The gardens burst with color, and Mary and David are busy in the kitchens creating all manner of preserves and poultices from our bounty. Delicious smells waft everywhere.

I hung your portrait in the hall upstairs. It is very strange to pass by it and look up at myself. I feel as though I'm being watched through a mirror. It's rather unnerving, but the others assure me that the image is quite fetching, so I'm sure I'll learn to live with it.

We are having more trouble with the Historical Society. They were at the gates of Briarwood just the other day... I fear they will make a submission to the Council soon in an effort to seize the castle.

The baby is healthy. My ankles are like melons and my skin glows. I love being pregnant.

Aline

And this one, dated a few weeks later, which I found particularly disturbing.

Robert,

Please come back to Briarwood, my love. The Historical Society are more bothersome than ever. I don't know who has given them the authority to come after us like this, but come they have, and they're not going away. We're trying to talk to the authorities, but it's as if they're anticipating our movements.

I toss and turn in the night. Sleeping had become uncomfortable with the baby pressing against my bladder and my worries pressing against my mind.

Please, come home soon,

Aline

Robert's letters, on the other hand, were erratic. Sometimes he sounded poetic and besotted. At other times – often in the same sentence – he'd switch to a grave and harsh diction.

Dearest Aline,

London cold is not Briarwood cold. The drafts of that old castle carry the ghosts of the past – venerable old rebels who fought for liberty and peace – not unlike us. But London cold is the cold of money just printed, of falling through ice, of bodies bobbing in the Thames.

I sleep, dreaming of your cunt.

Robert

Aline,

They won't sell me a sandwich. I have money. But I asked Robert did he want smoked cheese or Swiss and they kicked me out. Cheese-scoffing French bastards.

Did you hang my painting?

Rob

Aline,

I'm going to die in this fucking city. Every breath is poison. I met a squirrel who was a banker. He's going to die, too. Send me your cunt in a bowl so I can drown in it.

Robert

Aline,

Destroy the portrait, I'm begging you. Throw it in the fire. Let the paint melt and dribble. I am painting you another, and it will be even finer and more beautiful, you will see. You must destroy the portrait, promise me. Don't ask me to explain.

Please, do this one thing for me.

Rob

And on and on it went. *No wonder Robert committed himself.* I didn't know much about mental illness, but if there was ever a case for schizophrenia or multiple personality disorder, this was it. But I knew that if I talked to a normal person about being a High Priestess and the fae and using orgies to increase my power, I'd sound just as mad.

Did all this stuff Robert was saying actually have some meaning? Were there coded messages that only my mother would understand? Why did he ask her to destroy the painting?

"Did you ever read these letters?" I asked Corbin's dad. "Did anyone else get correspondence from Robert or other witches?"

Andrew shook his head. "Most witches don't socialize outside of their coven. It's dangerous. If anyone is discovered and persecuted as a witch, then there's less chance they'll be linked to others. There are only a few ways of getting news from the witching community, such as visiting Isadora in London. Aline had some contact with other High Priestesses leading up to the final ritual, but this handwritten communication was only between her and Robert. If I'd known about it at the time, I'd have advised her not to do it."

"Does any of this nonsense look like code to you?" I showed him the letter about the squirrel. "I'm just thinking about the Historical Society references. Some of these other things might have a hidden meaning. The squirrel?"

"If it's code, it's nothing I can fathom." Andrew picked up another letter from the stack. "But that's a very astute observation. I'll keep looking. Maybe something will jump out."

While we worked I snuck looks at Corbin and his dad, smiling at their identical habits. The way they both bent over the letters, the rest of the world fading away as they focused on research. The way their eyes lit up when they uncovered some interesting detail. After a while, they started to read aloud particularly interesting sentences, and even got into an argument about the science of graphology that included at least seven words I never knew existed (psychogram? Iridology? The Barnum Effect? You had to be kidding me).

But after awhile, even watching Corbin reconnect with his dad couldn't keep down the creeping sensation that we weren't finding anything useful. I tossed the last letter down and stared forlornly at the page of notes I'd made, most of which consisted of the words, 'ROBERT = CRAZY?' with a million question marks.

"There isn't anything here." I tossed the letter back into the archive box.

"Agreed." Corbin frowned at the sketchbook in front of him. "I feel as though we're circling the edges of the truth."

"Maybe that's because we're approaching this like historians, instead of scientists." An idea glimmered in my mind.

"What do you mean?"

I held up a handful of the letters. "We're reading old conversations, old news, completely out of context." I jabbed my finger at the stack of letters on the table. "We've got no way of knowing if these are the insane ramblings of a sick man or a code between Smithers and my mother. Since Robert's the only person alive who can decode this mystery, I think it's time we paid him a visit, even if we have to break the law to do it."

34

FLYNN

After Maeve's revelation yesterday, there was no way I could enjoy Oxford without several pints of ale in me. Arthur was being a right tosser about my request for inebriation. He only agreed to go to a pub if it was the one his favorite author, J. R. R. Tolkien, used to drink at, so he dragged us across town – past several perfectly respectable-looking drinking holes – to arrive at the *Eagle and Child*.

The pub was too bright and filled with happy-looking tourists. The ale was okay. I'd have expected more from Mr. Hobbit himself. Arthur couldn't stop grinning at he sat down at Tolkien's own table. Kelly and Jane had disappeared into some shop next door. They seemed to get along really well, always whispering and laughing together and ducking off on some secret mission. That sounded preferable to sitting here listening to Arthur and Rowan and Blake talk about how amazing Maeve was.

Arthur and Rowan got up to order more food, and Blake leaned in and tapped my shoulder. "Maeve's pissed at you."

"Is it that obvious?" I slurped the foam off my drink.

"What'd you do, tell her you'd found unequivocal evidence that world is actually flat?"

"How do you even know the word 'unequivocal'?"

"Maeve said it once. I had to look it up on your phone." Blake poked my arm. "Out with it, mate."

"She told me she loved me."

Blake shrugged. "She told Corbin and Rowan, too."

I winced. I hadn't known that. "Yeah, but they probably did the polite thing and said it back."

Blake sighed. "Everyone is so concerned that *I'm* the one lying all the time, but you can't even admit the truth to yourself."

"And what's that?"

"That you're hopelessly in love with Maeve just like the rest of us."

I shook my head. "I'm not in love. Maeve and I... it's just a bit of fun."

"I thought that, at first." Blake squeezed vinegar over his basket of chips and shoved three in his mouth. "But you gave yourself away, mate. You've got it bad, but for some reason I can't fathom you don't want her to know that. You push her away and—"

I stood up, pushing my chair out. "I'm going to bed."

"Don't be daft. You haven't even finished your pint, and it's your round next."

"Fine." I threw a few pounds down on the table, and headed for the door, my heart racing. "I'm not thirsty anymore."

35

MAEVE

I helped Corbin and his dad place the letters neatly back in order inside the archive boxes. I knew I should feel defeated that we still didn't have any answers, but my blood sizzled with excitement. The more I read, the more I was certain there was something going on between Robert and my mother beyond their physical relationship and the magical bond they shared, something they were trying to keep everyone else out of.

I'd never get to confront my mother, but Robert… Robert was alive. We could ask him. We had to at least try.

"I'm sorry you didn't get the answers you wanted," Corbin's dad said as he shrugged on a long black gown.

"That's okay. You've given me something even more precious today – a glimpse into my mother's life." Andrew moved his hand toward me for another shake, but I decided to take a chance. I pitched myself at him, wrapping my arms around his body, the same build as Corbin's but not as toned and muscled. "Thank you so much for helping us," I whispered into his ear.

He froze. I hugged him tighter. After a moment, he raised

an arm tentatively and patted my back. "You're welcome, Maeve," his voice cracked.

I pulled away. A tear streaked down the side of Andrew's face. "I'm glad we finally met." He blinked, then turned to his son. "Corbin, could I speak with you for a moment? Maeve, would you be okay if—"

"Of course. I'll just wait outside." I stepped out of the archive room and wandered around the museum. Shelves of slinky Egyptian cats glared at me with eyes of onyx and lapis lazuli, so different from Obelix, the rotund castle cat who stalked around Briarwood. I wandered into a picture gallery, but all the exhibits were static and dull. I didn't see any science displays. I checked the archive room door. Corbin and his Dad were still inside. I went down to the lobby.

Beside the usual tourist brochures and Oxford-themed gift stand was a stack of pamphlets and booklets about the university. One title leapt out at me, and I pulled out the thick booklet.

Department of Physics Prospectus.

I flipped open the prospectus, looking at pictures of smug-looking students peering into microscopes and laughing from the parapets of the medieval buildings. Scientists in white lab coats bustled around gleaming laboratories and lectured on international stages. My eyes scanned down the subject list, my heart hammering.

Research areas: Astrophysics.

I devoured the text, reading about the department's research into dark matter and dark energy, into the formation of black holes, their design and building of ground-based research instruments, and their involvement in many of the largest telescope projects across the world. Graduates had gone on to be top research scientists and astronauts at NASA and the European Space Agency...

I let out a breath I didn't realize I was holding. I flipped to the next page, which was information for prospective students, and a list of available scholarships—

"Maeve?" Corbin's voice came from behind me. I dropped the prospectus and whipped around. Corbin stood next to his dad. They weren't holding hands or touching or anything, but the tension that had cracked through the air when we'd first arrived had completely disappeared. "Are you ready to go? Dad's going to introduce us to some of the best Oxford pub grub."

"Huh? Yeah, sure." I yanked my coat over my shoulder and, with a final glance at the abandoned prospectus, I followed the two Harris men out the door.

36

MAEVE

*D*inner was amazing. We went to a pub that was older than every building I'd ever visited in America and had bangers and mash and cider and I sat back and listened as Corbin and his Dad argued about Shakespeare and Chaucer and whether the new BBC series about Roman Britain was historically accurate. When we left the pub, Andrew embraced Corbin, wrapping his arms tight around his son and whispering something in his ear before he hopped on his bike and pedaled off.

Corbin couldn't stop smiling. He barely spoke about the painting mystery as we walked back to the apartment we'd rented in Oxford for the night. All he talked about was his dad and how they talked and how amazing it was that I'd got him to open up.

"I had nothing to do with this," I said as we climbed the stairs to our rented apartment. "It was all you. It was just time for you and your dad, and he knew it."

"Maeve, you're back!" Kelly threw her arms around me as soon as I entered the room. "Look at the new dress I got!"

She danced around, revealing a wrap dress boasting the

Union Jack flag in garish sequins across the front. "It's... quite something," I said, wondering if the rest of the evening was going to consist of a *Next Top Model* fashion show.

"Hey, where's Flynn?" I asked as I scrolled through the news on my phone to check no weird fae attacks had made the headlines. My favorite science blog popped up with a new update, but I closed the notification without reading it. The Oxford University prospectus flashed in my mind, but I waved the thought away. I couldn't even think of anywhere except MIT, and besides, it was fae first, real life later.

Blake shrugged. "He went for a walk, said he needed to be alone."

"Flynn? Alone? But who would listen to his naff jokes?" Arthur smirked as he slumped down beside me and wrapped his arm around me, the way a boyfriend would. I grinned at him, hoping I'd get the chance soon to be alone with him and tell him how I felt, and ask him about the cut on his arm.

Kelly wanted to wear her new dress out, so after she and Jane changed and did their makeup – and Jane handed a sleepy Connor over to Rowan, who'd offered to babysit – we went for a pub crawl. Each venue was older and narrower than the last. Kelly and Jane sat off to the side and gossiped about movie stars, while Corbin and I managed to fill the guys in on what we found and what we were going to do next.

"Is this really going to help us?" Arthur said. "What if this guy is so crazy Google can't even translate him?"

I groaned. "Can we leave the Flynn jokes to the resident expert? I don't think I can take any more."

Arthur shrugged. "The opening was there. I took it."

"Where is Flynn, anyway?" Corbin asked. "Has someone texted him?"

I didn't want to talk about Flynn any more. I entered the bathroom just as Jane emerged from one of the stalls.

"Quick," she whispered. "Kelly's chatting to some football twat at the bar. Give me the gossip."

I filled her in on the content of the letters. "I feel as though we're getting close." I shrugged. "So we're going to Avebury next. Corbin says there's another coven there who may be a little more accommodating. Will you come, too?"

She nodded. "It's good to get out of Crookshollow for a few days, blow the cobwebs out. I'll keep Kelly occupied while you guys get your witch on."

"Thank you for looking after her. Flynn's been shirking his duties, big surprise there. I'm glad she's having fun with you."

"No need to thank me," Jane shrugged. "It's fun. Kelly's awesome."

"Does she—" I lowered my voice. "Does she ask you about me?"

Jane nodded. "She's... suspicious. She's been here a few days and you've hardly spent any time with her. And when you are around, you're tired and distracted. She thinks you don't want her to be part of your life over here."

I sighed. "That's ridiculous."

"I know that, and you know that, but look at it from Kelly's point of view. You made her a promise back in America."

"I'll always be there for you," I mumbled, gripping the edge of the sink.

Jane nodded. "Just because she's not in the hospital anymore and she's got her pink backpack doesn't mean she doesn't need you. But you're always off with the guys doing some 'research project' and you won't tell her anything and she thinks it's just your way of telling her to piss off. You need to show her that's not true or she'll take that ridiculous backpack of hers and leave."

"I know." Tears pricked the corners of my eyes. "I know,

but I'm so tired. The whole world is falling apart around me. I can't do it all. I can't keep up. Arthur's being weird and Flynn isn't talking to me and in a week the Slaugh are going to be *here* and I don't know what to do about any of it."

"Can I make a suggestion? You need to tell Kelly the truth."

I shook my head. "I can't."

"You can. You're Maeve Moore. You're a fucking witch. You can do anything. At least tell her about the guys. She's worried you're cheating on Arthur with Corbin. Remember, you're asking them to lie for you, too. Don't tell me they can all be relied on. She'll find out eventually, and it will be even worse if you don't tell her first."

"Have you told her about you?" I asked. "She grew up in a conservative Christian household. Even if she's a good person, she still believes prostitution and fornication are sins."

Jane pursed her lips. "So I can't be friends with Kelly because of my *job*?"

"You know I don't believe that, but she will."

Jane laughed, scorn digging at the back of her throat. "You're the one who keeps bringing it up. Maybe you don't know Kelly as well as you think you do. Maybe if you weren't so busy with the guys, you'd have bothered to talk to her and you'd see—"

Her comment stung. "I'm trying to save *your* son," I snapped. "I'm doing the best I goddamn can. You can't possibly understand the complexity of what I'm dealing with. It's not just about one single mom who doesn't even know who her kid's dad is. It's the whole damn world—"

"Fuck you, Maeve. You don't get to hold that over my head." Jane whirled around, her hair flying behind her. The bathroom door slammed shut.

I pressed my cheek against the cool mirror. *Shit.* Why the hell did I say that? How had that gone so wrong, so fast?

Of all people, Jane understands what it's like to be on the receiving end of religious fervor from people you care about, I thought. *Let her tell Kelly what she does for a living and feel the sting of that judgement.*

I slunk back outside. Flynn had just arrived, and he was smiling and laughing with the others like nothing was wrong. *Great, just what I need.*

Arthur reached for my hand. "We're leaving now," he yelled over the Irish band caterwauling in the corner. "Corbin wants us all to pack our bags in case we can get on a train tonight."

Jane and Flynn both avoided looking at me as we filed out of the pub. I walked back to the apartment on Arthur's arm, fuming in silence as I stared at the back of Kelly's head while she chatted to Flynn.

Jane's ugly words rattled around in my head. *She thinks you're cheating on Arthur. Just because she's not in the hospital and has her pink backpack doesn't mean she doesn't need you.*

I'd prove her wrong. Jane didn't know my sister like I did. Kelly was *fine.* She was better than I was. She always bounced back from anything. That was her – the great bouncing Kelly. *I'll prove it. I'll talk to her, tonight.*

As I waited for the others to enter the apartment ahead of me, Flynn grabbed my hand and yanked me down the street.

"What are you doing?" I hissed. I glanced over my shoulder just in time to see Kelly's head poking out the apartment window, watching us. She jerked her head inside as soon as she saw me. *Great.*

"The other guys have all had a little bit of Maeve time. I wanted to get my fix," he smiled.

My fingers itched to slap that smile off his face. I used to find Flynn's cheeky grin a comfort, now it burned my flesh like a knife. "I've tried to be alone with you several times. You always avoid me or drag one of the others along." I shrugged. "I get it. This is just a bit of fun for you. It never meant anything. You don't have to rub it in my face."

"Is that what you think I'm doing, Einstein?"

"Don't call me that," I snapped. "Only Kelly's allowed to use that name."

"You never had a problem with it before."

"That was because I thought you cared about me."

Flynn looked away. I seethed. I'd given him the opportunity to tell me otherwise, but he'd ignored it, because I was right after all. I wanted to go back and find Kelly, but curiosity kept me beside him. He was a member of the coven. He might be showing me something important, something that could actually help. It would be the first time Flynn had ever done something helpful.

Flynn led me down a narrow cobbled lane to a tiny jetty where a line of tiny rowboats were tied up, the water slapping against their wooden sides. He sat down on the end of the jetty, the toes of his sneakers digging into the water, and patted the wood beside him.

I remained standing, my arms folded. "What are we doing here, Flynn?"

"I needed to be by the water," he said. "Things like this are always better said by the water."

"Things like?"

Flynn kept staring across the idyllic river. "I love you, Maeve."

The words sucked the breath from my lungs. They pulsed in my head like a radio wave. My first thought was that he was mocking me. "If this is a joke, it's a cruel one."

"No joke. I love you, Maeve Moore, and I'm terrified of it."

"Why?"

He sucked in a breath, and his shoulder shuddered. "Every person I ever tried to love in my life has left me. My pa left me in the coven's ritual, another victim of the fae. Ma left me for drugs and horrible men because she couldn't handle his death or… or maybe the guilt of what they did that night. My uncle never cared about me. He was too busy running a crime empire. I never had a friend I could count on until the coven. When Corbin found me and asked me if I wanted to come live at Briarwood, I up and left the next day. No one came after me. No one reported me missing or stuck my face on a milk carton." Flynn laughed bitterly. "That shows you how much value I have in this world. I'm nothing. I've always been nothing."

I sat down beside him. "Why couldn't you say all this to me? Why couldn't you be alone with me?"

"Because I've felt something for you ever since I first laid eyes on you, all those years ago in an Arizona classroom. But I was afraid, afraid I'd fall for you and you'd leave, so I figured it was better to do what I always did," he flashed me his signature grin, his smile wavering at the edges. "I played the fool. I smiled. I told jokes. It's the only thing I'm good at. Well, that, and bollocksing everything up."

"That's not true. You're very definitely not nothing. I mean…" I struggled through the double negative. "You are special. Your smile has kept this coven together more than you ever realize. If it wasn't for you, Corbin and Rowan and Arthur would have drowned in their own sorrow years ago. You make us remember that there are good things in the world worth fighting for."

"You sound like a bloody Hallmark card." Flynn rested his head on my shoulder.

"I know, but it's all true. I never told you before because I was embarrassed, but I do remember you from when you were in Arizona. I thought you were so hot, but I knew that in a million years someone popular like you would never be interested in a nerd like me. You think you're not worthy of me? I didn't think I was worthy of you. But it's all *bollocks*. We get to be together and love each other and bugger the whole world if they try to stop us. You don't have to push me away. It's okay to be scared, but we can get through it together. The coven needs you, Flynn. *I* need you. More than that, I *want* you. I love you."

I rested my head against his shoulder. Across the water, couples strolled along a path lit by fairy lights, laughing as they shared ice cream cones and made up silly dance moves to music playing only in their heads. I wondered if I'd ever get to have a normal date with Flynn or any of my guys.

My phone beeped. I pulled it out and checked the message from Corbin. "Where are you? Get back here! Clara's convinced the Avebury Coven to get us inside the institution for a meeting with Smithers tomorrow. We're leaving Oxford tonight."

My stomach fluttered. As much as I'd fallen in love with Oxford, we had shit to take care of. Namely, finding out who Robert Smithers really was, and what.

I tucked my hand into Flynn's. "Come on, it's time to leave this river of shit behind us."

"What are we going?"

I grinned. "Toward a giant mountain of shit. But at least we'll be climbing it together."

37

MAEVE

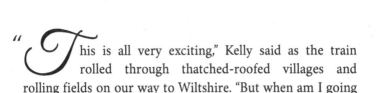

"This is all very exciting," Kelly said as the train rolled through thatched-roofed villages and rolling fields on our way to Wiltshire. "But when am I going to get to see Briarwood?"

There was an accusatory tone in her voice that I'd never heard before. "Soon, I promise. We just have a few things to do in Wiltshire first, for our research project."

"You and Corbin?" Kelly's voice was light, but I remembered what Jane had said to me in the pub in Oxford. I had to be careful or she was going to start trouble.

I shrugged, as if it was neither here nor there to me. "Well, he's the one interested in history."

"Why is this project of yours so important? Couldn't it wait? Do you really have to travel all over the country with all the guys like this?"

"It's about my mother, Kelly. I'd have thought you'd understand. I never got to even meet her. The Crawfords knew nothing about her, but now I find out she was a famous artist's muse and I just... I need to know more, okay?"

"It just seems like...." Kelly played with a strand of her golden hair. "If I didn't know better, I'd say you were going with Corbin, instead of Arthur. But then you seem so close to Arthur, too. All of them, actually. And you barely know the guys. It's weird, is all."

"It's hard for you to understand because you have a mother—"

Kelly's face fell. "Fine," she said shortly, standing up.

Too late I realized what I'd said. "Kelly, I didn't mean—"

"No, you meant every word." She whispered as she grabbed her purse from the seat pocket. "You always do."

Kelly hurried down the carriage and sat down beside Jane, whispering something in her ear. Jane reached into Connor's enormous diaper bag and pulled out some baby wipes. Kelly dabbed at her face. Jane glared at me over her shoulder.

I buried my face in my sleeve. How was I messing this up so badly? Arthur slid across from his seat and wrapped an arm around my shoulder. "You okay?" he whispered.

I shook my head. "I'm bollocksing everything up."

"In what way?"

"With Kelly. She's asking questions. She thinks I'm cheating on you with Corbin. Jane thinks I should tell her the truth."

"I heard what she said when Flynn made his polyamory joke. It might've just been because it was Flynn saying it, but she didn't sound like the kind of person who would accept something like this. But she is your sister, and I don't know how much longer we can hide it. We're close quarters in the apartments. She's bound to walk in on something."

"But if I tell her, and she leaves, then I can't protect her from the fae." I rubbed my forehead against Arthur's Blood Lust shirt. "This is a nightmare."

"Maybe there's a chance today to start the conversation."

"What do you mean?"

"Do you know what Avebury is? It's the largest megalithic stone circle in the world. Our ancestors – pagans, from before there even was such a thing as pagans – used to perform rituals and fertility rites there, probably involving wild orgies, because that's what people did instead of watching telly in Neolithic Britain. The stones have been standing for longer than Kelly believes the earth has existed. Maybe you guys can start a conversation."

I squeezed his hand. "You're pretty smart, you know, for a Viking."

"Thanks."

At Swindon we changed to a bus. Kelly and Jane rushed on ahead of us and took a seat right at the back. There were no other seats around them, so the rest of us had to crowd up the front near the driver. It was past midnight now, and I could barely keep my eyes open. I leaned against the window and fell into a sleep haunted by terrible dreams.

"Maeve," Arthur shook my arm to wake me. "Time to go, luv. We're here."

I dragged my weary body off the bus. A woman stood with Corbin, helping him pull out our backpacks from storage. Arthur swooped in and grabbed Kelly's pack for her, grunting under the weight as he staggered away from the crowd of passengers.

"Maeve Moore." The woman's round, kind face broke into a smile as soon as her head turned toward me. She looked a little like a witch you'd seen in a movie – probably in her fifties, with strawberry-blonde hair reaching down past her waist, thousands of bangles and bracelets that clinked together when she moved, and laugh lines crinkling at the corners of her eyes. She clasped my hand in hers. "You look so much like your mother. The Avebury Coven welcomes you with open arms."

"The what?" Kelly's head whipped up.

"Oh, um…" My sleepy brain grasped for an explanation.

"Oh, poor gullible Yank," Flynn drawled, wrapping his arm around Kelly's shoulders. "This is Gwen's act for the tourists. Because of the stone circle, many of the locals pretend to be witches The 'Avebury Coven' is just the name of her artist's collective. Isn't that right, Gwen?"

The woman nodded. "Yes. We have ten artists who all produce work inspired by the history of Avebury. I'd be happy to show you around our studio space and gallery shop if you're interested."

"Oh," Kelly looked relieved. "Cool. I'd love to see the gallery, as long as it's not too New Agey? I'm not into all that occult stuff."

Gwen glanced from me to Corbin, her grey eyebrow raised, but she didn't give us away. "Follow me," she said. "You must be tired. I've made up your beds all ready, and we even have some food waiting."

Gwen hurried us to her house as fast as she could – just as well, because my teeth chattered from being out in the crisp night air. She lived in a beautiful ancient cottage on the edge of the village. An enormous rock stood pride of place in the middle of her front garden, surrounded by beds of herbs and wildflowers. "It's not original, you mind," she explained as we traced our fingers over the rough surface. "After the archae-ologists mapped the site and released the probable locations of other stones, I decided to erect this one where one of the ancient stones stood."

Beside me, Flynn smirked. I jabbed him in the ribs, real-izing he was giggling about the word *erect*.

Gwen held the door open for us and we hurried inside. She flicked on the light, revealing a long, low-ceilinged sitting room where several air beds and cots had been erected in front of a roaring fire. The warmth enveloped me, and I instantly felt at ease. "I've set the girls up in the spare bedroom, so you can have privacy with the baby, but I know Maeve might like to sleep out here. I know it seems mad to have the fire on in summer, but I thought you'd appreciate it arriving so late. it gets cold in this old house. Plus, I think it gives the stew a great smoky flavor."

The scent of hot meat wafted across my nostrils. My stomach grumbled. Gwen went to the fire and swung out a large cauldron on a long hook and gave it a stir. "All ready. My daughter Candice will be along shortly with the bread."

"Here you are." A beautiful girl about my age with ice-white hair down to her waist entered, holding a large wooden tray upon which was perched two loaves of crusty bread. From the smell of them, they'd just come out of the oven.

"Gwen, you're too kind." Corbin said, taking a stack of plates from Gwen and handing them around.

"The only way you could be kinder is if there was some Irish whiskey available," Flynn mused, accepting a heaped plate of the meaty stew and a slice of bread.

Grinning, Candice produced a bottle from the folds of her skirt.

"A woman after my own heart," Flynn grabbed her around the waist and hugged her close, his grin wide as he swiped the bottle from her hand and took a huge swig.

We all sat down around the room, some on Gwen's floral-patterned sofa, others perched in the deep window seats or kneeling beside the fire, and finished our food in companionable silence. I admired the artwork hanging from every spare inch of wall space – some bold abstracts, some ethereal illustrations of fairies and nymphs, some that seemed to depict astrological signs and constellations and the arrangement of the stones. Candice sat with Flynn and told him all about the studio in their barn that she and Gwen shared with eight other local artists, and the gallery shop in the village where they sold their work. He couldn't stop staring at the paintings.

I didn't blame him. They were captivating. Candice pointed out two of hers, which leapt out from the rest – the visible brush-strokes almost dancing across the canvas, as though she'd captured the sound of music.

"I'm beat," Kelly announced as soon as she was finished her food. "I'm going to brush my teeth and crawl into bed."

I hugged her goodnight. The hug felt stiff, forced, but I didn't know how to fix it. The rest of us moved into the tiny kitchen to give Kelly some quiet. Gwen made hot chocolate in a pot on the old-fashioned wood-fired range, and we talked about Avebury and art and the sights we'd seen in London until I couldn't keep my eyes open any longer. I kept trying to go off to bed, but Corbin held my hand firm at his side.

Gwen poked her head into the living room and beckoned me over. "Is your sister asleep?" Gwen asked. I nodded, watching Kelly's slumbering figure, her mouth hanging open and emitting tiny, wheezing snores.

"When she's snoring like that, not even the Slaugh could wake her."

"Good." Gwen pulled the back door open, sending a cold gust of air across the room. She grabbed a long, gnarled staff and a white robe from beside the door. "Grab your coats and shoes. Hurry now. The rest of the coven is waiting for us."

~

I shivered between Blake and Flynn. We stood inside the area of what Gwen called the Southern Inner Circle, beneath a tall standing stone called 'the obelisk.' Women wandered around the outside of the circle, where only a few stones remained, carrying flaming torches high as they chanted in a language I didn't understand.

"They're speaking Breton," Corbin said. "That's so cool. I've never heard it spoken aloud before. Gwen's coven trace their ancestors back to the earliest druids, who used to worship on this site after the Neolithic peoples abandoned it."

Druids. I barely understood what that word meant beyond vague memories of stories of human sacrifices and cannibalism. I watched Gwen move to the center of the circle, her white robes fluttering around her plump body as she led a ritual that I didn't understand. Flynn nudged me and whispered, "I've been to a druidic ritual before. They make no bloody sense, but the best thing is that at the end there's a feast."

"Do you think there will be curry?" Blake asked hopefully.

The ritual seemed to be winding down. The chanting stopped. Gwen tossed down her staff and she extended a hand to me. "Come, we have welcomed you and asked our gods to bless and protect you on your sacred mission. Join us now as seal our bonds with bread and wine. We have much to discuss."

Our two covens sat in the center of the field, forming two lopsided circles around Gwen and I. Baskets of bread, sharp cheese, relish, and small walnut tarts were passed around, as well as drinking horns filled with mead. Candice sat behind her mother, holding her staff and the still dribbling candle. Was she the magister? I wondered. But surely Gwen didn't have a sexual relationship with her own daughter. There must be all sorts of different traditions and ways of doing magic, just like there were a hundred different Christian churches and denominations.

I chewed on a slice of bread while I summed up for Gwen, as succinctly as I could, exactly what had happened at

Briarwood and what we knew so far about the fae. Unlike the nervousness I felt around Isadora, I found the words came easily here.

And even though the words I spoke were of terrible things, I felt a tremendous sense of power wash over me. Standing out in the crisp wind, with the stars blanketing our ritual, something kindled inside me. I glanced up at the Milky Way streaking across the sky and fancied I saw a silver thread streaking through the cosmos, connecting us all the way back into prehistory and beyond.

"… so I don't know what to do," I finished. "I know my mother asked you to Briarwood twenty-one years ago to perform a ritual. I know that ritual involved something so dark that you may wish never to speak of it, but my very existence means that you can't have seen what you think you saw."

Gwen placed her hand on my shoulder. "Aline was the most powerful witch of her time, and that night her power was bolstered by the rest of us. I was part of the inner circle, and I saw a terrible thing. She intended to kill you, and yet you did not die." She rubbed my hand, squeezing my fingers when they started to tremble. "That is magic I've never seen before, the power of life or death."

"I'm afraid…" My heart thudded in my chest. "I'm afraid that in order to stop the Slaugh I'm going to have to do a terrible thing."

Gwen rested her hand on my shoulder. "Somehow, I do not believe so. Your mother found a way to cheat the fae of their price. You are clever, and you are bolstered by other clever witches who love you. You will find the answer, and we will help you in any way we can. Where you lead, we will follow, Maeve Moore. We have so much here that's worth protecting. We will fight for you, for us, for all of humankind."

"Thank you." I squeezed her hand. "I'm sorry that this all has to be done in secret. I'm scared my sister—"

"Oh, precious girl. We're all scared. That's why we must work together. Because—" Gwen stopped mid-word, her head snapping up. "Someone is there," she whispered. "Behind the stone."

I focused my gaze on the large stone she was staring at. My heart stopped as a dark figure broke away from behind the monolith and sprinted back toward the village. In the darkness it was impossible to recognize it, but it looked slight, the churning limbs thin and spindly. I thought I caught a flash of blonde hair.

Like a fae. Like Liah.

MAEVE

I woke to the smell of bacon frying and voices laughing. Arthur snored beside me on the foldout sofa, one enormous arm pinning my body to the mattress. I slid out from under him, noting that the rest of the guys were already awake. I peeked into Kelly and Jane's room, but they weren't there, either, and Connor's stroller was missing.

I ducked under a particularly low beam into a tiny bathroom to gargle. Gwen's tinkling laugh and Corbin's loud groan echoed off the dark wood. Flynn must've told one of his patented dumb jokes. I stepped into the kitchen and three guys wrapped me in a morning hug. Flynn's lips brushed mine while Rowan pressed his to my ear and Blake nuzzled (nuzzled? Blake? I'm in heaven) the nape of my neck.

"Welcome to the land of the living." Candice called from in front of the stove, where she flipped sausages and bacon like a pro.

I tried to extricate myself from the guys before Candice noticed, but Flynn shoved his tongue down my throat. "It's okay, Einstein, I told her about us."

Candice nodded. "It's typical in our coven for the High Priestess to take many lovers. Mum's no exception. These days she... how do you say it in America? She bats for the other team."

I recalled the sea of female faces who regarded me from within their snow-white hoods last night, and the way Gwen would touch one on the shoulder or laugh with another. Candice's revelation didn't surprise me at all.

"Candice said she'd show me the coven's studio after breakfast." Flynn looked hopeful. His eyes darted to one of Candice's paintings on the wall above the stove. "I had an idea for a new piece and I thought... I'm not much use otherwise..."

"Go." I waved a hand. "I'm starting to realize that making art *is* useful. Has anyone seen Kelly? It's not like her to miss bacon."

"She and Jane went out for a walk about an hour ago." Blake tucked into his eggs and bacon with gusto. "I guess they'll come back when—"

"Omigod, I smell bacon!" The front door slammed and Kelly came rushing into the kitchen. She frowned when she saw us all around the kitchen table. "Were you even going to save any for me?"

"Of course, Kelly. There's plenty. Here." I held out the plate for her. She didn't take it.

"I have to wash my hands." Kelly disappeared from the room.

A hand touched my shoulder. Rowan. Of course he was the one to notice the tension between us. "It will be okay," he whispered.

I wasn't so sure.

Our appointment wasn't until the afternoon. Gwen had to work a shift at the gallery shop, so Corbin took all of us – except Flynn, who didn't want to leave Candice's studio – on a tour of the Avebury henge. We walked around the enormous stone circle that encircled the village, and hunted for any sign the fae might have been nearby last night. We found nothing, but the memory of that figure still haunted me. I touched the stones, digging inside them with my spirit power to feel the hum of magic still clinging to them.

"Starting in the late medieval period, people came to live in the village, and they destroyed many of the stones – some because they needed the space for the walls of their house, and some because they didn't like the pagan rituals the stones represent." Corbin pointed to the two towering stones in the center of a green field. One was skinny, the other a vaguely diamond shape. "Fertility rites were very important to our ancestors. These stones represent the male and female entities that must come together to create new life, both in the womb and in the earth."

"If these sites are so important, how come there isn't a stone circle at Briarwood, or near any of the London covens?"

"There actually was a stone circle at Briarwood," Corbin explained. "It was quite close to the sidhe. We don't know anything for sure because there's no written history pre-Romans, but we believe Neolithic peoples got along quite well with the fae... well, there was a kind of uneasy truce, anyway. It's possible witches and fae even worked magic together, for instance to help the wild places to produce enough food for everyone, or to keep mutual enemies at bay."

"What happened to destroy that friendship?"

"Technology, science, civilization, the smelting of iron," Corbin shrugged. "You name it. If it's part of human enlightenment, the fae took exception to it. They want us to live like Neolithic people, but the human mind can't help but innovate."

"They wanted to protect the wild places," Rowan said.

"Humans burned forests to make fields. We slaughtered entire species for food or sport. I think the fae thought they were trying to save us from ourselves, to remind us where we came from."

"Liah said she could hear the ghosts of the trees howling in pain," Blake added.

"That's probably true. The humans saw it as the fae trying to halt progress. Over the years the human race progressed and the rift between us grew greater," Corbin shrugged. "Even witchcraft changed. Many of the ancient sacred places – including the circle at Briarwood – were destroyed for farming or war. Modern covens realized that it wasn't stones that gave them power. Although a witch can draw power from an ancient place like Avebury, it's nothing like the magic you hold within yourself."

"Then why do—hold on," I hissed, watching as two figures jogged across the field toward us. "Kelly's coming."

Arthur slid in beside me – the perfect boyfriend – just as Kelly and Jane stopped in front of us. "Maeve, can we talk a minute?" Kelly asked, her voice cold.

"Sure." I dropped Arthur's arm. "You guys keep going with the tour. We'll just be over by the male/female stones."

We walked a short distance away in silence. Jane shifted Connor from one shoulder to the other. When we were out of earshot of the guys, Kelly blurted out, "Why did we come here, Maeve?"

"It's an interesting tourist site. I thought you'd like to see it."

"That's a lie and we both know it. You'd never choose to come here. There's not an observatory or a science museum for miles around. Why are you suddenly so interested in pagan worship sites? Why are you so desperate for me to believe in all this mystical witchy stuff? We always disagreed about theology before and you never cared, not really. What's going on?"

"Nothing. I mean, being here in England where everything's so ancient… it's brought home just how stupid it is to believe Earth is only six thousand years old—"

"I don't care how old the stupid earth is," Kelly hissed. "I want to spend time with my sister. I came here because you asked me, remember? Because you said you'd look after me so I didn't feel like I was alone. But it's exactly the same as when you were a thousand miles away. I'm completely invisible to you."

"Kelly, that's not true."

"It *is* true. You didn't even notice that I changed my hair."

I stared at her blonde locks, hunting for something different about them. Did she get layers? Was her hair a little shorter? I honestly couldn't tell. "I never notice when you change your hair," I said.

"I saw you last night," Kelly hissed. "You were standing by that tall stone over there while all those ladies in white robes danced around you, like some Satanic ritual or something. What was that all about?"

No. It wasn't Liah running away from the ritual last night. It was *Kelly.* Of course. I'd seen a flash of blonde hair. Kelly must've woken up and heard us leaving and followed us. My mind reeled, searching for an excuse I could give her, some explanation for what she'd seen that wasn't, 'I'm a witch.'

"That was Gwen's idea," I said, frantically trying to think of an excuse. "It's a performance art piece and she wants—"

"If you're not going to tell Kelly the truth, then we're done here," Jane fumed. "Come on, Kelly. I saw an ice cream shop in the village. Leave Maeve with her *boys.* That's what she wants, anyway."

Kelly glared at me a final time, then stormed off after Jane.

I watched them flee toward the village, my stomach churning. *Kelly saw the ritual. She knows I'm hiding something from her. How long until Jane breaks down and tells her the truth and I lose Kelly forever?*

MAEVE

Kelly and Jane avoided me for the rest of the morning. They didn't go back to Gwen's house, and when I saw them coming out of the village teahouse, they quickly turned and fled in the other direction. My heart sank into my shoes. I didn't know what to do.

The guys and I ate lunch in a thatched roof pub. Our table was right next to an old stone well descending right through the flagstone floor and deep into the earth. I ordered beef and Guinness pie and didn't eat a bite. Kelly's words pounded against my skull. The guys gave up trying to get me to talk about it and just ate their lunch in silence.

Corbin pushed his chair back. "Maeve, we have to go."

I nodded miserably. Yesterday I'd been so excited about the possibility of meeting Robert Smithers and getting to the bottom of this. Today, I couldn't care less. None of it seemed to have any point without Kelly.

Corbin turned to Blake. "Can you join us? I have a theory I'd like to test out."

Blake shoveled in a last mouthful of curry and grabbed his leather jacket. "Sure."

We left Arthur and Rowan sampling local chocolates at the pub and hopped on the bus out to the asylum. I expected an imposing Victorian building with spindly trees, like something out of a horror film. Instead, we walked into a bright, modern building of glass and steel. Solar panels dotted the roof and colorful vegetable gardens and flower beds lined the winding driveway. A nurse admitted us with a smile. "He doesn't get many visitors," she said. "Follow me. He's in the reflection room. If he starts getting agitated, press the call button by the door and we'll come to assist you."

She ushered us into a small room. Two walls held large canvases depicting what I might describe as "tranquil" scenes – a calm beach surrounded by palm trees, and water rippling over rocks on the edge of a wooded stream. A white recliner sat under the window, facing the garden beyond. A head of dark hair with flecks of grey poked out over the top of the chair.

"Robert Smithers?"

The man didn't answer. I stepped forward, coming around the side of his chair until I could see his profile. His handsome features had sagged a little with age, his sharp cheekbones softened, his strong jaw less defined, but the resemblance to the artist in Clara's book was unmistakable. My heart fluttered against my chest. I knelt down beside him, placing one hand on the arm of his chair. "I didn't mean to disturb you, Mr. Smithers. We were just wondering if we could speak to you."

Still no reply. Blake leaned against the forest scene, his eyebrow raised nearly to the ceiling. "Look, Maeve, this painting is so realistic it's almost as if I'm leaning against this tree."

Corbin smirked. I ignored him. "Robert, I'm Maeve Moore. Do you remember Aline Moore, from Briarwood? Well, she's my mother. You might have believed I was dead, but I'm alive and I very much want to talk to you about a painting—"

"Bloody rubbish," the man in the chair muttered.

"What's rubbish? The part about me being alive, or about being Aline's daughter?"

Robert raised a shaking finger and pointed it at the forest painting. "Not real," he muttered. "No soul."

Of course. We were speaking to an artist. Even I with my total lack of any artistic ability could see that those murals were garbage.

Blake's face broke into a grin. "That's right. They're complete rubbish. And you'd know, wouldn't you? You were one of Britain's greatest living artists for a time. How come they didn't ask you to paint the contemplation room?"

Smithers shook his head frantically. "Not me. I can't make the colors work anymore."

"I know who you are." I pulled out the Smithers' book from my bag and opened it on his lap. "You used to be an artist, didn't you? These are your paintings."

"I painted that one," he mumbled, jabbing his finger at a dry portrait of a Duke. He moved his finger over another portrait, this one of a woman with flowing red hair. "Robert painted that one."

"Robert? But you're Robert."

The man tapped his head. "Robert lives in here. Sometimes he paints instead of me when I get tired. But we don't paint anymore."

"How come?"

He shrugged. "Nothing left to paint. Robert doesn't want to."

"And you always do what Robert says?" Blake asked with a twitch of his mouth.

The man shrugged again. "Robert knows best. He knows

so many things about the world. Robert's been everywhere. To the moon and the stars."

Ooooo-kay. "So if you're not Robert, then who am I talking to?"

He whistled, his eyes rolling toward Blake again. He reached out toward the tree beside Blake, his fingers scraping over the plaster. He blinked. When he spoke again, his voice had completely changed. Gone was the throaty rasp. Instead, his words were crisp, clear, bitter.

"I call him Rob, the other one. He gets more of a look in these days. I don't really have much to interest me in this place."

I glanced at Corbin, then back to the man in front of me. Weirdly, even his face looked different. His skin tighter, his lips forming a pout. He would have been so handsome when he was young. If my mother was anything like me, I could see what attracted her to him. "So, we're speaking to Robert now?"

Robert Smithers gave a tiny wave, and a mischievous grin. "Howdy. Rob and I don't always get along, y'see. He's not a fan of my artwork. Thinks it too bold, too daring. I think he's pussywhipped."

Corbin met my gaze, his eyes betraying his disappointment. He shook his head sadly. I knew he was thinking this was hopeless, but I wasn't convinced. We knew from Robert's letters that he had this split personality or whatever it was going on, but that didn't mean we couldn't get anything useful out of him.

I flipped to the page of the book that showed the portrait of my mother, and laid down a photograph of the painting from Briarwood on top of it. "Do you remember this lady? Which one of you painted her?"

He stared at the page for a moment. "Aline was special. We

both painted her. She's the only one we had to both paint. Rob insisted." He waved his hand in the air, like he was flapping at invisible mosquitoes, and picked up the photograph. "This was mine. She liked it best, that's why she kept it close to her."

"Why was she special?"

"Just look at her, a..." Robert's eyes rolled back, and a moment later, her blinked. "What... did I fall asleep?"

"No, Mr Smithers. We were just talking to, er... Robert."

"That bastard," he swore. "What was he saying to you? What lies was he telling about me?"

"Nothing. That is, I just wanted to know about this painting." I touched the photograph again. "About the lady in it. You painted her, didn't you? But not this image. This one in the book here that hung in the National Gallery, right? Why did you and Robert both paint her?"

He shoved the book away. "Don't let her look at me."

I snapped the book shut. "It's okay. She's not looking at you anymore. Can you tell me about her, about Aline?"

"I loved her," he sniffed. "I loved her with my heart and soul and spleen and every other part of me, but she only loved Robert. She had no time for poor Rob. I poured everything I had into that portrait, I tried to show her what she meant to me, but she chose him instead."

"How did she choose Robert? What did she say?"

"She wanted to go, go, go, up to the stars. He was always talking about his home in the stars, where he built a castle of stardust and a throne of skulls. I made her a writing desk, but she needed the skulls."

Skulls... that didn't sound good. Why did my mother want skulls?

"Were you there that night, Rob? The night of the ritual? The night Aline died?"

His eyes fluttered shut. "She didn't tell me anything," he

301

whispered. "She only shared with Robert. Only Robert was inside the circle."

"But did you see what happened inside the circle? Did Aline stab her child?"

"So much blood…" Rob's eyes closed. He opened them again, and burst out laughing. Robert was back, his eyes crinkling at the edges as he laughed at my pain.

"You were there, weren't you, Robert?" He only laughed harder. I balled my hands into fists. Desperation clawed at my veins. I needed answers, but talking to this guy was worse than talking to Flynn.

I tried a different line of questioning. "Do you remember my father? He was a fae named Daigh and he would never have come inside the castle. He might have been disguised. Did Aline speak of the man who made her pregnant?"

Robert's whole body convulsed with laughter. "She fucked a fae?" He choked out. "Oh, you're full of wild stories, girl. Aline spread her legs for me, wrapped those silky gams of hers around my head. Her cunt was like—"

"Hey, Princess…"

Blake's smile was easy, but his hand slipped against the chair, and he nearly toppled over. Corbin caught him on the arm, steadying him.

"No problem," Blake murmured. "I just need to step outside for a bit."

"Blake—" but he was already gone, the door slamming shut behind him.

"Excuse me a minute." Robert was too busy laughing to notice anything amiss. Corbin glared at me as I raced from the room, slamming the door shut behind me.

I glanced around frantically. Blake sat on a bench seat in front of a wall of glass looking out into a tree-lined courtyard, his head in his hands. I slumped down beside him, placing my hand on his knee. "Okay, spill the beans."

"I don't have any beans, Princess." Blake moaned, rubbing his head.

"It's an expression. It means 'tell Maeve what happened in there so she can stop freaking out'."

"Nothing happened."

"You suddenly felt the need to contemplate the nature of your existence?" I pointed to a sign on the wall that invited residents to sit and do exactly that.

Blake groaned again. "Seeing that guy in there, it hit me that I could have been looking at myself."

"What do you mean? Best I knew, you've never referred to yourself in the third person."

"I mean, inside that man's skull is a human mind wrecked by fae magic. That could be me if I'm not careful."

"Explain."

"Fae magic and human magic – they're connected, but different. They both harness and manipulate the basic elements, but in completely different ways. That's why the fae can't shoot fireballs like Arthur and we can't compel people. Except when we can." Blake rubbed his head. "Daigh taught me some simple fae magic – very simple glamour and compulsion, a couple of other tricks I haven't shown you yet. I shouldn't be able to do them, but I think he might have done something in my head to make that happen. Every time I do them, I lose a little piece of myself. It tears apart bits of my mind."

"Neurons," I corrected him.

"Right, neurons. If I'm not careful, you could be sticking me in a place like this. Because Robert Smithers, he's been broken by fae magic. I looked inside his head. It's a mess."

"So he's been doing fae magic?"

"That's what I thought at first, but no. Remember I told you a fae could only compel for a half hour at most? Robert was compelled for *years*. The scars are all over his head."

The horror of that shuddered through my body. "You're telling me that Robert had a fae literally hitchhiking around in his brain?"

Blake nodded, misery scarring his crystalline features. "I had no idea that was even possible, but the neurons don't lie. A fae fucked him up."

"He must have been fighting against that voice, seeing it do things with his body and being completely unable to stop it." I ran over the broken conversation we'd had with Robert. "That's why he said someone else painted those portraits. Because someone did. Rob is the person, Robert is the fae."

"No."

"No?"

Blake placed his hand in mine, curling his fingers between my digits until our palms pressed tight together. "You're right about Robert living with two people inside his head. But the fae is no longer present in his mind. Robert is entirely an invention of Rob's mind. After so many years sharing his mind with another, he must've got lonely when the fae left, and just decided to continue the conversation."

"He's so used to feeling his body and words controlled by another, he kept going on believing he was two people, even after the fae left." *It's horrible.* So many details slotted into place. How Robert Smithers the artist suddenly appeared on the art scene with an unheard-of talent. How he survived the ritual at Briarwood, but never painted again...

... because he couldn't.

Tears welled in the corners of my eyes. Was there anything the fae wouldn't corrupt, any witch of Briarwood whom their cruelty couldn't break?

"You two get back in here *right now*." Corbin poked his head out the door. "This guy's talking a load of gibberish and he's demanding I hold his bedpan."

"Rob or Robert?" Blake called back.

"They're the same bloody person!"

"No," I whispered. "No, they're not."

Corbin stormed over to stand front of the bench, his arms folded. "This is a lost cause. The guy's completely deranged. We'll have to go back to the letters and—"

I held up a hand. "Just let me think for a moment. Both of you, tell me everything you know about fae compulsion."

"What? Why? What's that got to do with bedpans—"

"Just do what the lady says, Mussolini," Blake grinned. "I think she's onto something."

Corbin sighed. "I don't know much more than you do. Compulsion is a fae power – Blake's the only non-fae I've ever heard of able to do it. It involves slipping inside another person's mind and giving them instructions, which they obey. The person can fight the compulsion, but it's difficult, especially if you don't understand what's going on. Most people will submit and do the will of the compeller. But compulsion uses a great deal of power and fae can usually only sustain the bond for a few minutes, half an hour at most."

"What happens to the fae while they're in the other person's head? Do they have to be asleep, or—"

Blake shook his head. "It's not like dreamwalking. You are inside your own head at the same time, but you can't really focus on both minds at once. You go a bit blank. Powerful fae with decades of practice can maintain a coherent mind in both their own mind and in their vessel, but that's rare."

"And if a fae is inside a person's head, would that person be susceptive to anti-fae wards or charms?"

Corbin shook his head. "No. We saw that already with Dora. A compelled person can pass through wards, although I'm sure a clued-in witch could create a charm specifically to root out compulsion."

"And what if a fae was inside a human's head while they

were, um, having relations with another human?" I turned to Blake. "Say, in the exact moment that a sperm impregnates an egg?"

"Then that fae would get a hell of a show," Blake grinned. "I don't know what would happen because that's never happened. The fae explicitly warn against it. They say it creates a binding, but I don't know what that means."

A binding. Holy shitballs.

"What is this about?" Corbin demanded.

"This is going to sound insane," I sucked in a ragged breath. "I think Robert Smithers was possessed by a fae when he lived at Briarwood. And I think he is my real father. Or, more correctly, *one* of my real fathers."

"*Y*ou're right," Corbin said. "That is completely insane."

"Sounds like Robert isn't the only one who should be committed, Princess," I added. "Daigh is your father."

"Do we have evidence of that? You know what we say – fae lie?" Maeve paced back and forth, her brow furrowed in that adorable way she had when she was thinking hard. Flynn called it her 'Mad Scientist Mode.' "I'll have to take a DNA test to be sure, but I'm almost positive I've figured this all out."

"Figured *what* out? What's going on?" Corbin was practically shouting now. A nurse wandered past with a cart of small pebbles in plastic containers and frowned at him.

"Okay," Maeve said, speeding up her pacing. "Hear me out. I have a hypothesis."

I rubbed my head, the echoes of Robert's scars still etched behind my eyelids. I had a bad feeling I didn't want to hear what Maeve was about to say.

"Here's what we know. Twenty-one years ago, Robert

Smithers the painter came to Crookshollow to live at Briar-wood with the coven. He knew it would be the perfect place to live a reclusive life where he could paint without his powers being discovered. While there, he falls in love with my mother."

"Yes, but—"

"Aline's letters say how they have no idea how the fae got so strong or were able to do what they did. She said it was as if they were anticipating the coven's movements. What if a member of the coven was somehow being controlled and possessed by a fae? By Daigh, to be precise."

Corbin looked skeptical. "He couldn't hold the compulsion for long enough to—"

I nodded my head, my mind racing. "I saw inside Robert's mind. I know it sounds impossible, but he's been compelled for months or years at a time."

"I don't know how he did it yet, but *if* Daigh had possession of Robert's mind he'd know all the coven's secrets," Maeve continued. "We know Robert was present at the ritual, and he was her magister – inside his head Daigh would know *exactly* what the coven was planning, how they were drawing the witches together for the ritual to stop the Slaugh. He knew *exactly* when to strike – while my mother was in labor with me and the coven would be at its weakest."

"Maybe that's exactly what your mother anticipated," I said. "That's why she kept the ritual secret from everyone except Corbin's parents."

Maeve nodded. "I think she figured out that Daigh was hiding in Robert's mind. She didn't trust any of the others, so she used fae magic – and how I haven't exactly figured out yet – to cast a glamour. To make them see what she wanted them to see; her plunging a knife through her newborn baby's heart. But what she actually did was hand me off to Corbin's parents, who squirreled me away to the orphanage and kept watch over me in secret, to make sure Daigh never found out he was tricked."

"Clever girl," I grinned. *Like mother, like daughter.*

"Daigh was inside Robert's head that night. He thought Aline was going to stab me. He intended to stop the ritual from the inside. Instead, my mother stopped him and stripped him of the power he needed to raise the Slaugh. And she died in the process."

"But this is impossible," Corbin said. "You're talking about *years* of compulsion. Even a powerful fae wouldn't be able to hang on to a human mind that long without being fought off."

"Except," I frowned.

"Except what?"

I didn't want to say what I was thinking. I'd already destroyed so much of Maeve's hope. But now that I thought it, I was sure I was right. "Except if he made a pact with a fae."

"Explain," Maeve said, her eyes narrowed.

"We're assuming Robert's mind fought the compulsion, which is usually why a fae can only perform it for a few minutes. Eventually, the conscious mind kicks out the interloper. But what if Robert gave his mind willingly?"

"Who would even do that?" Corbin growled.

"Of course," Maeve slapped her hand on her forehead. "Remember what Hendricks at the art museum said? Robert Smithers' last painting – painted just before he committed himself – was terrible. He never painted again after that. I'd assumed it was because he was mentally ill. But maybe it's because he *couldn't.*"

That bloody wanker. "Robert said just before that he didn't paint anymore. He probably couldn't paint before he met Daigh, either. Daigh just took a promising mind from the street and plied him with promises of fame and money and power. Robert got all Daigh's talent in exchange for sharing his skull. But he had to remain reclusive so that people wouldn't notice he couldn't paint when Daigh wasn't inside his mind."

"A deal with the devil," Corbin breathed. "Holy shite."

"Think about it," Maeve said. "It explains why the letters were so drastically different. Some of them were written by Robert Smithers, some of them were written by Daigh, in control of Robert's mind and his hand. It was Daigh who painted all those famous portraits and made Robert Smithers' name, at least in the beginning. Robert said he painted some of them – maybe toward the end he was exerting more influence over Daigh. But they never received the same critical reception."

"But Daigh's not possessing him now." Corbin jabbed a finger at the room. "So why is he so bonkers?"

"We figured that out, too," I said, beaming at him with pride. "If you'd spent years of your life hearing another voice inside your head, you might continue to live with that voice, even when you couldn't hear it anymore."

"Daigh painted the portrait of my mother." Maeve's body trembled.

"What if it's more than that?" I said, thinking back over every wicked art-related prank Daigh had pulled over the years. "What if he didn't just capture her likeness? What if he somehow captured part of *her* inside it?"

"A – that's impossible," Corbin ticked off his fingers. "And B – we'd have found a trace of fae magic on the painting. All we found was the mark of a witch."

Maeve's eyes narrowed. The expression on her face could've halted an army. She turned on her heel and stalked back into the bedroom.

Corbin met my eyes. Both of us got to our feet and sprinted after her.

I stood behind Maeve as she sank to her knees in front of Robert. I considered reaching into her mind for what she was thinking, but it was already written on her face.

"Can I speak to Rob, please?" she snapped, her eyes blazing.

"Robert's gone away," he whispered in that horrible rasping voice. "He's laughed himself to sleep."

"That's good. I want to talk to Rob. Hello, again. You said you were in love with Aline?"

"She wanted to visit the stars," he whispered. "To me, she was the stars. And the moon and the sun and the whole bloody universe."

"And Robert was in love with Aline, too?"

He let out a strangled sob, his head lolling to the side.

Maeve grabbed his knee, her nails digging in. "Rob, did you do something to Robert so you could have Aline all to yourself?"

"I can't hurt Robert," he whispered. "If I hurt Robert, I hurt. If he dies, I die. So we both must live."

"But you did something to punish him that night, didn't you? You made sure he'd never be able to have Aline." Maeve shook his leg, her shrill cry echoing off the painted walls. "What did you do, Rob? Tell me. *Tell me!*"

Robert's eyes rolled back in his head. His mouth flapped open and a moment later, a loud snore shook the room.

MAEVE

I walked out of the institution in a daze.

It's true. It's all true.

Robert Smithers hadn't given us much, and not even Corbin's vigorous shaking could wake him up again, but I just *knew*... everything Blake and Corbin and I had figured out was true.

I sat on the bus, staring out the window at the rolling fields and munching sheep. My mind reeled. I *finally* had answers. I glanced down at the Smithers' book in my lap, running my fingers over the edge of my mother's portrait.

I never got to meet you, but now I feel like I know you just a little bit. You were really clever. And when I figure out exactly what Robert and Daigh did to you, I'm going to make him pay.

But it didn't mean anything. We were still no closer to figuring out how to actually stop the fae. I stared out at the green meadows. Somewhere under the grass, in the depths of the earth, Daigh waited. The souls of the dead clamored to be free, the restless spirits begged for their chance to feast on the living.

I didn't even believe in souls, and the whole thing had me scared shitless.

I jumped as a hand landed on my knee. "Hey," It was Corbin. Of course it was, staring at me with those kind, concerned eyes. "We've got this."

I shook my head.

"We do, Maeve. We made so much progress today. Your hunch paid off. We know what really happened that night."

"It doesn't help us. The past never does." The words stuck in my throat.

"Spoken like a true scientist." Corbin grinned. "Luckily, you've got an historian, and a warrior, and a baker, and an artist, and a lady of the night, and a sister, and a whatever the hell Blake is, on your side."

"Hey, I heard that, Mussolini," Blake called.

A bitter laugh escaped my throat. "I don't have Kelly or Jane, not anymore. What are we going to do now?"

"Come here, Priestess." Corbin raised his arm. I collapsed against his shoulder, letting his warm strength envelop me, falling into his kind eyes. He patted my arm, and kissed the top of my head.

It was only later, as my eyes fluttered shut and I fell into an uneasy sleep, that I realized neither of them had answered my question.

I want to make art like you do," I told Candice over a pint.

We'd taken a break from the studio to head down to the pub. I'd been so engrossed in the painting I was creating that I hadn't even noticed my stomach growling or the tickle at the back of my throat. Now that we were at the pub I'd already downed one pint and was working my way through a plate of fish and chips drowned in vinegar.

I hadn't painted in a long time. It felt too dainty to me, too controlled. I liked big sculptures, scrap metal with jagged edges that looked like they'd exploded out of a junkyard. Stuff that was once useful clamped together like a post-apocalyptic Frankenstein. But since my talk with Maeve the other night, a whole bunch of weird emotions sloshed around inside me like so much fine Irish whiskey, and pigment and a brush and a square 30cm canvas seemed the only logical way to expel them.

"You already do, you idiot." Candice grinned, spooning a mouthful of sticky date pudding into her mouth. "Your painting is beautiful."

"Sure, but it doesn't do what yours does." I lowered my voice. "There's magic in your work. I know it. I can sense it."

I'd noticed it as soon as we'd entered Gwen's house. It was obvious, now that I knew Maeve's mother's portrait was infused with magic. All the paintings were brilliant, but Candice's shone with a radiance that invited your eye and drew up emotions you'd rather be left alone. If I stared long enough, I fancied I saw the edges of the paint shimmering.

"I can show you how," Candice whispered. "Mum says I shouldn't do it. She says it's a waste of my magic – once you place it in the painting, you can't get it back. But it's only a tiny piece. That's what art is all about, isn't it? Giving pieces of yourself to the world."

I downed my pint in one gulp. "I am your willing student."

Back in the studio, Candice admired the painting I'd been working on. "This is for someone specific, isn't it?" She dabbed her hand in the pink jet across the corner. "Maeve?"

I nodded. She smiled. "Good. Then you're halfway there already. Finish the piece, and then I'll show you what to do."

Candice turned on the indoor fountain (it was nice to know other water witches had the same habits) and went back to her sketch. I dabbed my brush in a lilac paint and dreamed of Maeve. Hours passed. I didn't realize how many until I looked up and saw it was dark outside, the sun long since disappeared behind the horizon.

I stepped back from the canvas, tilting my head this way and that. Did it need a little more silver in the corner? Should I try and lighten the green a little? Had I captured the color of Maeve's eyes? My brush hovered in the air, unsure of what to do next.

I'd painted Maeve's portrait in an abstract style – her face made of streaks of watercolor and speckles of white acrylic to create an effect like a swirling galaxy bursting with stars.

A pink nebula became the streak in her hair and her eyes were two green planets teaming with life. That was the idea. In reality, it looked like a child's finger-painting. And not a precocious savant – a child who was really shite at painting.

I hate painting. I am so not a painter.

Candice came up beside me. "I think you're ready."

"It's rubbish. I should cut my ear off. Maybe a nice blood splatter will make it halfway decent."

"I think it's perfect. All it needs now is a finishing touch." Candice pulled up a stool beside me. "Are you sure you're ready for this? You are literally trapping some of your magic inside. Nothing's ever gone wrong before, but Mum's always telling me it's dangerous."

"Dangerous and potentially life-altering magic? Sign me up. What do I do?"

Candice took my hands and placed them about the still-drying paint. Her magic hummed through her fingers, lapping against my skin like water bubbling on the edge of a stream. I'd never known that water magic could feel so powerful before. And she'd been placing pieces of her magic inside her paintings? *Bloody hell, I can learn a lot from this woman.*

"Close your eyes," Candice said, her voice soothing. I slammed my blinkers shut. "Picture Maeve's face when you first realized you were in love with her."

Easy. That image had been carved into my memory for years. Maeve as a teenager with her short hair and vivid hazel eyes and t-shirt with a picture of a nebula and 'I need my space' written on it. Her nose buried in a battered copy of *Astrophysics for People in a Hurry* as she navigated through a crowd of football jocks in the hall without even looking up.

She wasn't like anyone else I'd ever met. I thought I'd never get someone like her to laugh. And then I made a joke about her already finishing *Mathematics for People Who Love a*

Brisk Walk, and she laughed, and it was the sweetest sound I'd ever heard.

"I got it," I said.

"Let the feelings flow out of you. Pour them into the canvas in the same way you pour water from your palms." She gripped my wrist and placed my fingers on the top of the still-wet paint. "Don't actually pour water on the canvas, though. That'll spoil all your hard work."

I focused the image in my mind, felt the fountain of water rising up inside me, pushing against my fingers as it begged to flow freely. With Maeve's laughing face still firmly in my mind, I imagined myself plucking out droplets from the well inside me and placing them into the paint, infusing my art with the part of me that called to Maeve.

Magic tingled in my fingers. I pressed them hard into the paint, sucking in my breath to hold back the torrent that threatened to spring forth like a garden hose after you undid a kink.

"That's it," Candice murmured. "You've got it. Now, close it off. You don't want to give too much."

I reached down inside of me and turned the tap off. The pressure on my fingers eased, and the fountain became a trickle. I took my hand away and opened my eyes.

At first I didn't see anything different. I squinted at the painting. At the edges, where the streaks of color met each other, I caught the faintest flicker of *something*. Whatever it was, it raised a shiver of excitement inside me. The white dabs that represented stars shimmered and sparkled like actual burning suns. I sucked in a breath. *Whoa. This is actually deadly brilliant. I've painted Maeve.*

"She's going to love it," Candice grinned.

My stomach twisted as I admired the likeness. All my feelings for Maeve rushed to the surface. I sank back into my chair, staring at my fingers, unable to believe that a tiny piece of my magic was now trapped inside the paint. Before, it was just a painting. Now, it was like it stripped away all the layers of bollocks I walked around with all the time, leaving just my raw, battered heart.

"This isn't…" I struggled for the words. "it doesn't make her feel anything that she doesn't—"

Candice shook her head. "What kind of a witch do you take me for? That canvas is all about you, Flynn. It's a window into your soul. How Maeve chooses to look through that window, and what she sees, is her own mind."

The paint was touch dry, so we wrapped up the canvas in brown paper and gave it a raffia bow. I found Maeve at the pub in hushed discussion with Corbin and Blake and Gwen. I knew I probably shouldn't disturb her, but if I didn't do this now, I'd never get the nerve again. I tapped her on the shoulder. "I was going to take a moonlit ramble around the stones, if you care to join me?"

She glanced over at the others, then pushed her empty glass across the table. "Sure. Corbin, can you take over here? I could do with a break."

"That's what I'm good for." I checked Kelly wasn't around, then extended a hand to her. Maeve took it, and we walked outside into the crisp moonlight.

"You doing okay?" I asked.

"Sort of. I think we've figured out everything." She held her free hand out as we walked around the stones, running her fingers over their rough surface as she told me what happened at the institution and what we now knew about the ritual. "So we're heading back to Briarwood tomorrow, as soon as we can get the bus and train…"

A dark figure emerged from behind the stones, heading directly toward us with long, purposeful strides. I yanked Maeve to the side just as the figure stepped in front of one of the floodlights and I recognized the golden hair.

"Kelly, hey!" I tried to wave, but I had the painting under my arm, so I just pointed a corner at her.

Kelly didn't reply. She glared at Maeve. I jumped at the hostility dripping from her. "Maeve and I were just looking at the stones. Did you know some people think aliens built the stone circle? As if. Aliens aren't into pythagoras. They do love getting stoned, though."

Neither girl even cracked a smile. Maeve yanked her hand out of mine. "Kelly, this isn't what it looks like."

"I came out to find you. Your *boyfriend* Arthur is looking for you," Kelly spat. Maeve reached for her, but Kelly yanked her hand away and fled across the field.

"What was that about?" I watched Kelly's retreating figure. "Should we go after her?"

Maeve's shoulders sagged. "Kelly hates me."

"She doesn't hate you," I said with more conviction than I felt. "What happened?"

"She's been getting weirded out by everything. I haven't been spending any time with her because of all the coven stuff, and she's seen me with Corbin all the time and she loves Arthur and she thinks I'm cheating on him. Last night she saw some of the ritual. She knows I'm lying about stuff. And now she's seen me with you—" her voice broke. "It's all messed up."

I leaned the painting against the stone and wrapped her in my arms. Maeve pressed her face into my shoulder and breathed hard. Her body felt so tiny and fragile in my arms. All I wanted was to take her pain away and see that smile of hers again.

Maeve drew away. "What's in the package? Has Blake stolen your credit card to feed his online shopping addiction again?"

"Thank fuck no. It's actually something I made for you today, but I can show it to you later, if you want to talk."

"I could actually do with the distraction." Maeve reached for it, but I hid it behind my back. "Come on, Flynn, hand it over."

"No, no, it's nothing. Let's go back to the pub and I'll listen to you..." I gulped as Maeve grabbed the package and pushed her nail under the tape. She slid the canvas out and held it up under the floodlight. My heart sank into my feet as I watched her face screw up in confusion.

"Flynn, it's beautiful," she whispered. Her face broke into that beautiful smile, and my heart hit the heavens. Maeve traced her fingers over the paint, angling the canvas so the light played off the shimmering stars.

Only one question burned in my mind. "Does it make you feel... different?"

"Not really," she tipped it on the side, and her grin widened until my heart wanted to fly out of my chest. "I'm just... a little bit blown away. No one has ever done anything like this for me before and... hang on. Flynn, have you... added magic to this?"

"How did you know?"

"It's got this... enchanting quality. A bit like my mother's portrait, or some of Candice's pictures back at the house."

"Candice showed me how to do it. It's just a tiny bit of magic. A smidge, really. It's supposed to say something that I can't say," I stared down at my shoes. "I love you, Maeve."

"I love you, too. But how did you get the magic to stay *in* there?"

"It's not dangerous, no matter what Gwen says. It was easy, really, but I think only some witches can do it. Candice said a lot of artists do it, because it's giving a piece of yourself to the audience, an extension of the painting. You really like it?"

"Omigod, Flynn." She hugged me. "Omigod!"

"That's pretty enthusiastic."

"No, you beautiful Irish fool." Maeve kissed me ferociously. "Of course I love it. I'd have loved it even if you hadn't shoved some of your magic inside it. But you've actually done it. You've shown me *exactly* how we can stop the fae."

BLAKE

"We're really, truly, going back to the castle?" I tossed my small parcel of clothes into the rack above my seat on the bus and slid in ahead of Arthur to nab the window seat. I was wearing a new t-shirt Flynn painted for me – it bore a runic quote from the *Hávamál* that I'd translated for him and the faint shimmer of his imbued magic. Ever since Candice had shown him how to channel his magic into objects, he'd been going nuts with the gifts. I was surprised he had any magic left.

"The boss says it's time to fly," Flynn grinned, stuffing his hands into his own new sweatshirt, which bore some ugly scrawled picture of a girl with a bunch of balloons that he kept telling me was some famous artist. The guy really had no clue about art. There wasn't even any naked cherubs. If Daigh had taught me anything, it was that you couldn't make real art without naked cherubs.

"Good. Because the curry here is rubbish."

"We've got one stop to make first," Corbin said, flicking a glance in my direction as he slumped down in a seat beside Rowan.

"We do?" Maeve asked.

He grinned. "Hey, Blake's not the only one around here who can keep secrets."

"Bite me, Mussolini." Corbin laughed. He didn't volunteer any more information about this unplanned stop. *Hmmmm. Mysterious.*

We rode in contented silence for twenty minutes. Kelly and Jane were the only two people who were talking. Those two never seemed to shut up about anything. They had a seat at the front of the bus and bounced Connor between them while they bent their heads together. Every time I looked over at them, Kelly had turned around in her seat to glare at Maeve, who was staring at an astronomy book and trying to pretend she didn't notice. Her hunched shoulders gave her away.

Interesting.

Flynn sat beside me and listened to that weird pounding music on his headphones, nodding his head like he had some kind of twitch. I stared at the window at the landscape, marveling how humans could idolize the rolling hills and wild woods of England at the same time they built towering metal shrines to their own egos in the scrawling, ugly cities.

For not the first time, I allowed myself to wonder what would happen if we did defeat Daigh. Would Maeve rule over the fae in place of him? Would the human race go right on paving over the whole earth with concrete? I remembered Liah's words about the weeping tree ghosts. I hoped I could convince Maeve to maybe do something about that.

Not that she'd listen to me. Or care about me at all. Maeve had told the others that she loved them. I overheard her saying it to Corbin and Rowan and Flynn during the private moments they didn't realize I observed. It made sense she hadn't said it to me. The fae did not value love in the same way that humans did. Fae did sometimes fall in love, but it was seen as a weakness, something to be mocked and ridiculed. Another being could not love you in return in the same way nature could. I had no concept of love.

At least, I always thought so. But the moment I'd first came to Maeve in her dreams, my heart had been entwined with hers. The idea of losing her made my chest ache and my fingers curl into a fist, ready to lash out at this invisible threat.

The idea of saying the words to her – and meaning them – made a chorus sing in my veins. But what if she didn't say them back? What if she didn't see me as part of the coven's future – then where would I go?

Not the city, I decided immediately. It was tempting to stay there just to spite Daigh, because I would never risk encountering another fae amongst all that metal. But the cities with their traffic jams and buildings like towering cairns were horrible – not even the superior curries would make me want to live in London.

I could return to Avebury. It did have a special charm about it – the hum of all that ancient magic still waiting to be unleashed – but I hadn't been lying when I said the curry there blew.

No place had sung to me like Briarwood. No other place felt like home. I hoped it would be my home for many years to come. But that all depended on Maeve. And right now I wasn't sure of my chances.

Ten minutes later the bus pulled into a small town station. Corbin stood up. "We're here."

"Where's here?" Maeve glanced out the window. "Corbin, this isn't Swindon. Why are we stopping here?"

"Will you relax? We don't need to change in Swindon. We can catch the train from the center of town directly back to Briarwood. It leaves every fifteen minutes. There's just one last thing we need to see first."

Everyone else stood up and gathered their bags. Arthur carried Connor's stroller off the bus. As I waited in the aisle for the line to move off, Jane slid out of her seat behind me.

"What's got your goat, cutie?" I asked her as she folded her arms and huffed.

She glared at me. "As if you don't know."

"I don't, actually. No one tells me anything."

Once we were all assembled outside with Kelly's enormous pack strapped to Arthur's back, Corbin pulled out his phone and typed in an address. "This way!" He strode off down the nearest street.

Jane jabbed her finger at the tearooms opposite the bus stop. "Kelly and I are just going to wait over there," she said. Kelly didn't say a word. She picked up her purse and trudged across the street.

Maeve's face crumpled. I reached for her, but she shrugged me off. "It's okay," she mumbled.

No, it's not. You don't have to be the strong one all the time. You can let us look after you.

We followed Corbin around the corner and down another street of brick terrace houses. He kept looking up from his phone, checking mailbox numbers. Suddenly, he stopped dead in the street. I ran up the back of him. "Sorry, mate."

I expected him to yell at me, which was usually his favorite thing to do. Instead he grabbed my wrist and yanked me out in front of him. "Blake, look at this."

I scanned the exterior of the house, expecting to notice something magical, some fae presence Corbin wanted my opinion on. But there was nothing about the house that gave off any magical vibe. It wasn't even particularly old or interesting – a recently built brick house with drab grey curtains and three blue gnome statues in the front garden.

I shrugged. "I've no head for architecture, but I don't think *Grand Designs* would give this place a second look."

Corbin tucked his phone into his pocket and inclined his head toward the house. "That's Darren and Colleen Beckett's house. Well, the land was purchased by a developer after the fire, and they built this place instead, but it's the same address. Blake, this is where your parents used to live."

My heart stopped. Of all the things I'd expected Corbin to say, that was not one of them. I stared up at the house, seeing it again with new eyes. A modest house where a family could grow and dream. A house with no room for magic and no portal to the fae realm in the backyard. A house where two traumatized witches could make a fresh start.

Even though I knew it wasn't the same place, I imagined a tiny little crib sitting under the upstairs window. I imagined my mother downstairs in the kitchen, heating up a bottle of milk. I pictured my dad – a real Dad who played footy with me and didn't torture me for fun – whistling as he walked up the path on his way home from work.

A lump rose in my throat. This was the first thing apart from my feelings for Maeve that had connected me to the human realm. For the first time, I belonged, even if it was to a house that didn't technically exist.

Maeve tucked her hand in mine, squeezing my fingers. She rested her head on my shoulder and I worried my chest might burst.

I reached out with my other hand, holding it in front of Corbin in the gesture of camaraderie he'd forced me into days earlier. For the first time, I actually wanted to perform this ritual with him. "Thank you."

Corbin cocked his head to the side, grinning like a Seelie caught in a trick as he cupped a hand over his ear. "What was that? I didn't quite hear you."

"You need to get your ears checked, Mussolini. I said thanks for this. It—" I swallowed. "It means a lot."

Corbin stared at my hand hanging in front of him. He stepped up beside it, lifted both his arms, and wrapped them around my body.

The only person in my life who'd ever hugged me was Maeve. The fae weren't exactly big on hugs. Corbin smelled like aftershave and ink. My throat closed up. I wasn't sure I was into it, but I patted him on the shoulder until he drew away.

"Welcome to the family, Blake," he said.

"Good to be here," I grinned. "Now, can we stop with the sentimentality? All these emotions are too much for my wee heart to take."

"Don't get used to it." Corbin waved us on. "Come on, let's get back to the castle. We've got some fae to slay."

CORBIN

*W*e found our way to the station and onto our train. Kelly and Jane went to another carriage, no longer making a secret of the fact they were pissed at Maeve. It had to be upsetting her, but when I asked her about it she shook her head.

"Not now." Maeve slid in beside me, squeezing my knee. "That was an amazing thing you did for Blake."

I shrugged. "Everyone else has had some kind of closure on this trip. I thought he needed some as well."

Across the aisle, Rowan glanced up at me and smiled, and my chest tightened the way it usually did for Maeve. *Fuck, that was unexpected.* My dick hardened too, just from a flash of memory of our last night in London.

Rowan was… as vital to me as breathing. For two years I'd fought to get that guy sober, and then to get the treatment he needed. I'd seen him go through every shitty thing it was possible to go through.

I couldn't save Keegan. Helping Rowan made that desperate ache in my bones recede, until I practically couldn't feel it at all. He felt as though I saved him, but it was the other way around – it was Rowan who saved *me*.

And now with this *thing* between the three of us... I didn't know where it was going to lead. I'd never considered that I might be anything other than heterosexual. I'd never even imagined another guy's dick in my mouth. But when I looked at Rowan, I didn't see another guy. I saw my best friend, someone who knew me better than I knew myself. He was a part of me, inked in my flesh like a tattoo. We'd already been through everything else together. The only thing that was a surprise to me now was that it had taken us this long.

Because we needed Maeve. She was the catalyst. She was the thread that bound us all together. From the moment she walked through the doors of Briarwood she was remaking us all, breaking apart all our walls and fitting us together again. We were all healing, together.

Almost all of us.

My eyes fixed on another face in the seat across the aisle, another guy I'd tried to save. *Arthur.* He wore a long-sleeved metal shirt, hiding his forearms. Was he cutting again? He seemed fine, joking around with Flynn and Blake. I hadn't noticed any erratic outbursts. He hadn't set anything on fire.

Maybe that was the problem. Arthur always said the cutting wasn't about wishing he was dead. It was about taking back control. I had no idea what he meant by that, but he seemed to be in control now. Or, at least, the illusion of control.

Watch him. Don't let him spiral down that path again. We need Arthur the warrior now more than ever.

Maeve leaned against my shoulder, jolting me out of my dark thoughts. "It's good to be going home."

Home. Home to Briarwood. Apart from the time I'd gone to Arizona, this had been the longest I'd been away from Briarwood in years. It had been more fun than I'd expected –

especially given the circumstances – and I felt proud of what I'd managed to achieve from outside my library. Maeve was right, you could learn a lot from scientific exploration, and experiments could teach us things we couldn't gain from books.

I just hoped like hell the experiment she had planned for when we got home would work. We wouldn't get another chance.

Speaking of libraries and books... I opened my backpack and ran my fingers over the book Dad had given me. It was a slim volume of poetry by the Romantics – Byron and Keats and Shelley and all of their ilk – the kind of volume a well-to-do Victorian lady would carry on her person for long train journeys or to read aloud at a dinner party. "I found this in a junk shop the other day, and I thought you'd like it," he had said softly as he handed it to me. "You always did have your head in the clouds."

Dad. I couldn't believe he was back in my life, and how easy we'd fallen into the same patterns, the same roles. We spent most of our dinner in Oxford arguing over medieval scholarship and I couldn't stop smiling. My heart ached to think of how many years or arguments we'd lost.

Everything was changing. Things were getting better, but was it just the apology at the end of the world, the death-bed confession? Had we built ourselves up only to lose at the final moment?

Not if Maeve has anything to say about it.

We got off at the station. The place was deserted. Even the ticket officer had gone on break or something. The sun shone bright, but my legs ached from being crammed into a narrow seat and we had Kelly's monolithic backpack to contend with. I asked Flynn to call us a ride share, but he said the app had a glitch. "I can see cars available, but it's like none of them can see us. Even if Arthur was out in the middle of the street in a black lace teddy, we'd still be invisible."

I sighed. *Of course, it falls on me to sort this out.* "Fine. I'll call a taxi."

I dialed the number of the local cabbie. He picked up on the third ring. "Hey, this is Corbin Harris. I'm wanting a taxi from the Crookshollow railway station out to Briarwood House. We're going to need to make two trips and—"

"I don't give rides to sorcerers," the driver snapped. The phone clicked off. I hit redial, but the line went straight to voicemail. I stared at the phone screen, listening to the driver's message. What the hell just happened?

I glanced up at the street. Pedestrians coming toward us veered off to cross the road. An elderly woman on the other side of the street stared at us from over top of her shopping bags. A guy took a wide berth around us on the path, crossing his chest and muttering something under his breath.

An uncomfortable sensation crawled over my skin.

"Corbin?" Maeve gripped my arm. "What's going on? Why do I feel like they're about to get out the tar and feathers?"

"I have no idea." I picked up my pack and slung it over my shoulders. "But I have a feeling we'd better get out of here soon, before they discover the garden store has a two-for-one deal on pitchforks."

MAEVE

*orbin called Clara, who closed *Astarte* and came in a
tiny Mini to pick us up. She took Arthur, Kelly, and
Kelly's ridiculous pack up to the castle so Arthur could pick
up his car and come back and get the rest of us. We sat down
outside the railway station, eating Hobnobs and Cadburys
from the concession stand and watching the pedestrians on
the street shun us.

"Witches!" a boy yelled as he zoomed past on his bike.

"Burn in hell," an elderly lady hissed as she took a wide
berth around us, dragging a tiny dog on a chain that barked
and snapped at Blake's ankles.

"Well, this is medieval," Flynn remarked, leaning against
the wall and snapping a stick of gum. "Arthur will be so
happy if they turn the high street into a jousting field."

"Better a jousting field than a gallows," Corbin muttered.

"Twenty-two people died in horrifying and mysterious
circumstance," I reminded Flynn. "We were there, and we
survived, and then we left town. I guess some people have
put those two things together."

A group of men gathered around the entrance to the lane.

They kept glancing over at us. Tension sizzled in the air. "You're not welcome here," one called over at us.

"You talk some shite, it's a public place." Flynn yelled back. Blake snorted.

"Flynn, don't."

One of them raised a fist. "Are you starting, mate?"

"Hope you like hospital food," Flynn yelled back. "Because you'll be eating that slop for weeks after we knack yer bollocks in."

"Flynn, shut up!"

Three of the guys approached the street, fists raised. One pulled his hand out of the pocket of his leather jacket, revealing a switchblade. My heart thudded against my chest. Arthur pulled up not a moment too soon, leaning on the horn. *I've never been so glad to see that stupid car.*

I yanked the door open and flung myself in. The guys piled in the back. "Hurry, go," I urged Arthur. He yelped as he saw the guys advancing toward us, and hit the accelerator. The car jerked to life, pulling away just as one of the guys swung his leg at the side, denting in the passenger door.

"Fuck!" Arthur swore. "He kicked my car."

"I'll marmalade them!" Flynn yelled out the window. He ducked as an empty can sailed past his head.

Rowan was white as a sheet. My whole body trembled violently. I didn't let out my breath until we left the village behind us.

Jane crouched in the front seat, cradling Connor in her arms. She looked up, her face streaked with tears, but when her gaze fell on me she expression shifted to one of complete hatred.

"What the hell is going on?" I managed to choke out.

"He kicked *my car.*"

"That's because Flynn provoked him," Corbin pointed out.

"Hey, they can't be starting like that around Connor." Flynn balled his hand into a fist. "I'll pan them out."

"Don't you pick a fight with them and make things worse. Our battle is with the fae, not the village idiots."

"Clara said it's been pretty tense in the village the last few days," Arthur said. "The Crooks Worthy vicar has been preaching fire and brimstone ever since the incident at the church, and the police are asking all sorts of questions about weird stuff going on at Crookshollow. Someone threw a brick through her shop window, and she said there have been people up at Briarwood at night, skulking around in the bushes."

We drove the rest of the way in silence, a chill settling over the car.

As soon as I stepped inside the familiar inner courtyard, with its towering walls of dressed stone and the outdoor beanbags scattered around, a sense of calm swept over me. Arthur had left his hookah pipe in a corner, and one of Flynn's weird spider sculptures crawled over the stone wall.

Home.

I'd missed the castle more than I'd realized. As soon as we were behind the walls, the tightness in my chest loosened. These walls had protected nobles and soldiers from powerful invaders. With a little help from our witchy magic, they could protect us, too.

"This place is *insane*," Kelly breathed, her neck craning right back to take in the full height of the sweeping staircase and double-height entrance hall. "You didn't tell me it was so *big*."

I beamed, happy she was talking to me again. "Yeah. I can't believe it's really mine."

"What's that hole up there?"

"Ah, now that's a really interesting feature of the original keep." Corbin came up behind me, slipping into his "Professor" voice. "If the enemy broke through the outer walls, the castle's inhabitants hid on the upper floors. Once the enemy broke down this inner door, the soldiers would pour hot water or pitch through the hole down on top of them. The castle is filled with all kinds of interesting details. Would you like a tour?"

"I'd love one," Kelly looped her arm through his.

"Me too," Jane shoved Connor into Flynn's arms and looped her other hand through Corbin's. "I've been hanging out here for a couple of weeks and I never knew that hole was defensive. Lead the way."

"I'll come too," I said.

"Don't you have a *project?*" Kelly said, her voice even. "I heard you on the train saying you had some important report to do for the *Historical Society.*"

My throat dried up. Kelly had overheard Corbin and I talking. At least we'd taken to calling the fae as the Historical Society, the same way my mother had. Corbin glanced at me, and he smiled. "Kelly's right. We've got all this info from our trip, and we should put it together before we forget anything. Maeve, why don't you get started on that while I tell the girls about the castle? I'll join you when we're done. We'll start on the second floor and then I'll show you the Great Hall and the stables."

"Yeah," I blinked, fighting the urge to cry. "I guess I've got some stuff to do. You guys have fun."

Corbin dragged them off, leaving the rest of us alone. I stared after them, watching Kelly's hair swinging behind her.

And then I realized what was happening. Corbin had just distracted Kelly so I could get on with my 'project' – which was preparing the painting ritual.

My bones ached with weariness. All I wanted to do was climb up to my tower room and go to sleep. But I was also desperate to find out if I was right about the painting.

No rest for the wicked witches.

"Get all the equipment we need," I hissed to Flynn and Blake. "Take it down to the sidhe."

"Right now?"

"Yes, of course right now, while Corbin's distracting Kelly. Did you really think he wanted to give a history lecture at this exact moment?"

"It's *Corbin*. Even if the Gestapo caught him he'd probably be trying to explain the provenance of their art collection."

"What about Kelly?" Blake asked. "Corbin can't exactly distract her during a ritual."

"I'll get Jane to take her somewhere or occupy her," I said, then remembered Jane's furious face in the car earlier. "Or I'll figure something else out. You two just get down to the sidhe with all the stuff. Corbin's started on the first floor, so when you hear them down in the Great Hall, it should be safe to sneak out the painting."

Flynn gave me a thumbs up. I raced off up the stairs. Corbin was just heading up the winding stairs to my tower bedroom, explaining how stairs in castles always turned clockwise because it gave the inhabitants an advantage when swinging their swords in the confined space. Jane stood at the bottom, Connor in her arms. I waved at her and she hurried over, a frown on her face.

"What do you want?"

"After Corbin finishes the tour, can you keep Kelly occupied while we go down to the sidhe? I know you hate me right now, but we might have found a way to defeat the fae, and that's more important than anything, even..." I trailed off, not sure what I was trying to say.

"Fine," Jane's face remained stony. "I'll distract her. But you're going to have to explain this to her."

'You know I can't—"

Jane grabbed my shoulder, her eyes locked with mine.

"Maeve, listen. I know you and I haven't been friends for very long, and I know you think you know what's best for your sister. But the girl who walked off that plane is not the same person you grew up with. The death of her parents changed her, same as it changed you. Did you ever stop to think maybe she deserves to know the truth about their deaths? Did you ever think that maybe asking me to lie for you is a really shite thing for you to do?"

"Why are you so invested in her?" I narrowed my eyes. "You hate girls like her, you told me so."

"She's different," Jane insisted. "You're so stubborn and pigheaded that you don't see how the rules can bend. People aren't *scientific*. They don't just act one way all the time. You know, you rail on and on about Kelly's religion making her blind, but you're blinded by your own prejudice, too. You can't see what's right in front of you. You better figure it out soon, because Kelly saw you with Gwen's coven and she saw you with Flynn. But I'm done. You want to ruin your relationship with your sister to avoid facing your own hypocrisy, then that's your decision. I don't bloody care."

She spun on her heel and stomped away.

"Jane, wait—"

She held up a hand, but didn't turn around. "I'm *done*, Maeve. If you're excuse me, I've off to lie to your sister for you."

46

MAEVE

*C*orbin ran into the library just as I scooped the grimoire up into my arms. "Jane's taken Kelly into the Great Hall. I think they're going to watch movies or braid each others' hair or something. What can I do here?"

"Carry this." I dumped the heavy book into his arms and stacked a bunch of candles on top, shoving one through the arrow hole so it stood upright. Corbin snorted. "Arthur and Blake have gotten the painting. Flynn's gone to his studio for the other supplies. Let's go down behind the topiary maze. I know it's longer, but it'll keep us hidden from the view of the Great Hall windows."

"Wait." Corbin went behind the desk and shuffled around in a drawer. He lifted out a small wooden box and tucked it under his chin. "We'll need this, too."

"What's that?"

"You'll see when we get there."

I grabbed my bag of supplies and followed Corbin down the secret staircase to the kitchen. It was so weird to see the enormous space empty, the counters bare of fresh-baked loaves and preserving equipment. Outside, we ducked and darted along the edge of the garden behind the topiary maze and through the orchard. The sweet tangy scent of the apple trees brought me back to the last time Arthur and I had come out here to practice our sword-fighting.

Was that really only a few weeks ago? It felt like another lifetime.

We passed Arthur and Blake as they shuffled over the uneven ground, the enormous gilt frame of the portrait bouncing awkwardly between them.

"Bloody heavy thing," Arthur growled as he dropped his corner and leaned against the frame, struggling to catch his breath.

"I told you we should have taken the frame off first," Blake shot back.

'Yeah, well, I thought all the banging and cursing as we tore the wood away would have alerted our guest." Arthur shot a look at Corbin. "Thanks for all your help, by the way. You just offered to take that tour so you didn't have to carry this bastard."

Corbin grinned as he squeezed past Arthur. "Got it in one. See you wankers down there."

Arthur yelled something abusive after us, and Blake cracked up laughing. Corbin and I tore down the slope and emerged in front of the sidhe. Flynn was there already, feeding dried kindling onto a small open fire. A canister of lighter fluid stood beside him. He wiped his hands on his jeans and stood up as I ran up to him.

"We don't have much time," I breathed. "I don't want Kelly to get suspicious and come looking for us."

"Do you have any idea what's going to happen when we do this?" Flynn asked.

"None whatsoever. But I do love a good experiment."

"I'd rather be experimenting in your bedroom right now," Flynn leaned over and pinched my ass.

Corbin dumped the grimoire in the grass in front of me. I bent down and started flicking through the pages. "After Flynn gave me the idea in Avebury, I remembered something in here from when we were searching all these books for a way to stop the— ah, here it is."

I leaned back, looking at the image. It showed a large hand, the fingers pointed down the page. A bolt of lightning shot from the tips into a small statue – a bulbous Mother Earth figurine like the kind we'd seen in the Neolithic museum displays at Avebury. A witch pouring her magic into an object, just the way Flynn had described doing with Candice. Corbin had placed a sticky note on the page – in his neat handwriting he'd translated the elements of the spell.

"If I remember my elementary witchcraft correctly," Corbin said. "In order to reverse this spell we kind of just do it backwards." He bent down and studied the spell carefully. "This is in Old Irish," he said. "It's one of the older spells passed down through the coven."

"Do you think Daigh saw this book?" I asked.

"If he was in Smithers' head, you can bet on it. For all we know, the whole reason he compelled Smithers for so long was to get access to these spells. When you combine this kind of power with fae magic, I can't even imagine what the results would be." Corbin glanced toward the painting. "I hope we're right about this."

Every word he spoke filled me with hope. I ran my finger down the list of instructions, feeling some comfort in seeing them written out in steps, like the experiments in a high school chemistry book. Crush those, mix take, light this, observe reaction.

"Right," I stared at my mother's face in the portrait leaning up against the side of the sidhe. "Let's get to work."

While Corbin hauled the painting into the center of our ritual area and called out instructions, Blake grabbed the

341

candles and set them out in a rough circle around Flynn's fire. Arthur waved his hand and the candles flickered to life. Flynn tossed a few crystals between the candles. Corbin handed me a container of salt and a candle.

"We're ready, Maeve. Cast the circle."

I followed the path of the candles the way I'd done once before, drawing a line of salt across the grass, then holding out the candle as I circled around again. While I walked, the guys stood inside the circle, chanting for the five elements to protect and guide us.

I stepped inside the gap I'd left, then closed it behind me with a line of salt. I faced my coven; Corbin radiating calm and confidence, Flynn with a wide grin and a dangerous glint in his eye, Arthur stoic, though his hand rested on the hilt of his sword. Rowan with his eyes focused on a spot at my feet. Blake's eyes twinkling. They all waited for me to begin the ritual.

"Right." I swept an arm dramatically through the air. "Um."

The scientist in me still wasn't comfortable with this whole leading rituals thing.

"One thing first." Corbin stepped forward. He held out the box in his hands. "We've never done anything official to mark Maeve as our High Priestess. We should do that now."

He pushed the box into my hands. My fingers ran over the rough wooden surface. I fumbled with the clasp and lifted the lid.

Tears sprung to my eyes as I beheld the treasure inside. Nestled in a bed of purple velvet was the three jewels of our coven – made of citrine – a stone that Corbin told me directed power, creativity, and decisiveness. *The ring. The pendant. The diadem.*

The same three jewels my mother wore in her portrait. I ran my fingers over the cold surface of the stones and the metal, dulled a little with tarnish. My heart clenched at the thought of her elegant fingers touching the same stones.

"We kept them in the drawer all this time," Corbin said, his smile wavering. "Waiting for you."

"I—" But I couldn't find any words.

Corbin's fingers left the bottom of the box. He dropped to his knees on the grass, bowing his head before me. He touched his fingers to mine. The air between us sizzled as his magic poured out of him and entwined with my own. He looked up again, his bright eyes meeting mine, wide and filled with love.

"Maeve Moore, my priestess, my love. I lay down my life for you."

Fuck. What the hell am I supposed to say to that?

The grass on my left rustled. I tore my eyes from Corbin. Arthur knelt in the dirt, the hilt of his sword in his hand, the blade pointing down toward the ground, toward our enemies. "Maeve Moore, my priestess, my love. I lay down my life for you."

Flynn dropped to his knees with a dramatic flourish. That wicked grin lit up his face as he pressed his fingers to my hands and said, "Maeve Moore, my priestess, my love. I lay down my life for you. And as an Irishman, it's worth at least two of these other fellas."

I laughed as tears streamed down my face. On my right, Rowan – precious, beautiful Rowan – sank to the earth, his voice as clear and loud and steady as I'd ever heard it. "Maeve Moore, my priestess, my love. I lay down my life for you."

My eyes met Blake's. He hesitated, pitching backward. For a moment, I thought he was going to turn and bolt. Then his face broke into a wicked smile. "Had you for a moment there, Princess."

He sank onto one knee, placing a hand over his heart.

"Maeve Moore, my priestess, my love. I lay down my life for you."

I glanced at each of their faces in turn, seeing their openness, their strength, their love. They had already dedicated their lives to keeping me safe, and now, here they were, promising more than I should ever have the right to ask of them.

My fingers itched to fling the box away, to sweep them all to their feet and give them the gift of their freedom, of a life without obligation to me and this coven. I wanted Corbin to go to university and Flynn to exhibit his art all over the world, and Arthur to join a metal band and Blake to open a curry shop and Rowan to realize just how amazing he truly was. But the tip of Arthur's sword bobbed over the dirt, and I remembered that this was so much bigger than us. None of us asked for this duty, but it was ours. While we still drew breath, we had to fight to save humanity.

I stared down at the glittering jewels. *In the movies, these sorts of things are always done for you by a nubile young slave.* But this was real life, and I already had all the testosterone in my life that I needed. I lifted the necklace out of the box. With trembling hands I pulled it over my head so the pendant hung between my breasts. The weight of it dragged my neck forward.

The ring next. I slipped it onto my finger. It fit perfectly.

I set the box on the ground and lifted out the diadem with both hands. I smoothed my hair down and placed it on my head. It felt weird, like a shackle. It hummed with power, warm against my head.

I opened my mouth. I found the words.

"I lay down my life for all of you, my warriors, my guides, my witchy men, my loves."

Five pairs of eyes stared up at me with such reverence it

stole my breath. My chest swelled until my heart threatened to burst through my ribcage.

Weirdly, standing out here with all my guys, the wind wisping my hair against the back of my neck, the grass cool beneath my bare feet, our magic spiraling around us, wrapping us in a warm, protective glow, made the magic rush through my body the same as when I'd kissed them for the first time. Even though we weren't touching, this ritual, this *binding*, was even more intimate than sex.

A tear rolled down my cheek. I swiped a hand across my eye. "Stand up, you guys. We've got work to do."

Arthur stood first. He adjusted his sword belt, then held up his palm. The fire in the center of the circle flared to life.

Corbin and Flynn dragged the painting over. I stared down at my mother's face, wondering again what would happen once we undid the spell. *If* we could undo the spell. I felt ridiculous with this diadem on my head, like a kid playing dress-up. If I hadn't seen for myself what we'd done in ritual together, I wouldn't even believe in this witchy stuff.

"Come forward," I said. The guys stood around the portrait and touched their hands to the frame. I pressed my palm against the oils that formed my mother's face. Now that were were out here, I was amazed I hadn't felt the magic emanating from it before. It sizzled against my skin, drawing up the pillar of my own spirit power, drawing that toward its embrace.

"On the count of three..." I met each of the guys' eyes in turn. "One... two... three..."

I focused my energy in my fingers, digging deep into the canvas, sensing the layers of paint and gesso. My spirit magic flowed out, searching, probing, reaching...

The tendrils of our magic entwined, forming a net that stretched across the entire canvas. We held fast. And then, we started to pull.

I hope this works, Princess. Blake's voice boomed inside my head.

Me too.

Maeve, you found me! The haunting, singsong voice of the painting cried with joy.

As one, we yanked our hands away from the painting. A surge of energy leapt down my arm, sending me toppling back into the grass. Arthur flung his arm back and hurled the painting into the flames.

47

MAEVE

The fire spluttered and sparked as the flames caught the oily paints. The gilt on the frame melted through the embers in golden rivers, and the carved wood beneath quickly went up in smoke. Noxious fumes wafted over us as the chemicals in the paint met the flame.

Tears sprung in my eyes as I watched my mother's face melt away, the canvas curling up as the paint ran into streaks that stained the charring wood. I touched my hand to the pendant between my breasts, mourning the loss of my mother's likeness.

Would the voice that haunted me go up in flames along with the portrait? Would the dark magic Daigh and Rob set into motion that night finally be undone?

I waited, my breath in my throat. The frame collapsed into the fire. Tears streamed down my cheeks. All that remained of the painting now was a pile of ash. The fumes wafted away on the breeze, carrying my hopes with them.

I was so sure...

Corbin reached for my hand. "I'm sorry, Maeve. We must've been wrong. It's just a painting after all—"

His words were cut off by an enormous BOOM.

The ground shook. The flames leapt up into an enormous column, stretching up twenty feet in the air, like the tail of a comet streaking across the sky.

Corbin and I braced each other, struggling to remain upright. Arthur yelled something, but I couldn't hear it over the roar of the fire. A high-pitched wail echoed in my ears and white-hot pain seared through my body.

Inside my head, the woman with the singsong voice screamed, and I screamed with her. *Make it stop, make it stop.*

My whole body screamed for release. From the column of fire emerged a dark shape swathed in flames. It moved toward me, separating from the fire and rolling across the ground, leaving a trail of flames across the dry grass. The shape bubbled and shifted, growing in height until it was almost another pillar itself.

A dark hole opened inside of it, and a scream tore through the night, no longer inside my head but free, and hurt, and desperate.

Water hit the screaming shape, and it sizzled as the flames died. I managed to tear my gaze away for a moment to see Flynn, who'd aimed both palms at the thing and shot a jet of water straight into its heart.

The flames fell away, revealing a figure beneath them, as solid and real as Corbin beside me. A long shift dress hung from its thin frame, the white fabric blackened and eaten away by the fire.

It lifted its head, and a face that was terribly, frightfully familiar to me stared out at the world. Eyes that were a mirror image of my eyes met mine, swimming with emotions deeper than anything I'd ever felt in my life.

My throat closed up. I couldn't speak.

"Hello, Maeve," the figure croaked, its voice dry and

hoarse. It outstretched its arms, lurching forward as if it intended to embrace me. "We meet at last, my daughter."

TO BE CONTINUED

≈

Need to know what happens next? Grab book 4, *The Castle of Wind and Whispers.*

(Turn the page for a sizzling excerpt).

≈

Can't get enough of Maeve and her boys? Read *The Summer Court* – a free Briarwood prequel novella – when you sign up for the Steffanie Holmes VIP list.

THE CASTLE OF WIND AND WHISPERS

"Hello, Maeve," the figure croaked, its voice dry and hoarse. It outstretched its arms, lurching forward as if it intended to embrace me. "We meet at last, my daughter."

My daughter.

The world froze. The apparition's words hung in the air, fuzzy and devoid of meaning. *It's saying I'm its daughter, but that's not possible, because my mother is dead.*

And yet ... the ice-blue eyes that looked at me with such haunting venerance were the same eyes that stared out of my mother's portrait. The delicate hands that had once been folded in her lap extended toward me. The bow-shaped lips that had once turned a mysterious smile out at me now trembled with anticipation. The only thing that was different from the portrait were long, thin cuts across its face.

It's impossible, but...

The citrine stone at my throat dragged against its chain, heavy and warm against my skin. The diadem around my forehead pushed my head toward the ground. My legs gave way beneath me. I sank into the soft grass, touching my

351

hands to the green blades as if they might give me some answer. "You... but... how?"

The apparition sank down beside me, white skirts fanning out around long legs like a ballet dancer. Behind its head the pillar of fire sank back, becoming a small blaze – like the campfires Andrew and I used to roast marshmallows over during our overnight astronomy trips. I could just make out the dark figures of my coven as silhouettes against the glowing flames.

The apparition reached out a hand to touch mine. The ring around my finger flared with heat as the hand approached. I jerked away. No way did I want the specter touching me.

That would make it real. And no way was this real. *No way.*

"I've been trapped inside that canvas for twenty-one years," the figure grinned, that beautiful smile like a knife through my heart. "You freed me, Maeve. I always knew one day you would. I just *knew* you would be the most powerful witch the world has ever known."

"We were only trying to release the magic trapped inside the painting," I said woodenly. "I didn't know about you."

Another figure dropped down beside me. Corbin's tattooed arm slid around my waist, and he pressed his lips against my cheek. "Maeve, I think this *is* the magic trapped inside. She might be a ghost or a wraith or just an imprint of her former life."

"Corbin, get back. We don't know what it is or what it can do."

"Corbin?" Its eyes widened as its gaze swept across his features. "Is that really you, all grown up? When I last saw you, you were a tiny toddler ordering everyone around. You have your mother's kind eyes." It turned back to me. "Does he look after you, my daughter? Does he protect you? His parents always protected me."

Corbin stiffened beside me. The figure swung around, its eyes leaping between the guys. "Arthur, that must be you with those huge muscles. You were such a big baby you nearly killed your mother during birth. I'd recognize that golden hair of hers anywhere. Flynn, you were always running after Corbin and getting into mischief. And Rowan, beautiful Rowan… you were only a babe when the fae came for us. You were the most peaceful baby, hardly ever crying or making a peep. Your parents loved you more than the moon and the stars."

Rowan made a strangled sound in his throat and staggered back. I felt a surge of anger toward the ghost… apparition… hallucination… whatever it was. It upset Rowan by talking about his parents, like it knew them, like they were friends.

It stretched long fingers out toward Blake, curling the ends as if beckoning him forward. Blake just stared with his smirk frozen on his face. "Blake Beckett… you were the sweetest boy. You used to bring flowers from the garden for your mother to make garlands for the rituals. You must have come into possession of your spirit magic by now – I hope it hasn't been a burden to you."

Blake said nothing, just kept staring and grinning.

Tears glistened in its eyes. "It wasn't supposed to turn out like this. We wanted to raise you all together – one big happy family. We wanted to teach you all about your powers and what miracles you are capable of. Instead, we abandoned you to fight our battle for us. I'm so glad you all found each other again… my heart just flutters with happiness." It clutched its hands over its chest like a melodramatic actress in the throes of passion. I might've laughed if its very presence hadn't robbed me of the ability to form sounds.

Corbin blinked. "Is she a ghost?"

"If she's a ghost, why isn't she falling through the earth?" Flynn asked.

His question stirred something in me, the innate need of mine to puzzle out strange phenomena, to subject even this terrifying vision to the scrutiny of science. I opened my mouth and found my voice.

"Ghosts don't exist," I said. "There's a logical explanation for what we're seeing. We've been breathing in God knows what chemicals from the burning paint, and it's caused this hallucination."

"If we're hallucinating, then why do we all see the same thing?" Arthur said from somewhere on my left.

"We're in a highly suggestible state – it could be possible—"

"I'm not a ghost, Maeve. If you touched me, you would know." The apparition raised its hand to its cheek and rubbed, then stretched its fingers out to me, palm out, begging me to try it. "I felt the heat of those flames against my skin. Right now, I'm wiggling my toes in the grass. The wind's blowing through my hair. I'm real, and all I've wanted to do these last years is hold my daughter in my arms."

I touched my finger to the Briarwood ring. The stone glowed with warmth. The metal seemed to have grown tighter around my finger. "I'm not touching you until I know for a fact this isn't some kind of fae trick."

It smiled. "So logical. So questioning. Such amazing hair." It tilted its long, slim neck, sweeping around to take in the five guys. "And commanding a coven of beautiful men? You are *definitely* my daughter."

"We'll let the DNA test confirm that," I growled. "Unless ghosts can't take DNA tests."

"I'll happily take any test you ask of me, my darling

Maeve. I'll walk over coals if it means I could hold you in my arms—"

Horror clawed at my belly as the apparition's words cut off with a hacking rasp. Its eyes rolled back in its head. It toppled forward, the body (that definitely appeared solid now) crumpling as its forehead slammed against the dirt. I screamed and darted back, my heart pounding against my chest.

"Aline?" Corbin cried, rocking forward to reach for it. I grabbed his arm.

"Stay back. Don't touch her!"

Her.

My mother.

But it's impossible.

I stared at her crumpled form, half expecting her skin to melt into a puddle, or ugly black spiders to crawl out of her white robes like they did in horror films. But she just lay still with her head and her arms draped at awkward angles.

She didn't move.

My heart leapt into my throat. *Why isn't she moving?*

Need to know what happens next? Grab book 4, *The Castle of Wind and Whispers*.

Can't get enough of Maeve and her boys? Get *The Summer Court* – a free Briarwood short story – when you sign up for the Steffanie Holmes VIP newsletter.

DYING TO KNOW WHAT HAPPENS NEXT?

READ THE CASTLE OF WIND AND WHISPERS TODAY

Now she's returned from the dead, Maeve's mother reveals the secret of how she defeated the fae twenty-one years ago. That secret will cost Maeve more than she could ever imagine.

Briarwood is no longer safe. The castle walls have been breached, and the coven's enemies batter at their doors. The coven have two options left – surrender, or die.

Maeve Moore doesn't do ultimatums, not when she's got five powerful men, an ancient witch, a prostitute with a heart of gold, a faithful sister, and the ghost of her dead mother on her side. Plus, her ancient castle still has a few tricks left to reveal.

If the fae want Briarwood, they'll have to come and take it.

The Castle of Wind and Whispers is the fourth in a brand new steamy reverse harem romance series by *USA Today* bestselling author Steffanie Holmes. This full-length book glitters with love, heartache, hope, grief, dark magic, fairy trickery, steamy scenes, British slang, meat pies, second chances, and the healing powers of a good cup of tea. Read on only if you believe one just isn't enough.

LOVE SO FIERCE IT TRANSCENDS EVEN DEATH.

When Elinor Baxter arrives at the dilapidated Marshell House to settle the estate of her law firm's oldest client, she can't help but feel a little spooked. The creaking gothic mansion is a far cry from her life as an adventurous party girl back in London.

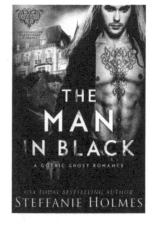

Then she meets Eric Marshell, a man dressed entirely in black with a wicked smile and the ability to float through walls. Eric was the violinist in popular rock band Ghost Symphony until a hit-and-run accident claimed his life. Now he's trapped inside his mother's house for all eternity, and the only one who can see or hear him is Elinor.

Eric and Elinor fight their attraction for each other as they dig into the mystery of Eric's death. But when they uncover a dark and sinister plot that threatens Elinor's life, their bond draws them into a world neither of them understands. Can their love transcend the boundary between life and death?

The Man in Black is a steamy gothic romance by USA Today bestselling author Steffanie Holmes, Set in the English village of Crookshollow, it's a standalone novel of love, redemption, and second chances. If you love clever BBW heroines, crumbling gothic mansions, and brooding rockstars who know what they want, then this book will have you shivering all over.

READ NOW: The Man in Black

THE MAN IN BLACK

AN EXCERPT

Elinor moved her hand, so her palm lay flat against mine. It was so odd to see her fingers nestled right inside my body, and even odder to *feel* them there, not as fingers usually feel, but as a hot ball of energy, emanating heat to a steady rhythm.

It took me a few moments to realise the rhythm was Elinor's heartbeat.

I stepped forward, my hand shifting against hers, her fingers dancing inside mine. I pressed my other hand against her back, my palm sinking into her flesh. If I were alive at this moment, I would push Elinor against my body, and relish the warmth of her, the shape of her, against me. But I couldn't do that, so instead I folded myself in closer to her. The front of my jacket brushed against her chest, sending waves of pulsing heat through my whole torso.

"This is amazing," Elinor breathed, her bow-shaped lips parting slightly. I didn't trust myself to reply, so I smiled back at her. I started to sway, pushing my right hip forward, moving the warmth through her leg. Elinor sensed the movement through her skin, and she moved backward, turning her body with me. I stepped again, and again we slid across the floor, our bodies sweeping and dipping with the music.

With my next step, I pushed myself closer, bowing my head slightly, so that my face hovered inches above hers. My eyes locked on those bow lips, ripe and delicious like the first berries of spring. I could feel my spectral cock straining against my boxers, ready for action. *God, I want this woman—*

"I like the music," Elinor said. Her voice wavered. She sounded nervous. I wondered if she was speaking because she sensed what I wanted to do, and she was trying to fill the space between us, to stop me from doing something I couldn't take back.

"Mmmm …" I shifted my fingers in her hand. The heat flickered, thrumming through my body with a quickened pace. She *was* nervous. *Interesting.*

"I love the … distortion. The way it crackles right through my whole body," Elinor breathed. "It's almost as if the music is mirroring the sensation when we touch."

"This piece is originally written by the composer Niccolò Paganini, a Greek violinist in the early nineteenth century," I murmured. If she wanted to talk, I could at least impress her. "He was known for making liberal use of the *diabolus in musica,* the devil's tritone, which creates that haunting dissonance you hear in the piece. Of course, Paganini's composition has been sped up and updated, and accompanied by the electric guitar, bass guitar, double bass, and drums, it's quite the feat of modern gothic rock."

"Who is playing the violin in this piece?" Elinor asked, her lips barely moving, struggling to form the words.

"I am, on Isolde. Ghost Symphony is my band."

"Eric …" Elinor's face turned up to me.

I leaned closer, I could practically taste the sweetness of those berry-red lips, feel the warmth of her mouth against mine. The air between us crackled with electricity. Elinor shifted her weight against mine, falling into me as she leaned forward, her lips pursed, waiting.

I brushed my lips against hers. It was like no other kiss I'd ever experienced before. The heat leapt through my body, twisting from my mouth right through my core. I felt as though I'd swallowed a hot coal, and though it burned me deeply, it was the most delicious thing I'd ever tasted. I leaned forward, my weightless body pressed against hers, my lips parting to devour her heat as our bodies hummed with pulsing energy.

READ NOW: The Man in Black

WANT MORE STORIES FROM THE WORLD OF CROOKSHOLLOW

Haven't read the Wolves of Crookshollow series yet?

Sink your teeth into the hot werewolf paranormal romance from *USA Today* bestselling author, Steffanie Holmes.

Now FREE on all platforms!

Anna

It's been five months since my boyfriend was tragically killed in a climbing accident. I didn't think I was over him ... until Luke walked on to the archaeological site.

Tall, dark, sexy, tattooed, funny, dangerous. Everything I want in a man.

But he's hiding something. He acts strangely in the moonlight. He won't tell me anything about his life. And I caught him trying to destroy an important find.

My body aches for him, but my heart tells me I'm not ready to make myself vulnerable again, especially not for a guy who isn't being straight with me.

If only ...

Luke

Anna Sinclair – archaeologist, geek girl, totally and utterly delectable.

I knew from the moment her intoxicating scent wafted across my wolf senses, she's meant to be mine.

And that knowledge is *terrifying*.

The last thing I expected was to find my fated mate on an archaeological site. Whenever I'm near her, all I want to do is claim her.

But she's broken. The last thing she needs in her life is a werewolf out for revenge. I'm here to destroy the site, to keep my family's past buried forever.

If Anna finds out the truth, she'd never speak to me again.

But I can't deny the bond between us. **I'll do anything to make her mine.**

Digging the Wolf is a standalone paranormal romance by USA Today bestselling author Steffanie Holmes. Read if you love archaeological mysteries, badass wolves, a broken heroine, and a hero so hot he'll have you howling for more.

OTHER BOOKS BY STEFFANIE HOLMES

This list is in recommended reading order, although each couple's story can be enjoyed as a standalone.

Briarwood Reverse Harem series

The Castle of Earth and Embers

The Castle of Fire and Fable

The Castle of Water and Woe

The Castle of Wind and Whispers

The Castle of Spirit and Sorrow

Crookshollow Gothic Romance series

Art of Cunning (Alex & Ryan)

Art of the Hunt (Alex & Ryan)

Art of Temptation (Alex & Ryan)

The Man in Black (Elinor & Eric)

Watcher (Belinda & Cole)

Reaper (Belinda & Cole)

Wolves of Crookshollow series

Digging the Wolf (Anna & Luke)

Writing the Wolf (Rosa & Caleb)

Inking the Wolf (Bianca & Robbie)

Wedding the Wolf (Willow & Irvine)

Fallen Sorcery Fae (shared world)

Hollow

Witches of the Woods

Witch Hunter

Coven

The Curse (coming in 2018)

Want to be informed when the next Steffanie Holmes paranormal romance story goes live? Sign up for the VIP Readers Club at https://www.subscribepage.com/briarwoodprequel *to get the scoop, and score a free bonus epilogue to enjoy!*

ABOUT THE AUTHOR

Steffanie Holmes is the author of steamy historical and paranormal romance. Her books feature clever, witty heroines, wild shifters, cunning witches and alpha males who *always* get what they want.

Before becoming a writer, Steffanie worked as an archaeologist and museum curator. She loves to explore historical settings and ancient conceptions of love and possession. From Dark Age Europe to crumbling gothic estates, Steffanie is fascinated with how love can blossom between the most unlikely characters. She also writes dark fantasy / science fiction under S. C. Green.

Steffanie lives in New Zealand with her husband and a horde of cantankerous cats.

STEFFANIE HOLMES MAILING LIST

Can't get enough of Maeve and her boys? Get *The Summer Court* – a free Briarwood short story – as well as two other free books when you sign up for the Steffanie Holmes VIP list.

Come hang with Steffanie
www.steffanieholmes.com
hello@steffanieholmes.com

COME HANG ON FACEBOOK!

hank you so much for reading and enjoying the Briarwood Reverse Harem series!

I've got a super-active reader group on Facebook. Join BOOKS THAT BITE if you want to talk about the series, get exclusive previews and bonus content, and meet some other awesome readers! I've love to see you there!

https://www.facebook.com/groups/1757403921176035

Printed in April 2019
by Rotomail Italia S.p.A., Vignate (MI) - Italy